Property of

SPIKE

Carol Dawn
International Bestselling Author

Property of Spike

All rights reserved. This book or any portion thereof may not be reproduced or used without the publisher's express written permission, except for the use of brief quotations in a book review.

Copyright © 2025 Carolyn Jacobs (Carol Dawn)
All rights reserved.

Published by Carolyn Dawn Jacobs
Cover by Carolyn Dawn Jacobs

Any references to historical events, real people, or real places are used fictitiously. Names, characters, and places are products of the author's imagination.

About This Book

Being President of the Iron Shadows MC isn't just a title. It's my whole damn life. Every day, another crisis, another burden weighing down shoulders that should've buckled long ago. But I don't break. I built this club from the ashes of a past better left forgotten, and now? We're known. We're feared. Nothing else matters.

Until Riley walks into my compound, her son against her chest, looking for protection. And just like that, my world shifts. The weight on my shoulders gets heavier, but for them, I'll carry it gladly. Because keeping them safe means more to me than the club, more than my own life.

I'll do whatever I have to do in order to protect them.

Even if it means going to war with the entire Palm Springs Police Department.

Trigger Warning

This book contains explicit content and may be triggering for some readers. It includes scenes of violence, abuse, kidnapping, and psychological trauma. There are references to physical and emotional harm. Reader discretion is strongly advised.

CHAPTER ONE

Spike

The weight of responsibility sits heavy on my shoulders, and I feel every damn pound of it as I lean over the maps spread across the table in the war room. Guns, shipments, and territory disputes. I've got my hands in it all, and the clock is ticking.

"Spike." A sharp knock on the door cuts through my focus, followed by Tank's voice. "You got a visitor. A woman. Says she needs to see the one in charge."

I don't even look up. "Tell her I'm busy."

Tank hesitates. I can hear it in the silence that follows. "She said it's important."

"They always say it's important," I growl, my fist landing on the table harder than I mean to. The maps shift under the force, but I don't bother straightening them. "I don't have time for some random chick showing up, thinking she can bat her lashes and get a meeting."

Tank shifts, his boots scuffing against the floor. "Should I..."

"Tell her to leave." My voice comes out sharp, cutting him off before he can finish.

Without another word, Tank retreats, the door clicking shut behind him. I pinch the bridge of my nose and let out a breath. Every day, it's something. Running the Iron Shadows isn't a job, it's a goddamn crucible.

A few minutes later, Tank comes back, knocking again before cracking the door. "She's gone."

"Good."

But as I stand there, staring at the maps and trying to focus on the job in front of me, a nagging thought creeps in. Women don't just show up at the Iron Shadows' doorstep unless they're desperate, stupid, or want to fuck. I have a hard time trusting, so biker bunny wannabe's need to go find a different fucking club to play in. Mine's off-limits, and they all know it.

So, she's either stupid or desperate.

I shake it off. Whatever her problem is, it's not mine.

"What's the problem this time?" Tank asks, his eyes narrowing as he leans over the table, scanning the maps.

I motion to the section I've been focused on, a jagged red circle marking the southern edge of our territory. "Got a call from Runner this morning at the south chapter. Says some new gang is trying to make camp here."

Tank snorts, folding his arms across his chest. "There? They must be desperate. That area's a shit hole."

"Exactly," I say, rubbing a hand over my jaw. "But that shit hole is still ours. If they think they can squat on it, they've got another thing coming."

He glances back at the map, his brow furrowing. "You think it's worth the fight? If they're that far south, it's not like they're threatening the heart of the club."

I level him with a glare. "The second we start letting small-time punks set up shop in our backyard, the vultures come next. We're not giving them a chance."

Tank nods, his jaw tight. "So, what's the move?"

"First, we confirm they're actually there. I've got Knuckles and a couple of prospects scouting the area now. Once we know what we're dealing with, we decide whether to smoke them out or send a message."

Tank smirks, a glint of violence in his eyes. "I vote for sending a message. A loud one."

I nod, my lips pressing into a thin line. "Yeah. We'll see how loud it needs to be. But we're not giving up an inch of territory, not to some wannabe gang looking to play house."

Tank taps the map, his finger lingering on the red circle. "Got it. I'll get the guys prepped, just in case."

"Good. Keep it tight. No screw-ups."

He steps back, heading for the door. As it clicks shut behind him, my eyes drift back to the map. The weight of the club feels heavier than ever, but there's no room to let it show. Weakness can be exploited and that's something I can't afford.

CHAPTER TWO

Riley

As I hide in the shadows of the local park, I don't know whether to scream, cry, or just give up.
Who am I kidding? Giving up isn't an option. Not anymore.
"Don't worry, sweetheart," I whisper, clutching the small bundle tighter against my chest. "I'll keep you safe. I promise."
The words feel hollow, even to me. Can I really keep that promise? My mind spins as I try to figure out my next move.
A motel? It's risky. They might find me there. A homeless shelter? Maybe they wouldn't think to look for me there, but that comes with its own dangers. Someone could steal the little cash I have, and I can't afford that.
The hospital. The thought lingers, tempting. It's the only place that feels remotely safe. I just had a baby less than forty-eight hours ago, and they might let me stay overnight. But would they look for me there? Is it too obvious?
I sigh, glancing down at Asher. The soft rise and fall of his breathing is the only thing grounding me right now. At least the hospital has security. I just hope there won't be any police officers around tonight. But do the security guards work with the police department? It's a risk I'm

going to have to take.

Decision made, I adjust the carrier around my chest and start the long walk back to Palm Valley Medical Center.

***

The hospital's emergency department waiting room is bright, sterile, and quiet.

"How can I help you?" the receptionist asks, her tone polite but distracted.

"I need to check into pediatrics, please," I say, doing my best to sound calm.

She slides a clipboard across the counter. "Just fill this out, and someone will call you back shortly."

Nodding, I take the clipboard and find a seat. Asher stirs in my arms, making those little noises that tell me he'll be awake soon. Hungry. I need to be somewhere safe before that happens.

But then my eyes land on the first line of the form: Name.

My stomach drops. If I check in, they'll know exactly where I am. Why didn't I think of that before? Could I lie and put some random name? Would the staff on the pediatric floor remember me and know that I lied?

Panic rises, tightening my chest. I force myself to stay calm, plastering on a polite smile as I stand and return the clipboard.

"I left my purse in the car," I lie smoothly. "I'll be right back."

The receptionist nods without question, and I turn away, my heart pounding.

Once outside, I pause on the sidewalk, staring into the darkness.

Now what?

The cool night air wraps around me, and the weight of the night presses harder on my shoulders. Asher's head moves, a soft whimper escaping his tiny lips. He's waking up. I bounce him gently, whispering soothing words, but my mind is racing.

The parking lot is nearly empty, just a handful of cars scattered under dim streetlights. I scan my surroundings, looking for anyone who might seem out of place. My heart beats faster when I spot a man leaning against a lamppost across the street.

He's too still. Too focused.

My breath catches in my throat, and I clutch Asher tighter, trying to convince myself it's nothing. Just a guy waiting for someone. That's all. I'm just being paranoid.

Don't panic. Keep moving.

I wrap my arms around the carrier and start walking down the sidewalk. Not too fast. Running would only draw attention. My eyes stay forward, but I feel his gaze on me like a weight.

He moves.

A quick glance confirms that he's stepping away from the lamppost, his movements slow and deliberate. My stomach twists, and my grip on Asher tightens.

I round the corner, my heart pounding so hard I can feel it in my ears. I need to think, but the fear is blurring everything.

A gas station comes into view ahead, its fluorescent lights flickering. It's not much, but it's something. I quicken my pace, practically running as I cross the parking lot and push through the door.

The clerk looks up, a bored expression on his face. "Evening."

"Evening," I mutter back, heading straight for the small seating area by the window. I settle into a corner, facing the door, my pulse still racing.

Asher starts to fuss, his cries growing louder. I bounce him gently, trying to calm him while keeping my eyes on the door. If that man followed me, I need to be ready.

Minutes pass. The door doesn't open. No one comes in. I let out a shaky breath, relief flooding through me. But it's short-lived. This isn't a solution. I can't stay here all night.

I glance around, my mind working through the options again. The hospital's out. The motels are too risky. I need somewhere they'd never think to look.

The clerk clears his throat, giving me a pointed look. "You okay there?"

I nod quickly. "Yeah, just...waiting for someone."

He raises an eyebrow but doesn't press.

Waiting for someone. The words linger in my mind and an idea flickers.

Maybe I do need to find someone. Someone who can help me. Someone who isn't tied to the people I'm running from. Someone they would be too scared to go against.

The problem is, I have no idea who that could be.

"I don't think it's a good idea, Butch," someone says from somewhere in the store. "The last time someone crossed the Iron Shadows, they lost an eye."

"I'm not afraid of those idiots," another says. "That man lost his eye because he's a fucking pussy. Let them try and come after us. I'll shoot 'em dead before they even park their bikes."

"You say that now, man, but I'm serious. You don't mess with that biker club. The President isn't one to play games. He shoots and asks questions later."

"You let me handle 'em."

I block out the rest of their conversation. The Iron Shadows. I happen to know a lot about them. I don't think anyone living in Palm Springs hasn't. But is it worth the risk to ask them for help? Would they even want to help? There's never been mention of the Iron Shadows doing charity work for scared and hopeless women. But maybe they secretly rescue damsels in distress without letting anyone know. Probably not, but I choose to think otherwise.

This group of bikers is well known for their not-so-legal activity, although it's never been proven. They're rough, scary, dangerous, and are all over Palm Springs.

It's risky, but maybe the risk is worth it.

I happen to know that they have a spy inside their club for the police department. Or rather, for one particular person associated with the police department, anyway. Maybe I can trade that information for a safe place to rest.

Asher's cries increase, so I head to the restroom. Maybe if I nurse and change him here, he'll sleep long enough for me to get us someplace safe.

***

They said no. They told me if I was having problems to go to the police. But I can't do that.

Now what?

CHAPTER THREE

Spike

"I'm telling you now, cousin or not, I'll kick your ass if you try to cross me." My voice is low and steady but sharp enough to cut through steel.

Billy leans back in his chair, running a hand through his greasy hair and sighing like he's the one under pressure here. "I wasn't trying to cross you, cuz. I just wanted to see if we could pass through to deliver a shipment to La Quinta."

"And I said no." I glare at him, the heat in my chest building as I fold my arms over my chest. "Why the fuck would I let an outside source cross my entire goddamn territory?"

"It's not like we're trying to set up shop," he protests, his tone edging on whiny. "Just passing through."

"Not to mention," Skip cuts in from the corner of the room, his sharp eyes fixed on Billy, "La Quinta belongs to us. You're talking about crossing our turf to deliver shit to our turf. That's not passing through; that's pissing on the Iron Shadows' name."

Billy rubs the back of his neck and looks between us like a cornered animal. "I know, Skip. But you all don't sell the shit you mule. If you let us cross and sell the Fentanyl, we'll give you a five percent cut of the profits."

I let out a humorless laugh, the sound harsh in the

tense room. "Five percent?" I lean forward, planting my fists on the table as I glare at him. "You think I'm gonna risk my club's reputation, our operations, and the safety of my brothers for five fucking percent?"

Billy's mouth opens, but Skip beats him to it. "You're out of your damn mind, Billy. We don't deal in poison, and we sure as hell don't play courier for anyone else's shit."

Billy's face twists, but he holds his tongue. He knows better than to push too hard, but I can see the frustration boiling under the surface.

"Let me make this real simple for you, Billy," I growl, my voice like gravel. "This club doesn't bow, doesn't bend, and sure as hell doesn't work for anyone else. If you think you're gonna waltz across our turf, sling your shit, and toss us crumbs like we're starving, you've got another thing coming."

He shifts in his seat, clearly uncomfortable. "I wasn't trying to insult you, Spike. I just thought…"

"That's your problem," I cut him off, straightening up. "You thought. Next time, save yourself the trouble and don't."

Billy sits there for a moment, his jaw tightening, but he finally nods. "Fine. I get it."

"Good," I snap, motioning toward the door. "Now get the fuck out of my war room before I decide family ties aren't enough to keep you breathing."

He doesn't need to be told twice. He's out of his chair and through the door in seconds, leaving a faint trace of cologne and desperation in his wake.

Skip shakes his head, leaning back in his chair. "Billy's always been an idiot, but I didn't think he'd have the balls to come in here with that bullshit."

"Family's tricky like that," I mutter, sitting back down

and glaring at the map again. "He's lucky he's blood, or I'd have made an example out of him."

Skip smirks. "You sure he's lucky? You scared him so bad he might piss himself before he makes it back to his car."

I grunt, a flicker of amusement breaking through the frustration. "Good. Let him remember that feeling next time he gets a dumb idea."

The humor fades quickly as the club's weight settles back onto my shoulders. Billy's little stunt is just one more thing on an already overflowing pile of shit. The Iron Shadows are mine to protect, and I'll be damned if I let anyone, family or not, jeopardize what we've built.

"Any update on that small gang?" Skip asks, his tone clipped as he moves toward the table.

"Tank's got it handled," I tell him, leaning back in my chair. "They've got twenty-four hours to pack up and clear out, or they'll be leaving in body bags. But that's not the only issue on our plate."

Skip mutters under his breath, shaking his head. "Seems to be a common theme these days. What now?"

I tap the edge of the map spread out before us, zoning in on the eastern border. "We've got a shipment coming through tomorrow night. Problem is, my inside man at the Calexico border checkpoint decided now was a good time to land himself in the hospital."

Skip exhales sharply and takes a seat across from me. "We really need more than one damn inside man at these borders. We're cutting it too close every time something like this happens."

"That's the plan," I reply, sighing and dragging a hand down my face. "But until we can get the right people in place, we're stuck scrambling when things go sideways."

He drums his fingers on the edge of the table, his brow furrowed. "What about a bribe? Whoever they assigned to cover his spot probably isn't gonna turn down easy money."

"Most people don't," I admit, sitting forward and resting my elbows on the table. "But I'm not about to throw cash at someone without knowing where they stand. I want Maverick to dig into whoever's taking his place. Find out if they've got a price or, better yet, something we can exploit."

Skip nods, a slow smirk tugging at the corner of his mouth. "Leverage is always better than cash. Costs less, too."

"Exactly. Money talks, but blackmail screams," I say, my tone sharp. "If Maverick finds something, we'll act on it. If not, we'll come up with a backup plan. Either way, this shipment doesn't stop, and it sure as hell doesn't get held up by some bureaucratic bullshit."

Skip leans back, crossing his arms. "I'll get Maverick on it. You want to pull anyone else in on this?"

"Not yet," I reply. "The fewer people in the loop, the better. But we'll reevaluate if we don't get something solid by morning."

"Got it." He stands and stretches his arms above his head, his expression softening for just a moment. "Anything else, or can I grab a drink before my head explodes?"

"Go. Take five," I mutter, glancing back at the map. "I'll be here if something else goes to shit."

As Skip heads for the door, the weight of the conversation lingers, adding to the ever-growing burden on my shoulders. Another crisis to handle, another fire to put out. It's the life I chose and the life I'll defend with every ounce of strength I've got.

***

The sound of boots hitting the concrete floor draws my attention, and I look up to see Maverick entering the room.

"I've got good news," he says, walking toward the table.

I raise an eyebrow. "Let me guess. You've got the border situation under control?"

Maverick smirks, a glint of satisfaction in his eyes. "Hell yeah. The guy who took over for your man? I found out he's got a gambling problem. He's deep in debt, and I'm betting he's more than willing to take a little extra cash to look the other way."

I lean forward, the tension in my chest easing just a bit. "Good work, Maverick. Get with Skip and come up with a number before making the offer. If he takes it, we'll move forward. If not, we'll figure out how to make him see the error of his ways."

Maverick nods, turning to leave. "You'll have an answer soon."

I watch him go, my mind already back on the shipment and the other fires that are still burning. One down, a thousand more to go. But that's the way it's always been, and that's the way it always will be. I've built this empire, and I'll be damned if I let anything or anyone take it from me.

The club's not just about the legal stuff. Hell, we don't operate on the legal side of things at all. Weapons, that's what we deal in. Illegal weapons. The kind of shit that keeps the world in balance for the highest bidder. We've got our hands in the dirt, but that's how it works. You want power, you want control? You play in the shadows, and sometimes, that means doing things that keep you on the edge of a knife.

But there's one line I don't cross. One thing I won't allow to be sold on our streets.

Drugs.

We don't sell drugs. Never have, never will. It's a matter of principle, even if it makes me a goddamn hypocrite. We mule the stuff across our territory, sure. Get paid a lot of money to do it. But I'll be damned if I let it poison the streets I've fought to protect. I've seen the damage it does, how it tears families apart, how it fucks people up from the inside out. I've been down that road before, and I won't let it happen again.

I'm a businessman, and I'm in this for the power and the money, but I'm not about to be the one who lets the poison spread. Not on my watch.

Which brings me back to Billy. He actually thought I'd let him sell the most dangerous drug on my streets? Fentanyl is fifty times stronger than heroin. Double that than morphine. Hell, even a tiny amount of two milligrams has been known to kill people. What the hell is he thinking?

Fucking idiot.

CHAPTER FOUR

Riley

"Can I help you, ma'am?"

"Oh, I just need to know where I can find the diapers," I smile at the kind woman.

"Isle five," she answers.

I thank her before heading that way. I'm so exhausted. I haven't slept more than ten minutes at a time in the past two days.

But I'll have to be more careful. I was almost found this morning because I fell asleep on a park bench. Someone saw me and called the police. Luckily, I was able to leave before anyone could arrive.

I've already decided to try the biker club one more time. I understand if they don't want to get messed up in my drama, but maybe they can point me to someone who will. Or, at the very least, point me in the direction of a safe place to sleep.

I just need a few hours, and I'll be good to go. My brain is too fuzzy to stay alert, and that puts my son's life at risk. I'm just so grateful that the weather has been warm enough that being outside isn't a danger.

If nothing else, I'll go to the library. There's a corner section where people go to read. Maybe if I'm holding a book, they will think I just fell asleep reading.

Taking a deep breath, I walk forward, pretending to

have all the courage in the world when, in reality, I have less than the cowardly lion. Purchasing the diapers and wipes, I place them in the diaper bag on my back and head towards the Iron Shadow's compound.

It takes thirty minutes to walk there, and by the time I reach their security gate, I'm about to keel over.

"Think you're in the wrong place, little lady."

I glance through the small window to where a single male smirks down at me.

"I need to speak to someone, please," I say.

"I'm someone," he says, his eyes filled with heat.

Gross.

The man looks like he kicks puppies for fun.

"I need to talk to someone in charge, please," I try again.

"He won't waste time on you," he laughs. "But, I'd be willing to help you out if you're willing to pay me back on your knees."

If I could reach through the glass, I'd throat-punch this man. But I don't want to risk my baby getting hurt.

Feeling defeated, I try not to cry as I turn and walk away.

"Fucking bitch," he yells.

But I don't care.

I'm too tired and in too much pain to care about anything anymore. Especially not this man's insults, his leering, or the fact that I just wasted what little energy I had left walking all the way here. All I care about is finding a safe place for my son. Just a few hours. That's all I need.

When I had Asher via c-section, they placed a waterproof bandage of some sort over the incision, but it still hurts like crazy, and I don't think I have any more pain pills.

Tears sting my eyes, but I keep walking, my shoulders slumping under the weight of the diaper bag. The sharp bite of the man's laughter follows me, cutting through my chest like shards of glass.

Maybe I should go to the library after all. Or perhaps just... sit on another bench somewhere and pretend to read. The thought is pathetic, but desperation doesn't leave room for pride.

"Hey!"

The shout is rough and deep, a stark contrast to the sneering tone of the man at the gate. I freeze, the hairs on the back of my neck standing on end. Slowly, I glance over my shoulder. A tall figure strides toward the gate from inside the compound.

Dark hair, a clean-cut beard, tanned skin. Broad shoulders and a body that looks like it spends more time lifting weights than resting. He's in jeans and a black shirt, his leather vest heavy with patches I can't quite make out from this distance.

Ruggedly handsome. Undeniably intimidating. And judging by the hard set of his jaw and the fire in his eyes... Furious.

"What the hell did you just say to her?" the man growls, and I realize he's speaking to the guy in the booth.

The smirking asshole stumbles over his words, suddenly all sheepish and nervous. "Nothing, Spike. She was, uh, she was leaving anyway."

"I'm not fucking blind." The man, Spike, steps closer, and the puppy kicker's face drains of color. "You think I don't know what kind of shit comes out of your mouth when you think no one's watching?"

Spike doesn't wait for an answer. He turns his full attention to me, his dark eyes scanning me with an intensity that makes me feel even smaller than I already do.

"You okay?" he asks, his tone softer now but no less commanding.

I nod, clutching the carrier tighter against my chest. "I just... I just needed to talk to someone in charge." My voice cracks on the last word, and I hate how weak it sounds.

"You're talking to him." His gaze sharpens, and I feel like he's trying to figure me out with just a single glance. "What's your name?"

"Riley."

"And what do you need, Riley?"

My throat tightens, and I have to swallow hard before I can answer. "A safe place to sleep. Just for a few hours. I...I have a baby, a newborn, and we've been on the run. I understand if you can't help, but... I didn't know where else to go."

His expression hardens, and for a second, I think he's going to tell me to get lost. Instead, he enters a code and opens the gate, his voice gruff but steady. "Come on in."

I hesitate, glancing back toward the leering man in the booth.

Spike follows my gaze and scowls. "Don't worry about him. He won't be a problem again."

Something in the way he says it makes me believe him, and for the first time in what feels like years, I take a shaky breath.

I step through the gate, clutching my baby like a lifeline, and follow Spike toward the largest building inside the compound, praying that I've made the right choice.

Spike

"That's the same woman from yesterday," Tank says, nodding toward the gate where a figure approaches.

"What's that she's holding?" I ask, squinting as I study her.

"I can't say for sure, but yesterday, I thought it was a baby."

"A baby?" My glare sharpens. "Why didn't you say something?"

"I thought I took care of it," Tank shrugs, unfazed. "It's my job to handle the little things around here. You've got so much shit on your shoulders as it is. You don't need some woman's issues. She looked scared, sure, but I told her that if she needed help, the best place for her would be the police station."

"Not sure she took your advice, brother," I mutter, rising to my feet. "Come on, let's go see what she wants."

As we approach the gate, I hear Pinkie's grating voice, loud and slimy as always.

"He won't waste time on you. But I'd be willing to help you out if you're willing to pay me back on your knees."

I freeze in my tracks, my fists clenching instinctively. Pinkie has been on my last fucking nerve for the past two months. He's prospecting to become a member, but with shit like this, he's not going to make it.

"Fucking bitch," Pinkie shouts when the woman turns to leave.

Actually, I might kill him for sport.

"Hey," I call out, my voice carrying enough weight to make the woman pause mid-step.

When I reach the gate, I glance back at Pinkie. His smirk falters, and fear fills his eyes.

"What the hell did you just say to her?" I growl, directing all my anger at him.

Pinkie stumbles over his words like the coward he is. "Nothing, Spike. She was, uh, she was leaving anyway."

"I'm not fucking blind." I step closer, towering over him even as he sits in the security booth and the color drains from his face. "You think I don't know what kind of shit comes out of your mouth when you think no one's watching?"

Pinkie stammers something, but I've already turned my attention to the woman. She looks exhausted, clutching the carrier against her chest like her life depends on it. Dark circles shadow her eyes, and she stands there with the kind of defiance that only comes from sheer desperation.

"You okay?" I ask, keeping my voice steady.

She nods, though her grip on the carrier tightens. "I just... I just needed to talk to someone in charge." Her voice cracks on the last word, and it's like a punch to the gut.

"You're talking to him," I reply, studying her. She's nervous but not fidgeting. Alert but not aggressive. She's running from something, and whatever it is has her scared out of her mind. "What's your name?"

"Riley," she whispers.

"And what do you need, Riley?"

Her throat works as she swallows, and it takes her a moment to answer. "A safe place to sleep. Just for a few hours. I... I have a baby, a newborn, and we've been on the run. I understand if you can't help, but... I didn't know where else to go."

Her words hit me like a freight train. A baby. Running. No one comes to the Iron Shadows lightly, and from the look of her, she's already been through hell.

My expression hardens as I weigh the risks. Bringing

her inside could invite trouble, but turning her away... That's not happening.

"Come on in," I say, punching in the code to open the gate. My voice is gruff, but I keep it steady.

She hesitates, glancing toward Pinkie like she expects him to stop her.

I follow her gaze and scowl. "Don't worry about him. He won't be a problem again."

The relief on her face is subtle, just a flicker, but enough to make me feel like I've made the right call. She steps through the gate, her grip on the baby carrier still tight. I motion for Tank to follow as we lead her toward the compound.

"Tank, have someone set up a room for our guest," I mutter under my breath. "She's gonna sleep, then we'll have a talk with her about what's scaring her bad enough to ask for help from the fucking monsters."

Tank nods, already pulling out his phone to send a message.

"And send Max to my office," I add before he gets too far. "He needs to deal with Pinkie before I do."

Max is my Prospect Leader. It's his job to weed out idiots like Pinkie before they become a problem. I don't know what the hell he was thinking letting that little shit in, but if he doesn't fix it, I will, and it won't be pretty.

Turning back to the woman, Riley, I gesture toward the main building. Our clubhouse. She looks like she's running on fumes, and I'm not sure how much longer she's gonna hold up.

"This way," I say, keeping my voice steady as I lead her inside and through the main rooms until we reach my office.

Once inside, I gesture to the couch in the corner. I don't

use it much for sitting, but it's damn good for the nights I crash here instead of going home.

"Have a seat, Riley," I tell her, grabbing a bottle of water from the small fridge in the corner. I make sure it's sealed before handing it to her. Don't need to add fear of being drugged to her shoulders. "I have someone getting a room ready for you. It shouldn't be long."

"Thank you," she whispers, her voice so soft I almost miss it. She opens the bottle and takes a cautious sip. "I can offer a little bit of money for your generosity, but I'm afraid it's not much."

"Don't want your money, babe," I say, leaning back against the desk. "You do realize who we are, right?"

"The Iron Shadows," she nods, her voice steady now. "Yes, I know."

"We're not good people," I admit, watching her carefully for a reaction. "We have a bad reputation."

"I'm aware," she says with a small smile that catches me off guard. "Which is why I asked for your help. I'm hoping you're scary enough to keep the monsters away long enough for me to get some sleep."

I bark out a laugh, but there's no humor in it. "Babe, we are the monsters."

"Nah," she chuckles softly, and the sound is so unexpected it makes me pause. "I've seen monsters. I've lived with them. You and your friends may not do things legally; you may even kill people, but you're nowhere near the monsters I know."

Her arms tighten around the baby carrier, pulling it closer to her chest. The slight tremor in her hands doesn't escape my notice, nor does the way her entire body seems to shiver at whatever memory is clawing its way to the surface.

"Trust me on that," she adds quietly, her eyes downcast now.

I don't reply right away. She's got a story. Something dark enough to bring her to our doorstep, clutching a baby and looking for sanctuary. Whatever it is, I'll get it out of her. But not now. For now, I give her what she needs: space and time to breathe.

"You need to rest," I say, my tone softening. "We can talk about what has you running when you wake up."

She nods, her grip on the carrier never loosening, her knuckles white with tension. It's a hell of a thing to watch, someone so fragile carrying so much weight. I step out of the room, giving her the privacy she clearly needs to gather herself.

"Room's ready, Prez," Tank says, appearing around the corner a few minutes later.

I nod in acknowledgment and head back into my office, ready to let Riley know she has a place to crash. But the words freeze in my throat when I see her.

She's slouched against the arm of the couch, her head tilted awkwardly to the side, fast asleep. The baby carrier strapped to her chest keeps the infant snug and secure, but the tension in her hands as they grip the straps hasn't eased, even in sleep.

Tank steps in behind me, his voice low and sharp. "Either she has no situational awareness, or she thinks she's safe." He pauses, then adds, "Not sure which one is worse."

I glance back at him, my jaw tightening. "She is safe," I say, my voice cold and edged with steel. I look toward the doorway, where a couple of guys are lingering. Nosy fuckers. "And if any of you so much as breathe wrong around her, you'll answer to me. Then to Bones."

The weight of my words makes the air in the room grow heavy, even catching me off guard with how fiercely they come out. Tank raises an eyebrow, but he doesn't comment. The guys outside quickly find something else to do.

"Really?" Tank mutters under his breath, smirking. "You had to bring up Bones? People are terrified of that bastard."

I ignore him and crouch next to Riley, frowning at the awkward angle of her neck. "You think we should take the kid out of the carrier?"

Tank crosses his arms, studying them both. "Hell if I know. Doesn't seem right to mess with them, though. She's got the baby in there tight, and the kid doesn't seem uncomfortable."

"Agreed," I say. "We'll leave them be and keep watch. If anything seems off, we'll figure it out."

I grab a pillow from the other end of the couch, carefully lifting her head just enough to slide it underneath. Her head rolls slightly, but she doesn't wake. Her breathing stays steady, the kind of deep exhaustion that comes from running on nothing but adrenaline for too long.

Standing, I pull a blanket off the back of the couch and drape it over her and the baby carrier. The blanket pools around her shoulders, and she shifts slightly, murmuring something I can't make out before settling again.

"She's out," Tank says, his voice softer now as he leans against the doorway.

"Yeah," I mutter, stepping back to take another look. "Let her sleep. Whatever's chasing her, it's not touching her while she's here."

Tank nods, but his gaze lingers on Riley for a moment

longer. "Guess that means you're not gonna let her just walk out tomorrow either, huh?"

I glance at her one last time, the weight of her presence settling in my chest like a challenge I didn't ask for but can't walk away from. "Not a chance."

This woman and her child just added more weight to my already buckling shoulders, but I'm strong enough to carry them both.

Shaking my head, I walk out and close the door, making sure to lock it so no one can get in. Riley will be able to unlock it from the inside, and Tank and I are the only ones with keys.

She's safe.

They're both safe.

I'm not gonna unpack why that matters to me.

But it does.

CHAPTER FIVE

Riley

"Riley, I need you to wake up."
Nope. Not happening. So sleepy.
"I know, baby, but I need you to open your eyes for just a minute."
Fear hits me hard, slamming into my chest and jerking me awake. My heart races as I look around, disoriented.
"Where am I?" I ask, my voice trembling.
"You're at the Iron Shadows' compound, remember?" Spike's calm, deep voice pulls me back to reality.
It only takes a couple of seconds for the events of my life to come crashing back. Asher's soft cries pierce the quiet, and I instantly spring into action. My hands fumble with the straps of the carrier, and I rush to pull him out, tossing the carrier to the side.
"I'm so sorry, sweetie," I say, my voice breaking as tears blur my vision. I cradle him close, running a soothing hand over his back. "I'm such a horrible mom. How long has he been crying? He's probably starving."
"My God, he's tiny," someone says, their tone skeptical. "Are you sure he was finished growing?"
"Shut the fuck up, Skip," Spike snaps, his voice sharp and commanding. "You've only been asleep for thirty minutes, Riley." His gaze softens as he crouches in front of me. "If you can hand me your bag, I can make a bottle and

feed him while you sleep some more."

I shake my head, my face heating with embarrassment.

"I breastfeed," I admit quietly, the words catching in my throat. "I need to change him."

"Alright," Spike says, his voice steady. "Then tell me what you need. Do you have diapers?"

"Yeah," I answer, pulling the diaper bag from my back. "I need to feed him first."

"We'll step out and give you some privacy," he says, standing.

I glance around nervously, my cheeks flaming. "I...uhm."

"You're safe here," Spike says firmly, his tone leaving no room for argument. "Nobody's gonna bother you, Riley. They wouldn't dare."

Tank mutters something under his breath, but I can't focus on it. Asher's cries are growing louder, insistent, and I know I need to act quickly. Swallowing hard, I nod and lay Asher on the couch next to me so I can adjust to a more comfortable position.

Spike steps back, his imposing presence hovering nearby. He doesn't move far, though, and something about his watchful gaze gives me the tiniest flicker of reassurance. For a moment, I dare to hope we'll be okay. Even if only for the next few minutes.

I settle into position, grabbing the pillow and blanket someone left earlier, and place them across my lap. Asher's cries quiet slightly as I lift him into my arms, but even as I prepare to feed him, exhaustion begins to tug at me again. My eyelids grow heavy, and I can already feel myself starting to drift off.

"Wait," I call out, my voice faint, as I notice Spike starting to close the door. "I'm afraid I'm going to fall asleep and drop him," I admit, my cheeks flushing with embarrassment. "Is there someone here who can maybe... sit with me?"

Spike freezes mid-step, his expression unreadable as he lets out a sharp exhale. "Fuck," he whispers under his breath, rubbing a hand down his face.

I immediately regret asking, panic blooming in my chest. "Never mind," I say quickly. "I'll figure it out. I'll stand and feed him. I won't fall asleep that way. I've had to do it several times already, so I know it works."

"I'll stay with her," Tank offers casually, his voice low.

Spike whirls on him, glaring with such intensity that even I flinch. "Over my dead fucking body will you watch her breastfeed," he growls. His tone is low, menacing, and full of an unfamiliar protectiveness that seems to surprise even him. "Is your sister here?"

"She and her husband left for a few weeks," Tank replies, his brows furrowing.

Spike curses under his breath again, his frustration palpable.

"It's okay," I say softly, trying to diffuse the tension. I quickly stand, ignoring the sudden onset of dizziness. "Really. I'll stand and feed him. I can manage."

For a moment, Spike stares at me, his jaw tight as though waging some internal war. Finally, he mutters, "No. You're not doing that. Sit down."

I hesitate, unsure of what he's planning.

"I'll sit across the room behind you so you can still have privacy," he says, his voice softer now but still firm. "You feed your kid, Riley. I'll stay here and make sure you don't fall asleep."

The softness in his tone takes me off guard, but I nod slowly, sinking back onto the couch. Asher fusses in my arms, but this time, the weight in my chest feels a little lighter.

"This will probably take thirty minutes," I admit as the door closes, and I'm alone with a man I don't even know. But, even still, I feel more safe than I have in years.

"That's fine, babe," he mutters from somewhere behind me. "Just feed your boy. I'll keep you both safe."

Using the blanket to shield myself, I do just that.

Spike

Longest twenty minutes of my fucking life.

Why the fuck did I get hard at a woman I don't even know breastfeeding a baby that's not mine? It'd make sense if it were my woman and my kid. But this?

This is caveman shit.

Just knowing she's feeding a baby is enough to make me want to grab her and claim her for myself.

Fucking idiot.

It's not like I saw anything. She's all the way across the room and covered up. My brain knows that, but apparently, my dick didn't get the memo.

My dick is a fucking idiot, too.

"Riley," I call out when her head starts to tilt to the side, her neck at an awkward angle. "Babe, you awake?"

No answer.

Damn it.

I move fast, kneeling in front of her and cupping her face. "Babe, need you to wake up."

She makes a soft noise, a little hum that tells me she's alive, but her arms begin to loosen. Shit. I quickly place my hands where hers were, holding the baby in place.

I pull back the blanket, and there he is, still nursing. And I freeze.

Holy. Fucking. Shit.

What am I going to do?

She told me about ten minutes ago she was switching sides, so I'm hoping this little guy is almost finished. I sigh and kneel there, my hands steady beneath his head and bottom, waiting. Five minutes later, he drifts off, his tiny mouth letting go.

"Finally," I mutter under my breath.

Carefully, I pull him to my chest with one hand and use the other to fix her bra and shirt. My fingers brush her skin, and I flinch like I've touched something forbidden. Hell, I have.

If she wants to punch me in the face for this later, I'll stand there and take it.

Once she's covered, I shift her gently, grabbing her shoulders and laying her down on the couch. I tuck the pillow under her head and spread the blanket over her body.

"Alright, little man," I whisper to the baby, his tiny weight warm against my chest. "You need to be burped and changed. We can do this."

I glance at her one last time, her face relaxed in sleep, and something in my chest tightens. It's not just the baby that's fragile. She is, too.

Tank walks into the room just as I grab the diaper bag.

"Alright, little man," I mutter, glancing down at the baby in my arms. "Let's get this over with."

I lay him down on the desk because, well, I don't have a damn clue where else to do this. Tank is standing in the doorway, his arms crossed and a shit-eating grin plastered on his face.

"You know how to change a diaper, Prez?" he asks softly, clearly enjoying my predicament.

"It's a fucking diaper, not rocket science," I snap, though I have zero idea what I'm doing.

The kid lets out a tiny squawk, and I freeze. "Hey, hey, none of that. We're figuring this out together, alright?"

I fumble with the straps on the onesie, which seems like it's been designed by an evil genius. After finally getting it off, I peel back the diaper and…

"Holy shit," I groan, turning my head as the smell hits me like a damn freight train. "What the hell has she been feeding you?"

Tank is outright laughing now. The fact that Riley is sleeping through it is a testament to how exhausted she really is. "Having fun, Prez?"

"Shut the fuck up," I growl, grabbing the wipes from the bag. It's only when I start cleaning him that I realize I should've been prepared for an ambush.

Warm liquid sprays up, and I barely dodge it. "What the?!" I shout, holding up my hands like I'm under attack. "Is this normal?"

"Yeah," Tank says, wheezing. "Boys will do that."

"Thanks for the warning," I grumble, wiping my arm and cut down with one of the baby wipes. I manage to wrestle a new diaper on him, though it's definitely crooked. Whatever. It'll hold.

Next is burping him. How hard can it be?

Removing my cut so the boy's tiny body isn't harmed against the rough fabric, I cradle him against my chest, patting his back a little harder than I probably should. He's tiny, sure, but he can take it.

"Come on, kid. Just let it out."

Nothing happens. I keep patting my hand like a steady drumbeat. Tank's still leaning in the doorway, looking way too amused.

"Maybe you're doing it wrong?" he says.

"I don't see you volunteering."

Finally, the kid lets out a burp that sounds like it came from a full-grown man. "There we go."

And then it happens.

Warm, sticky spit-up slides down my shoulder, soaking into the sleeves of my shirt. I freeze, staring at Tank in disbelief.

"You're fucking kidding me," I say.

Tank's laughter echoes through the room. "Oh, man, that's gold. You're a natural, Prez."

"Natural, my ass." I grab another wipe, trying to clean the mess while the kid gurgles, apparently pleased with himself. "Next time, you're on diaper and burp duty, Tank."

He shakes his head, smirking. "Nah, looks like you've got it handled."

By the time I've got the baby cleaned up and my dignity in tatters, Riley blinks groggily, looking at me with a mix of confusion and surprise. The loud fucking laughter must have woken her.

"You... changed him?"

"Yeah," I grunt, holding the baby like he's a ticking time bomb. "Don't get used to it."

But as I hand him back to her, a tiny part of me wonders why it wasn't all that bad.

"Here," Bones, our Enforcer, says, entering the room. "It's not much, but your baby can rest on this while you sleep."

"Oh. Uhm, thank you, scary-looking dude."

Bones hands me the cot, nods, and leaves the room.

She has no idea how scary that man actually can be.

Laying down the sleeping cot, I reach out for the

baby. She has a slight hesitation but hands him over. She already has him wrapped up like a burrito, so I lay him down and slide the cot close to the couch.

"Lay down and sleep, babe," I order. "You've slept less than an hour so far, and you need far more."

"He'll wake back up in three to four hours to feed again," she yawns.

"So soon?" I ask.

"Every three to four hours," she answers. "It's exhausting, but I love him, so it's worth it."

Every three to four hours? I glance back at Tank, shocked. But his eyes are dancing with joy.

Fucker.

"Sleep, Riley," I grunt. "I'll check back in soon."

With that, I turn and walk away. But not before making sure she did as I said.

CHAPTER SIX

Spike

"The shipment made it through border patrol and is on its way to the warehouse," Maverick reports. It's six in the morning, and I didn't get any sleep last night. Deciding not to go home in case Riley needed me, I pretty much sat at my desk all night and watched her.

"Thanks, brother," I reply, taking a long gulp of my coffee.

Maverick's not technically a member of the Iron Shadows. He's what they call an Outlaw. He plays by his own rules and answers to no one. But he likes us well enough to stick around every once in a while. I've asked him more times than I can count to patch in, but every time, he turns me down.

"Not the type to be tied down," he always says.

Fine by me. Patch or no patch, he's still one of us whether the stubborn bastard admits it or not.

"What's up with the little lass in your office?" Maverick asks, his voice cutting through my thoughts.

I glance around the room, a sigh slipping out before I answer. The Iron Shadows run four chapters in Palm Springs. The main compound, where most of the club and the officers are based, and where we're currently at. Then we've got three satellite chapters scattered across our territory. Each one answers to me and follows my officers' orders, but still, they each keep their own corner of things. In all, there are roughly a hundred members. Give or take a few.

Currently, I'm here with all of my officers and Maverick.

Tank, our Vice President.

Crusher, Sergent-at-arms.

Skip, Treasurer, and the craziest fucker you'll ever meet.

Knuckles, our Road Captain.

Bones, Enforcer. One scary-ass bastard right there.

Max, Prospect Leader.

And our very own outlaw, Maverick.

Maverick's question has the entire room at attention. I stare at him for a moment, trying to gauge his tone. The guy has always been the kind to go off on his own, never sticking around too long in one place, and yet he's standing here, asking about her like he's actually concerned.

"The little lass in my office?" I repeat, lifting an eyebrow. My voice is rougher than I mean it to be. "She's not your concern, Maverick."

He doesn't back down, though. The Outlaw never does. His gaze stays steady, and he leans back in his chair with that lazy half-smirk he's perfected over the years. "I wasn't asking to get in your business, Spike. Just curious why you're keeping her under lock and key in your office. She seems a little... lost."

I can feel my jaw tighten, my grip on the coffee cup tightening with it. I remind myself that I trust the Outlaw with my life. "She's fine. She needed a place to rest, and she's got a kid with her. That's all you need to know for now. When she's awake, we'll sit her down and see what she's running from."

I take a deep drink of my coffee, hoping the silence will push him to drop the damn subject. But of course, Maverick's the type who doesn't let things go, especially when they pique his interest.

He leans in, elbows on the table, his voice low but sharp. "Something's off, Spike. I can see it. You're not the type to just take in some random woman, no matter what the story is. What's really going on with her?"

Fuck, I can't explain it. I don't even understand it myself. But something about her... it triggers something deep inside me, something primal, protective. I don't like the feeling, but I can't push it away either. And to hell if I'm gonna let Maverick know how much I'm already tangled up in this shit.

"She just needed a place to fucking sleep, Maverick. Would you have me turn her away, knowing a newborn is attached to her chest? Now, if you don't mind, I'd like to drop the subject."

Maverick doesn't say anything more, but I can tell by the look in his eyes that he isn't convinced. He's too damn sharp for his own good, and he knows when there's more to a story. But I'm not about to let him dig into it.

I stand up and walk over to the window, letting my gaze drift over the compound. There are fifteen houses built inside the compound walls, with the clubhouse being the center. My plan years ago was for members to live here with their families so we can keep them safe. But most of the men with families decided to live outside of the compound. Seven of the houses are being used by myself and my officers. Who knows where the hell Maverick lives. The other houses will be available to members as they earn them.

"What's next on the agenda?" I ask, trying to shift the

focus. The club's operations don't stop, even with all the chaos swirling around Riley and her kid.

"The shipment's through," Maverick says, his tone finally shifting back to business. "Should be in the warehouse by noon. We'll need to move it fast, but we've got backup from the other chapters."

I nod, satisfied with the report. "Good. Let's keep this clean. No mistakes. Have the eastern chapter grab the payload and get them secure. Crusher, you take point. I want those weapons sanded, polished, and ready for shipment by next week. We've got two hundred grand waiting on us after they're delivered."

"Got it," he says.

"Next."

"As of two hours ago, the gang has packed up and left," Tank says. "The south chapter had to force the issue, but it wasn't a big deal."

"Good," I sigh. "I'll have to meet with Runner. He never should have let them make camp to begin with."

As the conversation shifts to something else, I can't shake the image of Riley's tired face from last night. She wasn't wrong when she said the baby would be up every few hours. It was like clockwork. Luckily, she was awake enough that she didn't need my help.

I wasn't disappointed by that. Not even a little bit.

Fucking liar.

"Your cousin left Palm Springs," Tank says, pulling my focus back. "But I wouldn't be surprised if he tries to sell under our nose. Might want to warn the other chapters to be on the lookout."

I let out a long sigh, pulling out my phone to send a quick message to a few of the guys.

If anyone catches Billy or one of his idiot friends selling shit in my territory, I want to know about it immediately.

I pocket my phone without waiting for a response from each chapter.

"I could just kill him, Prez," Skip offers, grinning like he's hopeful. "Might even take away that tic in your eye every time his name comes up."

"Ask me again in a week," I respond, deadpan. Billy's pushing his luck, and if he keeps it up, I won't hesitate to let Skip handle it for me.

Before the conversation can go any further, I hear a soft voice. "Uhm, hi?"

We all turn to see Riley standing just outside the war room door, looking a little out of place.

And still fucking beautiful. She has curves that make my mouth water, not just soft little curves, but enough to make me want to pull her close and feel her against me. I bet she's soft all over. Those thick thighs would shake as I pound into her.

Fucking delicious.

Her auburn hair is pulled up into a messy bun on top of her head, and her green eyes, wide with apprehension, make me want to hunt down whoever made her look so fearful.

"You look better," I say, my voice softening. "How do you feel?"

"Much better," she replies, offering me a small smile. "I just wanted to say thank you before I left."

Left? Not happening.

"Why don't you take a seat," I say. "Tell us what has you so scared."

"Oh, uhm. It's nothing," she smiles. "I just needed sleep."

"So, you mean to tell me that you feel perfectly safe

leaving the security of my compound with your newborn son? And I'll warn you now. I won't tolerate a fucking liar."

Harsh? Yeah. But I'd rather her stay here out of fear, knowing she won't get hurt, than let her leave and walk straight back into whatever chased her here to begin with.

She gasps, taking a step back.

That's right, little girl, see who the real monsters are.

"No one is gonna hurt you, Riley," I sigh, running my hands through my hair. "Listen, I have to take care of some club business, so please, just sit down and talk to us. Let us see if we can help you."

"I promise not to bite," Skip smiles. "Too hard."

"Skip," I warn.

"Fine," he sighs dramatically. "Alright, tiny female, tell us who hurt you."

"I'm anything but tiny," she says.

And isn't that fact fucking delicious.

"You okay Prez?" Skip grins. "You need a cold shower? I know I do."

"Fuck off," I tell the asshole. "Get up and let her have your seat."

"Here you go, tiny female," he stands and gestures… you guessed it…dramatically. "It's already warm for you."

"Thank you, strange man," she says, her voice light but cautious as she carefully settles into the chair. Her little bundle is snug once again in the carrier, cocooned as if the outside world doesn't exist.

"Jealous, Prez?" Skip grins, throwing a playful glance my way. "She called me strange."

I watch as she relaxes slightly, a little tension easing from her shoulders. Skip has a way of disarming people, whether he means to or not. I guess I'll let him live... for now.

"You ready to talk, baby?" The words are out before I can stop them. Shit. I meant, *babe*. Not that it's much better.

"Not really," she admits softly, hesitating as her fingers graze the edge of the chair. "But I guess I might as well give it a try. I'm warning you now, though, you don't want to get mixed up in my problems. I just needed somewhere safe to catch my breath, that's all."

"Why don't you tell us what's going on and let us decide if we want to get mixed up or not," I say, my tone sharper than I intended. She's putting me on edge without even trying, and it's pissing me off.

Her gaze flickers toward mine, and after a moment, she sinks a little deeper into the chair. "I guess that's fair," she murmurs. "Alright... a little over nine months ago, I found out I was pregnant. My husband and I were so happy. Or at least, I thought we were."

"Husband?" I ask, my eyes catching on her hand. No ring.

"Well, he's not really my husband," she confesses, her voice low. "That's just what he tells everyone. Anyway, Chuck wasn't always... gentle. Especially after a bad shift at work. When things didn't go well, he came home looking for an outlet for his anger."

"Did he hit you?" Skip asks, his usual humor gone, his voice steady but cold.

Riley looks up at him and nods, her expression haunted.

Motherfucker.

"After I found out I was pregnant, I did everything I could to keep him calm," she continues, her voice trembling slightly. "A friend of mine works with him and would call me on his rough days to warn me. Those days, I tried harder. I didn't want to risk him hitting my stomach."

The room feels like it's holding its breath, every man in it silently seething. I clench my fists, imagining the piece of shit's face under them.

"A few months ago, I found out he was cheating on me," she continues, her voice quieter now. "Not that I cared. But one night, I overheard him on the phone, saying that once my baby was born, he and whoever he was talking to would raise him together. He was planning to take my son away from me."

"It's not easy to take a child from their mother," Max says, trying to sound reassuring.

"Maybe not for most people," Riley replies, her arms tightening protectively around her baby as she gently rocks him. The motion seems to soothe her more than the sleeping child. "But it wouldn't have been hard for him. I have no family, no home, no money. No real way to take care of Asher. They wouldn't let a homeless mother keep custody over a father with a stable career and a house."

No one argues because we all know she's fucking right.

"No family at all?" Maverick asks.

She smiles sadly, shaking her head. "None. I was an only child, and my parents had me late in life. They passed away years ago. If they had any relatives, they never told me about them."

"What happened next?" I ask, my voice steady, though my blood's boiling.

She takes a deep breath. "About a week ago, Chuck came home in a rage. Something about a case he was working on falling through. I asked him if he'd like me to bring his dinner to him, thinking it might help him calm down. But apparently, he didn't like that I spoke." Her voice cracks slightly, but she keeps going.

"He came at me and grabbed me by the hair. I tried not to scream, but it didn't matter. He threw me to the ground and kicked me really hard. Right in the stomach." Her hand moves instinctively to her midsection as she talks, her lips trembling. "I was just a week away from my due date."

She pauses, swallowing hard. "The doctors were worried at first, but Chuck told them I fell while mopping the floors. They believed him. I ended up having an emergency C-section. Asher's alright, thank God, but he's so small."

Her voice trails off as she looks down at the baby in her arms.

"Two days ago, Asher was born," she continues, her voice barely above a whisper. Her eyes never leave him. "But I was alone in the hospital. As I nursed my baby for the first time, I realized I couldn't stay. I had to leave." Her voice trembles, but she pushes through. "So, I checked myself out, ran home to grab a few things, and I haven't been back since."

"What about going to the police?" Bones asks, his tone cautious but firm. "Surely they know of a battered women's shelter that can help hide you."

A single tear slips down her cheek, landing on the edge of the carrier. She brushes at it quickly, her hand trembling.

"I can't," she says, her voice breaking. "Chuck is the Police Commissioner of Palm Springs."

No. Fucking. Way.

That bastard hates me.

"And Chuck," she adds bitterly, a hollow laugh escaping her lips, "happens to despise all of you. He's been trying to get your entire club disbanded for years."

She's not wrong.

Crusher steps forward, his expression hard as steel. "Did you come here to gather intel?" His voice is deadly, the accusation cutting.

"What?" she shouts, her wide eyes snapping to him before darting back to me. "No, I swear. I'm not a spy. Please, believe me."

I hold up a hand to stop Crusher, my eyes locked on Riley's. Her fear is palpable, but there's something else. Determination. She's terrified, but she hasn't broken.

"Crusher," I say, my voice low but firm. "Stand down."

He hesitates, then backs off, muttering something under his breath. Riley's shoulders relax a fraction, but her grip on the baby carrier tightens.

I take a few steps forward and look down at her. "Riley, you've got to understand where we're coming from. Chuck's been gunning for us for years. You showing up here? It's a huge risk for us. Not one we can take. But I'm not about to throw you out without hearing the whole story."

She nods slowly, her lips pressed together as if to keep her emotions from spilling out.

"I know it looks bad," she says. "Coming here. But I didn't have anywhere else to go. I thought... I thought if anyone could hide me away for just a few short hours, it would be you." Her voice cracks on the last word, and she looks down, blinking rapidly.

I exchange a glance with Tank, who shrugs like he's just waiting for my call.

"Why us?" I press. "Out of everyone you could've gone

to, why a club of dangerous men?"

Her lips quirk into the faintest of smiles. "Because Chuck is scared of you. He talks about you like you're the monsters of Palm Springs and not him. But I don't see monsters." Her eyes flicker up to meet mine, and for a moment, I can't look away. "I see people who might actually fight for what's right regardless of the illegal stuff you do. And I was so exhausted. I just needed a place to rest where people weren't afraid of him. A place he would never expect me to hide."

The room falls silent, her words hanging heavy in the air.

Tank clears his throat, breaking the tension. "What do you need from us, Riley?"

She hesitates, her fingers trembling as she brushes a strand of hair behind her ear. Her gaze flicks to the baby in her arms before returning to Tank. "You already gave it to me," she says softly, a small, tired smile tugging at her lips. "I honestly just needed some sleep. Now, I really should get going."

Her words catch us off guard, and the room goes still.

"I don't want to bring trouble to your doorstep," she continues, her voice steady but laced with resignation. "If Chuck finds out I'm here, he'll use every bit of power at his disposal to get me out of here and have you all thrown in prison. He'd probably spin some lie about the scary biker club kidnapping his wife and baby. And the worst part? People would believe him."

"Not if we've got the truth on our side," Bones says, his tone sharp.

Riley shakes her head, a sad laugh escaping her lips. "You don't know Chuck like I do. He doesn't lose. He'll twist the truth until it looks like something else entirely.

He's good at it. Too good."

"Maybe so," I cut in, my voice low and deliberate, "but we're good at what we do, too. And we don't back down from a fight."

Her eyes widen slightly, searching mine as if looking for any sign of hesitation. Finding none, she exhales shakily.

"But this isn't your fight."

"Riley," Maverick says from across the room, his voice softer than usual. "You came here for a reason. If you didn't think we could handle this, you wouldn't have walked through our gate, right?"

She bites her lip, glancing down at Asher. "I guess I just didn't think anyone would actually want to help. I didn't think anyone could."

"Listen," I say, kneeling in front of her, "Chuck's a problem. We get that. But problems have solutions. And if he's stupid enough to come for you here, he'll find out real quick why we're feared."

A flicker of hope crosses her face, but it's quickly replaced by doubt. "I don't want anyone getting hurt because of me."

"That's not your call to make," I say firmly. "You're here now, and we don't let anyone mess with what's ours."

Her head snaps up, her eyes locking on mine. "What's yours?"

I nod. "You, Riley. You and Asher are under our protection now. Chuck wants to come knocking? Let him. We'll be ready."

For the second time since she sat down, a tear slips down her cheek, but this time, it's not fear I see in her eyes. It's relief.

Police Commissioner Chuck.

Double fuck.

"Meet me back here in ten," I tell the men.

While I may be the president of this club, I respect the opinions of the men in this room. This might not be a decision I make on my own.

"I'm gonna show you to the guest room, Riley," I say, standing and holding out my hand. "You can rest in there for a bit. Kitchens fully stocked. Eat whatever and whenever you want. Feel free to move about the building. Just know that my men will be in and out throughout the day."

"That room even has a TV," Skip says, his body relaxed despite the fire in his eyes.

"Oh, I forgot to tell you about the sp…"

"Tell us later, babe," I say. "You need more rest, and my men and I need to talk."

"But it's…"

"Later," I say gently.

Taking my hand with a sigh, I help Riley up and lead her to her room.

I nearly buckle as the added weight of fucking Police Commissioner Chuck lands on my shoulders.

***

"This is a bad fucking idea, Prez," Knuckles says as I step into the room. His face is a storm cloud, his arms crossed tightly over his chest. "The last thing we need is the police sniffing around."

I think about the newly arrived shipment of guns and ammo stashed in the warehouse and the drugs that my guys will be running across Palm Springs in the coming days. He's not wrong. Hell, I can't help but agree.

"I know."

"The fucking police commissioner," Crusher growls, pacing the length of the room like a caged lion.

"I know," I sigh, the weight of it pressing down on me.

"He's been riding our asses for years," Skip chimes in, his tone sharp.

"I know," I say again, the words clipped.

"This could very well be the downfall of the Iron Shadows," Maverick throws in, ever the voice of cheerful pessimism.

"I know," I reply, nodding.

"Not just the club," Max adds. "The tattoo shop, the gym, the fucking bike garage. Everything we've built."

"I fucking know," I say through gritted teeth, dragging a hand down my face.

"We have to help her," Bones says quietly, cutting through the tension like a blade.

The room falls silent.

"I know," several of us admit in unison, the words heavy with inevitability.

This isn't just about Riley anymore. It's about who we are. Who we've always been. The kind of men who step into the fire, even when it burns. Especially when it burns.

"The best thing we can do right now is to keep her hidden," I tell the room, my voice firm, brooking no argument. "As long as she stays within the walls of this compound, it shouldn't be an issue."

"Maybe," Tank says, his arms crossed, his tone skeptical. "But we can't hide her forever."

"No," I agree, nodding. "But we can hide her long enough to dig up dirt on Chuck. There's no way he's as clean as he wants people to believe."

"I'll look into it," Maverick volunteers, leaning back in

his chair, a calculating look in his eyes.

"Good," I say, my tone hardening. "Bribe who you have to, extort all you want, but don't get caught. And keep Riley's name out of it."

Maverick gives me a dry look, his lips quirking into a faint smirk. "Not stupid, Spike," he says with a sigh. "I'll get back to you when I can."

With that, he stands, his chair scraping against the floor, and strides out of the room, already plotting his next move.

I turn my gaze back to the others. "The rest of you, continue business as usual. No slip-ups, no mistakes. We can't afford any missteps right now."

The room hums with tension as my brothers nod, their jaws set and their expressions grim. They know what's at stake. And they know, just as I do, that this is the calm before the storm.

She didn't mean to, but Riley just put everything I worked years to build on the line.

The Iron Shadows are about to go to war with the Palm Springs Police force.

Fuck.

CHAPTER SEVEN

Riley

The guest room is small but comfortable. It has a soft bed, fresh linens, and a cot for Asher. It was more than I could've hoped for when I ran. But even with the quiet hum of the ceiling fan and the steady rhythm of Asher's breathing, I can't relax. I don't feel safe enough in this room, even though I know I am.

Something about these men, especially Spike, makes me feel safe. I don't care if they do illegal things or not. I know deep in my heart that Spike isn't the monster he says he is.

Voices seep through the thin walls, low and muffled but still clear enough to send a chill down my spine.

"She's put us all at risk," one of them says, his deep voice sharp with irritation.

"Spike should've said no. Now we've got the goddamn police commissioner breathing down our necks. For what? A woman and her kid?"

"She's got nowhere else to go," another replies, but there isn't much conviction in his tone.

"Yeah, and now we might lose everything. You think she's worth that?"

My chest tightens, my pulse thundering in my ears. I didn't want this. I didn't want to ruin their lives.

Asher stirs in the cot, and I go to him, brushing my

fingers across his tiny hand. His warmth grounds me, even as my thoughts spin. We can't stay here. We won't.

Moving quickly, I shove the few things I took out of my bag, diapers, wipes, and the blanket Asher had been wrapped in at the hospital, back into it.

When I have everything packed, I tuck Asher into his carrier, slinging the strap over my shoulder. His soft coo almost shatters my resolve, but I force myself to stay strong. I can't be the reason all of these men go to prison. I just can't. I'll find another place to hide. I have enough money to buy a bus ticket out of Palm Springs, but where would I go? What would I do when I got there?

The building is quiet as I make my way outside and to the gate, the darkness cloaking me. The cool night air nips at my skin, but I welcome the sting.

Inside the four solid walls of the compound are houses. A few windows are lit up which tells me that the reason the main building was so quiet was because everyone probably went home.

As I approach the gate, I silently hope it's not the same guy as before. A few steps closer, relief washes over me when I see it isn't. The gate guard stands tall, his silhouette imposing in the moonlight. He's not standing inside the booth like the guy before but is leaning on the wall. His sharp eyes lock onto me the moment I approach.

"Where do you think you're going?" he asks, his voice steady but curious.

"I need to leave," I say, trying to keep my voice calm and even. "Please, open the gate."

"Can't do that," he grunts, his stance solid as the stone wall surrounding the compound.

"Why not?" My voice cracks despite my best efforts.

"Orders from the Prez," he replies, his expression

softening just slightly. "Nobody comes in or out without his say-so."

My stomach churns. "Am I a prisoner?"

The man steps fully into the security light, and I see his face. He looks slightly familiar. Must be one of the men we passed on our way to the guest room.

He shakes his head. "No, ma'am. But I've got my orders."

Before I can say another word, the sound of heavy boots crunching against gravel makes my breath hitch. I turn to see Spike stepping out of the shadows, his expression a storm cloud of anger.

"Where do you think you're going?" he asks, his tone low and dangerous.

I tighten my grip on the carrier strap and straighten my spine. "I'm leaving."

His eyes narrow as he strides closer, his presence as commanding as ever. "The hell you are. Let's get back inside before you get yourself sick. Thanks for the heads-up, Mike."

I glance back at the guy at the gate, but he just flashes me a smug smile.

"See you later, little miss," he says casually.

"Why does everyone insist on calling me little?" I grumble as Spike gently steers me back toward the building. "I outweigh most of you."

Spike just grunts, not bothering to respond, as he leads me inside and back to the room he took me to when I first arrived.

With a heavy sigh, I drop onto the couch, instantly feeling some of the tension leave my body. I couldn't relax in the other room, but I guess I just needed to clear my head.

Yeah, right.

"Want to tell me what you were thinking, babe?" Spike's deep voice pulls my attention. He's leaning against the desk, his arms crossed, his eyes locked on me.

"Oh, um," I start, stalling.

"Don't lie," he growls, the command in his voice making me freeze.

Dang it. Why does he have to be so intimidating?

"I heard some of your men talking outside the room I was in," I admit reluctantly. "They were saying how I'm putting everyone here at risk. They sounded angry that you didn't just tell me to leave. I don't want that, Spike. I don't want to be the reason Chuck finally finds a way to toss you in prison, and I don't want to cause problems between you and your friends."

"Fuck," he mutters, dragging a hand down his face. Something he seems to do a lot. "Did you see them? Catch the names on their cuts?"

"Cuts?" I blink at him, confused.

He gestures to the patch on his black leather vest that reads *Spike*, with *President* stitched above it.

"That's called a cut?" I ask, raising an eyebrow. "Weird."

"Riley," he says, sighing heavily, clearly unimpressed by my tangent.

"Sorry," I mumble. "No, I didn't see them. I was in the room you gave me. I just heard their voices."

"Listen closely," he says, his tone hardening as he steps forward, crossing his arms again. "This isn't a democracy. What I say goes. Not everyone's gonna be happy with the decisions I make, but they, and you, need to trust that I know what the fuck I'm doing. Got it?"

I bite my lip, unsure how to respond, but his steady gaze leaves no room for argument.

"Got it," I sigh.

"Good," he nods. "Now, let's get you back to your room. It's midnight. You should be sleeping."

Not wanting to seem ungrateful, I stand and follow him down the hallway. I'd spent most of the day holed up in my room, only venturing out a few times to find food and stretch my legs. Spike wasn't lying when he said people would be in and out all day, but not once did I see him until now.

I don't know why that bothers me. Why does it leave this hollow ache in my chest?

"In you go, babe," he says, opening the door to my room. "Get some sleep. Night."

And just like that, he's gone.

I'm alone. Again.

I lean against the closed door, letting out a shaky breath. I tell myself not to compare this to my life with Chuck, but it's impossible not to. He did this kind of thing all the time. Sent me away, told me to go home when I brought him lunch, and made excuses about why I couldn't come to his work parties.

Not that it mattered much in the end. Chuck and I hadn't so much as shared a room since I got pregnant. Five years together, and it never really felt like we were *together.* I was just something convenient, someone he could use when he needed and hurt when he wanted.

The truth is, I don't think I ever loved him. I think I was just desperate. Desperate to feel wanted, even for a moment. Someone like me, someone big, someone who doesn't turn heads, grabs onto that feeling, and clings tight, too afraid we'll never feel it again.

But when Spike shut the door and walked away, it hit harder than I expected.

Why doesn't anyone ever want me around?

CHAPTER EIGHT

Spike

Riley and Asher have been here for three days now, but I've only stopped by to see her once. Call me a coward, but she makes my head fuzzy, and I can't afford that.

Especially not today.

"Who's running today?" Tank asks, his arms crossed, his expression sharp.

"Knuckles is leading the East Chapter," I reply, scanning the room. The men gathered around the table look calm, focused, but I know better. Tensions are always high on transfer days, and for good reason. We're transporting over one million dollars worth of rock candy. While we don't sell the shit, this transfer alone is making us twenty-five hundred grand.

"They'll carry the majority of the goods. I want all thirty of them on two wheels for this. No exceptions. I also want four more men in vehicles, flanking the front and back. I'll take the rest with ten men from here. Tank, you'll drive the car. We'll follow five minutes behind. The buyer will meet us at location five, at the edge of Palm Springs."

The bikes are for show. A distraction. The vehicles will be the ones transporting the goods. They have hidden compartments designed to keep even the damn drug dogs from finding them.

Tank nods, but his brows pull together. "That's a lot of heat, Prez. You expecting trouble?"

"Always," I say. "But this isn't just about moving product. It's about making a statement."

"Got it," Tank says, but there's a flicker of concern in his eyes. "And if Chuck catches wind? He always has his goons watching us like a hawk. They might get curious as to why there are so many bikers together."

"If Chuck wants to stick his nose where it doesn't belong, he'll regret it," I say, leaning forward. My voice drops low, carrying a weight that silences the room. "This is our territory. Our rules. And we're not about to roll over for anyone. Not even the fucking police commissioner."

There's a murmur of agreement around the table, and I nod, satisfied.

"Knuckles, you and Tank will make the handoff and stay until the buyer's out of our territory. No one leaves their posts until I get the all-clear."

"Got it, Prez," Knuckles says, his voice steady.

I glance around the room, meeting each set of eyes. "And remember, no mistakes. Not one. We've got a lot riding on this run, and I don't need to tell you what happens if we screw it up."

They all nod, the air thick with tension.

As the men disperse to prep for the run, I catch Tank's eye. He hesitates for a moment, then says, "You sure you don't want to sit this one out, Spike? Let someone else take the reins?"

I let out a humorless laugh. "You know better than that, Tank. I don't sit out."

But even as the words leave my mouth, my mind drifts back to Riley. To the way she looks at me as if she's trying to figure me out. Like she sees something I'm not ready for her to see.

I shake my head, forcing myself to focus. There's no room for distractions today. Not when the stakes are this high.

***

The roar of forty bikes pierces the stillness, shaking the building as engines ignite in unison. The men fall into formation, the rumble of their machines a warning to anyone foolish enough to cross us. I sit at the front, my fingers gripping the handlebars tightly. The weight of this run presses heavy on my shoulders. It's not just about the money or the product. Each run, no matter the reason, is a statement. A reminder. This is our territory.

Knuckles and the East Chapter take point, rolling out first. I wait five minutes before signaling my team to follow. The bikes surge forward, engines snarling like a pack of lions on the hunt. Between us, the vehicles trail in formation, their cargo secured in hidden compartments only a select few know about.

The first stretch is uneventful. Too uneventful. The eerie quiet prickles at the edge of my nerves. Deep in our turf, things should be smooth, but silence like this is rarely a good omen.

Tank's voice cuts through the comms. "Eyes on us, Prez. Couple of cars keeping pace."

He doesn't need instructions. Tank's a pro. He knows the drill: make the delivery, get paid, and clear out. But nothing's ever as simple as it should be.

I glance back. The bikes fan out, shielding the vehicles from view. It's a tight formation, a perfect cover. The only variable now is whether someone's bold or stupid enough to make a move.

"We're at location five," Knuckles reports, his voice clipped. "Buyer's here. No signs of trouble."

I nod, though unease gnaws at me. Everything's lined up, but there's always that damn gut feeling, like a storm on the horizon.

Bones comes on the line. "We've got company, Prez. Bikes slipping in at the rear. Not ours."

Grinding my teeth, I give the signal for everyone to tighten up. No way we're letting anyone break formation.

"Knuckles, take lead. You and Tank handle the handoff. Don't stick around. I'll deal with this."

Knuckles doesn't argue. He knows what he's doing.

As we approach the meeting spot, my eyes scan the area. The buyer stands next to a black SUV, far too polished for this dust bowl. A suit like his screams, *'Look at me'*. Attention is not something we want right now. I'll need to make it clear at our next handout that proper attire is expected. Idiots.

My men have the SUV surrounded when we arrive, just as Tank slows, pulling the lead car to a stop beside the SUV. Knuckles dismounts and approaches, staying sharp.

Then I see it.

A blacked-out truck lurks at the edge of the lot. Far enough to avoid immediate attention but close enough to set alarms blaring in my head.

"Something's off," I growl into the comm. "Be ready."

The truck's doors fly open. Two men step out, armed, and start closing the distance.

"Shit," Bones mutters. "We're blown."

My engine roars to life as I swerve sharply, skidding to a stop between my men and the advancing gunmen. Drawing my pistol, I bark into the comms, "Move! Finish the transfer and get out!"

Instead of shooting, the men exchange glances, smirking before retreating back to their truck. Moments later, two bikes pull up behind them. Likely the same assholes who tailed us earlier.

Chaos ignites. The men scramble as Knuckles and Tank toss the goods into the SUV. The buyer, pale but resolute, climbs in and floors it, kicking up a storm of dust.

"Go, Spike!" Knuckles shouts. "I'll cover the buyer."

"You know what to do, brothers," I say over the comms. "Break formation and take your detours back. Meet back at the compound."

My club is well-trained for any situation that may happen during a run. Tonight, they know to separate into small groups and take random routes back to their sectors. However, today, I want them all to return to the main clubhouse. This hour-long trip will take two to three to get back home. But the safety of our family comes first. Some of the brothers have wives and kids that live on or near their clubhouses.

Holstering my gun, I take the lead of my small group as the truck trails us, headlights glinting in my mirrors. My hand brushes the grip of my weapon. If this turns into a chase, things are gonna get ugly fast.

"Tank, hard right!" I order.

Tank veers off-road, his vehicle bouncing across the uneven terrain. We follow suit, bikes tearing through the desert as the truck struggles to keep pace. A series of sharp turns finally leaves them in the dust. By the time we reach the compound two hours later, they're long gone.

The men regroup, pulling into the lot. I dismount, my jaw tight as Knuckles pulls in behind me.

"Buyer's safe," he says, shutting off his engine.

Nodding, I survey the group. They're waiting. Tense.

"We have a fucking traitor," I yell. "Go to the basement and choose a fucking cot to sleep on. No one leaves until I find out who the fuck to kill."

Skip falls in beside me as we head inside. "Could've been on the buyer's side."

"Thought of that," I admit. "But it doesn't add up. Why ambush us during the transfer instead of waiting for the buyer to be alone?"

Knuckles grunts. "And why follow us back? It's likely they already know where to find us. The compound isn't exactly inconspicuous."

I turn to Tank. "Get me a list of everyone who ran today. Apart from the East Chapter, us, and the ten men I handpicked, who else knew about the drop?"

"Just the buyer and seller," Tank replies. "We've dealt with both for years. We've never had an issue. It doesn't make sense."

"None of this does," I mutter. "Tell Mike to lock the gate. No one in or out until I give the all clear. And order food. We're not starving just because I'm pissed."

Tank nods. "Got it, Prez. What's next?"

"Right now, I'm gonna grab a beer and go check on our guest."

Yeah, that sounds like a good idea. Doing just that, I grab my beer and race up the stairs. I'm not any less pissed off by the time I reach her door, but I refrain from banging harshly, knowing that Asher is probably asleep. No answer.

"Riley," I say. "It's Spike. You awake?"

Again, no answer.

Probably sleeping. I just need to peek in and make sure she's alright, for sanity's sake.

However, when I open the door, she's not there. I know

she didn't leave. Mike would have texted me. Pulling out my phone, I double check and don't see any missed messages.

Rushing to the kitchen, I only find Skip eating.

Bathroom. Maybe she's showering. Not caring one bit for her modesty, I stride right in but find it empty.

"What's up, Spike?" Maverick asks.

"Riley's gone," I say. "Where the fuck is she?"

"Check the cameras," he says. "You know Mike didn't let her through the gate. That means she's still here somewhere. Probably just wandering."

Heading toward my office, I open the door and freeze. Riley is fast asleep on my couch, and Asher's asleep on the floor cushioned by a blanket. Riley's hand is resting near his head almost as if she was reaching for him in her sleep.

"I'll keep everyone out," Maverick whispers. "We'll talk tomorrow."

Nodding, I walk in and shut the door. As I stand here taking in my two newest burdens, my pulse settles for the first time this evening.

Removing my cut, I hang it up and grab the extra pillow. I settle my body on the floor next to Asher. It may not be the most comfortable place I've ever slept, but it'll do just fine. Reaching out, I place my hand next to Riley's and can't help but wonder what the fuck is going on with me.

The next time I open my eyes, Riley's gone. But Asher is wide awake and looking right at me.

"Good morning, bud," I smile. "Does your back hurt, too?"

Standing, I crack a few things before bending over and picking up Asher.

"Let's try this changing shit again, but I'm warning you, no pissing on me this time."

He doesn't respond, but his eyes say it all. *Try and stop me.*

Luckily, I get him changed with no issues.

I make a note to buy some more diapers because it looks like there aren't many left in his diaper bag.

"Let's go search for your mom," I say. "I need your help in talking some sense into her. Every time I turn around, she's gone."

Asher shoves his fist in his mouth in agreement.

"If I had known that the Prez was allowing club whores into the main clubhouse, I'd have asked for a transfer."

Surely, I didn't hear what I think I did. And surely, it's not directed to the woman under my protection.

"I'm not a whore. And if you don't remove your hand, I will stab it."

"Damn, you need to be shown your place."

Turning the corner, I see Riley cornered by Seth. Some fucker from the East Chapter. She's facing toward me, and he's plastered against her back. His hand was on her shoulder, but he reaches around and grabs her tit.

I. See. Fucking. Red.

Before I can react, Riley takes the fork she's holding and jams it into Seth's hand. He screams and tumbles backward.

"What the fuck is going on?" Tank asks as he rounds the corner to the kitchen.

"Hold Asher," I growl with barely restrained anger.

"No way, Prez. He's too small," Tank says, taking a step back. "I'll accidentally break him."

"Tank, take him. Now."

Sighing, he nods as I place the baby against his chest

and move Tank's large hand to hold him in place.

As soon as the baby is safely out of my arms, I fucking attack.

Seth doesn't have time to react. My fist connects with his jaw, sending him sprawling across the floor. He scrambles to get up, but I'm already on him, pinning him down with one knee as I grab the front of his cut.

"You've got a death wish, asshole," I snarl, pulling him closer until our faces are inches apart. "Touch her again, and I'll fucking burn you alive."

He spits blood, glaring up at me with defiance. "She just stabbed…"

I don't let him finish. My knuckles crash into his face again, silencing him. The satisfying crunch of his nose breaking echoes in the room.

"Enough, Spike!" Tank's bored voice cuts through the haze of my rage. "You'll kill him."

I glance back at Tank, then to Asher, who's watching from his arms. The baby doesn't cry, but his little fist is shoved into his mouth, and drool runs down his arm. I'm taking that as approval.

Reluctantly, I release Seth, letting him fall to the floor in a groaning, bloody heap. My chest heaves as I try to rein in the storm raging inside me.

Riley's voice brings me back. "You didn't need to do that," she says, her tone even but firm. "I had it handled."

"He grabbed you, Riley. That's not something I'm just gonna let slide."

She doesn't flinch, meeting my glare with the same fiery resolve she had when she stabbed him. "And I handled it. You didn't need to go full berserker."

Tank chuckles under his breath. "She's got a point."

I ignore him, stepping closer to Riley. "You're under my

protection. No one puts their hands on you. Got it?"

After a few seconds, she smiles softly. "Got it," she says.

"Get this piece of shit back down to the basement," I bark.

Handing the baby to Riley, Tank nods, motioning for two nearby prospects to drag Seth out. Once the room clears, it's just me, Riley, and Asher.

I look back at her, trying to calm the fire still burning in my chest. "You okay?"

She sighs, setting the bloody fork on the counter. "I'm fine, Spike. But, just because he's a creep didn't mean you had to hurt him."

I smirk, unable to help myself. "He deserved worse. And for the record, you stabbed him first."

Her lips twitch like she's fighting a smile. "Fair point."

Asher lets out a squeal, breaking the tension.

"Come on, little man," she murmurs, her voice softening as she cradles him. "Let's get you fed."

I watch her walk away, the heat of the moment finally giving way to something else. Something I can't quite name but feels just as dangerous.

I'm in deep and I don't even know anything about her apart from her first name.

And the fact that she's beautiful.

And makes my head spin.

I need coffee.

"Hey, Prez," Skip says. "Just got a call from Runner. He found something online about your girl. Said he sent it to your email."

Pouring myself a cup of coffee, I head back to my office.

I haven't even begun to sort out the Riley situation. That's next on my agenda once I figure out who the traitor is.

My mind is a million miles away as I open the office door and head inside. Three steps in, I notice Riley sitting on the couch nursing Asher.

"I'm so sorry," I mumble. "I'll come back when you're finished."

"It's alright," she smiles. "I'm completely covered."

"Not to sound rude," I say, rubbing my neck. "Why are you in here and not in your room?"

"Oh," she whispers, a blush rushing across her face. "I can't seem to relax in there. I feel like I'm being watched. But when I'm in this room, I feel safe. I know it's weird. I'll go to my room."

She goes to stand, and the blanket that was covering her falls away.

"No." My voice is rougher than I mean it to be, and I force myself to soften. "Don't. You're fine."

She hesitates but nods, her gaze dropping back to Asher. Her fingers move gently over his tiny head, soothing him as he nurses.

I should turn around. I should leave. But my feet don't move.

Instead, I step inside, shutting the door behind me.

Moving to my desk, I sit, though I barely notice doing it. My eyes stay on her. On them.

The outside light catches the gold in her hair and the soft curve of her cheek. Her focus is completely on Asher, her expression calm and... serene.

It's the most beautiful thing I've ever seen.

And the most unsettling.

Something stirs in me. Something I don't understand. I've seen women nursing before. Hell, half the guys in the club have kids, and no one blinks an eye at the old ladies who breastfeed out in the open.

But this is different.
She's different.

CHAPTER NINE

Riley

"I have to call him," I say, staring at the article on Spike's computer, my heart pounding.

"Absolutely not," Spike growls, his voice sharp enough to cut glass.

"If I don't, he's going to turn this into a manhunt," I argue, refusing to back down.

"Maybe she could call the police station instead," Max suggests cautiously. "She could let them know she and the baby are safe without speaking to Chuck directly."

"That won't work," Maverick interjects. "He'll just claim she was coerced into saying it. The best thing to do is stay hidden."

"For the rest of my life?" I snap, my frustration bubbling over.

Spike's jaw tightens. "What did you expect to happen when you left?" he asks, his tone cutting. "His woman and his son vanish from the hospital without a trace, and you think he'd just let that slide? You knew he wouldn't stop."

His words sting, but I refuse to look away.

"We're risking a hell of a lot to keep you safe," he continues, his voice lowering but no less intense. "Going up against a Police Commissioner isn't a small thing. One slip, one phone call, and it could all come crashing down. Do you understand that?"

"I do understand that," I say firmly, refusing to waver under Spike's intense glare. "But he doesn't have to know where I'm at."

"Your call could be traced," he snaps, frustration clear in his tone.

"Then maybe I go to the police station instead," I counter. "If they see me in person, they'll know I'm okay. I'll explain that I left because I didn't feel safe."

A thought hit me. The spy. What if he already knows I'm here? I open my mouth to tell him about it, but he speaks first.

"And walk right into his hands?" Spike growls, taking a step closer, his towering presence making the room feel smaller. His dark eyes flash with unrestrained anger, his voice dripping with derision. "How fucking stupid can you be, Riley? You might as well have stayed and let him use and abuse you while he raised *your* child with another woman."

His words hit like a slap, the weight of his anger and contempt pressing down on me, squeezing the air out of my lungs. My brain freezes every thought as I try and process his anger.

"Fuck, Spike," someone mutters under their breath, the tension in the room crackling like a live wire.

I feel lightheaded, my pulse pounding in my ears. For the first time since arriving here, I want to be anywhere else but here. For the first time since I met him, I don't feel safe.

"If this is how you make decisions," Spike continues, his voice harsher now, "maybe you don't deserve that kid. Did you think about him when you packed up and ran? Or did you just decide to gamble with his life and hope for the best?"

I can't breathe. My chest aches, and every word he spits feels like a dagger sinking deeper. "That's not fair," I whisper, my voice trembling as I try to hold back tears.

"Fair?" Spike's laughter is cold and hollow. "You want fair? Fair would've been that asshole rotting in a cell while you and Asher got to live your lives in peace. But instead, you come here, dragging your mess behind you, and now we're all in the crosshairs. So yeah, forgive me if I don't give a damn about *fair* right now."

The room is deathly silent except for the sound of my uneven breathing. My legs feel like jelly, but I force myself to stay standing, even as the walls seem to close in around me.

I stand frozen, his words tearing through me like a storm, my chest tight with the ache of trying to hold myself together.

"Do you even get how bad this is, Riley?" His voice rises, every word sharper than the last. "We're not just talking about your mess anymore. You put every one of us in danger when you walked through those doors. Hell, for all we know, you already led him here, and we're just sitting ducks."

He paces the room now, running a hand through his hair as though trying to rein in his fury but failing miserably. "And what's your big idea? Stroll into a police station and hope for the best? God, you're not just naïve. You're reckless. You think that bastard's gonna let you walk out of there once he's got his hands on you?"

The silence that follows is deafening, every pair of eyes in the room glued to the scene unraveling before them.

His words are sharp, each one cutting deeper than the last, but he doesn't stop there.

"You don't think, Riley. That's the problem. You never

think. And now, we're all cleaning up after your mess. We're gonna have more targets on our backs because you couldn't handle your shit. Maybe you should've stayed where you belonged. At least then the rest of us wouldn't be stuck risking our lives for someone too selfish to see what's at stake."

I stand frozen as the final blow lands, my body trembling from the force of his words.

My vision blurs as I step forward, scooping Asher from Tank's arms. My hands shake, but I clutch my son tightly, cradling him to my chest like a shield.

I don't say a word. I can't.

The silence in the room is suffocating, every pair of eyes watching as I turn and walk out of the room. My legs feel heavy, my steps slow, but I refuse to stop until I'm back in the guest room with the door closed firmly behind me.

Only then do I allow the tears to fall, each one burning as it escapes.

Spike's right. I didn't think of anyone else but myself. I was so afraid of Chuck taking my son away that I took him from a stable home. Sure, his father would have most likely kicked me out and moved in the woman he's seeing, but at least Asher would have a home.

I allow myself half an hour to cry and feel sorry for myself before wiping my face and packing Asher's bag. I only have one outfit, but it's been washed and dried. I make sure to fold the borrowed shirt and shorts on the bed. I don't know who they belong to, but they aren't mine to take.

Besides the outfit, I leave the rest of my money. It's the least I can do for them helping me. I'm not going to need it, anyway.

Time to make another stupid decision. But at least this one isn't about myself.

With Asher in his carrier, I head downstairs, keeping my head held high despite the knot of anxiety twisting in my stomach. The clubhouse feels eerily quiet as I step outside and walk toward the gate.

Mike is standing there, arms crossed, his expression unreadable. He straightens when he sees me approaching.

"I need you to open the gate," I say firmly, stopping a few feet away.

Mike hesitates, glancing back toward the house. "I, uh... I gotta check with the boss first."

I tighten my grip on Asher, the weight of Spike's words from earlier still lingering in my chest. "Unless I'm a prisoner here, Mike, you'll open the gate and let me leave." My voice is steady, though my anger simmers beneath the surface.

Mike shifts uncomfortably, clearly torn. Before he can respond, heavy footsteps echo from behind me.

"What the hell is this?" Spike's voice cuts through the air like a whip.

I turn to face him, my spine straightening. His expression is hard, his jaw clenched, and his dark eyes filled with fury.

"I'm leaving," I say simply, meeting his gaze head-on.

"Leaving?" He takes a step closer, his towering presence making the air feel heavier. "Where else can you go to hide, Riley?"

"That's none of your business," I reply, my tone sharp but even.

"The hell it isn't," he snaps. "You don't get to waltz in here, put us all in danger, and then just decide you're done. That's not how this works."

I take a breath, forcing myself to stay calm despite the anger radiating off him. "Please, just open the gates so I can leave. No one will ever know that I was here. None of you will be in any danger."

His eyes narrow, his lips curling into a sneer. "You want to leave? Fine. But don't come crying back when he finds you. And he will find you. You think you're protecting that kid?" Spike continues, his voice harsh. "You're just dragging him down with you. And when Chuck gets his hands on him, it'll be because of you."

I don't flinch, though his words feel like jagged shards slicing through me.

"Open the gate, Mike," Spike barks, his voice cold and final.

Mike hesitates for only a moment before stepping aside to press the button. The gate creaks open, the sound echoing in the tense silence.

I walk past Mike but stop and look at him for a few seconds. He really does look familiar. Hmm.

Turning, I look at Spike and try to smile.

"Thank you for your help, Spike," I say, trying my best to keep the tremble out of my voice. "You and your friends have been very kind to me. I'll always remember that. I'll always remember you."

I take a few more steps before pausing and looking back one last time.

"Not everyone close to you is trustworthy."

There are too many people around, and I don't want to risk the spy hearing. I have no idea who it is. But maybe I can trick Chuck into telling me, and I can find a way to warn Spike. Just because he hates me doesn't mean I hate him. No matter what he said tonight, I know he's not a monster. Even if my heart is saying otherwise.

I know he was just speaking out of anger. His words were harsh, but they were also what I needed to hear. I'm going to make everything right.

Without another word, I turn and walk away, holding Asher tightly as I step out of the safety of the compound. My chest aches, my legs feel weak, but I keep moving.

Spike's voice rings in my ears long after the gate closes behind me, each harsh word replaying in an endless loop.

I don't look back. I can't.

Because despite everything that just happened, I'll beg him to let us stay.

CHAPTER TEN

Spike

The TV screen flickers as Chuck's smooth, calculated voice fills the room. He looks polished, every word carefully measured to sound sincere. It's enough to make my blood boil.

"I can't thank God enough for bringing my family back home," he says, pausing like he's choking back some fake emotion. "However, due to this incident, security in the hospital will be increased. How many other women have up and left because of postpartum depression? How many new mothers and children weren't as lucky as my wife and child?"

He shakes his head, playing the role of the concerned man to perfection. "That's all the time I have right now. I just want to get my family home."

The screen cuts back to the anchor, but I don't hear a damn thing they say. My fists clench at my sides, rage simmering under my skin. Two days ago, she walked through my gate, and I haven't stopped thinking about her since. The anger hasn't lessened.

"Why the fuck would she go back to him?" I say through gritted teeth.

"Oh, I don't know," Skip says, his eyes glaring daggers at me. "Could be something along the lines of, '*Maybe you should've stayed where you belonged. At least then the rest of us wouldn't be stuck risking our lives for someone too selfish to see what's at stake.' But that's just a guess."*

"Yeah," Maverick agrees. "You're a fucking idiot."

"She wasn't putting us at risk," Bones adds. "And you damn well know it. You were just too pissed at the thought of her being near Chuck."

"We all saw the way you looked at her, Prez," Tank says. "We saw how protective you were. Hell, we even saw how you were with that baby. We also saw you avoiding her because she messed with your head. You had a great opportunity there, and you blew it."

Fuck. Fuck. Fuck.

"It's for the best," I lie. "I've got too much shit on my shoulders as it is. Riley is back where she belongs. Let's get to work. The Black Serpents are asking for permission for seven of their men to make a run through our territory. We need to contact their President and see the reason why before I make a decision. Also, I'm sending the men in the basement back to their sector. I'll deal with this traitor business next week."

The men look at me clearly wanting to say more, but they won't.

The sound of a fax coming through breaks the silence.

"I'll get it," Skip grunts. "It's probably for me anyway."

He's right. The only faxes that come through are things involving money. That's Skip's domain.

"I'll make contact with the Serpents," Tank says, breaking the silence. "When are they wanting to come through?"

"Next Friday," I say, flopping down in my chair.

"Should be fine on our end as long as their reasoning is sound," he tells me. "By the way, your brother called. Said to tell you that you can't avoid him forever. He'll be here next month."

"Call him and tell him I'm busy all next month," I demand.

"He wouldn't listen if I did," Tank chuckles. "Just as stubborn and hardheaded as his big brother."

My mind keeps circling back to Riley and the way I tore into her. It's my fault she went back to that bastard. I was so angry at the thought of her walking straight into the police station, right into his hands, that I couldn't stop the words from spilling out. Every venomous thing I said feels like a weight on my chest.

"You listening, Prez?" Tank's voice cuts through my spiraling thoughts.

"No," I admit, shaking my head. "He *hits* her. She told us that herself. And she just *walks* right back into his arms?"

"Spike, you know damn well she didn't go back to him because she missed him," Maverick says, his tone calm but firm. "She went back to keep the cops off our doorstep. I'm not saying it was the right call, but her heart was in the right place."

"She didn't even give us a chance to help," I say, frustration lacing every word. "We've got someone digging into Chuck's background, but she bailed before we could get anything useful."

"Because you *pushed* her away," Skip snaps, his anger clear as day. "You couldn't pull your head out of your ass long enough to hear what she was trying to say before you tore her apart with your words. Of course, she left. Why the hell would she stay after that?"

"Skip, back the fuck off," I warn, my voice low.

"I don't think I will, Spike." He steps closer, glaring at me. "Forget for a second that you clearly felt something for her and her kid, though you were too much of a coward to face it. Let's focus on how fucking stupid you were with your words. I watched you tear her down, blow by blow. Every time you opened your mouth, I saw the trust in her eyes shatter. And you," he jabs a finger at my chest, "you let it happen."

The room falls silent as Skip steps back and tosses a thick folder onto my desk.

"We haven't gotten anything on Chuck yet," he says, his voice tight, "but we've got plenty on Riley Hayes. It came in about an hour ago. I made it through five pages before I had to stop."

My stomach knots as I flip open the folder. The first page freezes me in place: a photo of a younger Riley, sitting in a wheelchair, her entire left leg in a cast. Behind her stands Chuck, smiling like the devil himself. A car accident report accompanies the image. It says Riley was severely injured, while Chuck walked away with little more than a few scratches.

Skip's voice is heavy with disgust. "She downplayed her entire life with that bastard. When I asked her if he hit her, all she did was nod. But it wasn't just hitting. He's been abusing her for years. And then *you*, with your shouting and the vile shit you said, hit her just as hard. I'm ashamed of you, Spike."

I take the verbal punch and turn the page. A police report stares back at me, detailing a mugging. Photos show Riley with finger-shaped bruises around her throat. I flip to the next page. A medical record of a swollen chin and black eye. The attached police report blames a man Chuck had sent to prison. Another piece of revenge Chuck orchestrated, no doubt.

"He's covering it all up," I mutter, the words bitter on my tongue. "Every single thing he does to her, he's got the power to bury it."

"Yeah," Skip says coldly. "Good thing she walked back into his arms, huh?"

He tosses another piece of paper onto my desk.

"One more thing," he says. "Apparently, Chuck has a damn spy inside the compound."

My blood runs cold as I grab the paper and start reading aloud.

The monster has eyes inside. I tried to tell you before, but something always got in the way. I don't know his real name, but I know the name he goes by over there. And I know his face. I won't mention names here in case I don't have the right fax number, but it hit me as I was leaving why he looked so familiar. It's your gate guy. Not the first one. Although, he was a creep. The one with the kind eyes. He's working for the monster. I'm not sure it's by choice, though. I overheard the monster telling someone a couple of months ago that if you-know-who didn't come through, then he'd lose someone close to him.

Please don't be too hard on him. Thank you for your kindness and generosity. Don't worry about us. Little Man is safe. I'll keep my ears to the ground and reach out if I hear anything you need to know.

Always,
Your Little (ugh, rolls eyes) Friend.

Skip's voice cuts through the heavy silence. "You're gonna fix this, Spike. Not for me, not for the club. For her. And don't screw it up this time."

I let the paper fall to my desk, my jaw tight and my mind racing. Riley's words echo in my head, mingling with Skip's condemnation.

"What the fuck did I do?" I mutter, the weight of my

actions suffocating me.

"A very stupid thing," Bones says, his voice calm but firm. "But you'll fix it. First, we need to deal with the problem at hand."

I take a deep breath, forcing all thoughts of Riley and Asher to the back of my mind… for now.

"Fucking Mike," I growl.

"Fucking Mike," Bones echoes grimly.

"Alright, let me think." I rise from my desk, pacing as I try to get my thoughts in order. "Max, I need you to get eyes on Riley and fucking Chuck."

Max frowns. "How the hell am I supposed to do that?"

"We need a damn tech guy," Knuckles says. "None of us are set up for this kind of thing."

"What about the guy we hired to scrub Bones out of that surveillance footage?" Tank suggests. "Fox or something?"

"Knox," Skip corrects with a nod. "The Obsidian."

"He charges a fucking fortune," Max points out.

"I don't care how much it costs. Make it happen," I snap. "When is Mike's shift over?"

"He's training one of the prospects on gate duty," Max replies. "His break is at three, then he's heading to the roof with the rifle for a couple of hours."

"Tell him to meet you in the war room to report on the prospect," I say, the plan forming quickly in my mind. That kind of request wouldn't raise any suspicion. Max is in charge of the prospects. It's routine.

Crusher speaks up, his brow furrowed. "I'll admit, I'm confused. Mike's been with us for years. There's no way he's been a traitor this whole time. What if Riley's lying? Or what if she's just wrong?"

"We'll find out soon enough," Skip says, his signature

mischievous smirk returning, tinged with a hint of malice.

***

Mike walks into the war room, and Maverick shuts the door behind him.

"Must be one hell of a prospect to have all the officers here for a report," Mike says, forcing a smirk. But I can see the nervous energy rolling off him. He's trying to play it cool and failing miserably.

"Have a seat, Mike," I say, nodding toward one of the many chairs at the round table.

He hesitates for only a second before lowering himself into the chair. I lean against the wall, arms crossed, waiting.

"What's going on?" he asks, glancing around the room.

"Do you know who Riley Hayes is?" I ask, cutting straight to the point.

His brows knit together. "Uh… yeah. She was the woman here with the baby, right? Why?"

"I meant before she came here," I clarify, my voice calm but firm.

His frown deepens. "No."

"You sure?" Bones interjects, flipping the chair next to him around and straddling it. "Maybe it was during one of your meetings with the Police Commissioner?"

Mike's eyes widen, panic flashing across his face. "Fuck," he whispers.

"Yeah, fuck," I echo. "So, do you want to try that answer again?"

He swallows hard, his gaze darting between us. "I swear, I never met her before she came here," he insists, holding my stare. "I'll explain everything. But what does she have to do with Commissioner Chuck?"

I shouldn't answer him. But Riley's words, her request not to be too harsh, echo in my head.

"She just had his baby," I say bluntly. "Now, you've been with us for years. You know exactly what we do to traitors. Start talking."

Mike scrubs a hand down his face, exhaling sharply. "Fuck, okay," he mutters. "Six months ago, my little sister got into trouble and landed herself in prison. A few weeks ago, during a visit, she told me one of the male guards was getting handsy with her. I went through half a dozen people trying to get Brittany transferred or at least get the guard fired. Nothing worked. Finally, I ended up at the Commissioner's door. At first, he told me he couldn't do anything. Said the prison wasn't his domain. Then, a few days later, he calls me out of nowhere and says if I do him a solid, he'll make sure Brittany's taken care of."

"A solid?" I repeat, voice dripping with venom.

"He wanted intel on the club," Mike admits. "I told him I wasn't in the inner circle, that I didn't know shit he'd care about. But that wasn't good enough. He wanted me to listen. Report back daily on what was happening."

"The mule run?" I ask, my hand twitching toward my gun. Mike was one of my ten.

Mike's eyes blaze with anger. "I haven't told him a fucking thing," he snaps. "I've lied my ass off. Gave him false info just to keep him off my back."

"What kind of false info?" Bones asks, watching him closely.

Mike smirks.

"I told him that the club was looking to expand into Arizona," he says. "That we were negotiating a territory split with the Vipers, but tensions were high. I made it sound like we were on the verge of a war."

Bones raises a brow. "That's some serious shit to lie about."

"Exactly," Mike says. "I figured if I fed him something big enough to keep him distracted, he wouldn't push for more intel. And it worked. He's been so focused on tracking some imaginary turf war that he hasn't asked for anything else."

I study him, searching for any sign of deceit. If he's lying, he's damn good at it.

"You expect us to believe you?" I ask, testing the waters a bit further.

He holds my gaze, unflinching. "I know how this looks, Prez. But I swear on my sister's life, I never gave him anything real."

The room is tense, the silence heavy. No one speaks for a long beat. Then Bones exhales sharply, shaking his head.

"So, let me get this straight," Bones says, his voice almost amused. *Almost.* "You got tangled up with the Commissioner to save your sister, played him with fake intel, and now we have to clean up your mess?"

Mike winces. "I can fix it."

"No, *we'll* fix it," I correct. "But first, we need to know exactly how deep this shit goes."

"I haven't contacted him in a few days," Mike admits. "He's been texting, asking for an update, but I've been stalling."

I nod. "Good. Here's what's gonna happen. You're gonna keep feeding him bullshit, but now, you're doing it under my orders. We're gonna turn this around and make him chase his own tail."

Mike's relief is visible. "I can do that."

"Damn right, you can," I say. "But make no mistake, you're on thin fucking ice. One misstep, and I won't hesitate to put a bullet between your eyes."

He nods, swallowing hard. "Understood."

I push off the wall, glancing at Skip. "Get Knox on the line. We're gonna need his help. Be sure to pull money from our offshore account to pay him. If Chuck's watching closely enough, I want to ensure the money trace doesn't touch the Obsidians."

Skip nods, already pulling out his phone.

"Mike," I say, leveling him with a look. "You're gonna set up a meeting with Chuck. Tell him you've got something big, something urgent."

Mike hesitates. "What do I tell him?"

I smirk, a plan already forming.

"Tell him the Vipers found out we were planning to move in on their turf," I say. "And they're fucking pissed."

Mike's eyes widen. "You want to make him think a war's already started?"

I grin. "Exactly."

Knuckles chuckles. "Shit, this is gonna be fun."

Mike exhales, nodding. "Alright. I'll set it up."

"Good." I glance around the room. "Everyone, stay sharp. When Chuck takes the bait, we're breaking into his house and getting my fucking woman back."

The brothers nod, the energy in the room shifting.

"Hey, Iron Shadow," a voice, Knox, I'm assuming, comes through Skip's speaker. The phone sits on the table while Skip focuses on his laptop.

"Obsidian," Skip greets. "Got a job for you."

"Aww, did widdle Skippy forget how to turn on his waptop?"

Skip sighs, trying to hide his smirk. "Fucker. I need you

to get eyes on Police Commissioner Charles Landry here in Palm Springs and the mother of his child, Riley Hayes."

"Ooo, a Police Commissioner," Knox sings. "That one's gonna cost you."

"We don't care," Skip says, his tone flat. "He's been abusing her for years. Hit her in the stomach at eight months pregnant and caused her to go into preterm labor. She came to us for help but went back to him out of fear for us. The bastard is out to ruin our club."

A different voice cuts in from Knox's side. "Why the fuck would you let her go back?"

"Stop listening in on my conversations, Papa. I mean, husband. I mean, dammit, go away," Knox snaps. A shuffle of movement follows, then a huff. "Anyway, sorry about that. So, she's with him now?"

"Yeah," Skip says, shaking his head. "Tell Taylor I said hey and that he still owes me that beer."

"Will do. Now, what about the baby?"

Skip looks up, a silent question in his eyes.

"I'm assuming he's with Riley," I answer. "But I can't say for certain."

"Oh, hey stranger," Knox's voice breaks in. "Okay, I have a Riley Hayes living in Palm Springs with her partner, Charles Landry. Uhm, no mention of a baby. Are you sure she had one?"

"I've got a milk-stained shirt to prove it," I reply, an uneasy feeling beginning to gnaw at me.

"She said Asher was born two days before she came here," Maverick reminds everyone. "She was here for three days, and now she's been gone for two."

"So, he was born a week ago," Skip observes.

"Give me a second," Knox says. "You said his name is Asher? What about his last name. Hayes or Landry?"

"We don't know," I admit, the frustration rising in my chest. I'm fucking pissed that I don't know.

Silence stretches through the phone line, broken only by the rapid tapping of Knox's keyboard.

"Interesting," Knox murmurs. "In the past two weeks, sixteen babies have been born, but not one to a Riley Hayes." A few more clicks follow. "Let me try Riley Landry... Nope."

"What the fuck is going on?" Tank's voice breaks through the tension.

"I'm looking at her medical records as we speak," Knox responds, his light tone gone, replaced by something more serious. "Here's what I'm gonna do. Give me a few hours to dig deeper, and I'll call you back. I already have Charles on my screen. He's at his office right now. I'll let you know if anything changes."

"I need your price," Skip says, already pulling up one of our bank accounts and preparing to transfer the payment.

"Pro bono," Knox says, his voice now devoid of the usual humor. "My payment is simple. You get her and that baby away from that bastard. If she needs a place to stay, let me know. I'll talk to my president, but I don't think it'll be a problem."

"Not happening," I growl, my voice low and dangerous. Once I get those two back, I'm never letting them go.

"Possessive. Sexy."

"PUP."

"Shit, gotta go. I'll be in touch."

The call ends, and the room feels heavier.

"Knox seems... interesting," Knuckles chuckles.

"I've only met him once," Skip says, grinning. "He's definitely fun to be around. Almost as crazy as me. But

Taylor and I go way back. He used to be a detective, and we crossed paths during one of his assignments. Sexy as sin. It's a shame he's married."

"Focus," I growl.

"Got the meeting," Mike says, looking up from his phone. "He can meet with me tomorrow at five."

"Let's hope The Obsidian can get back to us with more information before then," I say, my jaw clenched. "I want to know why Asher's birth records don't exist."

CHAPTER ELEVEN

Riley

I think I've made a terrible mistake coming back. But, at the same time, I don't regret my decision. If Chuck ever finds out that they helped me, he would rain hell down on their heads. He'd give up looking for something and just lie his ass off to get them thrown in prison.

Frankly, I'm surprised he hasn't done that already.

"I said, stand the fuck up," Chuck yells, his voice seething with rage. "What kind of worthless woman are you?"

I flinch but keep my eyes on the floor, biting my lip to stop myself from crying. "I'm sorry, Chuck," I say, trying to steady my voice, my hands shaking. "I cooked the chicken the way you like it."

"No, you didn't," he snaps, his voice rising. "Now, get your fat ass up and clean up this mess. Casandra's on her way, and we need to make plans."

I hesitate, my heart pounding. I can't do this anymore.

"You're not taking my son," I say, my voice trembling but firm. I feel the defiance rise in me, a small spark of courage.

Chuck freezes for a moment before his expression hardens into something darker. "What did you say to me?"

It's only then I realize how badly I've pushed him.

"You heard me," I say, trying to stay as calm as possible, though my hands are clammy and my stomach twists. "I'm not letting you take him. I know you plan to leave me and raise my son with someone else. I won't let you do that. He's MY SON."

The words feel like a weight lifted from my chest, but I immediately regret speaking them. His face contorts into a look of pure fury, eyes flashing with an intensity I've seen before, but never this close to the surface.

"You really think you have a say in this?" His voice is low, deadly calm. "You're lucky I don't throw your ass right back out the door. You're nothing but a fucking burden, Riley."

I take a step back, but Chuck is faster. He grabs me by the wrist, his grip like iron, yanking me toward him. The force causes my breath to hitch, the pain in my arm flaring up.

"You're MY property," he growls, his words dripping with venom. "And you think you can stop me? You think you can stand in my way and have any fucking say in what happens to MY son?"

My pulse races, fear clawing at me, but I refuse to back down. I struggle to hold my ground. "I'm his mother, Chuck," I spit, my voice shaking with both fear and anger. "I don't care what you think you own. I won't let you tear him from me."

His eyes narrow, and before I can react, he shoves me hard against the kitchen counter. My head slams into the edge, and a sharp, sickening pain shoots through my skull. The world spins for a moment, but I push through, trying to focus.

Chuck looms over me, his chest heaving with rage. "You think you're going to stop me?" he growls again.

"You're pathetic."

Before I can react, he slaps me across the face, the impact ringing in my ears. My cheek burns, and my eyes fill with tears, but I bite my lip and refuse to let them fall.

The slap is nothing compared to what I've endured over the years, but this time, something feels different. This time, it hurts more.

"You're nothing without me, Riley," Chuck sneers, stepping closer, towering over me. "No one will ever want you. You'll always be my problem to deal with. You'll always be mine."

A sob rises in my throat, but I force it back down. I'm done being afraid. I refuse to be scared of him anymore.

"I'll fight you," I whisper, my voice broken but steady. "I'll fight for him."

Chuck laughs darkly, the sound mocking. "You're a fool, Riley. You really think you can take me on? Do you think anyone will believe you?"

I open my mouth to respond, but before I can get the words out, he grabs me again, this time by the throat. His fingers dig into my skin, cutting off my breath.

"You're nothing," he repeats, his voice cold and final. "I'm done with you."

The world around me starts to blur, the pressure on my neck making it harder and harder to breathe. My vision fades, and just as everything goes black, the last thing I hear is his voice, filled with anger, ringing in my ears.

"Nothing," he says before everything goes silent.

Spike

"PREZ."

Skip's shout cuts through the night like a gunshot, stopping me dead in my tracks.

I turn, my muscles coiled tight, already knowing I'm about to hear something I don't want to.

Skip comes to a stop a few feet away, his eyes lock onto mine, and I see something I don't like. Hesitation. Like he's trying to figure out how to say whatever the fuck he's about to say without setting me off.

"Just got confirmation on Riley," he says after a few seconds, his voice clipped. "She's in the hospital. She was attacked. The report says she was mugged."

I don't wait for details.

I'm already moving.

My boots slam against the pavement as I stalk toward my bike, my heart a violent rhythm in my chest. The air around me turns razor-sharp, my vision narrowing to one singular purpose... Getting to Riley.

"We have to go about this rationally," Skip says, keeping pace beside me, his voice lower now, more controlled. "If we're gonna get her and Asher away from Chuck, it's best if he doesn't catch wind of us being there."

Rational.

I don't feel fucking rational.

I feel like putting my fist through the first wall I see. I feel like hunting that bastard down and making him wish he'd never laid a hand on her. But I grit my teeth because Skip's right. I can't go in guns blazing, no matter how bad I want to.

I don't just want Riley back. I need her back. I need them both more than my next breath, and that confuses the fuck out of me.

"I have an idea," Maverick calls from the clubhouse doorway, arms crossed, eyes unreadable. "But I'm gonna need you to trust me."

I exhale sharply, clenching my jaw so hard it aches.

I don't like trusting shit I don't control.

But right now, I don't have time to argue.

I nod.

"Lose the cut," he orders. "Meet me outside the gate in thirty minutes. Bring Bones with you in case shit goes sideways."

Then, without another word, he swings his leg over his bike, revs the engine, and speeds off towards the gate.

I stand there, fists clenched, staring after him. My mind is a storm, my pulse hammering in my ears.

Riley is in the hospital.

Hurt.

Probably scared.

Where's Asher?

And if Chuck had anything to do with this, I will burn his fucking world to the ground.

Turning on my heel, I stalk toward the clubhouse, already yanking off my cut.

Time to get my girl back.

Twenty-five minutes later, I'm outside the gate with Bones, both of us in civilian clothes. The night air is thick, heavy, like it knows shit's about to go sideways. Bones leans against the gate, arms crossed, one boot propped up against the metal. He looks calm and collected, but I know better. His mind is a million miles away.

"What's up?" I ask, my voice steady, even though my insides are anything but.

Bones doesn't answer right away. Just exhales slowly through his nose, his gaze locked on something in the distance. Then, without looking at me, he says, "Maybe you should stay here. I'll collect them both and bring them back."

My whole body goes tight. "Not fucking happening, Bones."

"Don't trust me?" he asks, finally looking my way, one brow arched.

"You know that's not true," I glare, my patience already razor-thin. "What the fuck is up with you?"

He shifts, dropping his boot and standing up straight. "Just a bad feeling," he admits. "My gut keeps telling me to keep you the fuck away from the Commissioner."

I let out a dry chuckle, shaking my head. "Don't you ever just ignore it?"

Bones gives me a look, the kind that says I should know better. "You'd be dead a dozen times over if I had."

He's right.

Bones isn't just my enforcer. He's my shield. The one who steps between me and the bullets I don't see coming. Which is exactly why Maverick wanted him here. I've got a list of enemies a mile long.

And after tonight?

Chuck Landry is gonna be at the top of it.

"I have to go, Bones," I sigh, running a hand down my face. "I can't explain it, but there's something inside me, something clawing at my fucking chest, telling me I need to get to her and that baby. I need them inside the compound walls where they're safe."

Bones watches me for a second, his face unreadable, then nods. "I know." His voice is steady, but there's something behind it. Something that tells me he gets it, even if I don't fully understand it myself. "We'll make it happen."

A set of headlights cuts through the dark as a gray car pulls up the short driveway and rolls to a stop several feet away. My body tenses instantly, my hand twitching toward the gun at my back.

Seconds later, Maverick steps out of the driver's side, and my eyes immediately snap to the passenger door as another man, one in uniform, climbs out.

My blood runs cold.

"What the fuck, Maverick?" My voice is low, dangerous.

Maverick just smirks. "Trust me?"

Fuck.

I clench my jaw, then give him a single nod.

"This is my friend, Alex," Maverick says. "He's safe. I give you my word he's trustworthy."

I don't like it. I don't trust cops, and for damn good reason. But I trust Maverick.

The so-called friend, Alex, steps closer. His hands rest casually on his belt, but he doesn't radiate the usual smugness I associate with most cops. He's watching me closely, but not like I'm the enemy. More like he's weighing his words.

"Maverick told me what's going on," Alex says. "And I'm not the least bit surprised the Commissioner is involved in this. The guy is shady as fuck, and I'm not the only officer who doesn't trust him."

I narrow my eyes, crossing my arms. "So why are you here?"

Maverick answers before Alex can. "Alex pulled some strings and got assigned to Riley's case."

"What the fuck for?" My patience is wearing thin.

"She told the doctor she was mugged," Alex explains. "The hospital is required to report cases like this, so we were called in. If she's stable, I can pull her from the hospital and take her in for questioning."

"Not. Fucking. Happening." The words come out as a

growl, my body practically vibrating with anger.

Alex doesn't even flinch. "Or," he continues, "I can have her discharged and escorted to a safe location. I'll bring her to the car where you will be waiting. But no matter what, I still have to ask her a few questions."

"She'll just lie," Bones says, speaking up for the first time. His voice is sharp, edged with something dark. "She won't say shit about Chuck."

Alex tilts his head. "You think she's protecting him?"

Bones scoffs. "No. I think she's protecting everyone else." His voice lowers, and the weight of his words sinks into my chest. "That bastard holds a lot of power and can destroy a lot of lives. Riley knows that."

I clench my fists, my teeth grinding together so hard I swear I taste blood.

Riley went back to hell to protect us. It's not her job to protect me. It's my fucking job to protect her. And I'm doing a shit poor job of it.

I'm about to burn the whole fucking city down to bring her home.

"I'm gonna need you in control if we want this plan to work without any complications," Alex continues. "Any markings to indicate your club need to be taken off or hidden. If, for some reason, you need to enter the hospital, leave your guns in the car. They will be detected if you bring them through the doors."

I don't like this. Not one fucking bit.

Walking into a hospital, unarmed, with Chuck's men probably watching? It's a recipe for disaster. But if this is the only way to get Riley out of there, I don't have a choice.

My jaw flexes. "Fine. But the second something feels off, I'm going in, and I don't give a fuck who sees me."

Alex, looking down at his phone, nods. "Alright, we need to go. I want to get her out of there before the Commissioner shows up."

Bones and I jump in the back of the car, and Maverick pulls out of the driveway.

"Her medical report just came through," Alex says reluctantly.

"What does it say?" I demand.

"Is he stable?" he asks Maverick.

"I'm very close to not being," I warn. "What the fuck does it say?"

Alex exhales sharply, "It's bad," he admits. "Worse than I expected."

The air in the car shifts, thickening with tension. Every muscle in my body locks up, my fingers flexing like they're itching for someone's throat.

"She's got a concussion," Alex continues, his voice tight. "Doctors noted dizziness, confusion, and sensitivity to light. There's also a deep laceration on her scalp. Likely from hitting something sharp. They had to stitch it up."

I grind my teeth, my jaw aching from the pressure.

"That's not all," Alex adds grimly. "Her cheekbone is bruised and swollen. Badly. And in her left eye, there's a burst blood vessel. The report says it's consistent with blunt force trauma."

Maverick mutters a curse under his breath. Bones clenches his fists, his knuckles turning white.

"There's more," Alex says reluctantly. "She's got bruising around her throat. Finger marks."

The world tilts for a second.

"He choked her," I say, my voice deadly quiet.

Alex nods. "Doctor noted signs of strangulation. She's

hoarse, likely from pressure on her vocal cords. They also note she's having trouble swallowing."

My vision goes red.

That son of a bitch put his hands around her throat.

Tried to squeeze the life out of her.

Tried to silence her.

"She say anything about Chuck?" I manage, my voice dangerously low.

Alex shakes his head. "No. She's sticking to the mugging story."

"Of course she is," I grind out, barely able to contain my rage. "Because she knows if she points the finger at him, he'll make sure she disappears."

"It does say that Chuck is the one who brought her in," he says. "He told the doctor that he found her a few blocks from their home. Dropped her off with the excuse that he had to go out and find the person who did it."

My hands curl into fists against my thighs.

"She shouldn't be in that fucking hospital alone," I snap. "That bastard could walk back in at any second and finish the fucking job."

"Then let's make sure that doesn't happen," Maverick says, pulling into the hospital parking lot.

"Does it say anything about her son?" Bones asks.

"No mention of a child," he answers. "But there's an attached picture."

Leaning forward, I get my first look at Riley. She's hardly recognizable. She's bruised and swollen, and one of her eyes is completely red.

I can't take it anymore.

I shove open the door before Maverick can even find a spot to park.

No more waiting.

I'm getting Riley out of here, and I dare anyone to try and stop me.

"Weapon," Alex hisses sharply. "Leave it in the fucking car."

Without breaking stride, I yank my gun from its holster and toss it back at a waiting Bones.

"Fuck," Alex mutters under his breath. "Don't say a damn word, or both of our asses will end up behind bars."

As we step through the hospital's sliding doors, I force myself to dial it back. My body is vibrating with the need to move, to get to her, but I know walking in like a raging bull isn't gonna help.

Alex takes the lead, flashing his badge at the receptionist. "Officer Alex Cooper. This is my associate, Ethan Turner. We're here to see Riley Hayes."

How the fuck does he know my real name? I'm gonna have to kill Maverick. What else has he told this fucking cop?

The receptionist nods, barely glancing up. "I've been expecting you. She's in room two-nineteen. Elevators down the hall on the right, second floor."

"Appreciate it, ma'am," Alex says smoothly.

I force myself to move at his pace, even though every instinct in me is screaming to shove past him and run.

Less than five minutes later, I'm stepping through her door.

And the second I see her, every bit of control I have left fucking snaps. Her eyes widen as she looks our way, but it only enhances her injuries.

"Don't lose it now, Spike," Alex whispers. "She needs you in control."

Taking a deep breath, I take in every bit of Riley and commit her injuries to memory.

Riley, who has a body full of beautiful curves... who should look soft and strong... looks small. Too fucking small, swallowed by the sterile white sheets and surrounded by beeping machines.

One side of her face is so swollen it distorts her features, her cheekbone a mess of deep purple, sickly yellow already forming around the edges. Her right eye is bloodshot, the whites flooded with red from the burst vessel. The sight of it makes something deep in my chest crack open.

And then I see the bruises.

Dark, angry fingerprints wrapped around her throat like a fucking noose.

I've seen bruises like that before. I know what it takes to leave a mark that deep. I know how long, how fucking hard, someone has to squeeze for them to form. That son of a bitch tried to choke the life out of her.

A bandage wraps around her head, strands of her auburn hair peeking out from the edges. I don't know how bad that injury is, but she must've hit something hard. Hard enough to cause a concussion.

Her lips part slightly like she wants to say something, but when she tries, nothing comes out. Just a raw, strained sound.

Her throat is too fucked up to speak.

Fuck.

My fists clench so tight my knuckles crack.

"Spike."

Alex's voice barely registers. I can't look away from her. I did this.

No, I didn't throw the punches. But I let her go back to him.

I was so fucking cruel, so brutal with my words, that I

sent her running straight into the arms of a monster.

And now? She's lying in a hospital bed, looking too fucking small, too fucking broken.

I step forward slowly, swallowing back the rage that's threatening to tear me apart. I don't want her to flinch. I don't want her to be afraid of me.

Carefully, I reach for her hand.

She fucking flinches.

It's barely noticeable, just a slight twitch of her fingers, but I see it. I feel it.

And I, it fucking wrecks me.

I pull back immediately, my stomach twisting in ways I don't fucking understand. She doesn't trust that I won't hurt her.

And maybe she's right.

Because right now, I want to hurt someone. I want to find Chuck Landry and end him. I want to make him feel every ounce of pain he's inflicted on her a hundred times over.

But first, I need to get her out of here.

Because if I don't do it now, I might never get the chance.

"Baby," I say around the knot in my throat. "I'm so fucking sorry. Please, let me take you back home."

Tears fall down her eyes, but she doesn't make a noise.

"Please, baby girl," I beg. "Please, let me hide you away."

"Asher," she whispers.

"I swear on my life that I will get him back," I tell her fiercely. "I won't stop until he's home with us."

"Do you think he's in danger with his father?" Alex asks.

Riley shrinks into the bed at seeing the man.

"I hate that fucking man with everything I am," he says

quietly. "I only hope that we can link those prints on your precious throat to the Commissioner so we can finally get his ass off his high horse and tossed in a prison cell for the rest of his life."

Her eyes widen in panic.

"Mug," she says.

"Don't Riley," I growl. "We know you weren't fucking mugged. Let's talk about this later. Come with me and trust me to get your boy back?"

I hold out my hand and hold my breath. If she says no, I don't trust myself to walk away. I won't. I'll carry her ass out of this building kicking and screaming if I have to.

After a few moments, she places her hand in mine.

Sighing in relief, I lean forward and gently kiss her forehead.

"Thank you, baby," I whisper. "I only hope you can forgive me for saying the shit I did. I won't give you any excuses. Just know that I'll never do it again."

"I'll go and get a chair and have her paperwork expedited," Alex says.

I tighten my grip on Riley's hand, careful not to squeeze too hard. She looks so fucking breakable right now, and I hate it. I hate that I let this happen. That I was the reason she walked back into hell.

Her fingers tremble in mine, but she doesn't pull away. That's something.

Alex steps out of the room, leaving us alone, and I take the opportunity to crouch beside her bed, leveling our eyes.

"Riley," I say softly, but my voice still comes out rough as hell. Raw. "We're leaving as soon as your paperwork's done, but I need you to tell me the truth about Asher. Where is he?"

Her breath shudders, and her lips part slightly like she wants to answer, but then she just closes her eyes.

No.

I can't fucking take that.

"Baby girl," I beg, my voice dropping lower. "Please. I need to know."

She swallows hard, her throat working against the bruises, and when she finally opens her eyes, there's something in them that guts me.

Despair.

Fear.

Hopelessness.

"Cassandra," she whispers, her voice nearly gone.

Cassandra?

"Who is Cassandra?" I ask, hating that I need her to talk just a little bit more.

More tears, and as much as I want to kiss them away, I'm terrified of hurting her.

"New mommy," she whispers.

What the fuck?

"Is she the woman you heard Chuck talking to that night?" I ask, remembering her mentioning it.

She nods.

His new mommy.

The words slice through me like a fucking blade.

Riley drops her head, her shoulders trembling, and it takes every ounce of control I have not to put my fist through the nearest wall. Or Chuck's goddamn face.

That motherfucker didn't just take her son. He replaced her. He ripped her baby out of her arms and handed him off like she never even fucking mattered.

I suck in a sharp breath, forcing myself to stay calm. She doesn't need my rage right now. She doesn't need to see me lose my shit when she's already barely holding on.

But fuck.

I crouch lower, trying to catch her eyes, but she won't look at me.

"Riley," I say, softer now. Controlled. "Look at me, baby."

She doesn't.

"Look at me," I repeat, and after a long, agonizing time, she finally lifts her head.

Her eyes are red and swollen, her lashes clumped together from unshed tears, her bottom lip trembling. And her face, her beautiful fucking face, is drawn down in agony.

I grit my teeth so hard my jaw aches.

"He's still your son," I tell her, my voice steady, firm. Unshakable. "And I'm gonna get him back."

She just stares at me, so fucking broken that it nearly levels me.

"You don't understand," she whispers. "Chuck has full custody now."

My blood runs ice cold.

Full custody?

"What?" The word is a growl, low and deadly.

She nods weakly, blinking away more tears. "He made me sign something before he left. I... I didn't even know what I was signing."

A slow, insidious rage creeps into my veins. That conniving son of a bitch.

He beat her senseless. Left her hospitalized. And while she was half out of it, he stole her fucking child.

I tighten my grip on her hand, my knuckles white.

"He doesn't own him, Riley," I swear. "I don't give a fuck what piece of paper he made you sign. That baby is yours."

Ours, I want to say. But I haven't earned that right. But I fucking will. And I'll work my ass off to earn Riley's heart, too. Because this woman already owns mine. She did the moment I saw her. I was just too fucking stubborn and set in my ways to see that.

She shakes her head, flinching as she tries to swallow. "You don't get it. Chuck is the law in this city."

"Not for long," I promise.

Because now?

Now, it's fucking war.

***

We pull up to the gate, and I jump out to help Riley out of the car. "Careful, baby," I warn, steadying her as she almost stumbles, standing up too fast.

Before I say another word, Alex steps forward, looking serious. "I hate to do this, but I really need to ask her some questions. Can I come in for a few?"

I shoot him a hard look. "No offense, brother, but I'm not letting a fucking cop inside my compound," I say flatly. "Ask her your questions here, and when she's feeling better, I'll bring her in if you got more."

Alex sighs. "Fine. But I'm about to turn my body camera on before I ask any questions. If you don't want to be recorded, then you need to step away from her.

I wrap my arm around Riley, placing my hand on her hip. I'm going fucking nowhere.

Nodding, Alex turns on his body camera.

"I'll come back in a few days to get a more thorough statement, Ms. Hayes," he says, his tone measured but firm. "But, for now, I have to ask at least one question. Did Chuck do this to you?"

I can see it before she even tries to lie, the denial in her eyes. I lean down slightly, my voice low and dangerous. "Don't fucking lie for him, Riley."

I watch, seething, as Riley's eyes flicker with a mix of fear and defiance. For a long, agonizing moment, she doesn't answer. Then, her voice, barely above a whisper, trembles out.

"Yeah... Chuck did it. He... he hit me."

Even though I already knew the answer, the admittance still hit me like a punch to the gut. I feel every ounce of anger surge through me, every heartbeat a promise of retribution. I clench my fists so hard that I can barely breathe.

"Fuck," I growl, my voice raw with rage and regret.

"To clarify," Alex says, pointing at the body camera. "Police Commissioner Charles Landry is the one who attacked you?"

"Yes," she answers.

"Alright, Ms. Hayes," Alex says, handing her a card. "Call me if you need anything. Before I go, would you like to place a restraining order against Charles Landry?"

"Yes," she whispers.

Nodding, Alex reaches up and turns off his camera.

The air feels thick and suffocating. Riley's holding onto that damn hospital paperwork like it's the only thing keeping her upright. Her whole body trembles and I can see the devastation in her eyes. It fucking kills me.

"What about my son?" She whispers, her voice nearly gone. "He made me sign that paper. Will I ever get to see him again?"

"According to the hospital records, you never came in and gave birth," Alex tells her. "As of right now, Asher doesn't exist."

As her knees give out, I shuffle behind her and wrap my

arms around her waist, holding her up.

"Riley." My voice comes out rough, low with a warning. "Baby, I'm gonna get your son back. No matter who I have to kill to do it."

Alex sighs. "Spike, you can't say shit like that in front of a cop."

I turn and glare at him, daring him to push it. "Don't pretend you don't agree."

He presses his lips together, looking torn for half a second before shaking his head. "Look, I get it. I do. But if you want to take Chuck down, you need to be smart about it. No reckless moves."

"I don't give a fuck about smart," I snap. "That bastard took her kid. I'll handle this the way I see fit."

The tension crackles like a live wire, and before I can get into it with Alex, Bones steps up, looking more on edge than I've seen him in a long time. His voice is firm, leaving no room for argument.

"Conversation's over," he says. "We need to get inside the compound. Now."

I don't like being told what to do, but I know he's right. This isn't the time or place. Chuck's men could be watching. The longer we stand out here, the worse it gets.

"Thanks for your help today," I say. "I owe you one."

"You owe me nothing, Spike. Just keep her safe. Once I release this footage to my boss, Chuck's name is going to go on blast. She needs to be hidden."

"She will be," Bones says.

"Come on, baby," I murmur, leading her toward the gate.

I feel her fingers tighten around my shirt like she needs something solid to hold onto. I don't say anything else. There's nothing left to say.

As we step through the gate, I throw one last glance at Alex. He's watching us go, jaw tight, arms crossed, but I know he's not our enemy. He wants Chuck to burn just as badly as I do.

Fine.

But I'll be the one to light the fucking match.

CHAPTER TWELVE

Riley

I don't know where I'm at. I don't know what I feel. I don't know what to do.

I'm lost.

"Come on, Riley," Spike says. "I need you to eat something. Anything, baby. Just, please, eat."

Glancing down, I watch as fresh tears fall onto the sandwich.

"Throat hurts," I admit.

The plate disappears, and in its place is a spoon filled with applesauce.

"Open up, baby," Spike says softly. "This is easier to swallow."

I stare at the spoon, my body heavy, my mind blank. Everything feels distant, like I'm floating outside myself, watching a life that isn't mine.

"Riley," Spike presses, his voice softer now, almost pleading. "Just one bite."

I don't know why, but I open my mouth, letting him feed me. The applesauce is cold, smooth, and easy to swallow, but I barely taste it.

"There you go, baby," he murmurs, brushing a stray piece of hair from my face. "Just a little more."

I take another bite, then another. It's slow, but he doesn't rush me. Just sits there, steady, patient, feeding me like it's the only thing in the world that matters.

And maybe to him, it is.

Tears well up again, blurring my vision. "I don't know how to get him back," I whisper, my voice barely there.

Spike goes still, his jaw tightening. His hand clenches into a fist on his thigh, but when he speaks, his voice is deadly calm.

"I do."

Something in his tone sends a shiver down my spine. A promise. A threat.

He's not just saying it to make me feel better.

He means it.

Spike

After making sure Riley is settled and asleep in my office, I head straight to the war room.

"Who do you want in on this?" Tank asks as I step inside.

"Just the officers, Maverick, and Mike," I say, scanning the room.

Tank raises a brow. "You trust him?"

I hesitate for half a second before nodding. "Yeah."

Ten minutes later, Mike's sitting in one of the chairs, his hands clasped together, tension rolling off him in waves.

"Was Maverick able to get your sister transferred?" I ask.

Mike exhales, shaking his head in disbelief. "I don't know how, but she's being released. She'll be under house arrest for a year, but at least she'll be home."

"That wasn't me," Maverick says. "It was the Obsidian."

"I've got news on that front, too," Skip chimes in, flipping through a folder. "Knox found someone to fill the tech gap we've got. Guy's name is Zane Foster. Thirty-seven. No family. And according to Knox, smart as fuck." He smirks. "Was arrested last year for hacking into the Secret Service database. They had him dead to rights, but all proof of his involvement disappeared, so they had to let him go."

Knuckles lets out a low whistle. "Why the hell did he do that?"

Skip shrugs. "According to Knox, just to see if he could."

The room falls silent for a beat.

I lean back against the table, crossing my arms. "And he's looking for a job?"

"Yep," Skip nods. "He was a firefighter but they refused to hire him back after he got released. Knox says he was bored."

A guy like that being bored? Dangerous. But useful.

"Set up a meeting," I say. "Let's see what he can do. Mike, I know things didn't go as planned, but did you meet up with Chuck?"

"Yeah," he nods. "But he was flighty. Felt like he was in a rush to leave."

"Did he say anything?"

"Not really," Mike says. "He just wanted an update on any incoming shipments."

"He gets his hands on a single transport, and we're fucked," Tank says. "Maybe we should back off for a little while."

"Agreed," I nod. "Let's focus on our legal businesses and leave the rest alone for a few months. When can the tech guy meet us? I have his test ready if he's really looking to join."

"In an hour," Skip says a minute later. "Or, I can have him come tomorrow."

"An hour is fine," I say, standing. "I hope he's as good as the Obsidian says. His first task is to help us find Asher."

"Oh, uh… forgot to mention," Tank says, rubbing the back of his neck. "Your brother called again. Decided not to wait until next month. They're driving up tomorrow. And he's bringing your sister."

I freeze. My jaw tightens. "My sister?" My voice comes out low and dangerous. "Why the fuck is he driving? He's not hauling her ass across the country in a damn car. She'll freak the fuck out. Call him back. Arrange air transport. Now."

Tank exhales. "He said it was something about having to travel for work," he says.

Fuck.

Abigail wouldn't stay alone for more than a day, no matter what. She may be twenty-five years old, but life has done a number on her, leaving her afraid of damn near everything. I've been trying to convince her to move into the compound for over a year, but the trip itself was always the thing stopping her. And now my dumbass brother thinks strapping her into a car for hours on end is a good idea?

Not fucking happening.

Once she's inside these walls, I'm not letting her leave.

I square my shoulders, forcing down the weight of yet another fucking problem. If I were a weaker man, I'd buckle under all this pressure.

But I'm not.

"Set up the house next to mine for Abigail," I say, not caring who handles it. Someone will.

"Which one do you want prepared for Riley?" Max asks.

I slowly turn my head, pinning him with a glare that has him shifting uncomfortably.

Tank smirks, catching on quicker than Max. "We'll set up Asher's room across from yours," he says. "Max, think before you speak. I'd rather not take over your responsibilities because you got yourself killed."

I don't bother responding. My mind's already moving ahead.

"Order everything a baby needs," I tell them. "Once Riley's feeling better and we get our boy back, she can add whatever else he needs."

Before I can say anything else, a scream rips through the compound.

Riley.

I don't think.

My chair crashes to the floor as I lunge to my feet, already halfway to the door, before the others even react.

"Handle this shit, Tank!" I bark over my shoulder.

I don't wait for an answer.

My woman needs me. And that's exactly where I plan to be.

I rush into the office to find Riley awake and crying. Shaking, her face pale, eyes wide with fear, and it breaks my fucking heart. My body moves without thinking, rushing to her side.

"Baby," I whisper, my voice rough and full of pain. "I've got you. You're safe now. You're with me."

She looks up at me, and I see the exhaustion, the terror, the weight of everything she's been through. It's all there in her eyes, that silent plea for relief. But I don't care. I'm gonna take every last bit of that burden from her. I'm gonna carry it all. I won't let her bear it alone anymore. I'll protect her from every single thing that hurts, every fear, every bit of pain that makes her feel small and broken. I'll carry it for her.

"I'll make sure nothing ever hurts you again, Riley. When we get Asher back, I'm not letting either of you out of my sight. You'll never have to face another day alone. Not while I'm still breathing."

"Spike…" Her voice is so soft, barely above a whisper, but it hits me like a freight train. Her pain, her loss, it's suffocating. She's not just hurting; she's unraveling, piece by piece, and I'll be damned if I let her fall apart like this.

Falling to my knees in front of her, I reach up, pulling her into my arms. I hold her tightly, her face pressed against my chest as she shudders with every sob. I can feel the heat of her tears soaking through my shirt, and it guts me. She's not just crying; she's breaking. The woman I've come to care about more than I ever thought I could is falling apart in my arms, and there's nothing I can do to fix it. Except carry it for her.

"Shh, it's okay," I whisper, brushing the strands of her hair away from her face as gently as I can. "We'll get through this. I swear I'll get Asher back. And I'm never letting either of you go."

Her grip on my shirt tightens as though she's trying to hold on to the last piece of herself, the last shred of something solid in a world that's turned upside down. But she doesn't say anything. She doesn't need to. I know what she's feeling. I can feel it in the way her body shakes against mine.

I can feel her fear, her sadness, her heartbreak…and I'm gonna take it all.

"Give it to me, baby," I murmur softly, my lips grazing her ear. "Let me carry everything for you. Let me take all of it, Riley. Everything that hurts, everything that scares you, everything that breaks you, give it to me. I swear I won't let you face it alone."

I feel her body go still for a moment, and I know she's holding her breath, fighting the battle between wanting to let go and not knowing if she can. But I'm not letting her keep this weight. I'm not gonna stand by and watch her destroy herself. I'll carry it for her, even if it crushes me. I'd do anything to take her pain away.

Slowly, she lets out a long breath, the tension in her body easing just a little as she finally, finally allows herself to lean on me completely.

I lean down, my lips barely brushing her forehead. As my lips move from her forehead to the soft skin of her temple, she closes her eyes, and I feel her tremble. This isn't a kiss for desire. It's not a kiss of passion. It's the kiss of someone willing to take her grief, her heartache, her soul-crushing fear and make it their own.

I taste her tears. Salty and fresh. And I take them in, feeling the weight of her sadness seep into me. My heart aches as I swallow her grief, and I promise, in this quiet, intimate moment, that I won't ever let her feel this fear again.

I pull back slightly, my breath shaky. "I'll get him back, Riley," I whisper, my voice rough. "I swear on everything I have. I'll make Chuck pay for what he did to you. And I'll get our son back, no matter who I have to kill."

Yes, *our* son.

My fucking son.

She nods, her fingers curling into my shirt as she lets the last of her sobs fade away. The weight of her pain is still there but a little lighter. Just a little. And I'll keep taking it, piece by piece, until she doesn't have to carry it anymore.

I'll make sure it's the last time she ever faces anything like this again.

Leaning down, I seal my silent promise with a barely there kiss on her lips.

CHAPTER THIRTEEN

Riley

Spike's in a meeting, but I don't care. I know he's talking about Chuck and Asher, and I want to be part of it.

So, pulling my big girl panties up, I march my way to the war room. Which I've only just learned is an empty room with a huge round table and a wall full of security screens.

"You can't go in there right now, miss," a man says as he steps in front of the door. "I'm afraid there's a meeting going on."

"I'm fully aware of that," I respond, my voice still a bit raspy from Chuck's attack. The bruises on the outside are nothing compared to how I feel on the inside. It hurts to speak, but I won't back down now. I take another step forward.

Without a second thought, the man reaches out and places his hand on my shoulder to stop me. He doesn't hurt me, doesn't squeeze too tightly, but instinct takes over. I rear my fist back and slam it into his throat.

He staggers back, shocked, but I can tell it wasn't enough to seriously hurt him. He just stumbles against the door, clearly surprised by my reaction.

"What the fuck is going on?" Spike shouts as he opens the door, causing Blue Eyes to fall back.

Blue Eyes points right at me, and I square my

shoulders.

"Baby, what are you doing moving around?" he says, ignoring his man and stepping over him. "You shouldn't be walking around on your own."

"What the fuck, Prez?" the man sputters, pushing himself up. "This fucking woman hits me, and you're acting like she's your goddamn prize?"

"Damnit," Max, at least, I think that's Max, grumbles from behind me. "I'm gonna lose all my prospects at this rate."

"She hit you?" Spike asks him. "Why?"

"How the hell am I supposed to know?" the man stammers, his face flushed with anger. "I just told her she couldn't go in the room."

"You touched her," Maverick's voice cuts through from somewhere behind me, calm but sharp.

"I did no such thing," Blue Eyes protests.

"You calling me a liar, boy?" Maverick steps forward, his posture menacing, his voice low but full of authority. "Don't forget that I'm not an actual patched member of this club. I don't need a good reason to kill a fucking brother. Slitting your throat will give me great pleasure."

"Sorry, Maverick," Blue Eyes whimpers. "I wasn't thinking. You're right. I did touch her. But I didn't hurt her."

"You touched my woman?" Spike's voice is a growl, filled with a dangerous edge that makes the air feel heavier.

"Your woman?" Blue Eyes asks, his face draining of color. "I didn't know, Prez. I swear."

"He hurt you?" Spike's eyes roam over me, taking in every bruise, every mark, but I know he doesn't see what he's looking for. There's so much damage on me, Chuck's marks all over my body, that I know Spike wouldn't even notice if Blue Eyes had added to them.

"No," I admit, the words slipping out as I glance at the floor. "He just put his hand on my shoulder when I tried to get in, but I'm so freaking tired of people touching me. I'm tired of being hurt." My voice cracks, and for a moment, I can't hold it in anymore. "I don't want anyone to touch me ever again."

I hate how weak I sound, how broken, but I can't take it anymore.

And despite everything I've just said, I lean into Spike's chest, feeling his arms come around me like a shield.

"Nobody but you," I whisper against his shirt, my voice barely audible. "Please, don't let them touch me."

I can't explain why I'm saying this. I can't explain why my skin crawls at the thought of anyone's hands on me. I can't explain why Spike feels like the only safe place, but I don't care. I don't need to. All I need is for him to promise me that I won't have to endure the touch of anyone else ever again.

"You don't ever have to worry about anyone touching you again. You're safe here. You're with me." Spike says, his voice tight, as though he's struggling to hold back his own emotions.

And I believe him. Maybe for the first time in a long while, I believe that I'll finally be protected. I'll be safe.

"Back to work," Spike says, gently pulling me away from his chest and guiding me into the war room.

"Uhm, Spike?" I ask as I sit in the chair he directs me to.

"Yeah, baby?" he replies, his voice low but attentive.

Everyone else is back in their seats, their eyes fixed on me. I sigh, feeling the heat rise to my face. I really don't want to ask this, but I have no choice.

"I need a pump," I admit, my voice barely above a whisper.

"A pump?" he asks, kneeling in front of me, his brow furrowing in confusion.

I can feel the embarrassment creeping up my neck, but I gather the courage to meet his gaze. My eyes drop to my chest, where wet spots have already formed over my nipples.

His confusion deepens, and I sigh before explaining. "A breast pump. Without Asher nursing every four hours, my breasts are full. I was able to pump at the hospital, but I haven't since then. If I don't pump regularly, my milk supply will decrease. I could lose my ability to nurse him."

Spike's brow creases and the intensity in his expression makes me smile despite the awkwardness.

"Manual or electric?" a broad man, one I've never seen before, suddenly asks.

"Uh," I hesitate, unsure if I should answer the stranger.

I glance back down at Spike, who's still kneeling in front of me, but now his eyes are fixed firmly on my chest, a dazed look in his eyes as if he's forgotten everything going on in the room.

"I'm not sure," I admit to the stranger, feeling my cheeks burn hotter.

"No worries," he smiles, looking down at the laptop in front of him. "Who has access to the club's funds?"

"That would be me," Skip answers, his tone sharp. "Why?"

"I have an order ready for her pump," the man says, fingers tapping away at the keyboard. "It'll be delivered in a few hours. Just need to make sure it's an approved expense for the club."

"Absolutely," Tank says, sitting back in his chair. "Since

our President's not mentally here right now, I'll override the voting process and approve it."

"Agreed," the rest of the room chimes in, their voices in unison.

"I'll input the bank info," Skip says, but the man just laughs.

"No need, Skip," he replies with a smirk. "Already did. I even added some extra bags so you can freeze the milk, ma'am."

"Please, call me Riley," I smile, embarrassed, my face feeling like it's on fire. "Thanks."

"How did you get our bank info?" Skip asks, still looking suspicious.

"With a few strategically placed ones and zeros. Don't worry, I made sure to use the main account," the man chuckles. "I also have some news on the baby. I'll update everyone whenever the club's President gets back from his... vacation."

With Spike still staring at my chest, I place my hands over the wet spots, trying to hide the evidence of my body's betrayal. This milk is for my son, and my body is wasting it.

Finally, Spike seems to snap out of it. He shoots a glare at the rest of the group, his jaw clenched with irritation.

"If a single one of you fuckers looks at her tits again, I'll stab you in the dick," he growls, his voice hard and unmistakably serious.

The room falls into a stunned silence as his threat lingers, and I feel a strange mix of amusement and comfort that he's so protective.

Standing, Spike reaches down, turns my chair slightly, and pushes me forward against the table.

Without another word, he removes his black vest,

shoves my arms through the slits, and drapes it backward over my body, effectively covering my chest.

I watch as he steps back, his eyes scanning my body. Once he's satisfied, he moves behind my chair, his large hands resting gently on my shoulders. His fingers press into the muscles there, a comforting weight that settles me even more.

"Better?" he asks.

I nod, a slight chuckle escaping me despite myself. "Yeah... much better."

The rest of the room remains quiet, and I can feel the tension ebb away, both in the room and in my body. Spike's got this way of making everything feel like it'll be okay, even if the world's falling apart.

"Now, what did you find out about Asher?" Spike demands, his voice low but firm, the weight of the question hanging heavy in the air.

"Oh, so you were listening?" Bones chuckles. "I just wonder what was on your mind that you couldn't remember how to talk earlier?"

"Fuck you, Bones," Spike mutters. "What do you have for me, Foster?"

The broad man, Foster, leans back in his chair.

"First, Asher's proof of life is now correctly filed at the hospital," he says. "It wasn't anything nefarious. There was a system crash that very morning and everything was done with good old-fashioned pen and paper. They're just now getting everything logged into the computers."

"I remember that," I sigh. "The nurses kept apologizing to me because they were having a hard time getting things done. They couldn't access the things they needed with a keycard, either. Which included most medications. It was chaos."

"I image it was," Foster smiles. "Now, for the other good news. The custody agreement that Ms. Hayes signed," he says, the smile widening. "It's null and void now."

"What?" I ask, leaning forward in my seat, my pulse quickening. "It wasn't legal?"

"Oh, it was legal," Foster says, holding up a hand to calm me. "That bastard made sure to file it with the court within an hour of leaving you at the hospital. But here's the thing. It's not legal anymore. It'll take about twenty-four hours for the courts to sort through all the logistics, but you'll have your son back by this time tomorrow."

"You're sure?" Spike asks, his fingers squeezing my shoulders a bit tighter.

"Without a single doubt," Foster smirks. "By this time tomorrow, baby Asher will be inside these compound walls."

"What do I need to do?" Spike asks. I'm thankful because my voice doesn't seem to work. My throat locks up, and my vision blurs with tears.

"You just need to send someone to collect him," Foster explains. "Give me the name, and I'll make sure they have clearance to remove the baby from Chuck."

"I'll do it," Spike says immediately.

"And by that, he means *I'll* do it," Maverick cuts in, his tone firm.

I want to fight them both. I want to stand up and say *no, I'm his mother. I should be the one to bring him home*. But the truth is, I know Spike won't allow it. I can barely stand without shaking. The thought of facing Chuck again makes me want to curl into a ball and disappear.

"The fuck you will," Spike growls. "That's my son. I'm the one bringing him home."

"And I'm *not* affiliated with the club," Maverick

reminds him. "You walk in there, and Chuck's gonna know exactly where Riley and Asher are. Let me handle it, brother."

The rest of their conversation fades into background noise as the tears finally spill down my face. The relief is too much. My body shakes under the weight of it, and before I can even process what's happening, I feel myself being lifted into strong arms.

Spike.

He carries me like I weigh nothing, his grip solid and unyielding. I don't fight it. I just bury my face against his chest and let it happen.

"If my son is inside this compound tomorrow like you said," Spike says, his voice filled with quiet authority, "you're fucking hired."

"Want to be a member?" Max asks as I feel Spike's chest vibrate with a chuckle.

"Not sure," Foster replies. "Let me think about it."

I sniffle. "My boobs hurt."

Spike shifts me in his arms. "We'll get you in a hot shower, baby."

I hear some amused chuckles, but I don't care. The moment the door closes behind us, muting the voices of the club, I feel the exhaustion set in deep.

"When we get our boy back," Spike murmurs, carrying me through the building and back into his office, "I'll tell you what I was dreaming about."

I manage a small smile, adjusting in his hold until I'm sitting comfortably against his lap when he lowers himself onto the couch.

"Even though Chuck is a monster, I know he isn't hurting Asher," I admit. "Every time he looked at him, he seemed happy. I'm not afraid for Asher's immediate safety. I just want my baby back. I want my son in my arms."

"Soon, baby."

"Yes," I whisper.

Spike exhales, tightening his hold on me. "Tomorrow, you and Asher are moving in with me."

I huff a small laugh, shaking my head. "You're making decisions for me now?"

"Damn right, I am," he grunts. "I don't want to hear shit about it being too soon. You're mine. Asher's mine. And you will be in my bed for the rest of your fucking life."

"I don't really want to be outside of the compound walls," I admit.

"Our house is inside the compound, baby," he tells me. "It's less than a minute walk away."

Despite everything, I giggle. "Alright," I whisper, not really wanting to fight him anyway. I've felt safer with Spike since I've met him than I have in my entire life. Maybe I was always meant to end up here. I just had to take a detour to bring Asher into the world first.

"The reason I always fell asleep in your office," I admit softly, "was because it was your space. I knew I could rest there when you weren't around. I felt... safe."

Spike strokes his fingers down my spine. "Then don't fight me on this."

"I won't," I say. "On one condition."

I feel his smile against the top of my head. "What's that?"

"What's your real name?"

His chest rumbles with laughter. "Ethan Turner."

I smile. "Nice to meet you, Ethan Turner." I pause, then tilt my head. "Now, tell me. Why did you freeze in there earlier?"

Spike groans, dragging a hand down his face. "Because I was picturing your tits engorged with milk."

My mouth drops open.

He smirks unapologetically. "I had this image of you sitting naked in our bed while I squeezed your nipples to relieve the pressure."

"You daydreamed that you were milking me?" I laugh, even as warmth spreads through me. "Caveman."

"I accept caveman status," he chuckles, shifting so I'm tucked securely against him. "Now, get some sleep. I need to be well-rested. I've got revenge to plan."

"We're getting Asher back," I remind him. "Why are you still plotting revenge?"

His entire body tenses. "Because that motherfucker *beat* my woman," he growls. "I'm gonna make sure he fucking pays."

"He's gonna *beg* me for mercy," Bones' voice suddenly cuts in as he waltzes into the room, "while I peel his skin from his fucking bones."

I shudder. Not because I'm scared of what he's saying but because I'm not scared at all. And *that* terrifies me.

"Graphic," I say.

"How do you think he got his name, baby?" Spike murmurs, running a hand down my back.

I glance over at Bones, watching as he leans casually against the wall. "Interesting choice of hobby," I say. "Is it hard to peel someone?"

Bones smirks. "Not if you have the right tools."

"Oh my," I mutter.

"Anyway," Bones continues like he wasn't just discussing skinning someone, "your siblings are about five hours out, Spike. I'll wake you when they're an hour away."

"You have siblings?" I ask as Bones disappears down the hall.

"A brother and sister," Spike says, pressing a kiss to the top of my head. "Samuel travels a lot for work, but my little sister, Abigail… she's different."

"Different, how?"

Spike sighs. "She's been through some bad shit. Has a ton of triggers. One of them is vehicles. This trip is gonna wreck her."

My heart aches. "We'll help her," I promise. "When Asher gets back, he'll help her too. Babies are magical when it comes to a broken woman."

Spike lets out a deep breath. "Thank you, baby. My little sister means the world to me. And knowing that my girl, my fucking universe, will be there for her? That means everything. And when we get our boy back, he's gonna heal her heart."

I swallow hard. "We're getting Asher back," I whisper, fresh tears falling. "Please, please, please let this work."

Spike pulls me tighter against him, shifting until we're lying down. His body surrounds mine as he moves me to lay between him and the back of the couch. His warmth presses against every inch of me, shielding me from everything else.

"Sleep, baby," he murmurs. "I've got you."

And with a deep breath, I close my eyes and actually believe it.

He truly does have me.

CHAPTER FOURTEEN

Spike

I smirk as Riley walks out of my office, holding two bags of milk ready to be frozen.

"I'm not sure how long these can be stored," she says, a little shy. "But I wrote today's date on them. Maybe I can buy a baby bottle, and you can feed Asher with this supply."

I fucking *love* that idea.

"Maybe after a week or so," I say, taking the bags from her. "I want him to nurse from you for a while when he gets back. You two need that bond, baby."

She nods, chewing her lip as she watches me store the bags in the freezer.

"Maybe we should mark them," she suggests. "What if someone grabs one by mistake? That would… make me feel weird."

Not to mention, nobody's taking a damn thing from my boy. That shit's *his*, and that's the end of it.

I turn toward the room and raise my voice. "Nobody fucking touches the milk in the freezer," I announce, making sure every asshole within earshot hears me. "If a single bag comes up missing, I *will* find out who took it, and I will hold you in place while my woman throat-punches you. *Then*, I'll take my turn."

Maverick nods solemnly. "Best listen to him. It's kind

of her thing," he says, rubbing his throat. "I've witnessed the madness firsthand. You don't want that kind of pain."

Riley gapes at the two of us like we've lost our damn minds. "You two are *impossible*," she mutters, then scans the room before landing on Skip. "You're my favorite of the day, Skip."

Like a fucking idiot, the bastard *skips* over to her, arms wide open.

"Touch her, and I'll break your fucking arm," I warn.

Skip freezes mid-step, pouting dramatically. "Damn it, Prez! I just wanted to give her a hug. I *am* her favorite of the day, after all."

Before I can explain to my beautiful woman that I'll always be her favorite *every* day, the front door swings open, and Tank walks in with my siblings.

Both of them are younger than me. Samuel by two years and Abigail by a whopping fifteen.

"I have to go," Samuel greets quickly, already looking at his watch. "I've got a meeting in D.C., and if I don't catch my flight, I'm not gonna make it."

"Hello to you too, little brother," I say dryly. "At least give me a damn hug before you leave."

Shaking his head with a smirk, he steps into my waiting arms. He's a fucking idiot for making Abby travel all this way, but I know why he did it. She wouldn't have made the trip on her own, *ever*.

"This is my woman, Riley," I say, wrapping an arm around her waist. "Next time you get a break, come stay for a while."

"It's nice to meet you, Riley," he says, stepping forward to take her hand.

I shake my head once, stopping him dead in his tracks.

She asked me not to let anyone touch her, and I'll be

damned if I let that start now. Works for me. I don't want *any* of these fuckers putting their hands on her.

"Bubby?"

At the small voice, I glance past Samuel and see my baby sister standing in the doorway, looking like she wants to be anywhere but here.

"I have to go, Abby," Samuel tells her gently. "I'm sorry I can't stay and help you settle in. But Bubby's here, and he's gonna take care of you. Love you, honey."

With a quick hug and a glance back, he's gone.

I press a kiss to Riley's head before stepping away, sending a silent glare to the room, daring any of them to lay a single fucking finger on her, before I head toward my sister.

"Come here, squirt," I say, pulling her into my arms.

Her little body trembles in my arms.

I tighten my hold, feeling just how thin she's gotten. She's lost weight. Too much weight. Fucking Sam. He was *supposed* to be taking care of her.

"It's okay, Abby," I sigh, holding her a little tighter. "You're safe here. I promise. *Nothing* can touch you inside these walls."

She lets out a shuddering breath, pressing her face against my chest. "I've missed you, Bubby," she whispers. "I'm sorry that I'm so scared to be here. But, at the same time, I'm *really* happy."

"And I've missed you," I murmur, resting my chin on the top of Abigail's head. "I was planning a trip out there for Christmas, but that was too damn long of a wait. You *do* realize you're not leaving now, right?"

She nods against my chest, letting out a small laugh.

"I figured," she admits. "And I'm okay with that. I love our brother, but he doesn't make me feel as safe as you do."

I close my eyes for half a second, exhaling slowly.

I have to remind myself that the person who hurt my baby sister is *dead*...by my own hands. But the thought never seems to calm me.

Because the damage was already done.

"Come," I say, pulling back. "I want to introduce you to someone."

Gripping her elbow, I lead her toward Riley, who's standing quietly, watching us with soft eyes.

"Abigail, this is my ol' lady, Riley. Baby, my little sister, Abigail."

Abby gives Riley a warm smile, holding out her hand. "Goodness, just call me Abby. I sure hope my brother dealt with whoever did that to you."

The reminder of the bruises on my woman reignite the fire inside of me.

"Not yet," I growl. "But I will."

"It's nice to meet you, Abby," Riley says, her voice gentle, ignoring my vow. There's a brief hesitation, but then she reaches out and quickly shakes Abby's hand.

"I can't believe someone *finally* caught my brother's attention," Abby teases, grinning at Riley before shooting me a playful side-eye. "I mean, you're so beautiful, it's no wonder."

Riley blushes, glancing away for a second. "I was just thinking the same thing about you. Is your hair naturally that blonde? It's almost white. And your eyes are so blue that I can practically see the waves of the ocean in them."

Abby laughs, running a hand through her hair. "It is my natural color. Believe it or not, I was born with dark hair. It just changed over the years. I usually keep it tied up to give it some dimension, but my head's been killing me, so I let it down."

"You should keep it that way," Riley says softly. "It's stunning."

Abby beams at her, and for the first time in what feels like years, something in my chest eases.

Then, her expression shifts. She tilts her head slightly, brows pinching together as she studies Riley. "Why are your eyes so sad?"

Riley freezes, and I see it. The guilt. For just a moment, she'd let herself forget. Let herself enjoy a simple conversation. And now, she looks like she wants to apologize for it.

She has *nothing* to be sorry for.

I step in before she drowns in it. "I'm afraid you've come to us at a rather hard time, baby sister. Let's go to my office, and we'll update you…"

"My son has been taken by his father," Riley blurts before I can take a single step.

Abby's eyes widen, shock flickering across her face before her gaze fills with tears.

"He's not even two weeks old," Riley continues, her voice tight. "He's the same reason I'm black and blue."

Abby's bottom lip trembles, her tears slipping free. Always so damn sensitive to other people's pain, my baby sister.

"Can't you get him back?" she asks, her voice barely above a whisper.

I tighten my arm around Riley, holding her steady as I meet Abby's gaze.

"We're getting him back *tomorrow*."

The words settle in the air, heavy with promise. And I'll be damned if I let anything stop me from making it happen.

***

"You really should've stayed home," Bones mutters, gripping the steering wheel tight. "Not just for your safety, but for Riley's. You're the face of this club, Prez. One look at you, and that bastard Chuck will know exactly where she and Asher are."

"I get your logic," I say, my voice steady. "I do, brother. But I *needed* to be here. I needed to be in this damn car when Maverick brings my son out of that house. I needed to be the one to hold him first, to take him back to his mother." I gesture toward the windows. "Besides, these are tinted past the legal limit. No one can see me."

Bones stays quiet, jaw tight. He knows I'm right, but that doesn't stop him from worrying. It never does. I don't know how many times I've told him he doesn't need to be my damn bodyguard, yet here we are.

"Here he comes," Bones says, relief bleeding into his voice.

My eyes lock past Maverick and land on Chuck, standing on his porch, arms crossed, scowling like the miserable bastard he is.

He may not be able to find my family yet, but he's gonna try. This won't be the last time I see Charles Landry.

Maverick yanks open the passenger door and climbs inside, slamming it shut. Before he even has a chance to hand Asher back, I reach forward, carefully taking my son into my arms.

"Hey there, son," I murmur, my voice soft and filled with relief. "Your mommy misses you very much."

I check him over, my fingers running gently along his tiny arms, legs, and belly. No bruises, no marks. He's warm and breathing. *Safe.*

Satisfied, I press a kiss to his soft little head before securing him into his seat.

"Get us the fuck out of here, Bones," Maverick growls. "Before I jump out and beat that bastard until he can't fucking function."

My blood runs cold. I snap my gaze up to Maverick. "What happened?" My voice is sharp, deadly. "Are you hurt?"

Sure, Maverick can watch out for himself. But, I'll kill any bastard who harms any member of my family. That includes the stubborn Outlaw.

I narrow my eyes, watching Maverick shift in his seat, gripping his thighs like he's trying to hold himself back from going feral. My patience is already hanging by a thread. I need answers.

"What happened?" I repeat, my voice cold. "Did he touch you?"

Maverick shakes his head but doesn't meet my eyes. "Not me." His jaw clenches tight, the muscles ticking. "But that fucker sure as hell wanted to make sure I passed along a message."

I already know I'm not gonna like this. "Spit it out."

Maverick exhales through his nose, looking out the window like it'll stop the rage from swallowing him whole. "He said to tell Riley to enjoy her time playing house. That it won't last. That he can't wait to have her back and under him so he can teach her a lesson. Took everything in me to turn and walk away, Spike. If I didn't have your boy in my arms, I wouldn't have."

The air in the car turns suffocating. *That motherfucker.*

Bones curses under his breath. "Knew this wasn't over. Does he know she's with the Shadows?"

"Not sure, but I wouldn't doubt it," Maverick says. "It's not even the words he said, brother. It's the way he said them. There was something almost wild behind his voice."

The only thing that stops me from leaving this car so I can put a bullet in Chuck's smug face is the tiny sound that comes from the infant seat. A small, soft noise.

Asher.

I look beside me. He's awake now, blinking up at the ceiling, completely unaware of the war raging inside me.

I exhale sharply, running a hand down my face, forcing the red-hot fury down before I do something reckless. I can't afford to lose my shit. Not here. Not now.

"Get us the fuck home," I mutter.

Bones nods, pressing his foot down on the gas.

As we pull away, I glance one last time toward the house. And there he is - Chuck Landry, standing on his front porch, arms crossed, watching us leave like he just won this round.

Then the fucker smirks. Lifts his hand in a slow, mocking wave.

The message is clear. He let us take Asher back. Because this isn't over. Because he's got something else planned.

"Drive carefully. I need to take the baby out of his seat," I tell Bones as I unbuckle Asher and lay him across my lap. "I want to check him for bugs. Chuck looks way too fucking smug for someone who just lost custody of his son."

Once his clothes are clear, I strip him of his diaper and inspect it. Sure enough, a small tear was made on the inside, and a tracker was placed within the diaper.

"I'm gonna swing by the bus stop," Bones says. "Shove

the tracker back inside the diaper and wad it up. Maybe he'll think she took the bus and left town."

Not a bad idea.

Grabbing a fresh diaper from the bag that Riley had us bring, I change him and place him back in his seat.

That bastard thinks he can hurt my family?

I clench my jaw so hard it aches.

You want a fucking war, Chuck?

Fine. You got one.

CHAPTER FIFTEEN

Riley

I pace back and forth as I wait for Spike to return with my son.

"You know," I tell Abby. "I'm not the only one with sad eyes."

Okay, yeah, I'm pushing for a distraction. But it's the truth. She looks like she's been through something horrible.

"How do you think I picked up on yours so quickly?" she smiles sadly. "I see that same look every time I look in a mirror."

"Want to talk about it?" I ask, finally sitting down beside her on the floor in front of the fireplace. There's no fire, but it's okay.

"No," she says. "But it always helps when I do."

Sighing, Abby turns and sits with her legs bent under her.

"A few years ago, I was on a trip with my friends," she starts. "It was a graduation trip because we had all just finished college. I had finally gotten my bachelor's degree in business administration and already had a plan to start my own business."

"What type of business?" I ask.

"I wanted to open a boutique store and sell my own clothing designs," she smiles wistfully. "Bubby already bought me the building as a graduation gift, and I was going to move here and get an apartment. It was my ultimate dream. Still is."

"What happened?" I ask softly.

Abby exhales slowly, staring into the empty fireplace like she's seeing something far away. Something she doesn't want to remember but can't forget.

"We took a trip to Mexico," she finally says. "It wasn't supposed to be dangerous. We weren't being reckless or anything. One of my friends had family there that was letting us crash at their place. We thought it would be a great way to experience a new culture before we all settled into our careers. Plus, it's just around the corner. I planned to come straight to Palm Springs right after."

I nod, encouraging her to continue.

"For the first few days, everything was perfect," she says, her voice hollow. "The markets, the food, the people - it was exactly what we'd hoped for. But on the fourth night, we were out late, celebrating, and we made the mistake of taking a route we weren't familiar with."

She pauses, swallowing hard, her hands clenching into fists in her lap.

"They came out of nowhere," she whispers. "Armed men. They didn't say a word, just grabbed us and shoved us into a van."

My stomach turns. I don't even know this girl that well, but I already feel sick imagining what she went through.

"They were insurgents," she continues. "Or at least some kind of militant group. Anyway, their leader saw us as a payday. American women? We were prime money. They planned to sell a few of us. To the rest, they planned things far worse."

I don't ask what *worse* means. I already know.

"Bubby found me," she says after a moment. "He and his men tore through their compound like the devil himself. I don't even know how they found us, but one second, I was locked in a room, and the next, gunfire was everywhere, and he was carrying me out."

A single tear slides down her cheek, but she wipes it away quickly.

"My friends didn't make it," she whispers. "They killed two of them first to make a point. The other three were either sold or killed elsewhere. I haven't heard anything from or about them since."

My breath catches.

"I was there for three months."

"Oh, Abby," I murmur, reaching for her hand without thinking. She doesn't flinch when I take it, just grips mine tightly.

"I should've died too," she says. "They had already decided we weren't worth the trouble anymore. I was next. But Bubby got there before they could do it."

I don't know what to say. What the hell *can* you say to something like that?

"At first, I stayed in my brother's house here inside the compound," she continues. "But being so close to the Mexican border terrified me. I was constantly on edge, always waiting for something bad to happen. So, my brother took me to stay with our other brother in Kentucky, hoping I'd feel safer there."

She pauses, shaking her head. "But I never did. If anything, I felt more vulnerable. I don't know why, but the further I got from here, the worse it got. The thought of traveling back was just as terrifying, but so was being alone. In the end, with the help of some pretty heavy medication, I let my brother bring me back."

"I'm really glad you're here," I tell her honestly.

She gives a small, shaky laugh. "Me too. So yeah, I guess I've got sad eyes."

I squeeze her hand gently. "You're stronger than you think."

She shrugs. "Bubby thinks so too. I'm not sure I believe it, though."

"Well," I say, offering her a small smile, "maybe one day, you will. Maybe one day, both of our sad eyes will be a thing of the past."

She gives me a watery smile in return. "Maybe."

And for the first time since I met her, I see just the tiniest flicker of hope in her eyes.

After a beat, I take a deep breath. "Well, since we're sharing, let me tell you my story."

"You don't have to," she says softly. "I can tell it's fresh. The pain is still raw."

"It's not any worse than yours," I tell her. "Just different. And I want to tell you."

So, I take a deep breath and lay it all out. The fear, the betrayal, the heartbreak.

When I finish, her face is pale, her eyes wide with horror. "And he just made you sign the papers while you were barely conscious? With a concussion?"

I nod, my jaw tightening.

Her expression hardens, her voice shaking with anger. "That's…Gosh, Riley. That's evil."

I swallow hard, pushing back the lump in my throat. "It didn't stop there. He took Asher and disappeared. Left me helpless, desperate, and with no way to get to my baby."

She shakes her head, furious. "No wonder your eyes are so sad. You went through hell."

I let out a shaky breath. "I'm still in it. At least until

Asher is back in my arms."

Abby reaches out, gripping my hand tightly. "But you're fighting. That's what matters."

I nod, squeezing her hand in return. "And I'm going to keep fighting. No matter what it takes."

Abby watches me for a moment before whispering, "Then I will, too."

It's quiet between us, but for the first time, there's an understanding. A connection forged in pain but strengthened by survival.

Before I can say anything else, the sound of an engine approaching the compound makes my heart stop. I shoot to my feet, my pulse pounding.

"They're back," I whisper, my legs already carrying me toward the door.

Abby follows closely behind, and as I throw open the door and step outside, my breath catches in my throat.

Spike is walking toward me, and in his arms, wrapped in a small blanket, is my son.

I fall to my knees in relief as every ounce of strength leaves my body.

"Fuck baby," he says, rushing to my side. "Come on, let's get you inside."

I don't take my eyes off Asher as Spike helps me back on my feet and ushers me inside. I don't reach for my son. I don't dare touch him for fear that it's all in my head.

Once in his office, Spike guides me to the couch, but my eyes remain locked on Asher. He's right there. So close I can reach out and touch him, but my hands tremble at the thought.

Spike kneels in front of me, his voice softer now. "Riley, he's okay. He's real. Take him."

My fingers curl into my palms as I shake my head.

"What if he's not?" My voice is barely a whisper. "What if I'm dreaming?"

A soft sound comes from the bundle in Spike's arms. A tiny whimper followed by a content sigh.

Spike presses him into my arms, and as I cradle my son, I feel the weight of him…solid, warm, real.

I pull him close, my hands trembling as I touch his soft skin. He's so small, so fragile, but so perfect.

"Shh," I whisper, tears streaming down my face. "Mommy's here. I've got you."

Asher makes a small, muffled sound, his little fists gripping the fabric of my shirt, but he doesn't open his eyes.

Spike hovers close, his hand on my shoulder, steadying me. "He's real, Riley. He's safe. He's unharmed. He's home."

I nod, my chest aching with relief, but beneath that relief, a spark of something darker simmers. Anger.

"He'll try to come after him again," I say, my voice steady despite the surge of fear.

Spike shakes his head. "He put a tracker in the boy's diaper. I double-checked to make sure he was clean before bringing him home." His jaw tightens. "Bones drove us past a bus stop to ditch the diaper with the tracker. Hopefully, that'll make him think you've left."

"Hopefully," I nod, but I can feel the weight of uncertainty hanging over me. "But it won't work forever. I can't stay hidden here. I have to leave these walls eventually. I need to find a job to take care of my son. I need daycare. I need somewhere to live…" My voice trails off as I freeze, suddenly aware of the way Spike is looking at me.

Spike's eyes narrow, his voice lowering to a dangerous level. "It seems I haven't been clear enough," he says, his tone almost cold with a hint of anger. "You and Asher belong to me. That means I'll supply you with everything your fucking heart desires. I'll take care of both of you in all ways. You don't need a fucking job. You don't need a fucking place to live. You don't need a fucking sitter. All you need to do is stay by my fucking side and let me handle everything."

I blink a few times, taking in his words, and can't help but smirk. "That was a lot of 'fuckings'," I say, trying to ease the tension in the air.

Spike doesn't smile, his gaze still intense, but I can feel the shift in the room. I cuddle Asher closer, helping to calm my nerves.

"I was with Chuck for a long time," I continue, my voice quieter now. "But even though we lived together, I never really felt like I was in a relationship. Not the kind of relationship where someone actually cares for you. Not one where I mattered. With him, it was always about what he wanted and how he could control me. And I... I got used to it. But not in a healthy way."

I swallow hard, trying to put words to something I don't fully understand myself.

"Then there's you," I say, my voice trembling ever so slightly. "You're different. I feel it when you're near me. Something about you... it just clicks, even though I'm not sure I understand how or why. It's like a part of me wants to be close to you, wants to never let you out of my sight. But another part of me... I don't know if I'm the woman you need. I don't know how to be that for you."

I bite my lip, feeling vulnerable, but it's the truth. Spike might want me, but I'm scared that I won't be able to give him what he deserves.

He leans in closer, his expression unreadable for a

moment, before his hands gently cup my face. "Riley," he says, his voice soft but firm, "You're not some perfect fucking woman with all the answers. And I don't expect you to be. All I care about is that you're here. You and Asher are mine now. And I'll take care of everything. All you have to do is trust me. Let me be the one to protect you, to make sure you're never in a situation like the one you were in with Chuck. You don't have to be anyone you're not. Just be with me."

His thumb traces my cheekbone, and I feel my heart race in response to the tenderness of his touch.

"I get it," he continues, his gaze softening. "You've been through hell, and it's hard to let go of that fear. I know you're not used to being treated like you matter. But you do. You matter to me. And I'll prove it to you every fucking day if that's what it takes."

I look into his eyes, searching for any sign of insincerity, but all I find is raw determination. And something else. Something deeper that tugs at my chest. Something I haven't allowed myself to feel in a long time.

"You don't have to be perfect, Riley," he adds, his voice low and steady. "You just need to be real with me. And right now, all I want… all I need… is you."

"I need you, too," I admit, my voice a little shaky. "But I also need us to go slow. I need to make sure that what I'm feeling for you isn't just because you saved me. I need room to find my place in this world. I know you want to take care of us, but I need to know that I can do that myself, too."

"I can do that, baby," he replies gently. "Whatever you want to do in life, I'll support you completely. But right now, all I really need is to kiss you. Is that okay? Just a small taste?"

Feeling shy and uncertain, I nod, my heart racing in anticipation.

"Thank fuck," he mutters before leaning in, his lips brushing against mine. He doesn't push for more but licks my lips softly, placing several long, tender kisses on them before pulling back.

I let out a small whine as his heat leaves me, and he chuckles at the sound.

"Time to feed our boy, baby," he says with a grin. "He smells his mama's milk, and he's on the hunt."

Looking down, I can't help but laugh. Asher's little mouth is wide open, and he's bobbing his head around like he's searching for a nipple to latch onto.

I look up at Spike, expecting him to leave, but instead, he smirks, crosses his arms, and leans against the wall, clearly settling in.

"Not going anywhere, baby," he says, his voice thick with desire. "Watching you nurse our boy is the sexiest fucking thing I've ever seen. Might even make it a club law that every time you nurse, you ring a bell, and all business stops. That way, I can sit down and watch you, no distractions."

"Caveman," I laugh, trying to summon the courage to pull my boob out, my cheeks flushing under his heated gaze.

I can feel Spike's eyes on me as I shyly pull my shirt up since the neckline won't stretch down far enough. I'm fully aware of my already plump body being even more so because of my belly, but I try not to think about it. I take a deep breath, trying to push past the shyness and shift Asher's little body closer before pulling my bra off one breast. His tiny hands instinctively reach for me, and I help guide him to latch.

His little mouth presses against me, and my heart swells with a mix of emotions. Love for my son, gratitude for Spike and his men, and something deeper. There's just something about Spike that calls to me. It can't be the fact that he saved me. He isn't the only one who has. Shoot, he isn't even the one who found a way to get Asher back. And yet…

Spike doesn't look away as I nurse. His gaze is steady, intense, as he watches the most natural, intimate moment I've ever had. There's no judgment, no rush. Just a quiet reverence in the way he observes. It feels… right.

I take a shaky breath, trying to steady myself. "I don't think I've ever felt this exposed, this vulnerable," I admit.

Spike tilts his head, his voice soft but full of conviction. "You're not exposed, baby. You're strong. You're doing the hardest thing in the world right now…taking care of him. And I admire the hell out of you for it."

His words settle over me like a warm blanket, soothing away the remnants of my unease. I meet his eyes and find something in them. Something I can't name yet, but it feels like safety. A kind of shelter that's been missing in my life for so long.

Asher lets out a soft, contented sound, and I look down, smiling at my son. "At least one of us is happy," I whisper.

Spike chuckles, low and rich, and the sound vibrates through the room. "You have no idea how happy you make me, Riley. And I'll do everything in my power to make you happy."

I shift slightly, cradling Asher a little more securely. "I don't know how I'm going to do all this," I say quietly. "Being a mom, a woman, and… everything else. It feels like there's too much."

"You don't have to do it all on your own," Spike says,

his voice low and reassuring. "You've got me. And I'm not going anywhere."

His words wrap around me like a promise.

We sit in silence for a moment, the only sound in the room the quiet rhythm of Asher feeding. I can feel the weight of what we've just shared, the unspoken bond growing between us. There's a future here. One that feels uncertain but also full of possibility.

All I have to do is reach out and grab it.

"Thank you," I say. "For helping me. For getting my son back. For just being you. For wanting me for me."

"You never have to thank me for wanting you, baby," he says softly. "It's my greatest pleasure."

CHAPTER SIXTEEN

Spike

"This is Asher's room," I tell Riley as I guide her through the house the following day. "And as much as I want you by my side, in my bed, for the rest of our lives, I promised you slow. So, I had Tank bring over a twin-sized bed for you yesterday. It'll stay in here until you're ready to admit that you've fallen madly in love with me."

"Madly in love, huh?" she laughs, the sound light, but there's something behind her eyes. A flicker of uncertainty I can't ignore.

"It's the only type of love I'll accept, baby," I tease, trying to ease the tension I can feel rolling off her. "I want you to be so in love with me that you'll go insane without me by your side."

She raises an eyebrow, her lips curving into a smile that doesn't quite reach her eyes. "Is someone capable of that type of love?"

I pause, taking a slow breath. I have to be careful. Too much, too fast, and I could scare her away. But the truth of how I feel about her is there, buried under layers of rough edges and past scars. I can't keep it inside even if I wanted to.

"It's taken forty years for me to find someone I want to call my own," I admit, my voice low, almost a growl, as I step closer to her and gently cup her neck. "I thought

I found someone years back, but what I felt for her isn't even on the same wavelength as what I feel for you. You're different, Riley. You're everything I never knew I was waiting for. I want you to be so in love with me that you'll go insane without me by your side."

I take a moment, letting the words settle between us, trying to gauge her reaction. I don't want to overwhelm her, but I need her to understand that what I feel for her isn't casual. It's not a fleeting thing.

"If you'd let me, I would lock you in this house and never let you leave," I continue, my voice a little rougher now, my grip tightening on the back of her neck as I fight the urge to pull her to me. "I want you all to myself. But, at the same time, I want the whole fucking world to know that I belong to you."

After placing a soft kiss on her plump lips, I take a step back, giving her space, even though it feels like I'm walking away from something that's already mine. She's been through hell, and I can't rush her. Not now. Not like this.

"So, yeah, baby," I say, meeting her eyes, my gaze hard and steady. "That type of love is possible."

I watch her face carefully, waiting as the weight of my words sinks in. She doesn't answer immediately, and that's okay. I'm not in a rush anymore.

It's the first time in my life I've been willing to wait. And for her? I'd wait forever if that's what it takes. No matter how long it takes to get through to her, I'm not going anywhere.

I shift my weight, feeling the tension in the air, but I don't push. The last thing I want is to scare her away. I've already said more than I should've, but it feels good to speak the truth, to finally lay it out for her.

After a moment, I clear my throat, shifting the focus, trying to make her feel less pressure.

"Our room is just over here," I say, gesturing toward our bedroom door on the other side of the hallway. "That's where I'll sleep every night. And no matter how long it takes for you to decide on us, I'll be there waiting for you. Now, I'll let you get settled in. I'm gonna make us dinner, and we can relax and watch a movie. Come down whenever you're ready, baby."

I leave it open-ended, giving her the choice to follow or not. It's in her hands now. She can choose to take that next step if and when she's ready. And if not, I'll give her space. No pushing. No rushing. With her, it's all about waiting for the right moment.

Riley

I stand frozen in Asher's room, looking at the bed Spike had set up for me. The reality of the situation is hitting me harder than I expected. He's offering me more than I've ever had in my life, but I'm not sure I'm ready to take it.

Spike's words echo in my mind, each one heavier than the last. *I want you to be so in love with me that you'll go insane without me by your side.* It sounds intense, too intense, but somehow, it doesn't scare me. What scares me is that it feels like the truth. A part of me wants to fall into him, to let him take care of me and Asher the way he says he will. But another part of me wants to pull away and keep my distance.

I try to laugh it off, but it doesn't come out the way I want. "Madly in love, huh?" I ask, the lightness in my voice hiding a flicker of uncertainty.

Spike's gaze sharpens, his intensity growing with every word. "It's the only type of love I'll accept, baby," he says, his voice teasing but with an edge to it. He steps closer, and I feel the heat of his body radiating off him. "I want you to be so in love with me that you'll go insane without me by your side."

I swallow hard. *Insane?*

"Is someone capable of that type of love?" I ask, my voice quieter. I meet his gaze, searching for something in his eyes, trying to understand what this all means.

His answer is slow, measured, like he's choosing his words carefully. "It's taken forty years for me to find someone I want to call my own," he says, his voice low and rough like he's speaking a truth he hasn't admitted before. "I thought I found someone years back, but what I felt for her isn't even on the same wavelength as what I feel for you. You're different, Riley. You're everything I never knew I was waiting for."

His words hit me like a punch to the gut. I want to pull away, but something inside me wants to lean in closer, to hear more, to feel what he's offering. But I hold back. My heart races as I try to process the weight of what he's saying.

Spike steps even closer, his hand reaching for the back of my neck, his touch tender but firm. "If you'd let me, I would lock you in this house and never let you leave," he continues, his voice rougher now, thick with emotion. "I want you all to myself. But, at the same time, I want the whole fucking world to know that I belong to you."

My breath hitches as he places a soft kiss on my lips. His lips are warm, but it's the gentle press of them against mine that catches me off guard. He pulls away almost immediately, giving me space to breathe, to think.

I'm not sure what I expected, but it wasn't this. *I want you all to myself.* That part hits me harder than anything else he's said. I want to say something, anything, but I can't find the words.

Spike doesn't rush me, though. He just watches me, his gaze steady but patient. "So, yeah, baby," he says, his voice low and commanding. "That type of love is possible."

I'm still processing what he said, trying to make sense of it all. His words are heavy, and for a second, I feel like I'm drowning in them. It's too much, too fast, but then again, it feels right. I feel like I'm standing at the edge of something big and terrifying and beautiful and I have no idea what comes next.

Spike watches me carefully, his eyes never leaving mine. He gives me a moment, waiting for me to say something, but I can't. My mind is spinning, my heart racing. I don't know how to respond.

He shifts his weight and clears his throat, breaking the silence. "Our room is just over here," he says, his voice softer now, easing the tension in the air. "That's where I'll sleep every night. And no matter how long it takes for you to decide on us, I'll be there waiting for you. Now, I'll let you get settled in. I'm gonna make us dinner, and we can relax and watch a movie. Come down whenever you're ready, baby."

He's giving me a choice. *No pressure.* He's saying all the right things, but I can't shake the feeling that there's more to this than I'm ready to handle.

I stand there for a moment, my mind racing as I try to figure out what to do next. I look at the bed, at the life Spike is offering me, and I wonder if I'm really ready to give in.

Spike walks away without another word, but I can feel

his presence in the room, like a constant pull, as if he's a part of me that I've only just started to realize I need.

I glance back at the door, then at Asher's small bed, and then back at the hallway leading to Spike's room. I feel torn in two. One part of me wants to follow him, to take the next step, to see where this goes. But the other part of me is still holding on to the walls I've built around my heart, unsure if I'm strong enough to let them fall.

I take a deep breath, push the doubts away, and move to the baby bed.

One step at a time, I remind myself. And for now, changing Asher and laying him down for a nap is the only thing I'm capable of doing.

Even still, I feel myself being pulled out of the room and down to the kitchen, where I know Spike is standing at this very moment.

I want you to be so in love with me that you'll go insane without me by your side.

Yeah, I have a feeling that type of love is possible, after all.

CHAPTER SEVENTEEN

Spike

"Foster, what do you have for me?" I ask as I enter the war room. Riley and Asher have been safe within my walls for four weeks now, and we haven't heard a damn thing from Chuck. It's making me antsy.

"As of last night, Charles Landry has put in for retirement," Foster answers, his fingers flying across the keyboard as he pulls up the official paperwork.

"He's not old enough for retirement. The bastard is up to something," Bones says, leaning forward, arms braced on the table. "We need to act before he does."

I nod my agreement, but my gut is already telling me this is more than just a career change. Men like Chuck don't walk away unless they've got a plan. A backup strategy to keep their hands clean while still pulling the strings.

"Anything else?"

Foster's screen changes, pulling up recent bank transactions and flagged activity. "He's moved large sums of money offshore in the last three days. Whatever he's planning, he's making sure he's got an escape route."

"He's getting ready to disappear," Crusher mutters, arms crossed over his chest. "Question is, does he run first or finish the job before he goes?"

My jaw clenches as I process the possibilities. I don't

like either damn option. If he runs, that means he's a loose end. But if he stays? He's biding his time, waiting for the right moment to strike.

"He's not gone yet," I say. "Which means we still have a window to hit first."

"What are you thinking, Prez?" Bones asks.

I drag a hand through my hair, my pulse steady despite the storm raging inside me. "I want eyes on him twenty-four-seven. Track his calls, his movements, everyone he comes into contact with. If he so much as sneezes in the wrong direction, I want to know about it."

Foster nods, already working on something.

"And Riley?" Bones asks, his voice lower now.

I exhale through my nose. "She's been through enough. I'm not telling her shit until I have to."

"You think she won't figure it out?"

"She will," I admit. "But I don't want her living in fear until I know exactly what we're dealing with."

Silence settles over the room, thick with unspoken thoughts. I know my men agree with me, but that doesn't make it easier.

I push back from the table. "Keep me updated. I'll be at my house."

I make my way out of the clubhouse and back toward my main house, my boots heavy against the ground. Four weeks of having Riley under my roof, and it still doesn't feel real. I see her every day. Hear her laughter when Asher gets her to drop her guard. Smell the damn vanilla and citrus scent she leaves behind.

And yet, she's still holding back.

I step into the kitchen, catching sight of her standing by the sink, staring out the window.

She senses me before I say a word, turning slowly, her

eyes guarded.

"What's wrong?" she asks.

Nothing and everything.

I cross the room, reaching for a glass of water to busy my hands. "Just checking in."

She doesn't believe me, but she doesn't push. And that? That tells me she already knows something is coming.

I just hope I can stop it before it gets to our doorstep.

Riley

"He's just protecting you," Abby says a few hours later, her voice gentle but firm. "It's ingrained in him to protect his family. He won't tell you anything that could put you in danger."

"I get that," I admit, rubbing my hands over my arms. "But isn't keeping me in the dark just as dangerous? The more I know, the better I can protect myself and Asher. How am I supposed to keep us safe if I don't even know what we're up against?"

Abby exhales, her expression filled with understanding. "And that's exactly the problem," she says. "In Spike's mind, *you* don't need to keep you and Asher safe because he's doing it for you."

Her words settle in my chest like a weight. "But what if something happens to him?" The thought alone steals my breath. Panic claws its way up my throat. "Oh gosh, Abby. He's practically declaring war on Chuck and his entire department. Chuck already hates him, and the second he finds out Spike's been keeping us hidden, he's going to lose it. If Spike gets caught in the crossfire…"

My pulse spikes. The room tilts. Black spots cloud my vision, swallowing everything.

The last thing I hear is Abby's voice calling my name

before the darkness takes over.

Distant voices pull me from the darkness, muffled at first like I'm underwater. My head feels too heavy, my body sluggish as I struggle to piece together where I am.

"What the fuck happened?" The deep, familiar growl slices through the haze, sending a ripple of awareness through me. Spike. He sounds frantic, his voice sharp with barely contained panic.

"She just fainted, Bubby," Abby's voice is calmer, soothing. "I think it was a panic attack. She worked herself up too much."

There's a rustling sound, then the warmth of a large, calloused hand cups my cheek. "Riley, baby, open your eyes. Come on." The demand in his voice is rough, edged with desperation.

I try. I really do. My eyelids feel like lead, but after a few blinks, I manage to crack them open. Everything is blurry, the overhead light too bright, but I can make out his face hovering over mine. His jaw is clenched so tight I can see the muscle twitching, his brows drawn low in worry.

"There she is," Abby murmurs, relief lacing her tone. "Just breathe, Riley. You're okay."

I try to sit up, but Spike's hands are on me instantly, keeping me in place. "No. Stay down." His voice is gentler now, but there's no mistaking the authority behind it.

My throat is dry when I speak. "What... happened?"

"You passed out, baby," Spike answers before Abby can. "Scared the shit out of me." His thumb sweeps across my cheek, his touch surprisingly tender despite the frustration vibrating off him. "You wanna tell me what the hell had you so worked up?"

It all comes back in a rush. Our conversation, the realization of just how much danger he's in. My chest tightens again, the panic threatening to rise, but Spike must see it because his hands move, one cradling the back of my head, the other gripping my fingers tightly.

"Hey," he murmurs. "You're safe. I need you to breathe, baby."

I focus on him, his presence grounding me. "I was just... thinking about something happening to you," I whisper, my voice breaking. "Chuck hates you. If he finds out you've been hiding us..."

"Stop," he orders, shaking his head. "You don't need to worry about me."

My eyes snap to his, frustration bubbling up. "How can I not? You're acting like you're untouchable, but you're not, Spike. You're going up against someone dangerous, and I can't just sit here and pretend that doesn't terrify me."

His expression softens, and for a second, something flickers in his eyes. Something raw. "I know," he says quietly. "And I hate that you're scared. But I swear to you, I've got this. Chuck isn't gonna touch you or Asher, and I sure as hell won't let him take me out either."

He leans in, pressing a soft kiss to my forehead. "I need you to trust me, baby."

I close my eyes, exhaling shakily. "I do trust you, Spike. That's not the problem."

He pulls back just enough to meet my gaze. "Then what is?"

I swallow hard. "The problem is... I don't think I can survive losing you. Weeks ago, you said, *I want you to be so in love with me that you'll go insane without me by your side.* Well, here I am, so deeply in love with you that the mere thought of you being taken from me is unbearable."

For the first time, Spike doesn't have a quick response.

He just stares at me, something unreadable in his eyes, before finally pulling me into his arms, holding me like he's afraid I'll disappear.

And I let him. Because for now, in his arms, I can breathe again.

Spike

"Abby," I say around the pulsing in my ears, my voice barely above a whisper. "Will you please take Asher for a few hours?"

Abby lifts a brow but doesn't question it. A soft smile tugs at her lips as she nods. "Of course," she laughs. "We're going to hang out in the main building. Maybe I can talk Crusher into playing his guitar."

I barely register her words as she gathers Asher and leaves. The door clicks shut behind them, leaving just me and Riley in the quiet room.

I hold Riley a little tighter, feeling the way her body trembles against mine. She hasn't spoken since Abby left, and I don't push her. Not yet. I just sit there on the floor, cradling her, stroking her hair, letting her feel me. Solid, unmovable, here.

Her fingers curl into my shirt, gripping tight, like she's afraid I'll disappear if she lets go.

"Riley," I murmur, pressing a kiss to the top of her head.

She pulls back just enough to look at me, her eyes shining with something raw. "I'm okay," she says, but I can hear the lie in it.

"No, you're not," I counter gently. "And that's okay."

Her breath shudders as she exhales, and then she does something that damn near breaks me. She buries her face in my chest and whispers, "I just need you."

I squeeze my eyes shut, my arms tightening around

her. "You have me, baby. Always."

She tilts her face up, and the look in her eyes steals my breath. There's vulnerability there, yes, but something else, too. Desperation. "Please."

That one word wrecks me.

I don't rush. I don't push. I just press my lips to hers, soft and slow, letting her feel my every desire.

Her hands slide up my chest, over my shoulders, pulling me closer. I shift, lifting her effortlessly, and carry her toward the bedroom. She doesn't protest, doesn't pull away. She just holds on, like she needs this as much as I do.

When I lay her down, I don't move right away. I brush my fingers over her cheek, tracing the curve of her jaw, memorizing her all over again.

"Are you sure?" I ask, my voice thick. "You just had a baby, Riley. I don't want to hurt you."

A soft smile tugs at her lips. "The doctor you brought in a few days ago said I was healed. I'm okay, Spike. I promise."

I search her face, needing to be certain because the last thing I ever want is to push her too soon. But she reaches for me, her touch warm, steady.

"I need you," she whispers, and I know she doesn't just mean physically. She needs me in all the ways I need her.

When I follow her down, it's not just about comfort or escape. It's about something deeper. Something more.

It's about reminding her she's not alone.

It's about showing her, with every touch, every kiss, that she's mine. That I've got her.

That I always will.

Riley

Spike moves over me with a care that steals my breath, his hands tracing slow, reverent paths across my skin like he's memorizing every inch of me.

"You're so damn beautiful," he whispers, his voice rough with emotion.

I reach up, my fingers threading through his hair, pulling him closer until our lips meet again. The kiss is soft, unhurried, filled with all the things we don't have words for. He kisses me like I'm something precious. Like I'm fragile and unbreakable all at once.

Somehow, he's removed both of our clothes, but I'm too caught up in the moment to admire his body or worry about the condition of mine.

His weight settles over me, solid and safe, and for the first time in weeks... years?... I feel like I can breathe. Like I can let go of everything outside this room and just be here with him.

He enters me slowly, kissing away my tears of pleasure as they fall down my face. I arch into him, sighing at the way he fits against me, inside me. The way my body recognizes him, like it was made for him and him alone.

"I love you," I whisper, the words spilling from my lips without hesitation.

His breath catches, his forehead pressing to mine as he murmurs, "Say it again."

"I love you, Spike."

A shudder runs through him, and then he's kissing me again, deeper this time, his body molding to mine like he's trying to fuse us together. Every touch, every lingering caress, speaks of something more than just desire. This is love in its purest form.

He moves with aching tenderness, his name a whisper on my lips as he guides me toward something I didn't realize I needed so desperately. The world fades away, leaving just us. Heart to heart, breath to breath, souls entwined.

And when we finally fall, we fall together.

After, he doesn't let me go. He falls to his side, keeping me wrapped in his arms, his hand tracing lazy circles on my back as our breathing evens out. I press my face against his chest, listening to the steady rhythm of his heart, feeling it beat for me.

"You're mine," he murmurs into my hair, his voice thick with emotion.

"Always," I whisper back, knowing with absolute certainty that no matter what comes next, we'll face it together.

"I love you, baby. So fucking much."

CHAPTER EIGHTEEN

Riley

The past week has been a strange kind of bliss. Spike loves me. He loves me. And I love him. Saying the words out loud was like taking a deep breath after drowning for so long. Every time he looks at me, every time he touches me, I feel it. This isn't just desire. It's something bigger, something neither of us is willing to lose.

He still works long hours, handling club business, but when he comes home, he holds me like he never wants to let go. And at night, when Asher is asleep, he whispers promises against my skin, words that sink deep into my soul.

I've never had someone like him. Never had this kind of love.

This morning, I woke up alone in our bed, but his scent lingered on the sheets, wrapping around me like an unspoken vow. I got up, fed Asher, and now we're outside, enjoying the warmth of the sun while I walk the perimeter of the compound.

The Iron Shadow's compound is my safe place, surrounded by a tall, solid wall, and the front gate is iron bars that keep out the world. But lately, my mind has been too focused on everything that's been happening, the chaos swirling in the distance, the feeling that something's coming.

Asher is content in my arms, his tiny fingers curled around my finger as we walk slowly along the grounds. The air is warm, the sound of the birds singing soothing, but the tightness in my chest doesn't loosen.

I stop near the gate, taking in the sights of the compound. The security guards are stationed at their posts, eyes scanning the area. This place is like a fortress. From an outsider's perspective, it's a scary no-go zone. But, from in here? It's warmth. Safety. Protection.

But then my gaze shifts to the car parked outside the gate. My heart lurches when I recognize the vehicle.

Chuck's black SUV.

My pulse jumps.

For a moment, it feels like the world freezes. The man who's been hunting me, hunting us, has shown his face. I can see the outline of his figure behind the tinted windows, watching me. The feeling of being trapped settles in my chest, but I try not to show it. I keep Asher pressed to my chest, my eyes locked on the gate.

I don't move. I don't want to make a scene, don't want to draw attention. But I can feel the weight of his eyes through the glass.

For a split second, he's just there, unmoving, watching me like I'm prey. The air feels thick, heavy, and my heartbeat is all I can hear in my ears.

As I stand there, the car still idling outside the gate, the realization hits me like a punch to the stomach. Chuck found us.

The tension that crawls up my spine feels suffocating, but I don't dare turn away. Not yet. Not when I'm afraid of what might happen next.

I feel Spike behind me before I even hear his voice. The heat radiating from him is undeniable, like a storm gathering in the distance, and I know he's already assessed the situation.

"Riley…"

His voice is low and dangerous, but I can't bring myself to speak. I don't want to admit how close I am to losing control.

I finally look at him, my breath shaky. "It's Chuck. He's here."

Spike's jaw tightens as his eyes narrow. He's already seen the car, already knows what's coming. His hand grips my shoulder, spinning me to face him.

"Stay close to me, baby," he says, his voice like gravel, rough with the need to protect. His eyes flash with fury as his gaze shifts to the gate, where Chuck's SUV sits, too still, too quiet.

"I don't care who he is. He's not getting near you. Not now, not ever," Spike growls as he reaches for his ever-present gun.

But before I can react, the sound of a door slamming shut rings out from the other side of the gate. My heart skips in my chest. Chuck is out of the car.

Spike moves to step forward, but I place my hands on his chest. "Spike, wait."

He looks down at me, his expression hard, but I can see the conflict in his eyes.

"I don't care what he says, Riley. This ends today."

But I shake my head, my voice barely a whisper. "He's still a cop. He can have you arrested, Spike. Don't do anything that will give him that advantage."

Spike's eyes flash with barely contained rage, but I can feel the tension in his body ease just slightly. He doesn't want to back down. I don't want him to. But I can't let him put himself in a position where Chuck can use the law against him.

Reluctantly, he tucks his gun away.

We stand there for a moment, silent, before I hear Chuck's voice cut through the air like a blade.

"Well, well, well, look who finally found a new plaything. Riley, you slut. You couldn't even wait until I was out of the picture, could you?"

The venom in his words makes my blood run cold, but I won't let him see the effect it has on me. I won't. I keep my back to him, my front plastered against Spike, Asher tucked safely between us.

"Guess the baby wasn't enough for you, huh? Just had to go and fuck some other guy, didn't you? I knew you were nothing but a whore."

Chuck sneers, his voice loud and dripping with disdain.

Spike's entire body goes rigid, his hand tightening into a fist. The sound of his breath going steady, trying to keep his temper in check, fills my ears.

But I can feel the change in the air. Like the tension before a storm. His presence is suddenly heavier, a force that vibrates in the very air around us.

I feel his hand, warm and steady on my waist, his fingertips pressing against the small of my back, the gentle reassurance that he's still in control. He doesn't need to raise his voice or throw a punch. He's the kind of man who makes you feel his anger without a single word. But then, in the silence that stretches, his voice comes, low, controlled, like the growl of a predator preparing to strike.

"You're pathetic, Chuck," Spike says, his voice like gravel scraping against metal. "You don't get to talk to her like that. Not anymore. And you sure as hell don't get to talk about her like that in front of me."

Spike gently moves one step forward, causing me to take a step backward, his boots heavy against the ground. The sound cuts through the quiet between us like a warning. Every muscle in his body is tight, and his energy radiates like a wildfire ready to spread.

I hear Chuck take a step, but he still tries to hold onto that bravado when he says, "Do you think it's a good idea to threaten me, Spike?"

Spike doesn't even blink. "I don't need to threaten you. The second you stepped onto this property, you already fucked up. One wrong move from you, Commissioner, and my man on that side of the gate will drop you before your next breath."

"You took my family away from me," Chuck says, his voice almost whiney. "I'm here to take them home."

Spike's voice is deadly quiet but filled with power. "Not happening. You can keep running your mouth, Chuck, but remember, I'm not the one who'll regret it. You're already digging your own grave."

The weight of his words hangs in the air, and even though Chuck is still standing there, I can practically feel the change in him. The uncertainty.

Spike's hand moves from my waist, sliding down to grip the hem of my shirt, pulling me closer against him. "This is your last warning," he says, his voice so steady and calm that it's downright terrifying. "Don't come near my fucking compound again. Cop or not, I'll tear your black heart out with my bare hands."

"Listen here, you can't threaten me," Chuck says nasally. "I can have you arrested right on the spot."

"It wasn't a threat, Charles. It was a fucking promise."

Whatever Chuck was about to say, Spike silences it with a look. Sharp, piercing, and full of promise. Chuck hesitates, and in that moment, I know he knows Spike means every word.

Finally, without another word, Chuck slams the door of his car, the engine roaring to life as he speeds away, leaving us standing there, undisturbed but for the silence that follows.

Spike watches the SUV disappear into the distance. He stands tall, unmovable, like the storm that's passed, leaving only calm in its wake. But I can feel the intensity, the fury still humming beneath his skin.

He looks down at me, his eyes softening, the fire in them dimming as he takes in the sight of me. His gaze lingers on Asher, tucked safely in my arms, before landing back on me.

"You okay?" he asks, his voice a little softer now but still filled with that same protective edge.

I nod, but there's a tightness in my chest I can't shake. "I think so. But... what if he comes back?"

"He won't," Spike growls. "And even if he does, he can't enter those gates without probable cause or a warrant. Which he has no reason for either. I own every bit of land my clubs live on. He has no legal rights to enter otherwise."

I swallow hard, still feeling the weight of what just happened, but in Spike's arms, I know that we're safe.

"You're mine, Riley," Spike says quietly. "Both of you. And nobody touches what's mine. Not ever."

There's something in the way he says it, a finality in his tone that makes my heart skip a beat. I lean back to face him, feeling the weight of his words settle into my bones.

"I know," I whisper, my voice catching as I look up at him.

"From now on, no walking the grounds alone," he says,

guiding me to the main building. "Anytime you want to take a walk, just let me know. If I'm not available, I'll make sure someone is. That goes for Abby, as well."

"What goes for Abby?" the woman in question asks as we enter the building.

"No more walking around without an escort," Spike answers.

"Oh, no worries there, Bubby," she says softly. "I don't even walk from my house to the main building unless there are several people outside."

"Let me rephrase," he says, stopping and staring down at both of us. "No more walking around without one of my officers by your sides. Now, Skip has decided he wants to cook for the club tonight, so I'm ordering something. How does fried chicken sound?"

Skip chooses that moment to walk in the room and his shocked face has both me and Abby laughing.

"Fucker," he says, trying to hide his grin. "I'll have you know that my chicken is a hell of a lot better than wherever you're ordering from. Abby and Riley are gonna love it."

"You're not poisoning my girls with your undercooked chicken, Skip," he says, pulling out his phone. "Meet me in the war room in ten. Chuck was just here."

"Are you alright?" Skip asks me, his eyes both worried and angry.

"Just shaken up a bit," I admit. "I pretty much had my back to him the whole time."

"Fuck chicken," he says, opening his arms. "You need a hug."

Before I have a chance to kindly ask him not to hug me, Spike grabs his cut and drags him away.

"War room," he says. "And I'm pretty sure I've told you

a dozen times already not to touch my fucking woman."

"Awe, Prez," Skip whines, "One of these days, you're gonna have no choice but to let me get some of those cuddles."

"Over my dead body."

"That could work."

"I'll haunt your ass if you so much as try."

Shaking my head at their antics, I follow Abby.

"These men are insane," she laughs as she pulls out the chicken Skip was preparing to cook. "Want to help me cook for thirty people?"

Nodding my agreement, I rush to the office to grab the rocker that Spike bought for Asher and set him up in a safe spot where I can still see him.

"Potatoes or chicken?" she asks when I return.

"I'll peel," I say, grabbing a bag of potatoes.

"You sure you're okay?" she asks as I take a seat and start peeling.

I nod, even though my hands tremble slightly as I reach for another potato. "I will be."

Abby sighs, setting down the knife she's using to prep the chicken. "Riley, you don't have to pretend with me. Chuck showing up like that…" She shakes her head. "That was messed up."

I take a slow breath, letting her words settle. She's right. Pretending I'm fine won't change the fact that my heart is still racing, that the image of Chuck's SUV idling outside the gate is burned into my brain.

"That man used to control my entire life," I murmur. "Every second, every decision. He made me believe I was worthless, that I couldn't escape him." I force myself to meet her gaze. "But I did. And I'm never going back."

Abby nods, her expression unreadable for a second

before something fierce sparks in her eyes. "Darn right, you're not."

I smile at that, the warmth of her support sinking into the cracks Chuck tried to leave in me.

"I was watching from the monitor in the war room," she admits. "My brother looked like he was ready to kill him on the spot," Abby continues, a small smirk tugging at her lips. "Honestly, I was kind of surprised he didn't."

I shake my head. "I stopped him."

Abby blinks. "You... stopped him?"

I nod, setting down the peeler. "Chuck's a cop, Abby. If Spike had done something, it could've given Chuck exactly what he wanted. An excuse to drag him in, to put him in a cage." My fingers curl into a fist, the thought alone making my stomach twist. "I couldn't let that happen."

She watches me carefully before letting out a slow breath. "You're good for him, you know that?"

I let out a quiet laugh, shaking my head. "Spike doesn't need someone to hold him back."

"No," she agrees, "but he does need someone who sees beyond his anger. Someone who reminds him that not every fight needs to end in blood."

I swallow hard, her words sinking deep. Maybe she's right. Maybe that's exactly what Spike needs. Someone who doesn't just stand beside him in the fire but knows when to pull him back before he burns everything down.

"Maybe," I say. "But I have a feeling that Chuck's ending will definitely be covered in blood. I just hope it's Chuck's and not Spike's."

The sound of heavy boots stomping down the hall has us both looking toward the kitchen entrance just as Maverick and Crusher walk in.

"Something smells good," Crusher says, patting his stomach.

"There isn't a single thing cooking," I laugh softly. "What you're smelling is peeled potatoes and raw meat."

"I stand by my words," he winks.

"Flirt with her again, and I'll break your face," Spike says, shoving Crusher aside.

"This is your fault, woman," Skip says as he, too, walks into the kitchen. "He used to be nice before he met you."

"Oh, please," Maverick grunts.

"Okay, nice is pushing it," Skip says, pulling Asher from his bouncer. "But he used to be tolerable. Now, he's an ass."

"That's President Ass to you," he says, taking Asher from his arms and cuddling him against his chest.

"What? Now I can't hold my own nephew? I'll have you know that I'm his favorite uncle."

"You wish," Tank says, grabbing a raw potato and eating it. "Ash and I already made plans to build his motorcycle. I'm clearly his favorite."

"He's an infant," I remind Tank with a smile. "And I don't think it's gut-healthy to be eating raw potatoes. I haven't even rinsed those off yet."

"We're planning on taking our time," he smiles, taking another huge bite. "And I'm a big guy, Riley. Me nor my gut are worried about a raw potato."

I raise an eyebrow, looking at Spike, then at the group of men crowding into the kitchen instead of being in the war room. "Shouldn't you all be in your super-secret meeting?" I ask, hands on my hips.

Spike smirks, completely unbothered. "Tried. Didn't last five minutes without you."

I roll my eyes, but before I can respond, he steps closer, crowding me against the counter. The kitchen goes completely silent except for a few amused snickers.

"Gotta say, baby," he murmurs, his lips brushing against mine, "being away from you? Not my thing."

Before I can react, he cups my face with his one free hand, the other still holding my son, and kisses me, slow, deep, and absolutely shameless.

The room erupts.

"Oh, come on!" Skip groans. "We get it. You two are disgustingly in love."

"Hey, some of us are trying to eat here," Tank complains around a mouthful of raw potato.

"Damn, Prez, at least give us a warning next time," Crusher mutters, covering his eyes like he's witnessing something scandalous.

Spike pulls away just enough to smirk against my lips, completely unfazed. "Don't like it? Get the fuck out."

Bones, the terrifying, emotionless enforcer, steps forward without a word and plucks Asher right out of Spike's arms. I tense for a second, but the sight of the massive, scarred man cradling my baby so carefully softens something in me.

"You let *him* take the kid, but I get threatened with a bullet every time I try?" Skip exclaims, throwing his hands up. "Where is the justice in this club?!"

Spike shrugs. "Bones doesn't run his mouth like you do."

"You wound me, Prez. You really do," Skip sighs dramatically.

Bones ignores the whole exchange, looking down at Asher with something bordering on tenderness. "Kid's getting heavier," he mutters.

"That's because he eats like Tank," I tease, looking pointedly at Tank and his raw potato.

Tank lifts the half-eaten spud in salute. "I'm a big guy. Need the fuel."

"Every single one of you are big guys," I remind him. "I'm not even sure we have enough chicken to feed you all."

Spike tightens his arm around my waist, completely content as he watches the chaos unfold.

I shake my head, laughing as Skip dramatically flops onto a chair, arms crossed like a petulant child. He, too, a giant man, makes the act even more hilarious. "You know, Prez, I could be your favorite if you just gave me a chance."

Spike deadpans. "I'd rather give Chuck a hug."

The room explodes with laughter, and as I lean into Spike, I watch as Skip bends his head to hide his grin.

"Is there a rule that all Iron Shadows have to be large?" I ask. "Why is it that every single one of you looks as if you spend your every waking moment in a gym?"

"You checking out my brothers, baby?" Spike growls. "Because if you are, I have to feed a bullet to every last one of them."

"She's not wrong," Abby blushes. "You're all like mountains. I think it's why I feel so safe here."

I glance over at Abby and smile in understanding.

"Yeah," I agree. "They're like our shields."

Skip straightens up at my words, puffing out his chest. "Damn right, I'm a shield. Best one you got."

"You?" Maverick snorts. "More like a decorative fence."

The whole room bursts into laughter as Skip glares at him. "A *decorative fence*?" he repeats, scandalized. "I'll have you know, I am a *fortress*. Impenetrable. Unbreakable. A damn tank."

"I don't know, man," Crusher chimes in, smirking. "You screamed pretty loud last week when that raccoon got into the clubhouse."

Skip scowls. "That wasn't a scream. That was a battle cry."

"Oh, sure," Tank says, taking another bite of his raw potato. "Real warrior-like."

Abby giggles beside me, and I shake my head. "Well, fortress or not, I'm not sure we have enough chicken for everyone."

Maverick stretches, cracking his knuckles. "Well, I guess we could always send Skip to get more food."

"Why me?" Skip protests.

"Because of your warrior status, of course," Maverick shoots back, grinning.

"I *hate* this club," Skip mutters, but he's laughing too. "Don't forget that I'm in charge of all of your money."

Bones, still holding Asher, smirks just the tiniest bit.

The room is filled with laughter, teasing, and a warmth that feels like home. Yeah… these men may be mountains, but they're *our* mountains. And I wouldn't have it any other way.

Spike looks down at me, and despite the laughter on his face, I can still see the worry in his eyes. He must have seen or heard my conversation with Abby, and that's why he ended the meeting before it even started. I know deep down in my heart that this group came in here to cheer me up.

Asher decides now is a great time to make room in his tummy for lunch number three. The sound coming from his little bottom even makes me cringe. Bones lifts Asher and kisses his head before walking over to Skip.

"Little tyke wants his favorite uncle," he says, placing Asher in Skip's arms and walking away.

Much to Skip's disgust, Asher takes a deep breath and

finishes his business.

Skip stares down at Asher, his face twisted in betrayal. "Unbelievable. First, I get demoted to decorative fence, and now I'm just a human diaper station?"

Tank slaps him on the back, grinning. "Tough break, favorite uncle."

Laughter erupts again, and when Spike presses a kiss to my forehead, I know, worry or not, he'll always find a way to make sure I'm okay.

CHAPTER NINTEEN

Riley

"Who are you?"

I jump at the sudden voice, the bread slipping from my hands and hitting the floor.

"Sorry," the man says with a smile, his tone apologetic. "Didn't mean to scare you. I don't think I've seen you around before. What's your name?"

I force a laugh, trying to shake off the surprise. "Riley. I haven't been here long."

"Riley?" He smiles again, his eyes thoughtful.

"Hayes," I answer, pushing the unease down. "Would you like a sandwich?"

"That would be lovely, thank you."

"Mayo?"

"Mustard."

"It's a bit warm for a hoodie," I tease as I grab a new slice of bread.

"It's a weakness," he laughs. "I'm always sweating like a dog by the end of the day, but I find them comforting."

He takes a seat, and I get to work making our lunch. The silence stretches between us, thick with something I can't quite name. It's not that he's done anything to make me feel uneasy. I just feel... on edge. There are always new faces passing through these gates, and the club's reach is a lot bigger than just this compound. So, it's not really surprising that I've never met this man. He must be okay, or they wouldn't have let him through the gate.

This isn't the first time I've made one of the strangers a quick lunch, but it is the first time I haven't felt completely safe doing it.

"I think I've heard your name on the news," he says, breaking the silence. "Something about the Police Commissioner?"

I glance up, surprised. "You have?" I hadn't realized I was newsworthy. Does Spike know?

"Yeah," he continues, his voice calm. "Mr. Landry was talking about how his woman and child were attacked in their home some odd weeks back. I'm surprised to see you here, though. Does he know where you are?"

The unease tightens in my chest. Where *is* everyone? There's usually a crowd of people coming in and out of the kitchen at all hours.

"He's not happy about it," I admit, keeping my voice steady. "But he knows we're here. Spike's protecting us. Chuck's not what he makes himself out to be."

"Most of us aren't," he says with a knowing shrug. "You must be something special for Spike to move you inside the compound. Hmm. Anyway, thanks for the sandwich. I'll get out of your hair."

He gets to the door, but I can't help myself.

"Who are you?"

"See you around," he says, his voice lighter, before slipping through the kitchen and heading for the front door.

I stand frozen, the quiet kitchen suddenly feeling very loud. As the door clicks behind him, I'm left staring at the empty space, my heart beating in my chest.

Something doesn't feel right. My thoughts swirl, each

one louder than the last, but I shake my head. I'm probably just overreacting. Walking to the door, I peek through the peephole, half expecting to see someone watching from the other side. But whoever he was is simply gone. The courtyard in front of the clubhouse is packed full of people, so he's probably chatting with his buddies.

Taking a deep breath, I head back to the kitchen.

"Everything alright?"

Again, I startle at the sudden voice and laugh when I see that it's just Tank.

"I think you men need to start wearing bells," I tease. "How is it that someone so big can make little to no noise?"

"Survival, darlin'," he smiles. "As I'm sure you're aware, our lives aren't always safe. You quickly learn small tricks in order to stay alive."

"Like moving without making a sound?"

"Like moving without making a sound," he nods.

"I guess that could come in handy," I admit. "Want a sandwich?"

Tank grins, flashing a bit of a teasing glint in his eyes. "Serving another man food? You trying to make Spike jealous, darlin'?"

I chuckle, shaking my head as I grab the bread. "No, just trying to make sure you don't starve while you're wandering around. What do you want on it?"

"Mayo," he says, already pulling a chair out to sit at the kitchen table. "And throw some extra meat on there. I'm a growing guy."

"I don't think it's physically possible for you to grow anymore, Tank," I laugh. "Your skin simply wouldn't allow it."

"You may be right about that," he grins. "But it won't stop me from trying."

This time, the silence as I make the sandwich is comforting and peaceful.

"Tank, do you ever feel like you're losing your mind?"

"With this crazy bunch?" he chuckles, accepting his food. "All the time. Why? What's going on?"

"I feel paranoid," I admit, nibbling at my own sandwich.

"That's to be expected, Riley," he says. "You've been through a lot. If you *weren't* losing your mind at least a little, I'd be worried."

"I suppose," I sigh. "But I think it's more than that."

Tank raises an eyebrow, his expression turning serious for the first time. "More than what?"

I hesitate, unsure if I should say the words out loud. It feels like I'm starting to unravel, and I'm not sure if I'm ready to face what's been weighing on me.

"I don't know," I say finally, setting the sandwich down. "Something's just... off. There's this feeling like there's something waiting to explode. Like the calm before a storm."

Tank chews thoughtfully, his gaze never leaving me. "You're not wrong. There's been a lot of weird energy around lately. The club's been... quieter. It's got everyone on edge. The shared anxiety is probably making you feel worse."

"You're probably right," I say, laughing it off. "Just moments before you arrived in here I was having weird feelings about one of your brothers."

"Did someone touch you?" he asks.

"No, nothing like that," I admit. "I was just talking to him, and I told myself that something felt off. I just didn't feel comfortable around him is all. You bikers sure can be scary."

"Who was he?"

"I didn't catch his name," I answer. "He was someone new, though. I hadn't seen him before. He was just as surprised to see me, though. He didn't know who I was, so that's why I knew he had to be from one of the other chapters of this club."

"He was *surprised* to see you?" Tank asks, shoving his half-eaten sandwich away.

"Well, yeah," I say, his tone causing that uneasy feeling to creep right back in. "Actually, he said he heard my name on the news a while back. I guess Chuck is telling everyone that I got attacked in his house. Idiot."

"Riley, I need you to focus. Why was he in here?"

"You're starting to scare me, Tank."

"Baby girl, I need you to answer the question."

"I don't know," I say, tossing my arms up. "I made him a sandwich, we talked for a few minutes, and he left. He didn't act as if he shouldn't be here."

"What did he look like?"

"You're not exactly helping my theory about me going crazy, big guy."

"Riley."

"Fudge. Fine. Uhm. A little under six feet. Red hair. Green eyes. Snarky, crooked smile. And he had his hair pulled back in a man bun."

"Was he wearing a cut?"

"Cut?"

Tank points to his vest.

"No, he had on a gray hoodie."

"Don't move from this spot," he says, turning and leaving.

Seconds later, he waltzes back in. "On second thought, come with me."

I swallow hard, my stomach twisting with a mix of nerves and confusion. "What's going on, Tank? You're starting to freak me out here."

Tank's face is all business now, his usual playful demeanor replaced by something darker, more urgent. He steps closer, lowering his voice so it's just for me. "That guy you described? He's not from one of our chapters, Riley. And if he's asking about you, that's a problem."

"Wait, what?" I step back, my heart rate picking up. "You mean... he's not part of the club?"

"No, he's not," Tank says firmly, his eyes scanning the room as though searching for any sign of danger. "There is a strict rule. If you don't live inside the compound, you don't remove your cut while inside the walls. I know every person involved in this club, Riley. As VP, I've made it my job to know all of their faces. He isn't one of us. I need you to trust me on this. Come on, let's go."

I nod hesitantly, the weight of his words sinking in. Every instinct tells me I should be more worried, but I follow him anyway, the knot in my stomach tightening. Something doesn't feel right, and now I know it's not just me. Tank's never this serious unless something's off.

As I follow him out of the kitchen, I glance over my shoulder toward the door, my mind racing with questions I can't seem to answer.

Who was that guy? Why was he asking about me? And why the hell is Tank so determined to keep me close?

We pass half a dozen men on our way to wherever we're going, and true to his word, every one of them wears their biker vests.

Eventually, we land in the war room. Spike looks up, his

smile fading when he sees the look on my face.

"What the fuck happened?" he asks, handing Asher off to Crusher.

He stands but doesn't move any closer.

Before I can get a word out, Tank lays the whole story on him.

"He could have been from one of the other Iron Shadows chapters," I add quickly. "Yesterday, a few came over just to hang out, remember?"

"You said he didn't recognize you?" Spike asks, not budging from his spot.

Why isn't he rushing over here to pull me into his arms?

"No," I answer honestly. "He asked who I was. He said he recognized my name from something Chuck said on the news."

"But he didn't know who you were?"

"Spike, there are at least a hundred people in your club," I snap, my voice rising. "If he came from another chapter, he *wouldn't* know who I am."

"Foster, call the other three chapters," Spike orders.

The big man nods, pulling out his phone. A few moments later, three separate screens light up on the big monitor mounted on the wall.

"Prez," multiple voices call out.

"Brothers," Spike greets. "Yell for those nearest to you to come into view."

It takes seconds for dozens of men to appear on screen.

"Quick question," Spike says. "Who is this?"

He glances at me, and Tank steps out of frame.

"Hey, it's the first lady."

"It's Riley."

"My old lady can't wait to meet you."

"We need to plan a visit."

"That'll be all, brothers. Thanks."

The screens go blank, and Spike turns back to me, his face deadly serious.

"Every single member of my club knows who the fuck you are, baby," he says. "They know your name. They know your face. They even know your voice. Every. Single. Member."

He takes a deep breath, then finally walks over, pulling me into his arms like he's afraid I'll slip away.

"So, who the fuck was inside my compound and near my woman?"

"I'm checking gate security," Foster says, sitting at a desk full of computers. "Looks like we had two visitors about half an hour ago."

"Why wasn't I notified?" Spike snaps, his voice razor-sharp. "Who was on gate duty?"

"Mike," Foster answers.

Spike's expression darkens. "Bring him to me. Now."

"I thought Mike was in the clear?" Skip asks, his gaze darting between them. "What the hell is going on, Spike?"

Spike doesn't answer right away. Instead, he turns to Max. "Once you get gate security in place, go find my sister. Make sure she's secure." His grip tightens on my arm as he guides me down into his chair. "Take my boy with you. If shit goes down, I don't want him anywhere near it."

The room shifts into motion around me. Men bark orders. Phones ring. The hum of tension is thick, suffocating. My pulse pounds in my ears as I struggle to keep up with what's happening.

Then the door swings open.

"What's up?" Mike asks as he steps inside, his

expression relaxed.

Spike's grip on the back of my chair tightens until I hear the frame groan under his fingers. "Did you let someone through the gates half an hour ago?"

Mike nods. "Yeah. Why?"

"You know no one gets in without an officer's approval," Spike growls.

"I had approval," Mike says, frowning. "Your cousin came by with a friend. Said he needed to talk to you about something. I called it in before opening the gate."

A murmur ripples through the room.

"Billy is blacklisted," Spike says, his voice eerily calm. The kind of calm that comes before an explosion. "No one would approve his entrance unless I said otherwise."

Mike stiffens. "I'm sorry, Prez, but I followed protocol. You can check the camera inside the box. I called it in."

"To who?" Spike demands.

Mike hesitates. "Max."

Silence slams into the room like a freight train.

"He's approved plenty of entrances before," Mike adds quickly. "It's never been an issue."

"He knew Billy was blacklisted," Tank says, his voice low, deadly.

"He also knew everything about that last run," Bones adds. "A team was waiting to take us out when we arrived at the buyer's location. This can't be a coincidence, Spike."

The air turns ice-cold.

"Where is he now?" Spike asks, his voice barely above a whisper.

Mike shifts uncomfortably. "He stayed at the gate when he sent me here."

A sudden, crushing realization slams into me like a tidal wave, stealing my breath.

"Spike," I whisper, my heart pounding so hard it hurts.

He turns to me, eyes burning with barely restrained rage.

"Max has Asher."

For a moment, the room is frozen. No one breathes. No one moves. Then Spike explodes.

"Find him!" he roars, sending a chair flying across the room.

Men scatter like a well-oiled machine, weapons drawn, barking orders into radios. My stomach twists, nausea clawing up my throat.

"Riley, stay here," Spike orders, but I'm already moving.

"Like hell, I will!" I snap, shoving past him. "That's my son, Spike!"

His hands clamp down on my arms, but I fight against him, desperation overriding reason. "I swear, if you waste time trying to keep me locked in here instead of finding my baby, I will never forgive you."

His jaw clenches. A storm rages behind his eyes, but after a beat, he jerks his head. "Stay at my side. You don't leave my sight."

I nod frantically, and just like that, we're moving.

"Mike, watch her fucking back."

"On it, Prez," he says, his voice heavy.

The clubhouse is in chaos and my mind is a blur, panic pressing in on all sides as I chase after Spike.

A sickening dread coils in my stomach as I look around, searching for any sign of Asher. My hands are trembling, my breath coming in sharp, uneven gasps.

Then, a crackle comes through the radio.

"Gate's wide open," comes a voice. "No one is here."

My knees nearly buckle, but Spike is already moving.

"Get eyes on every camera between here and the

highway!" Spike shouts. "Find that fucking traitor."

Foster jogs up, his expression grim. "Security feed shows Max leaving with two others. They didn't have your boy."

"What's going on, Spike?"

Abby steps out of her house, cradling Asher against her chest.

As the realization slams into me, my knees buckle, and I collapse under the weight of it all.

Spike takes Asher from Abby, holding him close for a brief moment before kneeling and placing him in my arms.

"Is Max okay?" Abby asks, her brows drawing together. "He dropped the baby off not long ago. Said he was in a hurry."

Spike's jaw tightens. "What else did he say?"

"Something about needing to sort something out. He seemed tense but didn't explain. What's going on?"

"That's what I intend to find out," Spike says, helping me to my feet. Then, turning to Crusher, he barks out, "Inform the security team that if they see Max, shoot to injure, not to kill."

"Got it." Crusher nods and strides off.

"Mike, send everyone else home," Spike continues. "Unless they live here, work security, or are an officer, I want them gone until further notice."

"On it," Mike nods.

Spike's gaze sharpens. "Any idea where Max would go?"

"Iron and Ink," Bones answers. "He spends a lot of time there, even when the shop's closed."

I swallow hard and turn to Foster. "Mr. Foster, did that man leave with Max?" My voice is barely above a whisper.

Foster gives me a small, knowing smile. "Just Foster."

I manage a weak nod. "Foster… did Billy leave with him?"

His expression darkens. "Yeah, honey. He's gone."

A heavy sigh slips past my lips as I lean into Spike's warmth.

"I'm taking my girls inside," Spike says, wrapping an arm tightly around me and ushering Abby closer. "Everyone else, meet me by the gate." His voice hardens as he issues his final orders. "Foster, Skip…you're staying here, protecting my family. There are guards around the perimeter and snipers in place. Mike, you're on gate duty until I get back. No one gets in without my personal approval. Understood?"

"Yes, Prez," Mike says. "I'll clear everyone out now."

As they disperse, the tension thickens, an unspoken understanding settling over us all.

Max betrayed us.

And whatever comes next… it won't end well for him.

Foster studies his phone, his expression unreadable. "What was Max's main job in the club?"

"He was in charge of all things regarding prospects," Tank answers. "Why?"

Foster's eyes darken as he swipes across his screen. "Because Skip's laptop was accessed late last night, and three transactions were deleted from his transcript records. And since Skip was with me, helping move shit into my new place during those timestamps, I know it wasn't him."

Skip stiffens. "Say what? I keep those transcripts off all servers. They can only be accessed through my personal computer. How the hell did you even gain access?"

Foster raises an eyebrow, and without hesitation, Skip turns and sprints toward one of the houses.

Spike's grip tightens around my waist as he rubs my back in slow, steady circles. "What did Max delete?"

Foster exhales sharply. "I won't know for sure until I get into Skip's system, but I'm guessing it was records from your last three runs. Skip left himself notes about contacting the dealers and upping the price due to increased risk."

Skip storms back over, his face flushed with fury, shoving the laptop into Foster's hands. "That two-timing, son-of-a-bitch, dead motherfucker," Skip growls. "Find out if he did anything else. He erased my records on three weapons scrubbings and changed the name of the Fentanyl buyer. He's covering his tracks. There's no doubt in my mind that he and Billy have been working together."

Spike's expression darkens, his voice dropping to something lethal. "Billy was pissed when I told him he couldn't sell that shit here."

Foster's fingers fly across the keyboard. "Then I'd say we just found his motive."

Max didn't just betray the club. He sold us out.

CHAPTER TWENTY

Spike

My chest aches under the weight of betrayal. Max has been part of this family for fifteen years. Long before I became President. Back then, the Iron Shadows were nothing but a no-name club, barely taken seriously. The President at the time didn't really give a shit what happened to his club or his men.

I spent years turning us into the feared name we are now, and through all of that, Max was right by my side.

For the past day, I've been trying to figure out why the hell he'd do this. He has no family alive, so blackmail doesn't make sense. He doesn't have money problems. My officers get paid well, on top of whatever cut they take from the club businesses they run.

Max has been in charge of our tattoo shop since we opened it, and I know for a fact he makes damn good money from it, even after the club takes its twenty percent.

So what the fuck is going on?

"He could have taken Asher," Tank reminds me.

"There was no reason to," Bones counters. "Max isn't working with Chuck. He's got his own agenda."

"Any luck at Iron and Ink's?" I ask.

"Nope," Knuckles says. "Maverick's checking out Max's house now, but I doubt we'll find anything useful."

A knot tightens in my gut. Max didn't just walk away from us out of the blue. He planned this.

"I hate to do this, Prez," Bones says. "But I need to lock down the compound until we sweep it for bugs. There's no telling what Max's play is, and I'd rather be safe than sorry."

"Alright," I sigh. "But keep the other three chapters running. There's a charity run tomorrow for the hospital's new rehab clinic. We're sponsoring it. I need at least thirty men on bikes representing us. Knuckles, since you're Road Captain, I want you outside the compound leading it."

"No problem."

"I'll take Abby, Riley, and Asher into the bunker beneath my house until the compound is clear," I continue. "It's not safe to take them outside these walls until Chuck is out of the picture."

Even if Max or anyone else planted a bug and is listening in, there's no way in hell they can access my bunker. Not without my eyes, my hand, and my fucking code.

"Uh, Prez, your sister is not gonna handle being in that bunker," Tank reminds me. "She'll flip the fuck out."

Shit. He's right.

"How long will you need?" I ask Bones.

"A day," he says. "Two at the most."

"Damn it. I can't sedate her for that long."

"I'll be fine, Bubby," Abby's voice comes from the door.

I turn to find her standing there, looking hesitant but determined.

"Sorry, I didn't mean to listen in," she continues. "I just wanted to let you know that Riley's ex is on the phone."

I freeze.

"Chuck?" I ask, my voice betraying my shock.

She nods. "He wants to talk to you."

And just like that, the air in the room changes.

"Oh, and I really will be fine in the bunker," Abby adds. "I've learned new techniques to deal with enclosed spaces. I might just need a little help from time to time."

"I'll help you, Abbs," Tank says without hesitation. "We all will."

I catch the way he looks at her, the softness in his tone when he speaks about my sister. He's been sweet on her since the day they met, and for whatever reason, he's never made his move.

If he thinks I wouldn't approve, he's dead wrong.

Tank is one hell of a guy, and I know he'd give Abby the love and life she deserves.

But right now, none of that matters.

Chuck is on the phone.

And I need to find out what the hell he wants.

I push myself to my feet, heading for my office with my brothers behind me, the tension hanging thick in the air.

Riley's sitting on the couch, Asher nestled against her chest, fast asleep. Her eyes are wide, a mix of concern and fear written across her face.

"Everything's gonna be alright, baby," I whisper, pressing a soft kiss to her temple.

I sit down behind my desk, hit the speakerphone button, and brace myself for whatever's coming.

"Commissioner."

"Spike," Chuck's voice booms through the phone, loud enough to make Riley flinch.

"What can I do for you?" I ask, trying to keep the calm in my voice, though my gut tells me this conversation is about to get a hell of a lot worse.

"How's my son?" Chuck asks, his tone dripping with something I can't quite place.

I don't answer, and he laughs, an unsettling sound.

"Anyway," he continues, "I'm just calling to warn you about a raid on your compound."

My pulse quickens, but I force my voice to remain steady.

"What reasons would you have to raid my property?" I ask, my hand signaling to Tank to start the protocols for an impending raid.

There's a beat of silence on the other end of the line. A game of cat and mouse.

If Chuck thinks I'm the mouse, he's got another thing coming. I'm the fucking wolf.

"Feds are circling," Chuck finally says, his tone almost apologetic, like he's doing me a favor. "They're getting close, Spike. I'm just trying to give you a heads-up."

I can hear the fake concern in his voice, but it doesn't faze me. He's trying to play the worried friend, but I know better. He's not calling to help me; he's trying to get me rattled.

I lean back in my chair, putting my feet up on the desk. "Chuck, as long as you've got the proper documentation for that raid, you're more than welcome to raid away. I've got nothing to hide."

There's a pause, and I can practically feel him trying to figure out what my response means.

"Are you sure about that?" Chuck presses, his voice lowering a notch, like he's trying to sound all confidential. "There's a lot going on, Spike. I just... I don't want you or your family caught in the middle of it."

I roll my eyes, unable to stop the small smirk that tugs at my lips. This is the oldest trick in the book. Play the concerned citizen. Make it seem like you're trying to protect the other guy's family.

"Chuck, I appreciate the concern, but you and I both know you don't give a shit about my family." I let the words hang in the air, cold and clear. "If you're really trying to warn me, save it. You don't have to act like you care. It's not gonna get you anywhere. And it sure as fuck isn't gonna get you near Riley and Asher."

Chuck's silence stretches out. Then, almost like he's swallowing back something, he responds. "I just don't want to see Riley or my son hurt, Spike. You know how dangerous things can get. I'm not asking for your trust. I'm just trying to make sure everyone's safe."

I lean forward now, dropping my feet off the desk, my voice low and measured. "Listen, Chuck. I know how dangerous things can get. And as for my family? They're under my protection, not yours. My compound's locked down, and unless you've got a warrant or something with more bite than your typical warning, I don't think you've got a leg to stand on."

Chuck doesn't reply right away. I can hear him shifting on the other end, probably trying to figure out his next move. But I'm already ten steps ahead.

"Just know," Chuck says, his voice hardening, "I'm trying to be civil here, Spike. You don't want to push me too far. I'm trying to help you avoid a situation where things go south. And you know damn well I'm capable of making that happen."

I laugh, the sound bitter and low. "Help me, Chuck? You've always been a snake in the grass. You've never been there to help anyone. If you're really concerned about Riley and Asher, do me a favor and stay the fuck away. They're Shadows now. Which means they're mine. You've touched Riley for the last fucking time."

The line goes silent, but I know Chuck is still there. I can feel the tension crackling through the phone.

"I'm done here," Chuck mutters. "But don't say I didn't warn you."

"Yeah, yeah, I've heard it all before," I say, cutting him off. "You can raid my compound all you want, Chuck. Just know I'll be here, waiting for you. You want to play games? Bring it."

I hang up before he can say anything else, staring at the phone in my hand.

"Protocols already active, Prez," Tank says, stepping up to my side. "We're ready if they make a move."

"Good," I grunt, my jaw tightening. "If Chuck thinks he's gonna walk in here and take my woman and child, he's sorely mistaken. Get the word out to the other chapters. Tell them to cooperate if they get raided. Bones, I need you to move quickly to get this place searched and cleaned for bugs. I need everything back to normal before the feds show up. Everyone else, contact any loved ones. Let them know you'll be out of contact for a few days. I want everyone in my bunker in three hours. Security needs to be changed every five hours. This compound is officially locked down."

***

Bones finishes the sweep in under twenty-four hours. And he doesn't find a damn thing.

Which only pisses me off more.

What the hell is Max playing at?

"Everything clear?" I ask Tank.

"They can tear this place apart, and they won't find a thing," he says. "Foster made sure every transaction tied to our banks is labeled for legit business."

"If they dig deep enough, they'll find unaccounted money," I mutter.

"I went all the way back to when you took over as President," Foster says, stepping into my office, a wide-awake newborn in his arms. "There's nothing for them to find. And I made sure Skip's records are locked down tight." He smirks. "Now, Riley said to bring you this little guy while she warms up a bottle. She's unthawing some milk from the freezer."

"Oh! Can I feed him?" Skip asks, practically bouncing into the room behind Foster.

"No, you fucking can't," I growl, taking my son. "If he's not nursing, then I'm feeding him. Now, what the hell do you want?"

"That baby's first word is gonna be 'fuck,'" Maverick comments from the doorway.

"What is this, a goddamn party?" I ask, scowling. "Don't you all have shit to do?"

"We're on lockdown, brother," Skip reminds me. "All work is on hold. But Max's prospects are handling grunt work at the Underworld, so at least that place is still running."

"Fuck," Maverick mutters as realization slams into both of us.

"No way," I say.

"What am I missing?" Skip asks, looking between us.

"The prospects," I say, my grip on Asher tightening. "Max personally vetted and chose every single one of them."

The room falls into silence, the weight of the revelation pressing down hard.

"What are the chances," I continue, my voice low, "that

he planted some of them as spies?"

Silence stretches across the room as the weight of my words sinks in.

"We need Max's records," I say, my voice hard. "I want a full list of every prospect he's brought in. I want to know where they came from, how long they've been here, and which chapter they're at now."

"I'll dig into it," Foster says immediately. "He kept files on every single one. I just need access to his laptop or his hard copies."

"Start with his office at the tattoo shop," I order. "If we don't find anything there, search his house."

"On it." Foster nods and turns to leave just as Riley steps into the office, a warm bottle in her hands.

The tension in my body eases slightly at the sight of her. She crosses the room, her eyes locking onto mine, reading the storm brewing inside me. But she doesn't ask questions. Instead, she gives me what I need.

Her steady presence.

"Here," she murmurs, handing me the bottle before crouching beside my chair. "Let me help."

I adjust Asher in my arms, feeling clumsy as hell. He's so damn small, and this is the first time I'm feeding him from a bottle.

Riley gently places her hand over mine, guiding the nipple to Asher's mouth. It takes him a few moments to accept the new nipple, but then he latches on, his little hands gripping my fingers.

"There you go," Riley whispers, her voice soft with affection. "Just like that."

A strange sensation settles in my chest. Something warm, something grounding. It's not just about Asher taking his first bottle. It's about this moment. Having

Riley beside me, steadying me, while the world outside this office threatens to burn down.

I exhale slowly, my focus narrowing to the tiny life in my arms.

For just a second, everything else – Max, Chuck, the raid, the traitor – fades into the background.

For just a second, all that matters is my son.

"I love you, boy," I murmur, staring down at the tiny bundle in my arms. "I hope you know that I'll always have your back. And so will all of your crazy, overprotective uncles. You're gonna grow up knowing exactly what it means to be fiercely loved."

Riley sniffles beside me, and I glance down to see her trying and failing to blink back tears.

Smiling, I reach out with my free hand and brush my fingers over her cheek. "And I love you, Riley. As much as I hate how it happened, I'm really fucking glad you ran into my life."

She huffs out a soft laugh. "More like bulldozed."

"Same thing."

Before she can respond, Skip clears his throat dramatically. "What about me, Prez? Do you love me?"

I shake my head, biting back a grin. "For some crazy reason... yeah. I love you too, Skip."

He smirks, turning to the others. "You hear that, losers? I'm his favorite brother."

"Hardly," Maverick scoffs from where he's still leaning against the doorframe. "That would be me."

Skip snorts. "Oh, puh-lease. You don't count, *Outlaw*."

Maverick just smirks. "Keep telling yourself that."

Across the room, Tank watches the exchange with quiet amusement, his arms crossed over his chest like he's enjoying a damn soap opera. Bones, on the other hand, just sits there, arms resting on his knees, expression blank, and indifferent to the playful bickering. But I know better.

Bones might not say much, might not waste his breath on bullshit, but he would kill for everyone in this room. No hesitation. No remorse.

I shift my focus back to Asher, who's still sucking away at his bottle, blissfully unaware that he's already at the center of this chaotic, dysfunctional, but fiercely loyal family.

CHAPTER TWENTY-ONE

Riley

I stare in absolute disbelief at the destruction around me. The clubhouse is wrecked. Some doors were kicked in, even though they had full access to every room. Furniture overturned, drawers yanked out and dumped, their contents scattered like someone took a snow globe of our lives and shook it violently.

And it's not just the clubhouse. Every single home inside the compound, occupied or not, has been torn apart. Even the garages, the vehicles, and the storage building where they keep old motorcycles weren't spared.

They made us sit outside for hours while they tore through everything, leaving nothing but chaos in their wake.

"Surely there's some rule stating they have to clean up after themselves," I mutter to myself, nudging aside a pile of clothes and papers that used to be neatly packed away.

The mess is so outrageous, so excessive, that I don't even know where to start. It's like they weren't just searching for something – they wanted to make a point. And they wanted us to feel it.

A heavy weight settles in my chest as I take in the destruction of Spike's house. This wasn't just a search. It was a message. A warning. Chuck must have told them to be extra destructive because there's no way this was just protocol.

I step carefully over the mess, my shoes crunching against shattered glass and scattered debris. It's not just overturned furniture or drawers yanked out. It's pure carnage. Mattresses slashed open, clothes ripped apart. Even the bathroom wasn't spared.

But when I reach Asher's room, the breath leaves my lungs.

The brand-new crib that Spike put together himself? Splintered into pieces. The soft mattress he picked out so carefully is sliced straight down the middle, its insides spilling onto the floor. His tiny blankets are crumpled and smeared with dirt like someone deliberately stomped over them.

Tears prick my eyes, but I blink them away, rage burning through the sadness.

This wasn't just about finding something. It was about breaking something. About making sure we knew that nothing – *no one* – was off-limits.

Below me, I hear some of the men enter my new home. Then I hear Spike cursing under his breath, the sharp edge of fury in his voice. Tank says something and I hear Spike respond, but I can't hear what it is they said. It doesn't matter though. I don't have to look at him to know his jaw is locked tight, his fists clenched.

They're all pissed. But when Spike sees this room?

I don't think even hell will hold him back.

Moments later, I feel them enter the room. I hold Asher tightly against my chest, knowing that he's feeling the tension.

Spike's footsteps are heavy, his boots crunching over the same broken glass I've been carefully avoiding. I hear him pause behind me, and I brace myself, knowing what's coming.

The silence stretches, and I can almost feel the rage building behind him. His breathing is shallow, controlled, but the anger in the air is suffocating. Then, it happens – he lets out a low growl, the kind that sends a shiver up your spine.

"What the fuck?" His voice cracks like thunder in the stillness of the room.

I turn to face him, and the sight of his eyes, narrowed, burning with a mix of fury and heartbreak, hits me like a punch to the gut. His gaze flickers to the shattered crib, the ruined mattress, and then to me, clutching Asher protectively.

He takes a step forward, his hands tightening into fists. But before he can say another word, Tank's deep voice cuts through the tension, calm but firm.

"We need to focus, Spike. We'll deal with the anger later."

Spike doesn't answer, but I know his mind is a hurricane of thoughts, each one more dangerous than the last. Bones, ever the silent observer, stands at the doorway, his face unreadable but his body stiff with tension.

I can see it in their eyes. They all want revenge.

I step forward, holding Asher tighter. "Spike... it's just stuff. We can fix this."

But the words feel hollow, even to me.

Spike looks at me then, his expression softening just a little. "It's not just stuff, baby," he mutters. "It's *our* life. It's our family."

I nod, but the heaviness in my chest doesn't let up.

Asher squirms against me, and I gently adjust him, brushing a strand of hair from his forehead. It's not enough to calm the storm inside me.

"Come on, let's get out of here for a while," I say, voice shaking. "We need to be somewhere safe."

Spike hesitates, his gaze lingering on the wreckage. But when he looks at me again, something shifts in his eyes – a mix of determination and love. "We'll stay in the bunker until we get this place back to normal."

Nodding, I take one last look around the room.

"There's no way this is protocol," I voice my thoughts. "Chuck is behind this damage. I know it deep down in my soul that he's told them to cause as much damage as possible. Might want to check for new bugs. He probably paid someone to place a few."

Spike's eyes widen before looking back at Bones.

"Already on it, doll," he says.

"I'm gonna get Abby and move her back down in the bunker," Tank says. "Skip has already made a call to a cleanup crew. Everything will be finished before we wake up in the morning. We're paying them double their amount to work through the rest of today and overnight."

"Good," Spike says. "Baby, I need to go out for a few hours. I need to go and check in on my other chapters. All four of us were raided at the same time. I need to make sure everyone is safe."

"We'll be fine," I tell him, even though everything in me doesn't want him out of my line of sight. But I can't be clingy. He has too many people depending on him.

"Order some new things for Asher," he says, handing me a black card. "We also need a new mattress and couch. Pick whatever ones you want. Just have them delivered here tomorrow. Pay whatever shipping fee is needed to get it done. I love you, baby. Please, stay in the bunker."

I nod, trying to steady my breathing as I hold Asher

close, but the tightness in my chest lingers. Every instinct in me wants to be near Spike, to stay within arm's reach, but I know he has to go.

I gently rock Asher in my arms, my mind racing as the chaos of the compound swirls around me. The wreckage. The broken things. It's all a physical manifestation of the mess we're in, and no matter how much cleaning gets done, it feels like we're never going to fix what's been torn apart.

"Spike, be careful," I say, my voice cracking a little, betraying the fear I've been holding back. "I know you have to go, but please be careful. You know Chuck won't stop until he gets what he wants."

Spike's gaze softens as he brushes a stray lock of hair from my face, his hand lingering for just a moment too long. "I'll be fine. I promise you." His tone is firm, but there's a spark of something deeper in his eyes. Something I can't quite read, but it's a promise that stirs something protective deep inside me. "I'll have Bones with me. That fucker can scare the devil. He'll have us all back together soon."

His hand reaches out, brushing Asher's tiny head, and for a moment, I see him – really see him – lost in the softness of the fatherhood that he's claimed. It's a fleeting moment, but it means everything to me.

"I love you, baby," he says, his voice low, almost a whisper.

"I love you, too," I reply, trying to keep my voice steady, though the words feel like they're wrapped in a thousand unsaid things.

As he turns to leave, Tank gives me a reassuring nod. "We got this, Riley. We'll keep everything tight until Spike gets back."

"I know," I say, swallowing the lump in my throat. "Just… please, be careful. Both of you."

Spike pauses in the doorway, turning back to look at me once more. His eyes harden, then soften all at once. "We will, baby. Trust me." And with that, he's gone, his heavy footsteps echoing down the hall.

I take a shaky breath and turn to Tank. "Thank you."

Tank just grins, that knowing smile of his on full display. "I wouldn't let anything happen to either of you. You're family."

I smile back, but it doesn't quite reach my eyes. All I can think about is Spike out there, in the thick of it, while I'm stuck here trying to hold things together.

But I know what I have to do. I have to keep Asher safe. I have to stay strong, even when every fiber of my being wants to collapse into Spike's arms and never let go.

"Let's go get Abby," I tell my large friend. "She hates the bunker, but I think if we spend the day snacking and watching movies, it will be easier for her."

Nodding, Tank leads me out of the room.

***

"Tank, you might want to come out here," Mike's voice says over the walkie. "The police are here and asking for Riley."

"Don't let them through the gate," Tank responds. "I'm on my way."

Tank doesn't wait another second before he makes his way out of the bunker. His glare over his shoulders tells me to stay, but I decide to ignore him.

"Abby, will you be okay on your own down here?" I ask.

"No," she says. "I'll follow you out, but I'll stay near the house."

Nodding, I follow the path that leads to the bunker's exit.

Why would the police want me?

I clutch Asher tighter against my chest, my heartbeat hammering in my ears. I know I should stay put, but there's no way in hell I'm hiding away when the cops are here asking for me.

By the time I reach the front gate, a line of police vehicles sits just beyond the entrance, their flashing lights bathing the compound in an eerie red-and-blue glow. Several uniformed officers stand at the ready, but it's the man in the middle that makes my stomach drop.

Chuck.

Dressed in a crisp button-up, his badge clipped to his belt like a freaking trophy, he looks entirely too pleased with himself. His arms are crossed over his chest, his smug grin making my skin crawl.

Tank is already standing in front of the gate, his stance wide, his arms folded as he stares down the officers. Mike and a few of the other guys are posted along the perimeter, tension rolling off them in waves.

"You got a warrant, Chuck?" Tank asks, his voice even but laced with barely restrained hostility.

Chuck lifts a piece of paper and waves it in the air. "As a matter of fact, I do." His grin widens as he steps closer. "Riley Hayes, you're under arrest for kidnapping."

The air is sucked straight from my lungs.

"What?" I whisper, clutching Asher protectively. "That's bullshit, and you know it."

Chuck shrugs. "Legal custody matters, sweetheart. And according to this," he pats the paper mockingly, "you took my son from me." His gaze drops to Asher, and something cold and possessive flickers in his eyes.

I knew he would find a way around Foster's work. He probably had someone inside push through new paperwork.

"Your son?" I spit, taking a step back. "You don't get to claim him just because your name's on some piece of paper."

Chuck lets out a fake sigh. "It's not up for debate, Riley. The birth certificate says I'm his father, which means legally, I have parental rights. And since you've denied me access to him, well... I had no choice but to get the law involved."

"You had a choice," I snap. "You could've left us the hell alone."

Tank steps between us, his voice dangerously low. "You're not taking her anywhere, Chuck."

Chuck tuts, shaking his head. "That's where you're wrong. I have a legal warrant for her arrest. If you interfere, that's obstruction." He lifts a second document. "And this one? Court order granting me emergency custody of my son."

The world tilts.

"No," I whisper, tightening my hold on Asher. "No, you can't do this."

Chuck's grin is razor-sharp. "Oh, but I can." He lifts his chin toward the officers.

The air crackles with barely restrained violence as Chuck lifts the warrant higher, waving it like a victory flag.

"Open the gate, Tank," he orders, his voice smug and grating. "You don't want this to get messy."

Tank doesn't move. His jaw is clenched so tight I swear I hear his teeth grinding. The veins in his neck bulge as he stands, unmoving, like an immovable wall between me and them.

Mike and a few of the guys shift behind him.

But then, the cops reach for their holsters.

A chorus of clicks fills the air as they draw their weapons and aim them straight at us.

"Last chance," Chuck calls, his smirk growing. "Open the damn gate, or I swear we will open fire."

My breath catches in my throat as I instinctively hold Asher closer. His tiny body trembles against mine, his cries muffled against my chest. My heart slams against my ribs as I glance at Tank.

His entire body is coiled so tight I think he might snap. His fists are clenched at his sides, his nostrils flaring as he breathes heavily through his nose.

Then, slowly, his gaze moves to me.

I shake my head. No.

But the fury in his eyes tells me what I already know. He has no choice.

"I'm so fucking sorry, Riley," he says softly. "Please, forgive me."

With deliberate slowness, Tank reaches for the keypad beside the gate. He hesitates for only a fraction of a second, like he's contemplating tearing Chuck apart with his bare hands right then and there. But in the end, he does what he has to do.

The gate groans as it slides open.

And then, everything shatters.

The moment the gap is wide enough, the cops storm inside. They move too fast, shoving past Tank like he's nothing more than an obstacle in their way. Before I can even react, hands rip Asher from my arms.

"No!" I scream, lunging forward, but someone

wrenches me back. Strong arms twist mine behind me, and cold steel snaps around my wrists.

"Riley Hayes, you're under arrest for the kidnapping of Asher Hayes Landry," an officer states, his voice void of emotion. "You have the right to remain silent…"

I don't hear the rest.

All I see is Chuck standing there, smirking, holding my son like he actually has a right to him.

Asher's screams pierce the air, his tiny fists flailing, his face red with terror. He's so young, but I know he's feeling my fear. The tension in the people around him.

"Give him back!" My voice is raw, desperate. I thrash against the cuffs, not caring that I can't break free. Not caring that I'm outnumbered.

Chuck just smirks down at me, then looks at Asher. "It's okay, buddy," he coos, rocking him slightly. "Daddy's got you now."

Something inside me snaps.

Pure, unfiltered rage overtakes the fear, overtakes the panic. I lunge again, but the cops shove me forward, forcing me toward the police cars.

Tank stands rigid, his fists clenched so tight his knuckles are white. His entire body shakes with fury, his nostrils flaring, his eyes dark and unreadable.

"You're making a big fucking mistake," he growls, his voice deadly calm.

Chuck chuckles. "We'll see about that."

And just like that, they shove me into the back of a cop car.

I barely have time to catch one last glimpse of Asher before the door slams shut, locking me away from my son.

CHAPTER TWENTY-TWO

Tank

Spike is gonna fucking kill me. And I'm gonna stand there and let him.

CHAPTER TWENTY-THREE

Spike

The roar of my bike is deafening, but it's not enough to drown out the blood pounding in my ears.

They took her.

They took my son.

Tank's voice still echoes in my head, rough and furious but controlled in a way that tells me just how bad this shit is. *Cops came in with drawn weapons. Chuck had a warrant. Riley's been arrested. They took Asher.*

I twist the throttle harder, pushing my bike faster, barely aware of the road beneath me. Bones is right behind me, his headlight glaring in my side mirror, but I don't slow down.

They took my fucking family.

My hands clench the handlebars so tight I'm surprised they don't snap off. I can't think about Riley being locked up in some cold cell, scared and alone. I can't think about my son – *my fucking son* – being in Chuck's hands.

That sick fuck probably planned this from the beginning. He couldn't get to Riley with his bullshit threats, so he used the goddamn system to rip Asher away from us.

A growl builds in my chest, low and dangerous.

The cops might've had the authority to take them. But I have the power to take them back.

I cut through town recklessly, barely stopping at lights, barely acknowledging the cars that blare their horns as I weave past them. The station comes into view, a squat, ugly brick building that's about to become a fucking warzone.

I rip into the parking lot, my tires screeching as I come to a sharp stop. Before my kickstand is even down, I'm off the bike and stalking toward the entrance. Bones is right behind me, silent, a storm brewing in his eyes.

The second I step inside, all heads turn.

Some of the officers shift uncomfortably, eyes darting toward the front desk. Others straighten, like they already know who the fuck I am, and don't want to deal with me.

Too fucking bad.

I slam my hands down on the counter so hard the desk sergeant flinches. "Where the fuck is Riley Hayes?" I snarl.

The guy behind the desk, some pudgy officer with a coffee-stained uniform, blinks up at me like I just kicked his dog. "And you are?"

My vision goes red. "You know *damn well* who I am," I growl. "Ethan 'Spike' Turner. President of the Iron Shadows. The *real* father of the baby you just fucking kidnapped and man of the woman you brutally took from my fucking home."

The guy has the nerve to sit back like he's unimpressed. "Ms. Hayes has been charged with kidnapping. The child was returned to his *legal* guardian."

Legal guardian.

Legal guardian?!

I lunge.

Bones' hand clamps onto my shoulder, stopping me before I can rip this guy across the desk. His grip is firm, steady, the only thing keeping me from committing a felony.

"Where. Is. She?" My voice is low now, more dangerous than when I was yelling.

The officer shifts in his chair, suddenly less confident. "She's in holding. Being processed. No visitors allowed."

I smile. It's not friendly. "We'll see about that."

The doors behind me burst open, and in walks the *last* person I need to see right now.

Chuck.

And he's holding my son.

He strolls in like he owns the place, that smug fucking smirk on his face, Asher tucked in his arms like a goddamn prize. The sight of him holding my son makes my entire body go tight with rage.

"Ah, Spike," Chuck drawls, rocking Asher slightly. "Didn't expect you so soon. I figured you'd be too busy dealing with the mess I left at your compound."

I take a slow, dangerous step forward. "Give me my son."

Chuck tuts, shifting Asher just enough so I can see his tiny, confused face. "*My* son," he corrects, his smirk widening. "And according to the law, he's right where he belongs."

All I see is *red*.

"Who the fuck are you?" Chuck snarls, glaring at someone over my shoulder.

The man steps forward, calm and composed, radiating the kind of authority that makes people listen. His suit is crisp, his expression unreadable. But his words? They cut like a blade.

"Zane Foster," he says smoothly. "Attorney representing Ethan and Riley Turner. I have here the official documentation stating that Riley Hayes Turner and Ethan 'Spike' Turner are the *legal* guardians of Asher Turner."

Chuck's face twists in fury. "What?" he barks. "His name is Asher *Landry*. And I'm his damn father."

Foster barely blinks. "Incorrect. Two months ago, Ms. Hayes was granted full custody of Asher Turner... *formerly* Asher Landry. Three weeks later, Ethan Turner legally adopted him right after he and Riley married. Their names have been updated accordingly in all official records. I have the notarized documents right here, including the one in which you, Mr. Landry, *voluntarily* signed away your parental rights."

Chuck's nostrils flare as he snatches the papers from the officer who just finished reviewing them. He flips through, his eyes darting over the legal jargon, before landing on the signature line. His face turns an ugly shade of red.

"This... this looks like my signature, but I never signed anything," he growls.

Foster doesn't even flinch. "These are original, court-filed documents, not copies. If you'd like to contest their validity, you are free to request an independent forensic analysis." His tone remains even, professional. But there's an edge to it. A warning.

Chuck glares at the officer. "You better have them checked."

The officer nods, but before he can speak, Foster continues, his voice firm. "Additionally, I am prepared to testify under oath that I was present at the time of signing. If necessary, I can also provide video evidence verifying Mr. Landry's consent."

Chuck's mouth opens, then snaps shut. His fury boils

over, his entire body shaking as he lets out a strangled, rage-filled scream.

Asher startles in his arms, his tiny face scrunching up before he wails in fear.

And that?

That's the final fucking straw.

"Give. Me. My. Fucking. Son."

Chuck just stares at me, his smug expression faltering for a split second. But before he can respond, a voice cuts through the tension.

"Give the kid back to his father, now, Charles."

A new figure steps into the room, a sharp-looking man with a commanding presence.

"It doesn't make any sense," Chuck mutters, still holding Asher, his voice tinged with desperation.

The man doesn't even blink at Chuck's outburst. "Mr. Foster faxed a copy of his documents ahead of time, and I've already verified their legitimacy." He turns to me, offering a brief but sincere nod. "My name is Ronald Blevins. I'm the Attorney General of Palm Springs. If I had all the information earlier, I would not have subpoenaed for a warrant. My apologies, Mr. Turner. Please, take your son and go home."

I'm still shaking with barely controlled rage, but my focus shifts. I move closer, finally reaching out for Asher. The second I hold him in my arms, all that anger boils over and fades into a raw, protective instinct.

But then one question arises, sharp and urgent. "What about my wife?"

Blevins doesn't hesitate, but there's a flicker of regret in his eyes. "Unfortunately, she will need to be processed. Regardless of the latest developments, your wife will remain with us until tomorrow morning, when I can get a judge to sign off on her release."

I feel like I've been punched in the gut.

"No," I growl, my voice thick with anger. "You're telling me you're keeping her in there tonight? Where that bastard has access to her?"

Blevins shifts uncomfortably as if he knows exactly where my mind is going, but the facts are the facts. "It's procedure, Mr. Turner. I understand your frustration, but this is how it has to be."

Frustration? That's not it. I want to fucking break something. Chuck has Riley in his grip, with all the time in the world to manipulate her, scare her, and make her life a living hell.

"Fuck that," I growl, taking a step toward Blevins. "I don't give a shit about procedure."

Another officer steps forward, his expression warning. "Mr. Turner, you need to calm down."

"Or what?" I snap. "You'll throw me in a cell next to her?"

That's not a bad fucking idea. At least I could keep an eye on her.

The officer looks ready to say something, but Blevins raises a hand. "Mr. Turner, I need you to leave. If you don't, you're going to land yourself in the men's jail on the *other side of the building.*"

The words hang in the air, a clear warning. He must have sensed my plan. But I'm so fucking angry, I can barely see straight.

"Let's go home, Spike," Bones says quietly from behind me. His voice cuts through the fog of my rage. "You don't need to make things worse. We'll get her out of there tomorrow."

His words hit me like a splash of cold water, and the

weight of the situation sinks in. Riley's not getting out tonight. I can't do anything about it.

Reluctantly, I turn, clutching Asher tighter to my chest. Every step feels like a fucking betrayal.

But the rage? That doesn't go anywhere. Not until I've got Riley back.

***

"I don't know how you did it, Foster, but I owe you my fucking life. You name it, it's yours."

Foster leans back in his seat, a grin pulling at the corners of his mouth. "It was as easy as pie, Spike," he says, his voice light. "Although, I've made a decision. I'm joining your club. And if you could do me a favor and skip the damn prospect stage, I'd appreciate it."

"Done," I say, not hesitating for a second to lock this man in as a brother. "Once we get my woman back home tomorrow, I'll patch you in officially. I want her to be here to witness it."

"So, you really are legally married," Foster laughs. "As well as Asher's legal guardian and adopted father. But I'm pretty sure Riley's going to want a ceremony."

"And she'll have it," I say. "I wasn't gonna ask her anyway. Asking gives her the option to say no. I knew from the moment I met her that I was gonna tie her to me."

We pull through the gates of the compound, the sight of my brothers' homes and the clubhouse almost bringing a sense of relief. But it doesn't feel like home right now, not without Riley.

The truck stops, and Tank is there. Standing by the gate, stiff as a board, his eyes locked on me with guilt written all over his face. As soon as I step out of the car, he's on me, his hands trembling as they reach out like he's about to crumble under the weight of whatever burden he's carrying.

"Spike…" Tank's voice cracks as he stumbles forward, his knees hitting the ground before I can even process what he's doing. "I…I'm sorry, man. I should've done something. I should've fought harder. I never should've opened the gates. I…"

Before he can finish, I drop to my knees beside him and place a sleeping Asher in his arms.

"Tank," I say, my voice surprisingly soft. "You did what you had to do. There was no other choice. If you hadn't opened those gates, it wouldn't have just been Riley and Asher they took. It would've been you, too. Or worse… they would have opened fire, and you'd be dead."

Tank's eyes are wide, filled with agony. "But I failed you, brother. I failed her. I failed my nephew. I let them take them. I didn't stop them."

"You didn't fail me, Tank. You kept them safe. You did the only thing that could've kept you alive, that could've kept us from losing even more. You protected them by not letting it turn into something worse. If you'd fought back, it could've cost you everything. But you kept them safe, and that's what matters."

Tank's breath hitches, and I can see the war inside him. The guilt still weighing him down, but also the realization that he made the hard call. The right one, even if it feels like failure.

He looks down at Asher and I watch as a single tear falls from Tank's face down onto Asher's cheek. I have never seen this man shed a tear for another living soul. Not even after his mama died.

"I should've protected you," he tells my son. "I should

have hidden you and your mama away. I'm so sorry, little one, that your mama won't be with you tonight."

Bones must have called him and updated him. He decided to wait for Maverick to arrive so Mav could ride my bike back home. They should both be here soon.

"Tank…" I start, my voice low, but sure. "You couldn't have done anything else. You were caught between a rock and a hard place. And you did the only thing that saved your life and theirs. I'll never forget that."

Tank looks at me, and for the first time since we pulled up, I see a flicker of hope in his eyes. His shoulders straighten, the weight of guilt lifting just a little, replaced by the resolve that I know will carry us forward.

"I'll fix this, Spike. I swear to you, I'll fix this."

I look down at Asher in my friend's giant paws and smile. The anger still simmers in my blood, but it's replaced by the sense of purpose that's always come when I fight for what's mine. My family. And we're getting Riley back.

"We're gonna bring her home, Tank," I say, my voice steady. "We'll get her back, and nothing… nothing…is gonna stop me."

Tank nods, a fierce glint in his eyes. He might have been on his knees a moment ago, but he's standing tall now, ready to fight. I can see it in the set of his jaw. The man who would burn the world down to protect his brothers.

"I'm with you, Spike," Tank says, his voice hard with determination. "When she comes home, I'm locking them inside the compound for the next five years."

I laugh at Tank's ridiculous promise but can't help but agree. I'll get my woman back. And when we do, when Riley's in my arms again, and they're both safe, there won't be a force on this earth strong enough to take them from me. Not ever again.

CHAPTER TWENTY-FOUR

Riley

I can't believe I'm sitting in a jail cell.

They didn't even put me in the cage with the other women. Instead, they shoved me to the back, isolating me in a tiny, cold cell, the door slamming shut behind me with a finality that sent a chill down my spine.

Tank's face as I was forced into the car flashes in my mind. I've never seen him so furious. But it was more than anger...it was a fire, a silent promise of death as he glared at Chuck.

Even I was scared.

A slow clap echoes through the hallway, dragging me out of my thoughts.

"Well, well, well. Looks like we've finally gotten some time to ourselves."

Chuck's voice slithers into the room like poison, making me jump.

I whip my head toward the bars, my stomach churning at the sight of him standing there, that smug, insufferable smirk plastered across his face.

"No need to be so jumpy, Riles. I just want to talk."

My throat tightens, but I force out the only question that matters. "Where's my son?" My voice is barely a whisper.

Chuck's smirk widens. "*My* son is at home with his new mommy." His tone is light like he's discussing the weather. Then his expression darkens, his next words slicing straight through me. "You'll never see him again."

I suck in a sharp breath, my body going rigid as he pulls a set of keys from his pocket and unlocks the door.

Panic claws at my chest. "You can't come in here," I say, my voice shaking as I instinctively press myself against the farthest wall, my hands bracing against the cold metal behind me.

Chuck steps inside, closing the door behind him with a soft click that feels deafening in the silence.

His grin turns cruel. "In case you've forgotten, *I* own the Palm Springs police department." He chuckles, the sound dripping with arrogance. "I can do whatever the hell I want."

And as he takes another step closer, the walls of my tiny prison feel like they're closing in.

His voice drops lower, sending a chill down my spine. "And Riles? I plan to do a *lot*."

I barely have time to process his words before his fist slams into my jaw. My head snaps to the side, pain exploding through my skull as I stumble, my legs giving out beneath me.

Before I can scramble away, his boot collides with my ribs. A sickening *crack* echoes through the tiny cell, but I can't focus on it. I can't focus on anything except forcing air into my lungs.

Another kick. Then another. My back. My side. My legs. My head.

I curl into myself, arms shielding my face as best I can, but it doesn't matter. The blows keep coming, relentless and punishing.

"I think it's time you learn a lesson in obedience," Chuck sneers, his foot slamming into my stomach so hard I nearly throw up.

I try to fight back, to move, to *do* something. Anything. But there's no chance, no opening, no mercy.

So, I close my eyes.

I force myself to picture my family. My baby boy, Asher. My love, Spike. All of my new friends.

Abby, Tank, Skip, Maverick, Knuckles, Crusher, Mike, Foster... and even Bones.

Although, if I'm being honest, he still scares me a little. But right now?

I *hope* he's the one who gets to Chuck first.

Eventually, the pain fades, even though the blows keep coming. My body feels weightless, floating upward, drifting further and further away.

I've finally died.

What a crappy way to go.

I was *finally* happy. I had someone who actually loved me, who wanted me. And now I'm being ripped away before we even had a chance to build the life we dreamed of.

I won't get to see Asher grow up. Won't hear his laugh, won't hold him close when he's scared, won't get to wipe away his tears or cheer him on when he takes his first steps.

He'll never know his mommy.

I can only hope and pray that Spike gets to him before Chuck poisons him. That my son grows up surrounded by love, with a real family, with good people.

Please, God, don't let Asher turn into Chuck.

The faces of my family fade, swallowed by the darkness as I drift higher.

Everything is quiet now. Peaceful.

Chuck

"Take her to the old warehouse on the outskirts," I say, rolling my shoulders as I shake out my fists. Damn, I haven't had a workout like that in a while.

Three officers – *my* officers – exchange a quick glance before nodding. They know better than to question me.

"What about the cameras?" one of them asks, stepping forward. "We can't have this getting out."

I snort. "Already taken care of. Footage will be wiped before anyone can even think about looking for it." I glance down at Riley's limp form, my lip curling. "Now, get her the fuck out of here before anyone starts asking questions."

One officer crouches, checking her pulse. "She's still breathing."

"For now," I mutter.

She should be grateful, really. I could've ended her pathetic little life right here. But where's the fun in that? No, I want her to *suffer*. I want her to know what it means to cross me. To take what's mine.

One of the officers grabs her arms, the other her legs, and they haul her off the ground like a sack of garbage. Her head lolls to the side, blood trailing from a gash on her temple.

I watch them carry her out of the cell and toward the back exit, a slow smirk spreading across my face.

She thought she could escape me. That she could run off with that *wannabe biker king* and play house. Thought she could take away *my* son?

Fucking stupid.

I lost my son because of her.

How fucking *dare* she side with those bastard Shadows, knowing damn well how much I hate them? How hard I've fought to dismantle that fucking club.

By the time I'm done with her, she'll wish she never betrayed me.

"Clean this mess up," I tell the remaining officer. "Leave the cage unlocked when you're done. They'll think the last dumbass on shift forgot to lock it, and she escaped."

"Got it, boss," he nods.

I rub my hands together as I make my way to my cruiser. I hope the bitch is awake when I get there. I've got something new I want to try.

CHAPTER TWENTY-FIVE

Spike

"What do you mean she's not here?" My voice is calm, but the fury behind it is barely contained. "I was told she'd be released this morning. So tell me. Why the *fuck* did you move her? And where the *fuck* did you take her?"

The officer in front of me swallows hard, his hands twitching at his sides. "Uhm, s-see, here's the th-thing…"

I step closer, towering over him. "Spit it out."

"She…she must have escaped," he stammers.

Silence.

Then, slowly, I repeat, "Escaped?"

Another officer jumps in, clearing his throat. "She wasn't in her cell this morning. We went in to bring her breakfast, and she was gone. The cage was wide open."

My blood turns ice cold.

Bullshit.

If Riley somehow escaped, she would have come to the compound.

"How long ago did she *escape?*" Bones demands.

The officer hesitates before answering. "When we checked two hours ago, she wasn't there."

Bones turns to me, his expression hard. "That's plenty of time for her to get to the compound. Even if she walked."

I nod, but every instinct in me is screaming that something is *very* fucking wrong.

"I want to see your security feed," I growl.

The officer rubs the back of his neck, looking anywhere but at me. "It's, uh... well, it was offline until about thirty minutes ago. We had to have someone come in and reboot the whole system."

Bones lets out a low, dangerous chuckle. "So what you're saying is your security system *conveniently* stopped working at the exact same time one of your prisoners *escaped*?"

Neither officer answers.

"Take us to her cell. *Right. Fucking. Now.*"

After a moment of hesitation, the second officer nods and leads us through several doors. Inside, there are three unoccupied cells.

I take one look at the empty space and feel my pulse hammer in my skull. "Why was she in here?" I demand. "We passed several cages out there packed with women in each one."

"The Commissioner requested she be isolated," the officer answers, shifting on his feet. "Said she was violent."

Rage crawls up my spine. Chuck. That piece of shit had this planned.

"She was in this one," he continues, pointing to the cell in the corner. "The door was unlocked when I checked this morning."

"No one checked on her in the middle of the night?" Bones asks, stepping into the cell.

"Just the commissioner," The officer's voice lacks confidence now. "He, uh... left right after."

Bones moves slowly, scanning the room with sharp, calculated precision. I want to storm in, tear the place apart, and look for any sign Riley might have left behind.

But I don't want to get in his way.

Pulling out his phone, he turns on the flashlight and checks under the single cot, running his fingers along the walls. It takes several minutes before he stills, swiping his finger against something in the far corner of the floor.

His jaw clenches. "Blood."

My whole body goes rigid.

"It's dry but not old." Bones straightens, turning to the officer. "Before Riley, how long had it been since you locked someone in here?"

"Months," the officer croaks, his face paling. "We only use these cells for dangerous criminals before transfer." He swallows thickly. "Maybe she just had a nosebleed?"

Bones shoves past him, already heading for the exit. "Let's go, Prez. We need to talk to our lawyer."

I don't hesitate. Foster will help us track down Chuck. And when we do – if that *motherfucker* has laid a single hand on my wife, I'll skin him alive.

Very. Fucking. Slowly.

Riley

I didn't die. Or I did, and I'm in hell.

I've screamed for so long that I don't know how my throat is still working. My voice is raw, my body a trembling wreck, but the pain doesn't stop.

"I know it hurts," Chuck says, his voice sickeningly gentle. "But think of it this way. When that biker finds your body, and I *will* make sure he does, he'll know just how much you love him."

He steps closer, his breath hot against my ear.

"After all, his name is carved into your back."

I squeeze my eyes shut, willing myself to disappear.

Chuck sighs, almost disappointed. "Although… the *E* doesn't seem deep enough. That's on me, of course. I couldn't see very well with all the blood."

He chuckles like this is some kind of joke.

"I would carve my name right across your ass if I had any intention of letting you live," he says as he walks behind me. "Then that fucking biker would think of me every time he fucked you. It's tempting, that's for sure."

My arms are tied to something from the ceiling, and I'm completely naked. I can touch the floor with the tips of my toes, and it takes some of the pressure off my shoulders, but I keep slipping in something, and I no longer have the traction to hold myself up. So, I let my body hang as I feel his fingers tracing something on my back.

"I'm just not happy with this *E*. Don't worry. I'll fix it."

I feel another wave of pain, but this time, no sound escapes my mouth as it's opened wide in a silent scream.

CHAPTER TWENTY-SIX

Spike

"Well, that was easy. He's in his company car," Foster says. "Which is a stupid move, considering they're all tracked."

"Where is he?" I demand.

"Just outside of Palm Springs," he answers. "At some old meat packing farm."

"Knuckles, you stay with Abby," I say. "Everyone else… Let's go get your first lady back."

The room erupts in determined cheers. I only hope that Chuck is there waiting for me. I've tortured my fair number of men in the past – mostly traitors – but this one is gonna be my favorite, by far.

"Spike," Bones says, stopping me before straddling my bike. "I hate to go there, but you need to call Patch and have him waiting for us. And it might be best to take your car. Just in case."

Just in case?

But I already know. Just in case Riley isn't in one piece when we find her.

I swallow hard, my grip tightening around my handlebars. I don't want to think like that. I *can't* think like that. If I let myself, I won't be able to function. And right now, I need a clear head.

Bones isn't wrong, though. I reach into my pocket, pull

out my phone, and dial the man who keeps my guys in one piece.

"Be ready," I say as soon as he picks up. "We're bringing Riley home, but she might need you."

Silence. Then a clipped, "Understood."

Patch is a brother that I would trust with my life. And I have several times in the past. But he keeps to himself and doesn't like to be involved in club politics. So, we call him in when he's needed. We always invite him on runs and to club functions, but he hardly ever accepts the invite.

I hang up and shove the phone back into my pocket, swinging my leg off the bike. My gut twists as I move toward my car, every instinct screaming at me to get there faster, to *run*. But Bones is right. If she's hurt, we'll need the space to get her out safely.

As I slide behind the wheel, Foster jumps into the passenger seat, his complete focus on his phone. "Got eyes on him," he mutters. "Chuck's been parked there for at least thirty minutes. He's not moving."

Good. That means he's settled in. Comfortable.

That means we can catch him off guard.

The roar of bikes fills the night as my brothers pull out in front of me, and I hit the gas, following close behind.

Hold on, Riley.

I'm coming.

CHAPTER TWENTY-SEVEN

Max

I didn't betray Spike and the Iron Shadows. Not in the way they think, anyway. But I don't expect them to understand my reasons.

Not that it matters. In the end, betrayal is betrayal.

The last drug run went to hell. We were supposed to deliver the merch to our buyer and walk away. Los Fantasmas was meant to stay hidden until we were gone. Then, they could take out the buyer and claim the packages. Simple. Clean.

But they got cocky. Greedy. They wanted to see if we had more than one buyer lined up that night. I told them a thousand times – *one damn run, one damn buyer.* All they had to do was wait and play their part. If they had, my debt would have been wiped clean.

But no. They had to push their luck, and now not only do I have the Iron Shadows out for my blood, but the damn Mexican Cartel, too.

Which brings me to my current situation.

I don't expect to earn my way back into the club. Maybe I don't deserve to. But I can do this one thing for them. Because no matter what they think of me, those men are still my family.

I just happened to be across from the police station last night when I saw two uniformed fuckers drag an unconscious Riley into a car and drive off. I tailed them the entire way here, and they never noticed.

They're either stupid or too damn arrogant. Which works for me.

One of the men at my feet groans, and I take intense pleasure in kicking his head hard enough to shut him up. Maybe I knocked him out. Maybe I killed him. Either way, all three of these bastards are dead before the night is over.

I glance back through the window. Riley is stripped down, and her arms chained above her head like a piece of meat on display. Blood streaks down her back, her bruised body limp. They weren't here long before I arrived, so they must have beaten Riley before they took her. Why the hell was she at the police station, to begin with? Where's Asher? Where the fuck is Spike?

It took everything in me to wait for the right moment to strike.

For twenty fucking minutes, I had to stand there, listening to that sick bastard torture her. If I'd gone in too soon, the two idiots, both armed with AK-47s, would've dropped me before I reached the door.

So, I waited.

And, just like I suspected, they let their guard down. One clean shot to idiot number one's head, and he was done. I needed answers, so idiot number two got a bullet to the knee before I knocked him out cold.

Even with my silencer, the shots were loud. But Chuck didn't hear a damn thing.

Shitty fucking cop.

Lucky for me.

Unlucky for him.

I slip inside the warehouse, the thick stench of rust

and old blood filling my nostrils. How often does our dear Commissioner bring people here to torture, I wonder?

The place is dimly lit by the few overhead lights that are struggling to do their job. Chuck stands with his back to me, admiring his own handiwork like the sick fuck he is.

Riley hangs limply from the chains, her body covered in sweat and blood. My hands clench into fists, but I force myself to stay calm. I need to do this right.

Silent as death, I step forward.

Chuck doesn't even hear me coming.

By the time he senses something is wrong, it's too late. My arm snakes around his throat, cutting off his air in an instant. He thrashes, trying to pry me off, but I'm stronger. He stumbles, his legs kicking against the floor as he gasps for breath.

I lean in, my voice a whisper in his ear.

"I'm gonna make this real easy for you, Commissioner," I murmur. "Consider this my gift to Spike. A nice little package, tied up with a bow."

His body jerks in protest, but his strength is already failing. I tighten my grip just a little longer until his body goes limp. I don't kill him. I know Spike will want that pleasure himself. But he's damn sure not waking up anytime soon.

I lower him to the ground and pull out my phone, typing out a quick message to Spike.

Me: *Meat packing plant outside Palm Springs. Two men on the side of the building. One dead, the other out. But don't worry, I'll handle them.*

Spike: *Max? What the fuck? We're already on our way. Thirty minutes out. Is Riley alive?*

Me: *I'm sorry about everything, brother. I hope one day you'll understand why I betrayed you and the club. Just know that I never would have brought danger to your door. Also, keep an eye on that cousin of yours. He's not who you think he is. Riley is badly hurt, but she's safe and waiting for you.*

I slide my phone away and turn my attention to Riley.

She stirs as I carefully release the chains, her arms dropping like dead weight. I catch her before she crumples to the floor, making sure to avoid the mess carved into her back.

"Easy, sweetheart," I say, crouching as she shivers against me. "I'm gonna lay you on your stomach and cover you with my cut."

Her lips part, but no words come out. Just a soft, pained whimper. It nearly guts me.

"I'm not going far," I promise, brushing damp strands of hair from her face. "Spike's on his way. I'll be close until he gets here. You're not alone, Riley. If you need me before he gets here, simply call out, and I'll come."

She nods weakly, her body sagging against me. I shift her into a more comfortable position on the floor, then step back.

Now, all that's left to do is get rid of the two idiots. But I'm gonna need idiot two's help with a few things first. I'm gonna take that fucking Cartel down even if I have to force my way into their ranks. I just need some inside intel from our local police department. Lucky me that I have a not-yet-willing participant to help me.

After tossing the two idiots into the back of my truck, making sure to tie idiot two up, I move into the shadows as I watch the entrance. It doesn't take long before I hear the low rumble of motorcycles and the distant roar of an approaching car.

Spike and the club move in fast, their presence swallowing the warehouse in an instant. As soon as I see Riley safe in Spike's arms, I let out a slow breath.

Chuck is tossed into the trunk like the trash he is, tied up just as promised. Riley is gently settled into the car.

Spike takes a moment to look around. It's nearly midnight now, so I know he can't see me, but I swear he looks right at me. For a few moments, he simply stares at the spot I'm hiding before giving a single nod and sliding into the backseat of the car with Riley.

And just like that, they're gone.

My heart cracks as they all drive away.

My friends. My family.

All gone because my fucking mother sold herself to the devil.

Her death resulted in a transfer of her debts. I was almost fucking done. I've been handing over buyer information for over a year now. I always made sure the buyers were sick fucks before doing so, and I was always adamant that the Shadows were never to be touched.

Well, they fucked up. They put my family in danger. Even if Spike hates me, I will still get my revenge for them being targeted.

Los Fantasma's, the fucking Ghosts, are going down.

Even if it's the last thing I'll ever do.

CHAPTER TWENTY-EIGHT

Spike

"Is it going to scar?" Riley asks from our bed, her voice laced with exhaustion.

Patch doesn't hesitate as he threads the needle through her torn skin. "Some spots will," he admits. "I'll get you a cream that should help."

My fists clench at my sides. Seeing the mess Chuck made of her precious skin has me seeing red all over again. And don't even get me started on the bruises.

The only reason I'm not with Bones, Tank, and Knuckles right now and making sure our *guest* is comfortable is because I can't bring myself to leave her side.

Once we made it back to the compound and Riley regained consciousness, it took a full five minutes just to calm her down enough to explain that Chuck no longer had Asher. Even then, she didn't believe it until she saw him with her own eyes. Only then did she agree to let Patch work on her back.

And now, watching her tremble beneath the doc's hands, watching silent tears slip onto our bed, I feel *helpless*.

"Can you give her another shot?" I ask, my voice tight. "She's in pain."

Patch shakes his head as he keeps working. "She can't

feel a thing I'm doing, Prez."

That doesn't matter. *She's still hurting.* Even if it isn't physical.

Shrugging off my cut, I shift onto my side, bringing myself closer to her. I reach out, wiping away a tear before it can disappear into the pillow.

"Everything is okay, baby," I murmur. "Chuck will never lay another hand on you again."

She blinks up at me, her eyes hazy but sharp with something I don't quite expect.

"You have to let him go, Spike," she whispers. "If he disappears, this place will be the first place they look."

I shake my head. "Foster already took care of it."

Her brow furrows. "What do you mean?"

"Chuck was planning on retiring. He put in his notice weeks ago," I explain. "After Foster embarrassed him at the station, people will assume he left town. Moved away. Foster is making sure there's a paper trail to follow, just in case."

"So... he's gone?"

Not yet.

But he will be.

"He'll never bother you again, baby."

She doesn't press for more. We lapse into silence as Patch continues, and I make it my mission to wipe away every tear before it reaches her pillow.

Finally, Patch leans back and strips off his gloves. "She'll need to sleep on her stomach for at least a week," he instructs. "No bathing until tomorrow, and nothing on her back that could pull at the stitches. She has a broken rib, but there isn't anything we can do about that except pain management until it heals. The pain will be a hell of a lot worse when she wakes up, but that's normal. Call me if it doesn't get a bit better over the next week."

I nod, but Riley is the one who surprises me.

"Why don't you live here?" she asks softly, glancing up at Patch.

He scoffs, already packing his supplies. "Not much of a people person. However, I hope you and that tiny boy plan to stick around."

"We do," she says without hesitation. "I just hope you'll come around so we can get to know you."

Patch pauses for a moment, then nods. "Just call if you need me, and I'll come if I can."

Turning for the door, he mutters, "No sleeping on that back, woman. Got it?"

"Got it," she smiles. "Thanks, Patchy."

Grunting, he leaves the room.

Riley shifts slightly, careful not to move too much. I can tell the numbing shot is starting to wear off, but she's fighting the exhaustion, her eyes heavy yet still locked on mine.

"I remember seeing him," she murmurs suddenly.

"Who?" I ask, brushing my fingers through her hair.

"Max," she whispers. "Before everything went dark, I saw him... I think he helped me."

My jaw tightens. Max. That traitorous son of a bitch. Except... something doesn't sit right.

"Yeah," I mutter. "He sent me a text telling me where you were. I don't know how he knew."

Riley shifts again, wincing. "Do you think he really betrayed you?"

I exhale heavily, staring at the ceiling for a moment before looking back at her. "I don't know," I admit. "The way everything played out, it damn sure looked like he did. But if Max was working against us, why the hell would he be there last night? Why would he take out Chuck's men and give me the location?"

Riley chews her lip. "Maybe… maybe there's more to his story than what we see on the surface."

I nod slowly, running my hand down her arm, careful to avoid any of her injuries. "Yeah. That's what I'm starting to think, too."

She stays quiet for a moment, and when she speaks again, her voice is barely above a whisper. "I hate that I was too weak to fight back."

I cup her cheek, forcing her to look at me. "Don't you dare say that, Riley. You survived him. Not just tonight. But for years. You fought in your own way. And now you're here, in our bed, where you belong. Loved. Worshipped. Safe."

Her lip trembles, and before I can say another word, a tear slips free. Then another. Then another.

I don't stop them. I just lean in, brushing soft kisses against her damp cheeks, wiping each one away before they can fall too far.

"I love you, Riley," I whisper against her skin. "I love you so damn much."

She sniffles, her breath hitching as she presses her face against my chest.

"I swear to you, baby… I will never let anyone hurt you again. Not so much as a damn splinter."

She lets out a soft, broken laugh, and I hold her tighter. Slowly, her breathing evens out, the tension in her body melting as exhaustion takes over.

I watch her for a long moment, running my fingers gently through her hair. Then, carefully, I slide out of bed and tuck the sheet around her, purposefully avoiding the heavy blanket.

Stepping out into the hallway, I find Abby lingering near the door.

"You'll sit with her?" I ask softly.

She nods. "Of course."

I squeeze her shoulder in silent gratitude before turning away.

Bones, Tank, and Knuckles are waiting with our guest.

And I've got unfinished business to handle.

***

Chuck is exactly where we left him. Stripped down, strapped to the chair in the middle of the room, and already looking half-dead. His head lolls forward, blood dripping from a gash at his temple where Knuckles got a little too eager earlier. But he's awake. Barely.

"Rise and shine, motherfucker," I sneer, gripping his hair and yanking his head up. His bloodshot eyes blink sluggishly, and I can already tell he's slipping in and out of consciousness. That won't do.

I nod to Bones, who steps forward and splashes a bucket of ice-cold water over Chuck's body. He jolts awake, coughing and shivering as the water seeps into the wounds Bones has already carved into him.

"I was wondering when you'd finally check in on us," Knuckles smirks, flipping the knife between his fingers. "We only played a little. Made sure there was still plenty of canvas for you, Prez. We even sat back and let Tank work out some of his anger issues before he left to deal with club shit."

Chuck groans, his head swaying as he struggles against the restraints. "Y-you... you're all dead... men..."

Bones snorts. "You still got jokes? That's cute." He crouches in front of Chuck, his expression darkening.

"You know, I gotta give you credit, Chuck. You haven't screamed very loud. Of course, we're gonna be sure to fix that immediately. But props to you, regardless."

Chuck spits at his feet, blood and saliva mixing together in a pathetic little puddle. "Fuck you."

I chuckle, rolling up my sleeves as I step closer. "Nah, see, that's the problem. You should've been more worried about fucking with me."

I reach for the blade on the table, testing its weight before pressing it just under his ribs. Not deep enough to kill him. Not yet. Just enough to feel it. Just enough to make him suffer.

Chuck hisses through his teeth, his body jerking, but there's nowhere to go.

"I'm not well adept at Bones' specialty. He's neat and tidy. A perfect carving. But, I can still make a blade slice through skin in my own way. This is for my son," I murmur, dragging the blade along his skin, carving deep enough to make him scream. I don't stop, not even when his voice cracks.

"There it is," Knuckles laughs. "I knew you had it in you."

"This is for Riley." Another cut. A bit deeper. But not deadly.

"For every goddamn thing you put her through." And another. This time, I may have pushed a bit harder than I wanted, but damn it, he fucking abused her for years.

Blood drips from his body, pooling on the floor beneath him, staining his skin, but I'm not done. Not even close.

Bones steps up next, gripping Chuck's jaw and forcing him to look up. "She begged for mercy, didn't she?" he asks coldly. "Begged for you to stop. But you didn't."

Chuck doesn't answer, his chest rising and falling in

short, pained gasps. Bones doesn't wait for a response. He simply pulls out a blade and slices a thin layer of skin from Chuck's face. His screams making my cold-hearted friend laugh.

Knuckles hums thoughtfully as he kneels beside Chuck. "See, we were gonna make this quick. But you took your time with Riley, didn't you? You beat her before you began torturing her, didn't you?"

He digs the blade into Chuck's thigh, twisting just enough to make him howl in agony.

"Please…" Chuck chokes out.

Knuckles' grin is all teeth. "Nah, not yet. I wanna hear you scream a little more. Bones needs your pain in order to feel something. I'd like it very much if my good friend could feel happiness for a little while. So, scream for him, Chuck. Scream as loud as you can."

And he does. Over and over again until his voice is nothing more than a wet, broken rasp.

By the time we step back, Chuck is barely breathing, his body trembling violently as blood seeps from every wound we've given him. His eyes are glazed, his lips cracked, and I know he won't last much longer.

Bones holds a layer of skin up to the light, inspecting it for whatever the fuck he's looking for. I shake my head at the sick fucker.

Crouching beside Chuck, gripping his chin between my fingers, forcing him to look at me one last time. "This is where I leave you," I say, my voice cold, merciless. "Bleeding out like the worthless piece of shit you are."

His head lolls forward, his breath coming in ragged, uneven gasps. He won't make it another hour. But it'll be an hour of pure agony.

"Make sure he stays awake until his last breath," I say,

stepping over the growing pool of blood and heading for the stairs. "I want him to feel every second of pain until the devil drags him home."

Bones clicks his tongue, shaking his head. "Damn shame we ran out of ice water," he mutters. He picks up a blowtorch from the table, the flame hissing to life. "Guess this will do just fine. Ever been torched on the heel of your foot, Commissioner? Hurts like a bitch."

Chuck flinches, but he's too weak to fight, too far gone to beg.

Knuckles grins, crouching beside him. "Too bad you won't last long," he muses. "I think you would've loved to hear how Bones got his road name. I mean, you've experienced some of it this evening, but not everything. Actually…"

I don't stick around to listen. My men will handle the rest.

I step outside, inhaling the cool night air, letting it cleanse me before I head inside the clubhouse to shower and wash away the blood, sweat, and the last remnants of that sick bastard before I go home to my wife.

My wife who is finally fucking safe.

CHAPTER TWENTY-NINE

Riley

"You really don't want a ceremony?" Abby asks for the third time. "I know your marriage is legal and everything, but you don't want to walk down the aisle to your future?"

"I already wake up to my future every morning," I smile at my best friend. "I don't need a ceremony to cement that. However, we could still have a party."

My ribs healed, and the bruises faded. But my back did scar. Spike's name is as clear as day from the top of my back to the bottom. Patch says that the cream he gave me should help in the long run. I know that it's my husband's name, but knowing how it got there has done some major psychological damage to me.

I've been working through the damage with a therapist. Abby insisted on it. She swears by them and says going to one helped her heal from her past. I couldn't say no, and I'm glad I didn't. It's been several months, and I can already feel myself healing.

"I think a party sounds like a grand idea," Skip says from the floor, where he's surrounded by puzzle pieces. "I'll take care of everything. Spread the word. This Friday, we're having a party to celebrate our newest Shadows."

Before I can respond, the door swings open, and in walks my husband, carrying a gift bag in one hand and

Asher in the other.

"First of all," Spike says, setting the bag on the table, "Skip, you run everything by Riley when it comes to any party."

Skip scoffs, waving him off. "She already gave me full control. Right, Riley?"

I nod. "Yes. But…" I add, seeing Spike's raised brow, "I do want to send a personal invitation to Patch."

Skip snorts. "Good luck getting him out of his cave."

"I'll handle it," Spike says. "Now, more importantly, Asher and I got you something."

Asher, oblivious to the moment, gurgles happily, chewing on his tiny fist as Spike hands me the gift bag.

Curious, I pull open the bag, my breath hitching when I see what's inside. It's a leather vest, almost identical to the ones everyone around here wears, except it looks softer. More feminine. I hold it up, the scent of leather filling my nose as I turn it around. On the back, in bold lettering, are the words: PROPERTY OF SPIKE.

Tears spring to my eyes, emotions hitting me all at once. "I…this is…" I swallow hard, unable to form words.

"She's crying!" Skip announces unhelpfully. "I knew she'd love it!"

Abby grins. "You officially broke her, Bubby."

I shake my head, laughing through my tears. "I don't mind being called your property, Spike. Not even a little bit." I pause, smirking up at him. "But just so we're clear, I will never bow down to you."

"That's cute, baby," Spike murmurs, leaning down until his lips are a breath away from mine. "But we both know you already have."

I blink. "When?"

"Every single time you get on your knees for me."

Skip groans. "I need to bleach my brain."

Abby throws one of Asher's soft books at Spike's head. "You're disgusting. I do not need to hear crap like that from my own brother."

Spike just smirks, wrapping an arm around my waist and pulling me into his chest. "And yet, you all love me."

I roll my eyes, still holding onto my gift. Yeah, I love this man. And no matter what life throws at us, I always will.

"Well, go on," Skip says gleefully. "Put it on."

"Yeah, baby," Spike smiles, stepping back. "Show the world who you belong to."

"Fine," I laugh. "If it will make you happy, I'll wear the vest."

"It's a cut," Skip glares. "Don't insult it by calling it a damn vest."

With my new vest…cut…wrapped around my body, I laugh. Never in my life have I felt such joy.

"Your name is on my back," I tell Spike, knowing he'll understand.

His eyes widen, but I shake my head.

"It's not the same, Spike," I tell him. "This is something I choose to wear. Something I'm proud of. Something given to me out of love and not hate."

Spike's expression softens as he steps closer, his fingers tracing the edges of my cut. "Damn right, you should be proud," he murmurs. "You're my old lady, my wife, and now, officially, part of the Iron Shadows family."

"Damn right!" Skip cheers, throwing a fist in the air.

I shake my head, laughing. "You just wanted to plan a party."

"Guilty," he grins. "But it's also about welcoming you the right way."

Abby crosses her arms, smirking. "I don't know. I think we should make her do some kind of initiation."

Skip gasps dramatically. "Oh! Maybe make her chug a beer, do a burnout on a bike, and wrestle Knuckles!"

Spike snorts. "I'm not letting my wife wrestle Knuckles."

I raise a brow. "Because you're worried I'd lose?"

He grins. "No. Because I'm worried you'd win, and his ego's fragile."

The room erupts in laughter, and as I glance around at the people who have become my family, warmth spreads through my chest.

I never thought I'd belong somewhere like this, but now, I can't imagine my life anywhere else.

CHAPTER THIRTY

Spike

Max is gone. I haven't seen or heard from him in weeks, but something about the way he left doesn't sit right with me. His actions aren't adding up.

"Have you found anything, Foster?" I ask, pacing the room.

Foster is now an official brother. To make the ruling legit, I had the officers vote to allow him to skip the prospect stage before fully initiating him in. It was a unanimous decision. Foster was voted in as an officer. Security and tech expert.

"Not yet," he admits. "I've got feelers out, but it's like he vanished into thin air. However..." He pauses, glancing down at his laptop. "I did find something interesting. Did you know his mother was working with Los Fantasmas?"

A sharp inhale from the doorway makes my head snap up.

Abby stands there, her face pale, her wide eyes filled with something close to fear.

"You okay, squirt?" I ask, my voice gentler now.

"Did you just say Los Fantasmas?" she whispers.

"You shouldn't be here," Tank growls, stepping up beside her. His protective instincts are on full display, but she doesn't so much as glance his way.

"Los Fantasmas?" she repeats, her voice stronger now, as if just saying the name steels her resolve.

"Yeah," Foster confirms, earning a glare from Tank. "Do you know them?"

Abby swallows hard. "I was kidnapped by one of their factions. Held hostage for a long time."

A dark rage simmers in my gut as I close the distance between us, pulling her into my arms. "They're all dead," I remind her. "They can't hurt you anymore, Abby."

She exhales shakily against my chest but doesn't relax. "You took out one faction, Spike. Just one. Los Fantasmas is the most powerful and influential Cartel in Mexico." She lifts her head, her eyes locking onto mine. "They're called the Ghosts for a reason."

A heavy silence falls over the room.

"Does this mean Max is working for them, too?" Knuckles asks, his voice low.

"I don't think so," I say, stepping from Abby and gently shoving her into Tank's arms. "Take her home."

Tank doesn't hesitate, guiding her from the room while she shoots me one last worried glance before the door closes behind them.

I exhale sharply, running a hand down my face. "Max said he hopes one day we'll understand why he betrayed us," I remind them. "But think about it. He saved Riley and handed us Chuck on a silver platter. His actions don't fucking add up."

"Maybe it has something to do with his mother," Maverick suggests, leaning forward. "Where does she live?"

"As of two years ago? Nowhere," Foster says. "She vanished. I can't even confirm if she's still alive."

I let out a frustrated sigh and drop into my chair, rubbing at the tension building in my temples.

"Until we find Max and get some goddamn answers,

there's nothing we can do," I admit. "But there's something else. He also warned us not to trust Billy. If Max has ties to Los Fantasmas, then I'd bet my last dollar my damn cousin does, too."

The room tenses at that.

"Until we get this shit figured out, we're not accepting any jobs that take us across the border," I say firmly.

Bones shifts beside me, arms crossed. "We already have weapons cleaned and ready to deliver," he reminds me. "Runner and his team are set to leave tomorrow. It's a two-hour ride to Tijuana before they head into Mexicali."

"Fuck," I mutter, sitting up. I'd been so focused on Max that I'd completely forgotten.

"Alright," I say, jaw tightening. "Warn them of the increased risk. Anyone who wants to back out has the option. If we don't have enough people to make the run safely, we'll handle it ourselves."

A few nods around the room, but the tension lingers.

What the hell has Max gotten himself involved in?

"I need someone running the tattoo shop," I say. "They don't need to be an artist. I just need someone to manage the store."

"Mike can do it," Knuckles says. "He told me that Max was training him to do piercings."

"I'll talk to him," I nod. "I don't want him piercing anything unless he's fully and legally certified. Luckily, the shop is already fully staffed. Next up, Riley and Abby want a pool. The contractors are breaking ground next Wednesday. I need the shit out back cleared away."

"Fuck yeah," Skip shouts. "I knew that woman was gonna make this place better. She wouldn't happen to want us to start a strip club, would she?"

Bones snorts. "Wishful thinking, brother."

Knuckles shakes his head. "You just want an excuse to spend more time around naked men and women."

Skip grins. "Like I need an excuse."

I roll my eyes. "Let's focus, yeah? Pool first. No strip club."

Skip sighs dramatically. "Fine, but if she ever changes her mind, I'm just saying...Skip's Sinful Sanctuary has a nice ring to it."

"Good heavens," Maverick mutters.

Ignoring him, I turn my attention back to Knuckles. "Talk to Mike. Make sure he's comfortable running the shop for now. If he wants the position long-term, we'll look into getting him certified. In the meantime, we keep things running as usual."

I glance around the room. "Any other business?"

"Nope," Bones says, standing. "Unless you want to finally admit that Riley is turning this place into a goddamn resort."

I smirk. "And what's wrong with that?"

He grumbles something under his breath, but there's no real heat behind it.

Meeting adjourned. Time to get back to my wife and son.

Riley

When Skip said a party, I thought there would be a dozen people here, maybe two dozen. But as I look around at the sea of bikers and their families, there have to be well over a hundred people here. Probably closer to two.

But, on every face is laughter as Skip tells one of his wild, and I'm sure untrue, stories.

Well, everyone but Bones. I'm not even sure that man has teeth.

"Congrats, little bit."

Gasping at the sound of a familiar voice, I turn and slam my body against Patch in the best hug I can muster.

"You came."

"I did, but I'm leaving," he says, hugging me back. "I just wanted to stop by to show my support."

"I know this isn't your scene," I smile up at him. "But I'm so happy you came. Even if it is for a few simple minutes."

"This is the only time you are allowed to hold my wife like that," Spike says, pulling me from my new best friend's arms. "Glad to see you, brother."

"You too," he laughs. "I'm actually leaving, though. Got you both a gift."

He hands me a book and I read the title: How to Survive Marriage to a Hardheaded Biker: A Guide for the Brave (or the Crazy).

I barely get through the title before bursting into laughter. Spike, however, is less amused.

He glares at Patch, crossing his arms over his chest. "Really?"

Patch smirks. "Figured she could use all the help she can get."

Skip, of course, chooses this moment to walk by and glance at the book. "Oh, hell yeah, I need a copy of that. Living with you, even one house away, is probably worse than being married to you."

Spike's glare intensifies. "You want to test that theory?"

Skip takes a step back, hands raised. "Hey, I'm just saying, man. We all know you're stubborn as hell."

Patch chuckles. "Exactly why I got the book."

I lean into Spike's side, still giggling. "You know, I might actually read this."

"Read it out loud," Skip suggests. "We can all take notes."

"That's it."

Spike lunges, but Skip is already running, cackling like the menace he is.

Best. Family. Ever.

"Thank you," I smile, stealing another hug. "Will you come back for a visit when it isn't so hectic?"

"Of course," he smiles. "Until next time, little bit."

"Bye, Patch."

With a kiss to the top of my head, he walks away.

What's his story? Why doesn't he want to be around the people who care about him?

"I said I was fucking sorry," Skip yells. "She doesn't have to read it out loud. We'll all just take turns."

"Someone give me a fucking gun," Spike growls.

Shaking my head, I walk over to Abby.

"He's loving the attention," she tells me with a nod at Asher. Currently, Runner is holding him and glaring at everyone who tries to take him away.

"That boy is going to be spoiled rotten, and there isn't a thing I can do about it," I sigh. "Anyway, look at the gift Patch gave me."

I hand Abby the book, and, as expected, she laughs.

She flips through the pages, a grin spreading across her face. Then, with a dramatic clearing of her throat, she reads aloud.

"Step one: Never let them believe they are the boss." She pauses, glancing at me with a wicked grin. "Bossy bikers, while great in bed, have fragile egos. To control them, let them think they're the ones in charge, but always be ready to remind them who really holds the reins."

I laugh, shaking my head. "Well, I'm pretty sure I already know that."

Abby continues reading, her voice getting a little more dramatic. "Step two: Don't let them make the decisions. The less they decide, the less they can mess things up." She smirks at me. "I think this one was written just for Spike."

Spike glares across the room, catching my eye. "You better not be reading that shit out loud, woman."

I smile innocently and shrug. "It's great advice. Especially since you guys are always so bossy."

Abby flips another page, reading, "Step three: They can't resist when you call them out in front of their brothers. Public humiliation works wonders."

"That's just mean," I laugh.

"I'm gonna shoot that fucker," Spike growls.

The book then moves from hand to hand as biker after biker and their families take turns reading something out loud.

This isn't the wedding party every little girl dreams about. This isn't the family everyone wishes to be part of. But I couldn't imagine a better group to call my own.

Laughter fills my ears as everyone takes turns reading ridiculous passages from the book, each one more outlandish than the last. Skip makes sure to read the most embarrassing ones loud enough for the entire group to hear, while Bones just sits quietly, clearly enjoying the chaos.

Spike glares at the crowd, but I can see the corners of his lips twitching, fighting back a smile. As much as he tries to act tough, he loves the camaraderie of his brothers.

"Alright, that's enough," Spike says, but his voice is more amused than angry. "Let's just get to the damn cake before Skip starts reading about 'how to keep your biker in check.'"

I smirk up at him. "I think you secretly want to read that part," I tease. "Maybe you have a humiliation kink."

Spike just shakes his head, pulling me closer and lowering his voice. "I'd rather be humiliated by you any day, baby."

I roll my eyes, but I can't help but smile. "I'll try my best to make that happen as often as possible."

The night goes on, filled with laughter, teasing, and joy, the kind of chaos only a family like this can create. Sure, it's not a traditional wedding or family get-together, but as I look around at the people I care about, the ones who have my back no matter what, I realize this is perfect.

It's my perfect.

And as Spike steals our son from another biker, wraps an arm around me, and talks to his brothers, I know he feels the same way.

"I love you," I say when there's a break in conversation. "Thank you for saving us. Thank you for taking on my crazy. Thank you for taking such a huge risk."

Spike's hold tightens as he smiles down at me.

"Wouldn't change a damn thing," he murmurs, kissing the top of my head.

Neither would I.

As the noise of laughter and the smell of leather surrounds us, I realize that in this wild, imperfect life, I've found exactly where I belong.

The End

About the Author

Carol Dawn, originally known as Carolyn Jacobs, hails from Maysville, Kentucky, USA. As a dedicated stay-at-home mom, she fills her days crafting peanut butter and jelly sandwiches, organizing toys, and showering her children with more cuddles than they might desire.

Carol's literary journey commenced at the age of five when she earned a reading medallion for devouring over twenty-one books in just an eight-week span. This early love for reading laid the foundation for her diverse creative pursuits, including poetry, songwriting, and short story composition.

Driven by a profound (some might say massive) fascination with alpha male/insta-love romance novels, Carol seamlessly transitions between being an avid reader and a passionate writer within the genre.

Beyond her literary pursuits, Carol is anchored by her deep love for God. Her faith serves as a guiding light, shaping her perspectives and inspiring her creative endeavors. Away from the world of words, she also indulges in her love for classic sci-fi, often immersing herself in re-runs of Stargate SG1 and Star Trek. Her other pastimes include culinary adventures, coloring mandalas, and entertaining an invisible audience with her favorite tunes.

In a nutshell, Carol Dawn is a multifaceted individual whose life revolves around the realms of literature, family, faith, and a diverse array of interests beyond the written word.

Also, by Carol Dawn

Infernal Sons MC, Series
Bear's Forever
A Very Beary Christmas
Chains' Redemption
Hawk's Choice
Ma
Trigger's Light
Brick's Fight
Ink's Second Chance
Sweet Baby Boy
Wolf's Hunt

The Renegade Alpha Pack
The Alpha's Omega
The Alpha's Scarred Omega

Once Upon A Forever
Red's Protector

Dark Souls Bound By Blood (Vampire Anthology)

The Phantoms MC
Cap
Axe
Beast
Reaper
Shadow

Bitsy

The Drexonians

The Drexonian's Mate

Obsidian MC
Echoes From Within
Echoes of Temptation
Echoes of Fear
Echoes of Obsession
Echoes of Danger
Echoes of Desire
Echoes of Secrets
Echoes of the Past

The Billionaire's Christmas Awakening

Audible
Bear's Forever audio

Printed in Great Britain
by Amazon

Voices Through Time:

Stories from the Workhouse

VOICES THROUGH TIME: STORIES FROM THE WORKHOUSE
Victoria Villaseñor d Nicci Robinson, Editors
Global Words Press
Copyright retained individual authors
Cover design by OcnFlame Photography
Cover image © The ational Trust
Internal photograph opyright by designated
Collection copyright © 2017 Global Words Press
Imprint Digital, UK
Cataloging informatin
ISBN: 978-1-911227-7-6

VOICES THROUGH TIME:
STORIES FROM THE WORKHOUSE

2017
GLOBAL WORDS PRESS
NOTTINGHAM, UK

Foreword

On behalf of National Trust property, The Workhouse, Southwell I am extremely proud to be introducing this book which captures the powerful words, thoughts and feelings of the people who have been involved with this project.

When we approached Global Wordsmiths to run a community based writing workshop working with people connected to this site and its stories, we did not know what the outcomes would be. On a regular basis staff and volunteers at The Workhouse can hear incredible stories, but to be able to give individuals an opportunity to document their own thoughts and stories and to then have these published offers another dimension and I hope a sense of real accomplishment.

The Workhouse, Southwell was acquired in 1997 and at the time marked a very conscious direction for the Trust to preserve and interpret a more diverse history of people and places. The property also joined the International Coalition of Sites of Conscience (ICSC) to 'use the lessons of history to spark conscience in people all around the world so that they can choose the actions that promote justice and lasting peace today.' With our strategy aim to 'move, teach and inspire,' we could not ask for a more powerful and relevant place in today's society.

I would sincerely like to thank all who have contributed to this book, including the Arts Council and MDEM for their assistance with funding. Each contributor has undertaken a journey which I hope has been one which has ultimately resulted in great pride in what they have achieved and produced, both collectively and individually.

~Sara Blair-Manning
General Manager
National Trust
South Nottinghamshire/North Lincolnshire

Preface

There's such a wealth of knowledge and experience gained through the simple act of living. Time slides past us, sometimes like a swiftly moving river, sometimes like a tiny creek. And as we find more years behind us than ahead, it is truly the moments we remember, the lessons learned, rather than the days.

It has been an incredible pleasure to work with the eleven authors in this anthology. One of the most difficult parts of memoir writing is figuring out where to start, and indeed, the writers in this group had a plethora of moments and lessons to choose from. Trials, triumphs, and, perhaps most clearly, love define many of the stories told here.

It's so important to listen, to learn, and to laugh alongside those of other generations. These stories of determination and survival are inspiring as well as heart-breaking, and I thank each author for showing us the meaning of vulnerability as well as strength.

~Victoria Villaseñor, Ed.

Contents

Tea and Sympathy by Samantha Ball — 1

My Sanctuary by Edmund Hutchinson — 5

A Worthwhile Experience by Ann Keen — 19

Footsteps and Chocolate Biscuits by Bridget Rogers — 25

The Green Book by David — 41

Unmade Beds by Karen Winyard — 49

Complicated Magic by Katrina Burrup — 63

History's Dramas by Kev Troughton — 71

Cooking with Care by Katherine Patuzzo — 75

Darkness, Darkness by Dinah Wilcox — 81

Seen But Not Heard by Rose Powell — 87

© National Trust

Tea and Sympathy?
by Samantha Ball

I like tea. I like the comfort tea brings. I like the feeling that whatever life throws at you, there is always a 'nice cup of tea.'

As I sit here in the bedsit, the light shining through thin curtains not made for the window, I look at the square table. I can see teacups, the green-blue colour of institution, which have their own functional appeal. A milk bottle and brown teapot complete the scene.

A table set for tea could be any table in any home. But this is different. This is a bedsit recreated by the National Trust from the memories of those who lived at Greet House from post-war days to the late 1970s. Six bedsits were created for women and children who had no home and were given temporary accommodation in an old workhouse building. Some families were here for weeks, some for months, and others for over a year. Throughout these times, mothers had to provide comfort and continuity during chaos. Love and warmth during despair.

As my role as a volunteer at The Workhouse, I listen to those who generously share their experiences of Greet House history. Those who have shared their bedsit memories, express deeply personal stories of an understandably difficult period in their lives. This is their history. Combined with The Workhouse, there are nearly

200 years of stories to tell. Powerful stories. Emotional stories.

These aren't the stories of great battles or military operations, or the histories of royalty, kings or queens which we all learnt at school. These are the forgotten histories of those neglected: ordinary people who find themselves in an extraordinary building.

As I sit in the bedsit I wonder what I would have done? As a mother myself to two teenage girls, how would I support my family if my world had come crashing down? How would I keep fighting? I would join the histories of numerous women and their children who found their temporary home in a room in a run-down workhouse with the associated stigma. I would join those who felt frightened, despondent, humiliated and homeless.

Am I overthinking this? I smile to myself when I remember the strength of the words of a woman who lived at Greet House with her three young boys. So matter of fact; so black and white. You just get on with it...

But, what if I just 'couldn't get on with it?' What would I tell my girls when they looked to me for guidance? I hope I would have the strength to provide answers. But, what if I couldn't? Or wouldn't? What happens when life is viewed through a black, depressed haze or when your tastes stretch to a drink stronger than tea? What if I gave up? What if I didn't care for my children and I was completely un-interested in making a family home in a bedsit, or indeed, in any home?

How does history expect women...no, I mean mothers, to behave? Do we look back and see victims? Or do we see women we can identify with and understand? Do we, as mothers, see women we can empathise with? (Mothers always do the best for their children, don't they? Well, that isn't always the case). No matter what lens we look through when we look back, sometimes women stick two fingers up to history; the history written by the victors, by those who can't understand, who categorise people in to what they should, and shouldn't, be. This is not neat history. This is complicated, inconvenient and messy history at its best. Or worst.

I sit here at my own kitchen table, a world away from Greet House, surrounded by the materialistic and technological advances of the last forty years. My favourite tea cup is embossed with the Welsh word 'cwtch': a word I find so great, (I am a very proud Welsh girl), one that has no literal translation, but everyone understands what it means. It is a familiar word in our house; for us, it's a loving cuddle or a hug. As mum to Lauren and Madeleine, I hope I will always be there to provide cwtch's: to soothe, to reassure, to love.

I do not know how history would have treated me had I been in Greet House, or how I would have fared, but I can look forward to the love I can give my girls. My family. I know I am lucky. History has not been kind to many workhouse women: an honest history which stares us straight in the face and forces us at times to be judgmental, harsh and cruel. For some, tea comes with no sympathy.

© E. Hutchinson

My Sanctuary
by Edmund Hutchinson

The Southwell Workhouse was constructed in 1824 by Rev John Becher, ninety years before the outbreak of WWI. It would later become a nationwide system for housing the poor and less than one hundred and fifty years after its construction I would be calling it my home.

Fifty-one years after the opening of the then Thurgarton Hundred Incorporated Workhouse, later named Southwell Union Workhouse, my great-great-grandfather on my father's side, James, would be born.

The 1901 census shows my great-great grandfather on my mother's side, who was sixty-one years of age at the time, was a pauper at the Bury Union Workhouse in Rochdale. Other ancestors were mainly cotton weavers working in the mills.

My grandfather, Harry, was born in Lancashire in 1913, the same year Britain had its deadliest tornado, killing nearly 500 people, but what was to come was to change the world forever. A year later, WWI broke out. Harry was one of thirteen children which included two sets of twins; it was quite common to have large families in those days.

Having survived the horrors and hardship during and after the war, Harry married my grandmother, Jennie in Tinsley, South Yorkshire in 1933. Life was very difficult in the thirties, with mass unemployment and poverty everywhere. Harry didn't have a career job he just got work here and there mainly labouring and delivering coal whereas Jennie was always busy with the children.

My father was born in 1937, the same year George VI was crowned King. He would be one of eleven children. Two years later, the country would be gripped with the beginning of WWII. So my grandfather would once again have to suffer the horrors and misery of another war. But this time, his son (my grandfather) would do the same, and he had seven children to look after and keep safe.

Soon after WWII started, ration books were introduced due to a shortage of food. Butter, eggs, milk, tea, and cheese were examples of foods to be rationed and it would be fourteen years before the end of rationing, when meat restrictions were lifted in 1954.

My father survived the war and eventually got married to my mother in 1958, the same year Christopher Dean was born (the eventual famous ice skater from Nottingham). This was also the year coal rationing ended and the first edition of Blue Peter was shown on TV. Considering the fact my father had ten siblings I knew very little about them I do know they survived the war and to date I continue to research their history.

I was born in Bolton one Sunday morning in 1962, the same year the Beatles released their first single Love Love Me Do. Only ten years later, I would be living in what is now the Southwell Workhouse, then named Greet House. My mother had seven children by the time she had reached twenty-four years of age. I am sure it had been very difficult for her, even at the best of times. I was the middle child of seven, with a sister and two brothers older, and two sisters and a brother younger. Apart from my oldest sister, we were all born in the Manchester area, and all but two of us were born in different areas, due to my father not paying rent and bills, which meant we moved quite a lot. My early life is vague but I do remember cobbled streets, terraced houses, and lots of children playing out on the streets with lots of open doors; no need to lock them in those days, as most people had nothing to steal and people were friendlier. Or so I thought.

Life was a huge struggle for such a large family and we had to rely on handouts from where ever we could. Memories of my father remain in the distant past, where they will stay, but his actions and their consequences will haunt me till I die. As I get older I realise violence in the sixties was quite rife and almost accepted as the norm. My mother did all she could to protect us and often took risks to make sure we had food to eat, which included sneaking bread to us at nights while we were in bed. She eventually found the courage and help from family and left him. A long journey from Manchester in the middle of the night, through Snake Pass, and we eventually got to Ingoldmells, which would be short lived. Ingoldmells was, as I remember, a fun place to be. We spent a lot of time walking to the seaside and spent the entire day there, walking around slot machines, waiting for pennies to drop, which we would fight for and spend on sweets and biscuits. We would go to the park, play on the witch's hat and chase cloud shadows in the playing field; we could play out all day until we came home, exhausted.

Due to leaky roofs and other conditions, the house had to be demolished, so we were again in need of a new home. My mother tried her best to get us a new home but Social Services stepped in, and much to my mother's anguish we were put in foster homes until suitable accommodation could be found. I didn't mind being in the foster home though, because it was very clean, had a lovely bed to sleep in, and the foster parents were very kind. It was just another part of the endless journey we seemed to be on. Our journey then took us to a farmhouse in Tuxford, which belonged to my new stepfather's sister. We stayed there while social services searched for a new place for us to live. A few weeks later we were finally on the move again, but this time it would be different. We were going to live in a big house where we all could be together. It was called Greet House, and I was just nine years old.

We left the farm house for Greet House and the closer I got, the more excited I got. I was expecting a posh house with a garden, so my first view got me really excited. It was comprised of two of the biggest houses I had ever seen. As we approached I just kept thinking of all the exploring we were going to do. We passed the first house and took a left turn to the next house and my excitement grew. We got out of the car and had to walk a little down the hill. I was met by my sister, who had arrived earlier, in a small yard at the end of the building. The first thing I noticed was how big the place was; it had loads of windows and went a long way across. It also had the smell of something I would later find was Jayes Fluid. I thought there must be loads of families living at a house that big, and looked forward to playing out with my new friends.

My sister invited me toward the concrete stairway with a look of disappointment, (to get to this stair way now you would have to go through the tea room and out of the other door, located at the back of the tea room), which was the exclusive entrance just for us. I ran up the steep stairs, past the first two windows, expecting to find lots of rooms and places to explore. Unfortunately, I was left somewhat deflated when I discovered it was only two rooms with four beds in each. Having two rooms would be short lived because we had to give one up for another family. The first room, which I still call the blue room, is pretty much the same now as it was way back in the early seventies. This is the room you can see when you take a tour of The Workhouse. This would be the girl's room.

The other room was much darker and had crude wallpaper. That was the room we were finally left with. It looked really big, probably because I was so little. It had two large windows with views of an overrun garden to the right, then a much nicer one over on the left. (Thirty years later, this would become the new gardens and a car park for visitors.) I wondered why the garden was split and made a mental note to explore it later. In the room were three sets of cast iron bunk beds in a u shape, with old blankets to keep us warm. There was a chest of drawers, a sideboard and some tea chests to keep our few belongings in. We didn't really have much as I can remember, thanks to us living in at least nine places in as many years.

The wallpaper room was similar to the blue room and would be the boy's room. There was a small cooker that had enamel coating on it, just like the one you can now see in the blue room, a table and some chairs, and there was a coin metre to pay for electric. We were used to having nothing, but this was nothing like I was expecting. All of us were going to share this single room, and there was nothing much to do unless you went outside. The bedding arrangements meant I would share a bed with my younger brother, and my two younger sisters would also share a bed, leaving a bed each for everyone else. I really couldn't understand why the house was so big, but we only had a small part of it to stay in. Eight of us were to share this room until Social services found us suitable accommodation.

Eventually, we were told that this was the only room allocated to us, and that the rest of the house was out of bounds. We weren't even allowed to go in the gardens. I was so ashamed; I'd been hoping for something so much better. I was getting to the age where I knew things mattered and that it was going to be embarrassing at school when people found out where we lived. The last few years had been pretty tough for us and I really thought it was our turn for things to get better, but no, it was just more of the same. I wanted to cry and run off somewhere, maybe back to my foster home I had loved so much. I can remember going outside to look around, and feeling quite angry that of all the space available in this big house, all we had was the yard and a half fallen down wall to play on. But playing was what we were good at, and we would soon find somewhere to play. We explored, and there was a wall around our yard which had mainly fallen down. There was a room next to the stairway we used to get to our room, and we found out that it was a larder, a pantry with food in it. Later we found out the house also had old people in it, and the larder was to feed them (the larder is now the tea room, and looking at the steps leading to the room you can see they are extremely worn with the traffic leading to the kitchens).

I walked around the side of the house, where there was a place for us to collect coal. But beyond that, mostly everything was fenced off or had big iron gates. We went on to explore different areas to see what we could find. I slowly walked up the lane constantly looking back to see how far I had walked, just in case I had to run back then I turned right to see how big the house was. I was small though, so could only see bits through bushes. The house was huge and seemed to go on forever, and I walked cautiously on, and then I discovered another big house, which I later found out was a children's home (Caudwell House). I continued right to the end of the road and then down the hill. The house seemed to disappear out of sight, then I found myself near a stream at the end of the lane. This was going to need more exploring later, I thought. Walking back up the lane you could see the top of the big house standing there like a big monster, looking down at me. We all got back and exchanged our findings, but the excitement had gone. It was replaced with hunger, and we had pancakes for tea because we had no food until my mother managed to get some money, which would be the next day. The house was really cold and the sense of adventure slowly disappeared. Coal was put on the fire to warm the room, then it was time to get in bed. I climbed into bed, noticing how coarse the blankets were. Sleeping was difficult because we didn't all go to bed at the same time, not to mention being in a really strange house and not knowing how long we would be there.

The next morning, we got dressed and after a bowl of porridge, off we went to school, not knowing this would be a life-changing experience that would change me forever.

My oldest sister took us to school, on a walk that seemed to take forever, but walking was what we were all very good at. Down the lane we went and turned right onto Kirklington road, up to the Ropewalk and then left, and at the top we could see Lowes Wong school. My section of the school was wooden huts, which I found quite scary; but we had milk in the morning which I loved and it gave me something positive to look forward to.

Within a few weeks I went on to the junior school, where troubles soon developed. When it came to the typical exercises where you have to tell your new school friends a little about yourself, I didn't really have much to say. I wanted to share anything other than where I was from and where I lived. Telling them I lived in Greet House caused a reaction I never expected; many of the children turned to look at me, and I went bright red with embarrassment. They looked me up and down as if I was something they had never seen before. I was really ashamed and couldn't understand what was so bad about living in the house. After a difficult day, I went home and told my mother how the other children reacted when they knew I lived in this house; she said it was only for a short time and to take no notice, but I could tell it was bothering her. I think the last thing she needed was us moaning, after all, she was having a difficult time, too. Days and weeks passed and things just got worse. We were classed as gypsy and soon became outcasts in Southwell; often we would have to run to the safe haven of Greet House to avoid humiliating teasing, and sometimes more, from the local children. Being ashamed, humiliated and taunted was soon to be the norm in Southwell. Once, my step dad made me dress up in my sister's dress and made me stand on top of the bunk bed in humiliation because I cried over something. I learned it was best to hide your feelings. We were good walkers but soon we became good runners, too. Most locals would never dare reach the road leading to The Workhouse due to fear or uncertainty about the place. It was, after all, haunted. Greet House, to the locals, was most unwelcoming, but to me, the sight of the house as I went home was most welcoming. It was my home and my fortress, my sanctuary where outsiders feared to venture. I knew as soon as I saw it I was safe. After living in so many places and having to deal with so much distress, I began to like the house. It was dry and the roof didn't leak, unlike some places I had lived. We adapted to the house as we always had everywhere else. Carrying the coal scuttle upstairs was hard but I began to like that too, because the determination to achieve something was quite rewarding. I knew I'd had far worse, so being here added more strength to my ever-building character. I was becoming strong and silent, like the house; we both had history and secrets that were just ours. I did look forward to going to school, because I loved the dinners and milk. School meals were a luxury I really wasn't used to, and having them really helped take my mind off things.

The concrete stairs leading to our room would be scrubbed at weekends, so the smell of Jeyes Fluid never seemed to go away. But we spent time playing in the trees around the small yard, sitting on the wall, even pushing more of it down just to pass the time of day and get away from the small room. As much time as possible was spent outside, because being in the room just made us frustrated and angry, and it often led to fights. We had a bath now and again; the boys would take it in turns with the same water, so I didn't spend much time in it because by the time I got in it was nearly cold and really dirty, not to mention the room was freezing too. The bath is still there, as is the toilet. During meal times we would have to take turns eating because of the size of the table, not to mention the cooker. Soup and mash, chip butties, stews and pies were common because it was easy to prepare and cook. My step father managed to get hold of a small black and white television, but to get a picture an aerial made from a wire coat hanger had to be dangled out of the window. There were other people living at Greet House, but it seemed each had their own way of getting in through different stairways. I very rarely saw anyone else, but could see lights on in the dark and sometimes hear them; I thought there was something wrong with us, or them, that meant we had to be isolated.

I do remember a well-dressed maintenance man who did odd jobs. He spoke quite posh and my sister nick-named him Flashy Pants because he wore a suit.

The school bullying carried on and we simply became accustomed to it. The stigma attached to living in the big house wasn't going to go away, so it was a question of having to live with it. Honestly, deep down I hated some of the kids. They made me feel ashamed, but I learned not to show it, as with most emotions. Some of the children avoided us, but a small minority would talk to us.

We continued to explore as much as we could; the stream that led to the mill is where we would spend lots of time, and the little lane next to the house is where we would also play. The tree next to the entrance had funny white berries on it like mistletoe, and it became our tree den. We often fought to get in the best spot. As children we had learned to make the most of what we had, and apart from the situation we were in, we had each other and enjoyed fighting each other, playing out, and exploring just like normal children did. Something I learned at an early age is that sometimes when you think you have nothing, you have everything. Life is what you want it to be. As children we'd play and make our own dens and toys, such as bow and arrows and catapults, and it was so rewarding. The fair came on Burgage Green and you could hear the noise from the house, and I remember being given fifty pence to spend at the fair. It was quite dark and I walked cautiously to the Green with my money in my pocket. When I got there I checked my pocket and the money was gone; it had fallen through a hole in my pocket. I was so angry and I went back down the lane searching for it. I never found it, it was too dark. So I went back to the fair and just watched the rides and listened to the exciting music before returning to the big house of sanctuary.

I can remember when, in 1971, the people from the papers and television came around to take our picture to go in the paper. My mother asked us to look sad while the pictures were taken, but I found it quite difficult because I was so excited. I'm the one in pyjamas, in the back. I think I had measles or chicken pox, so I wasn't at school. The article was something about all of us having to live in one room, but to me it was normal to live on top of each other. That's how it was for us for many years; that and the violence. We had been there about five months, then, after the news people had talked to us, we were allocated a house on Lower Kirklington Road. We'd lived at Greet House for a total of six months.

When I left the house, my sanctuary, I was torn between going to the new home and missing the safe place. But we were out now and there was no going back. We all settled into the new home, life went on, the bullying continued, but we wore it down. We were very often ridiculed for being at Greet House even after we'd left it, and when I was old enough I was glad to leave Southwell behind, along with the emotional memories that surrounded it. I didn't realise they would stay with me forever, even though I'd left the area.

After finding out the National Trust had added The Workhouse to its portfolio, I discussed the house many years later with my partner and her mother. Her mother couldn't believe people had spent time in The Workhouse as late as the seventies, and like so many, didn't even know the house existed. So a visit was arranged and even though I didn't want to go, I plucked up the courage to visit a part of my life which I had tried to bury for nearly forty years.

On my way to visit, I was extremely apprehensive, and if I said I was a bag of nerves, it would be an understatement. I still get nervous and angry when I go through Southwell, so we skipped around it and went the Kirklington way. When I saw the house, my heart raced and my hands trembled.

I entered the house for the very first time in over forty years through an access I had never been in, and it dawned on me the house had so much more going on than I could ever have imagined. It was so cold and thought-provoking. I was in awe as I walked around the concrete corridors, then something amazing happened. I could smell the Jeyes Fluid and I followed the smell instinctively, even though I didn't know what part of the house I was in. I followed the visitors until I came into a room where a curator was standing by, and I mentioned I had lived here some years ago. She was totally startled and listened to my story, and by this time my partner's mother realised it was all true. She, too, was in shock as to why at the time people were having to stay in the conditions Greet House had to offer. I felt like I was an imposter but the truth was, I felt safe all of a sudden. I relaxed, knowing I was back in the safe haven. No one but a few would know the feelings going through me in those moments. Things had changed in that room, but not enough to make me feel like a stranger. I reminisced and I smiled, knowing the people around me were visiting me in the past, even though I was there in the present. There is part of me in the big house and part of the house in me.

I wonder, all those years ago when my grandfather and father were stuck in the horrors of the war, how they would have loved to have had the luxury of staying in Greet House sanctuary, rather than struggling to make ends meet each and every day.

Thank you to the National Trust for saving part of my memories. I can now say I am proud to have had the privilege to have lived in the Southwell Workhouse.

*Though I have mentioned how Southwell rejected us for being in The Workhouse it's important to say not all Southwell people treated us poorly. There were very kind people I will always remember: thanks to Ray Smith, Kevin Harper, Neil Plummer, and Mr Gadsby who gave me my first ever job from leaving school.

Edmund Hutchinson, 'My Sanctuary', in Voices Through Time: Stories from The Workhouse, ed. by Victoria Villaseñor and Nicci Robinson (Nottingham: Global Words Press, 2017) pp. 4-17

© National Trust

A Worthwhile Experience
by Ann Keen

Departure, withdrawal, seclusion, retreat, just a few of the words used to describe that stage in your life: retirement. Nobody pays you for your knowledge and expertise. You're not needed any more. I'd had a life time of working when I felt that I was needed by society. As I approached retirement, I started to wonder if I still had a purpose in the world at large. While I discovered what it was, I thought I would volunteer at a National Trust property. That's what people do when they retire, don't they?

I'm not a historian. I didn't even like history at school, but somehow I ended up at The Workhouse; mainly because it was the nearest National Trust property to my home. I had thought about going to one of the big country houses, but my final decision was based on travelling distance.

I had visited many National Trust properties and one time when my aunt came to stay, I took her round The Workhouse. I remember driving into Southwell, looking for the brown signs that lead you to places of historical interest. We had expected The Workhouse to be a small house in the middle of Southwell, but the brown signs kept leading us onward and out of town. Finally, we saw a sign which pointed to the car park. I wasn't expecting the enormous grounds. The Workhouse was built out of the way, out of sight, so the town's folk didn't have to see it and the poor souls who were sent there. At that time, retirement was beginning to feel the same. I felt as if I was being sent away, out of sight.

Once we turned the corner we were astounded to be confronted by the imposing building. I certainly wasn't expecting such a large, extraordinary façade. The experience was already becoming uncomfortable; the long walk along the path and the overpowering building. I don't know what I expected to see, but it wasn't such a commanding structure. It felt quite overwhelming. I can't even imagine the desperation that the paupers felt when walking up this path.

The tour was interesting and informative and started me thinking about the people who had lived there. My mum was always talking about the local workhouse in later life. At the time it was meaningless to me, but I was beginning to understand. She related care homes to the workhouse, and I can understand why she didn't want to end her life there.

When I did retire, I saw an advert for discussion volunteers; I didn't know what they were, but it sounded useful. So, with some trepidation, I contacted The Workhouse. My journey started.

I was taken into the volunteer room, which was bursting with lively people. That, in itself, felt quite daunting. Everyone seemed to know what they were doing, except me. I was provided with endless historical facts and felt overwhelmed by the sheer volume of knowledge that I needed to absorb. It felt rather like learning to swim, by someone pushing you into a swimming pool without a life line.

I don't know why I kept coming back, but I was somehow drawn to the place. I read about the history of The

Workhouse and other room guides patiently answered my questions. Gradually, I learnt. I had stimulating conversations with visitors who told me endless stories about their relatives who had been in workhouses. I have never had so many conversations with builders who shared their knowledge of building construction with me. I watched people crying with both sadness and joy when they related their experiences of this Workhouse. I met people who had visited their friends living here, as children. I spoke to people who talked to me with tears in their eyes, who had lived here themselves as children. I began to experience other people's lives. Slowly, I started to soak up the information and to get to know the people whose lives I became wrapped up in, whether they're still with us or have passed on. I was beginning to feel a sense of place; this is where I belong.

    I became involved in the everyday life of the National Trust Workhouse. There were endless opportunities for different roles. I started as a room guide, got involved in school visits, took tours around and participated in living history events. I learnt about the lives of people who lived in this Workhouse. As I walked around the building, I started to feel the weight of its history and the stories contained in its walls. I joined the team telling stories of The Workhouse to community groups. Our stories are based on Workhouse life, some true, some fabricated, but all reflect the lives of the people who passed by here. I was given a pauper costume and I took on the persona of a fictional inmate: someone who could easily have lived here. We were always told to have a back story when we put a costume on and soon, I became Annie. Her husband lost his job and ran off to the army, leaving her with six young children. She tried to earn a living by taking in washing and doing 'needleworking' but she couldn't feed all those mouths so had to go into The Workhouse. Not true, but she could easily have existed. She has become my alter ego. As soon as the costume goes on, I turn into Annie. I know how she would react and I know what she would say to people, and I understand her motivation. No-one has given me a script of Annie's life, but I become her; I walk in her shoes (or rather, her clogs). What is it that makes me identify with Annie? Perhaps I can see my mum and dad in Annie's existence, always struggling to keep their heads above water with the threat of The Workhouse looming over them.

As storytellers, we are a happy band of people who enjoy performing. This isn't something I ever imagined I would do. I am learning new skills and enjoying new experiences. Someone once said to me, "You have found your voice." I suppose I have. I feel strangely 'at home' in The Workhouse. I don't know why. I have no previous connection with this building or its people, but I have become integrated into the fabric of its history.

The inmates were considered unimportant as citizens, most of them had no status or 'worth.' But I hope I have contributed in validating their lives and making the stories of their lives notable; people like Elizabeth Griffin. She was a pregnant vagrant when she came to The Workhouse and asked to stay until she'd had her baby. The Master and Matron were both ill in bed with influenza and were incapacitated, so were unable to carry out their duties. Despite asking to stay for her confinement, after a few days, she was discharged by the porter. She moved on, against her will, to Mansfield Workhouse to join her husband. The Master there reported her neglectful treatment at Southwell and the case was investigated. It was reported in the Newark Advertiser, although The Workhouse staff never admitted any wrong doing. After much deliberation the case was closed. The last few sentences published in The Newark Advertiser in 1891 stated, "The chairman asked, Is the case finished?" To which the Inspector replied, "Oh yes; it is finished, nobody will hear any more about it."

Well, they have heard about it. Over 100 hundred years later, a volunteer researcher found the report and she gave it to me and I have told Elizabeth's story to visitors. Perhaps she has finally received some recognition. I feel I have helped to give her a voice, to speak out for the voiceless people of the past.

Humanity requires us to remember the downtrodden, the underdogs, and those in need. The people who are now in The Workhouse, whether they're staff, volunteers, or visitors, have all helped to make the previous occupants important, and to make their lives worthwhile. Perhaps I am needed to help tell this story. Perhaps that has become my purpose at this new stage in my life. Over time, people have been so ready to condemn the workhouse system, but surely its function is, and always has been, to help those who feel worthless realise that their lives are worthwhile. After all, the Reverend Becher stated, 'An empty workhouse is a successful workhouse.' His intention was to support those in need as well as to help them move on.

It appears that I haven't retired. My role now is to help visitors understand the people who lived here and to continue contributing to the future history of The Workhouse.

Do they pay me? Yes, in cups of coffee, cake, and biscuits.

© Stuart Crump 2016

Footsteps and Chocolate Biscuits
by Bridget Rogers

The pencil drawing of the train on the back of the photograph was crude and childish but that was allowed after all, it was a child who drew it over ninety-five years ago. Little did my father realise that this particular photograph was going to have such an impact on his daughter eighty years later. The photograph was of his Great Grandfather a Victorian Railway Director on the Isle of Man, standing proudly next to the engine named after him, the George Henry Wood. An internet search quickly revealed George's life, along with a large and fascinating family. It became a catalyst for my already keen interest in the Victorian period. My family tell me it's because I can find photographs that I connect so easily with the people and events. They are of real people photographed going about their daily lives, some born as long ago as the eighteenth century. Their lined and weary faces look back at me clues to their lives all around them, witnesses to a period of immense change. To some extent I would agree with the comments, but for me it's more than that. I studied the period for O and A level history and even managed to work it into my degree, making my background knowledge of the period both comprehensive and useful.

But how did one childish drawing lead me to The Workhouse? It hasn't been because my research has revealed that one of my ancestors trod that desperate path; although one might have done had it not been for the family keeping and supporting her and her daughter. My family like so many of the period did have its connections. It was whilst researching George Henry that I discovered that his father, Thomas, was a Relieving Officer for the Huddersfield Union. The social worker of his day, Thomas worked with the poor and desperate in his community his role amongst others, to gain admittance to the workhouse for the paupers of the area. Whilst searching newspaper archives I was both surprised and moved to find him mentioned several times in newspaper reports and later, of two of his sons and a grandson who followed in his footsteps. Suddenly they had become far more than names on a census return. Their stories lost to members of my family generations back, were speaking across the centuries, kept alive along with those of the people they helped, becoming very real to me.

Recently I discovered how terrible the conditions were in the earliest workhouses of the area, including Slaithwaite where my family had lived for generations. Dating from the 1770s, workhouses were little more than converted houses, and the sick and the young were woefully neglected. An official inquiry uncovered dreadful conditions in the infirmaries, infectious disease rife, filthy bed linen on beds that were little more than bags full of straw and shavings laid on the floor. A second report found forty children occupying a room twenty-four feet by fifteen feet, sleeping ten to a bed.

I've always known that conditions in many workhouses were dreadful but reading this has shaken me. Did my family know of the dreadful conditions inside the workhouses, but turned a blind eye? Faced with the desperate, helpless and sick, did they believe that anything was better than starving to death? I'll never know but reading a report in the Huddersfield Chronicle in which Thomas, one of the younger generations of Woods, showed great kindness; I am filled with a real sense of pride and a feeling that I would have liked him. Thomas had helped two young children, William, eight, and Edith, four, in 1892. Abandoned all day the children were described as being covered in vermin, lying on a bed fully clothed due to the cold; the only other furniture in the room being three broken chairs with just a crust of bread to eat. On several occasions he took them food and at one point he'd taken William to his own home to get him warm. The children's parents were working but the money coming in just wasn't enough. Eventually it was agreed that the children should enter The Workhouse for two weeks; at a cost to their parents of seven shillings and sixpence. Try as I might I have yet to find out what happened to Edith and William as, like so many children of this period, they seem to have disappeared without trace. Thomas comes across as a very caring person desperate to help these children in any way he could. Their circumstances must have been truly dreadful for him to recommend their removal to the Workhouse, knowing that they would have been separated not only from their parents and home, but from each other. As children, society saw them as innocent and blameless, reserving the harsh judgements for their parents whose only crime was to be poor and desperate.

    I knew nothing of this story until after I started volunteering twenty months ago. Living locally, I had watched the changes to the site take place from my car en-route to Newark. I had made acquaintance with the Reverend Becher long before I turned up at the Porter's Gate, as his portrait had sat in an office just down from my own in the Minster Chambers many years before. Little had

I realised back then how he was going to impact upon my future life and that I would become a part of the system he influenced so greatly; his story becoming entwined with mine. I could have volunteered in a variety of different ways but have always wanted to do so for the National Trust. Colleagues in a former life back in Cheshire had influenced me with their stories of volunteering at Quarry Bank, so I knew it was something I always hoped I could do. Retirement gave me the opportunity, my passion for the period, and the drive. This, combined with my desire to know more about Thomas (my Great, Great, Great Grandfather), and the work he did, made it inevitable that I would find myself walking the Pauper Path towards the imposing and yet, beautiful building that is The Southwell Workhouse.

   Now, as I put on my costume, tie my clogs and push my hair into a bonnet, I leave the trappings of modern life behind. The face reflected in the mirror devoid of makeup looks grey, lined and instantly older. Although warmer and in better condition than anything a pauper would have owned, the workhouse uniform was designed to rob a person of their individuality, and it worked. As role players, the uniform helps us to become the paupers we play, easing our passage backwards in time; however, you do have to excuse the occasional bit of Velcro and the extra layers we slip underneath in the colder months, an option unavailable to genuine paupers of the past! As I switch off the dressing room lights it's like turning off the twenty first century and becoming my cue to walk backwards in time.

   The perfect blue sky's reflected in the many windows looking down on me in the Women's Work Yard. The eerie cries of two buzzards circling above are haunting and sad joining the noisy bleating of the sheep in the neighbouring field. Only the sound of the occasional passing car reminds me that I am not back in the nineteenth century. The air is fresh and perfect with only the slightest hint of the sweet and sickly smell of the sugar beet factory a few miles away. How different it would have been back in the 1840s with the stench of The Workhouse chimneys mixing with those of carbolic soap, and unwashed human bodies. Standing in the yard I can't help but wonder how the previous occupants must have felt on days such as this, although, I doubt they would have been at liberty to stand still long enough to notice them, or to feel the warmth of the sun on their backs. I glance up at the windows and can almost feel faces looking down at me not ghosts, but the spirits of ordinary men and women, children like Edith and William looking out of the windows, gazing at the fields beyond The Workhouse walls.

Running a hand down my blue and white costume I contemplate who I'm going to be today. Shall I be Hannah, whose husband died so tragically in a farming accident; or Mary, whose husband was transported for sheep stealing? Then there's Elizabeth Tether, whose three year old daughter died in a tragic accident in the very yard where I'm standing. The child had fallen into a tub of scalding water being used by the women for the laundry, and died from burns four hours later. Real people, their stories told in great detail in Newspaper Archives for the period, brought to our attention by our dedicated volunteer research team. Suddenly they aren't just names but individuals, many victims of circumstances beyond their control but at the time frequently labelled 'the idle and profligate.' Bringing their stories to life is more than 'entertaining,' it's giving them a voice so that they aren't just forgotten, consigned to the past. I hope that I do them justice when I recount their stories. That they would understand what I'm trying to do, that I genuinely believe that they have a voice that should be heard, stories that should be told no matter how distressing and sad.

That thought stays with me as I sweep the yard and prepare for the class of children expected that morning. They, like me, won't have walked miles to get here, nor will they be hungry, cold and aching from sleeping in hedge bottoms. They too will be travelling back in time dressed in pinafores, bonnets and shawls, albeit accompanied by a wonderful array of multi-coloured glasses and footwear. Dressing up is the part that the children enjoy the most, covering up their school uniforms, taking on the persona of someone else. Likewise, they carry the identity and story of a real child who entered through the Porter's Gate but, fortunately for them, they won't suffer the indignity of being stripped of their clothes and scrubbed by strangers. Nor will they be separated from their loved ones and forced to work for long hours in the classroom, laundry or kitchen. Safe in the knowledge that at the end of the day they like me, will return to their homes and families and the comforts of modern life. At the click of a latch we're all transported back to 1841 and our time together begins.

Putting my broom aside I scuttle across the yard to greet them, clogs ringing out as I go. I know who is Matron this morning and that I'd better get the girls organised and rehearsed pretty sharpish or suffer the consequences of her tongue lashing, all part of a well-rehearsed routine. Matron enters the yard and is greeted by a lovely line of bobbing bonnets rather like gulls on the sea. She utters the first harsh words, and naturally it's me who gets both barrels! As a Learning Centre we feel that the children should understand the harshness of Workhouse life for all who entered child and adult alike, a role we take very seriously. Life for the majority of Victorian children was incredibly hard. Punishments such as beatings were commonplace. A lack of food, clean water, warm clothing and shelter were a way of life. We want the children to empathise with the paupers of the past, the real children whose names they have taken, along with their stories. Rules and regulations dominated Workhouse life and were there to enforce control; after all there were only three to four paid members of staff and upwards of 158 pauper inmates. However, this isn't at the expense of a few laughs I might add; like the time Master accused me of stealing a bottle of gin and instead of sending me to the refractory threatened me with a day in the refectory to which I raised an eyebrow and tried very hard not to answer, "Thank you very much sir, I'll enjoy a cup of tea and a slice of cake!"

Wide eyed and in most but not all cases nervously, the children recite their stories visibly relieved when it's over; well prepared by their Teachers and our own Group Leaders. On the odd occasion our pauper children are a little overwhelmed by the setting and the adult in front of them, and freeze unable to recount their few lines. As experienced role players we get around this but, I have to admit, it is rather hard at times to keep a straight face when we have twenty-three Marys, all of whom are orphaned; or on occasions when asked their names they reply with Maddison, Brooke, Jade, or Jessica; not such well known Victorian names, but it all makes for an interesting start to the day.

Entering through the Porter's Gate would have been such a different and frightening experience for little Edith and William. Someone must have taken them there was it their parents Caroline and Lewis, or were the children accompanied by Thomas in his capacity as Relieving Officer?

That would have been so hard for all concerned, for the parents whose heads may well have been filled with tales of cruelty and neglect; but no easier for Thomas breaking up a family taking the children away from everything and everyone they knew. The children must have been terrified with no friends or family to look to for reassurance, no hand to hold, just strangers in what must have been a very daunting place. Scrubbed and de-liced, their clothes taken away to be fumigated, made to wear the coarse unfamiliar uniform of The Workhouse, I hope someone smiled at them and maybe took them by the hand.

Whilst registration takes place, I do my best to provoke some kind of reaction from Matron, usually by dropping the metal bucket, leaning on a wall or talking to a fellow pauper. Talking or singing gets the best reaction, enabling Matron to threaten all sorts of dire punishments, and as we look suitably remorseful the children look horrified, glancing sympathetically in our direction.

It's in the Committee Room that all the children, both boys and girls, get to see each other dressed as paupers. Gone are the smiles and laughter from the dressing room as they line up either side of the Guardians' table. It takes a brave or foolhardy child to misbehave once the Workhouse Master has entered the room. Resplendent in long green coat, yellow waistcoat and top hat, Master makes for an imposing figure. Usually the children stand in awed silence, but there has been at least one occasion when a boy has been heard to mutter under his breath, "He's not scary, he looks just like Willy Wonka."

Having been a role player for twelve months now, I am accustomed to the slamming of the book on the table but, like everyone else in the room I still jump when it happens. Tapping his hand with his walking cane the Master emphasises the importance of manners, behaviour and compliance as he's watched by the children, desperately trying to keep still and on rare occasions, not to giggle. As paupers we expect to get shouted at and humiliated, all enacted under the watchful gaze of Reverend Becher looking down at this scene from his portrait on the wall. Quite what he would make of it I'm not entirely sure, but there's no avoiding his stare as it's one of those portraits where the eyes follow you wherever you stand! The boys are dismissed and escorted around the building by a male pauper who, like me, attempts to make their experience as real as possible. The girls file quiet and subdued, into the schoolroom and my fellow pauper and I hit the Volunteer's Room in search of coffee and the chocolate biscuits, essentials for any National Trust Volunteer!

Refreshed, and possibly regretting that coffee, my role as a pauper really gets going as I greet the children after their lesson and take them into the kitchen. My fellow female pauper starts in the dormitory upstairs. It's at this point that you find out whether the earlier role play has succeeded in getting the children 'on side'. The pauper stories are true and by telling them we hope to make The Workhouse more real. Sometimes we've done such good a job that the children are convinced that they're staying and a supper of gruel and a night in a dormitory beckons. Obviously we do our best to abate these fears but we are back in 1841 and need to stay in role!

The biggest problem for me has been the accent. Having been brought up to pronounce my t's and h's and to finish my words properly, I've had to work hard at this. I am aware that my accent varies throughout my performance; sometimes it has a slight Welsh lilt, and I blame my husband for this, whilst at others it definitely leans more towards

Cockney or Devonian. When talking about the vegetables I'm unable to say the word 'fertiliser' without sounding like one of the 'Wurzles' and find it very hard not to smile when I do this. The other big pitfall is the dreadful, never to cross our lips...okay. Not a word I used much until I started texting and not in common use in 1841, but every now and then when rushed it slips out, catapulting us forward in time.

Another big concern is that of timing, critical for the smooth running of the day. As Paupers, we are accompanied by a wonderful person known as a Group Leader. Their role, amongst other things, is to prepare the children for the morning ahead, which makes a huge difference to their experience and is vital for ours. They get the children into costume and down to The Workhouse ready to take part in the morning ahead; sometimes faced with an impossible shortage of time due to a school being delayed. As paupers in 1841 we wouldn't have had wristwatches since they hadn't been invented yet, and it's unlikely that we could tell the time. To get around this we rely on a system of hand and finger gestures to indicate how much time is remaining. Unfortunately, there are times when the best efforts of the Group Leaders get missed due to the over enthusiasm of the role players who have much to get across. I have to confess that I myself am guilty of forgetting to look at these adults in the room for which I apologise now. Once in costume I become totally absorbed in the world that I'm creating completely lost in 1841, taking the children back with me. This means that the subtle time warnings are wasted on me and a certain amount of helicopter hand waving, loud coughs, sighs and even jumping up and down is required to get the message across.

The kitchen is a wonderful room in which to talk about Workhouse life as, for the girls, it's where the majority would go on to spend their working life. I start with my story of how I came to be a pauper in The Workhouse. Usually I'm a widow with a family unable to leave until my youngest finds work or an apprenticeship. I point out that although the daily routine is gruelling and the loss of liberty hard, it's the separation from my children that is hardest to accept. It's important that the reality of life 'outside' is understood, that they appreciate that those who entered The Workhouse had no choice that they owned nothing except the clothes on their backs and their names. Talking about the dietary I point out that paupers in The Workhouse received three meals a day including meat three times a week, something unheard of for the majority of the population. Whilst dropping the tin plates on the table I demonstrate how everything had to be both practical and cheap; simultaneously giving Master or Matron an excuse to threaten me with punishments such as no meat that day, or the loss of a chance to see my children the following Sunday. By this point the majority of children are so absorbed in the story they believe every word I say and I have to take care to avoid actual tears! Listening to their responses I can't help but think how grateful Edith and William must have been for those three meals a day, no longer forced to survive on just a crust between them, or begging from neighbours. They, like so many others, must have felt the food luxurious if a little dull and repetitive.

As the kitchen range, flooring, tables and benches are reproductions, I don't feel the same closeness to the past as I do in the yard, on the staircases, or in the cellars. It's as I walk through the doorway into the Women's Work Yard that I really connect with the past; my clogs walking where others trod well over a hundred years ago, their passage clearly visible by the wear on the doorstep. I think the children feel it too, gathered around the pump, small and insignificant, daunted by the sheer size of the building that wraps around them. Whilst they try their hand at pumping water for use in the laundry, I explain where that water comes from and what it's used for and how as paupers they'd be expected to wash every day in the yard. This is when the occasional slip forwards in time occurs, as the children talk about washing machines and daily showers, all making staying in role challenging, particularly when a child reads out the sign saying 'Do not drink the water,' but we have an answer for most things!

    Like the Pied Piper, I lead the children down to the cellars, the air getting colder with every step. With my hand on the rail and my clogs echoing on the hard, well-worn steps it doesn't take a great deal to imagine the horror of working in the bowels of The Workhouse. The children feel it too, and follow uncertainly, their heads filled with my tales of the rats that sometimes frequent the building, and of walls covered in flaking paint and green mould. They squeal with delight when I produce my toy rat and wave it before them, entering into the spirit of things and often encouraging me to add chopped rat to Matron's dinner. They know it's not real but at that moment they're more than happy to pretend it is. In the cold, damp atmosphere of the cellar I explain the work the women were forced to do with only candle light; at times up to their ankles in water, with only the rats for company. It must have been horrendous down there and I can only try to imagine the fear of working in such conditions, especially when locked in with the roughest of women. It's here that I talk about segregation and how it meant the women never seeing the men in the Work Yards or Vegetable Gardens; how Matron supervised everything so no contact could made between them, and how wives and husbands were separated no matter how old they were. Listening to the dripping water from the overflow pipe, feeling the cold, damp air it's not hard to imagine the desperate conditions underground, and it makes me shiver. The laughter of the moment before is forgotten as the stark reality of everyday life sinks in. The locked doors, rough and sometimes violent women working together in dreadful conditions, the shame of being in The Workhouse; it all becomes a little more real to the children with me.

Tiptoeing up the Master's staircase, quiet as mice and rarely uttering a sound, we proceed to the dormitories. In what would have been their dormitory, they imagine what it would have been like sleeping two or more to a bed with a bucket to use as a privy at night. Separated from their mothers from age two and a day, they may have had a sibling with them but the majority were orphans; I paint a picture of loneliness and just a little fear. They wrinkle their noses and laugh at the prospect of bed sharing, but I think they get the message. Not many talk about the comfy bed they slept in the night before, or having their own bedroom, but for some it comes as something of a shock! Pausing in the doorway I glance back at the room where so many young children have slept. How hard it must have been for four-year-old Edith back in 1892; forced to share a bed with a total stranger, shut away in the dark with no brother to comfort her, and uncertain as to when she'd see her parents again. Did she wet the mattress? She probably did. Was she punished for doing so like so many Workhouse children? I'd like to think not.

Along the corridor in the Old and Infirm Women's Dormitory, the children get the chance to sit on a bed. Old hospital beds from the period are as close to the real thing the National Trust can get. Instantly, the children complain about the hardness of the mattress and the scratchiness of both blankets and nightshirts. I describe the horror of being locked in at night with no candle or fire. Windows were locked open in all weathers to alleviate the smell of unwashed human bodies. They guess at the contents of the mattresses, and this is when they compare them with those at home, describing soft duvets and warm pyjamas. Of course I have to portray total bewilderment at such things, quickly steering them back to the nineteenth century by getting them to guess what the object under the bed is called, and what it was used for. Now most responses to this question are potty or chamber pot but that's not the one I'm looking for. Avoiding the term 'piss pot' which was probably the actual term used, I talk about a 'gazunder' and ask them why it's called that. On one occasion the reply was, "That's easy...it's because it goes under your bum"! Although not the answer I was expecting, I couldn't fault the child's logic!

It's in the dormitories whilst in costume, that I get a real sense of the loneliness the inmates must have felt as I gaze out at the gardens below. Maybe a wife caught sight of a husband, son or friend, but they might as well have been on the other side of the world for the use it did her. The view from the rooms on the top floor span further away, but whether it's the smaller windows making the rooms darker and sadder, or the original dark and peeling paint on the walls, I find the atmosphere palpable. I have never been up there whilst in costume and don't think I ever will; for me it's too disturbing, far too sad.

The mood lightens as we descend the well-worn staircase to the Old and Infirm Exercise Yard, all carrying imaginary gazunders on route to the privies. It's here that I point out the windows angled so that Master and Matron could watch you all the time. I have them 'looking out for me' in case Matron sees us wasting time and appears threatening more punishments. Then it's to the privy they go, two by two, each with imaginary gazunder to empty the imaginary night soil. Their faces are priceless when they come out, unable to contain the shrieks of laughter and they're all genuinely appalled at the very thought of actually using one. Building on this, I describe what they're like in hot weather, overflowing and smelly, and ask them who do they think will empty them? Tentatively they ask if it's them and are visibly relieved when it isn't. Eventually, they finally guess it's a punishment for the boys and are predictably delighted! As a parting shot I explain what happens to the contents of the privy, how it's mixed with the wet straw from the mattresses and the ashes from the fires; how it's left to rot down and then put on the gardens to make the vegetables grow including those I'm going to prepare for their dinners. This always gets a great reaction and it's at this point that I bid them good-bye.

Crossing the yard on my way to change, I pause and look up at the windows of the children's dormitories. I can almost visualise the faces of others, such as Edith and William, gazing forlornly down on the yard below. How must they have felt after being taken away from everything and everyone they knew? The conditions they'd left behind were appalling but after all it was the only home they knew. Were they grateful for the regular meals, warmth and security that The Workhouse offered? Did they stay for a fortnight or did it stretch into years, only for them to be separated again when William found work or an apprenticeship? Were they ever reunited or did William, aged thirty in 1914, suffer the fate of so many of his generation, that last and final separation? And what of Edith, what was life going to be like for her? Was it a life of servitude or would she too be affected by war, widowed only to return to The Workhouse once more? As yet, I don't know. Maybe one day I'll find them. I hope so.

Standing by the pump with a broom or a bucket in my hand, I wonder what the women who worked in that yard would make of me. Would they appreciate what I do or would they be angry that I, someone who has never experienced true hardship, think she can tell their stories, recall their lives? Would my ancestors, Thomas, William, Joseph, and the younger Thomas, understand my reasons for putting on The Workhouse uniform, becoming an inmate from the past? Would they be appalled by what I do, even horrified that a member of the family would volunteer to be in a workhouse? I'd like to hope they'd understand my reason for being there; in the same way as I try to understand that they believed what they were doing was best for the families they met across the years of the workhouse system.

Climbing the stairs to the dressing room, and turning on the lights, I return to the twenty first century. Whilst removing my bonnet and hanging up my costume, the pauper I'd become fades into the atmosphere around me. Dressed and make up applied, I gather together my things and make my way back across the yard. The children don't recognise me now as they queue up to use the modern day facilities before their lunch of sandwiches, crisps, and fruit juice.

And what of that photo of George Henry Wood and that pencil drawing of a train that started all of this? The photo remains but sadly the drawing is faded and barely visible now, lost to future generations; but I know its story and, like those of the paupers who stories we tell, that story will live on. I make my way to that well-worn step and into the Volunteer's Room, there friendly faces greet me along with a hot cup of tea and of course... another chocolate biscuit.

The Green Book
by David

In 1972, my wife and I were going on holiday to Majorca from Luton Airport. We were excited and looking forward to our foreign holiday. After checking in and standing by the gate to board the plane, a man standing by the wall near the gate beckoned me over. There were not many people around us, and he didn't have a uniform on, but was very smartly dressed. He told me on my return from holiday I should apply for a new birth certificate, as the one I had was insufficient, as it was a small square paper with only a name and town on it. This was so strange! Who was this man? How did he know of me and of my birth certificate? At the time I didn't think to ask any more questions, but I did think about it on my holiday and on my return.

You see, I grew up in a small village near to Southwell, not far from The Workhouse. I was adopted when I was four weeks old, and I knew that fact from the time I was still a young child. They were not technically my mum and dad, but I was someone special. I was too young to fully understand what this meant.

I lived on a small farm with my new mum and dad, sister, and grandad. I shared a bedroom with my grandad for over nine years. The farm was my playground; with all the animals, the shire horses, and a pony. There was no machinery, electric, or gas. Over the years I would ask about my adoption, as I was curious and wanted to know more about my roots. They didn't know anything of my true mum and dad or where I came from, only that I was collected from a house in Newark next to the Church, and my legs were in irons to encourage my baby bones to straighten out. It was sixty years later that my adopted sister told me that she, my aunt, and my mum went to the house to collect me from my true mum. She also told me that my new mum destroyed my adoption papers by setting fire to them, so that at the time, I couldn't find out any information about my birth and my birth mother.

    I have lots of happy memories of the farm and I loved the rural life in Southwell. Thrashing time was a big event with lots of men, and the thrashing machine and tractor driving it always excited me. I can recall the sound of it to this day. At nearby Manor Farm the owner wanted to make a big lake next to the lawn and big house. A big excavator (drag line) was put to work to dig out the hole for the lake, and every day I sat on the wall to watch this massive digger at work. As a little boy, it was something special to me. After I'd watched for several days, the digger stopped and the driver came over to me.

    "Do you want to have a go in the digger?"

    Well, I leapt at the chance! He helped me climb up into the cab. I stood in the front seat, holding on to the levers while the driver worked the foot pedals and I pulled the levers. The big bucket swung out and dug into the ground, and the other lever pulled the bucket back, swung around and emptied it out. I went home so excited that day! This is a special memory for me, but strangely enough, I can only remember leaving the farm three times with my father to go on trips. But, farming life was hard and he was needed close to home, seven days a week. Life on the farm meant that we were separate from the rest of town and at times I did feel isolated, an outsider bullied by the 'town' children at school. That is why I enjoyed the farm, where I felt safe. It's also why the memories of seeing the farming machines, and driving the excavators, are so special to me. I have continued to have a lifelong fascination with engineering machines.

By the late fifties, I had finished my school days and started work in Newark, so I passed The Workhouse many times over the next ten years. From the bus, I remember looking over at the children, and thinking of the people in The Workhouse. Sometimes the bus would stop and wait at the railway crossing below The Workhouse. I was aware of what the building was, but as a teenager I didn't really understand it or why people lived there. But it was always a presence, a constant on my landscape.

In the sixties, Dad received an unexpected letter from one of his family in Canada, named William. He wanted to correspond and keep in touch with his family back in Nottinghamshire, but Dad refused to even reply. Although Mum tried to encourage Dad to answer the letter, he wouldn't. I asked Dad to explain why not and if he would make a family tree so we could know something of his family, but again Dad refused. I was intrigued. Who was this mysterious man from Canada and why didn't Dad want to know more about him?

In the farm house, we had a small green book about Oxton Village with stories of life and folk in Nottinghamshire. (I still have it.) I took a look in this book and there was William, a local Methodist preacher who later migrated to Canada. So, this must be the William that sent the letter to Dad! With Dad refusing to tell his family history, and Mum refusing to speak of my adoption, I stopped asking questions, thinking I wouldn't find any answers to understand my past, a fact that was highly disappointing, as there were things I wanted to know. I was aware that there must have been family secrets, but I didn't really think much of it.

Until, that is, that day at Luton Airport. This is where I began to search for answers to my life and began to play detective, although at the back of my mind, I always thought, perhaps with a little bit of apprehension, what will I discover?

After the events at the airport, I applied for a new birth certificate. This one was much bigger and had far more detail, and most importantly, it had my birth mother's name on it as well as my place of birth, information I'd never had before. This was the turning point in my search. With the support of my loving wife, I began to look for my birth mother.

I was a war-time baby, and I discovered after a lengthy and costly search, that my mother worked in the RAF as a shorthand typist. My home for the first four weeks of my life was St Catherine's House in Newark, under the care of Southwell Diocesan Council for Family Care. It was from here that my new family collected me to take me to the farm in Southwell.

After many twists, wrong turns, frustrations and disappointments, I found my birth mother and she confirmed my birth, (although this was through a 'go-between', not directly). I sent my first letter to my mother, who agreed to one meeting, on the understanding I did not contact any family members. I agreed to her wishes, but I was full of so many emotions! I was nervous, excited, and apprehensive. Was she going to accept me?

With my wife and daughters by my side, I met my mother and her husband. It was very pleasant, but she gave no information on her time in the RAF, or any information about my father. 'Pleasant' seems such an inadequate word to describe a mother and son meeting for the first time in nearly fifty years, but this is exactly what it was. There was a distance: a gap that couldn't be bridged. She was on her guard and the meeting was on her terms. But, I suppose in the end she had more to lose. She could have refused to acknowledge me at all, and I am so pleased I had the opportunity to meet her. I found it very disappointing that she didn't give any information about my father, but I set out to do what I intended. I met my birth mother, and she met me and my family, and she could see that I was happy. I wanted her to understand that I had no ill-feeling towards her: what happened to her during the war-time was unfortunate (she was an unmarried mother and it must have been very frightening for her), and I have no bitterness. I did discover, though, that I have siblings: two sisters and a brother, but I was told by my mother to have no contact with them, and I have respected her wishes.

The search for my father has proved to be trickier. Again, I paid a researcher to help me and as we knew that he was also in the RAF, we looked for him by base and his age. Attempting to contact the RAF Personnel Centre is difficult, as I'm not next of kin and they won't release any information to non-family members. I have persevered, however, and through searching local history of airbases and placing many adverts in RAF magazines, I believe that I have my father's pilot number and name. This does give me some comfort, but as I am not 100% sure, there remains some doubt, but I will keep searching...

In 2014, I was looking for a new interest and my love of history led me to start as a volunteer at The Workhouse in Southwell. It seems strange that as a teenager I'd been looking at the building from the outside, and now I'm looking from the inside. After I'd been there only a short time, I'd discussed some of my family history with a researcher, and soon, he gave me a note from the Guardians Account Book. There were records for an outfit given to a child called William; the same William from the green book at the farm! It turns out, he was my grandad's brother! (The grandad I'd shared a room with for nearly ten years!) I don't know if Grandad was also in The Workhouse, and the records don't tell me where the boys' parents were. By coincidence, I also discovered that Grandad married into a family which included a Guardian at Southwell Workhouse, a place he would have been quite familiar with. My family history shares both sides of The Workhouse story; poor William eventually moved away to start a new life in Canada, a success story of sorts. Imagine living in The Workhouse, and then going on to travel and become successful? After all these years, I'd ended up volunteering at the very place I'd had a mysterious family member once live.

    As a volunteer I walk in the footsteps of the small boy William, and I think about his start in life. Was this family secret the reason why Dad didn't want to correspond with William? At the moment, I'm content with the information I have, though a part of me will always be curious about details I may never obtain.

    I have spent half my life searching. From that strange day at Luton Airport, I chose to open a book which was firmly closed, and search for answers to questions about my history, my story, and my identity. Although both my mothers are gone now, I continue to search for the rest of the green book mysteries. I have found a new interest in local history and am discovering more about the history of my adopted family. As I enter a new chapter in my life as a volunteer at The Workhouse in the rural town I grew up in, and where I enjoyed my childhood on the farm, I reflect upon my hidden history and the secrets of those before me, like William's. This story is my DNA, this is me.

One final thing: my new birth certificate also included my birth place. I was born at 105 Stockwell Gate, which is familiar to all those from Mansfield. I was born in a workhouse.

© Adam Phillips

Unmade Beds
by Karen Winyard

It was a dull day in February, or maybe early March, when I first came to The Workhouse as a prospective volunteer in 2003. I came almost by accident. A friend spotted a notice in the local paper and thought it would be something I'd enjoy. I was at a bit of a loose end so I thought why not? I didn't know anything at all about The Workhouse but I was in need of a new challenge.

There was a half-hearted drizzle of fine rain and everything looked grey. I was feeling grey myself, grey and washed out. By then I'd been married for over twelve years and I had two young children. I'd left a demanding job to become a full time mother and housewife even though I hate housework with a passion and I'm not good with children. But I've always felt that family is the most important thing in life. I don't know if that's because my own childhood felt isolated and lonely, without strong roots in an extended family; or whether it's a legacy from the stories Mum told me about her larger than life family.

My mother never said as much but I suspect she didn't like my volunteering at The Workhouse. She was the youngest of nine surviving children and was born and grew up in Nottinghamshire. They were poor, something she was always ashamed of. My mother would have understood the stigma attached to The Workhouse. I think she would also have shared the nineteenth century belief that, on the whole, paupers were idle and profligate. She could be harsh and unforgiving in her opinions. Never towards her children but there were times growing up when she really shocked me by something she said or believed. When that happened it was frightening. I felt as though I didn't really know her very well. As it turned out, I didn't.

Although I must have driven past The Workhouse any number of times, I'd never noticed it. If I had any expectations of the place, they would have been coloured by Mum's stories of her childhood. I imagined a row of picturesque tumbledown cottages that had seen better days, a terrace of alms-houses straight out of "Cranford" or "Lark Rise to Candleford". As I rounded the corner to drive up the hill and saw the house for the first time it quite took my breath away.

It is actually rather grand in typical Georgian fashion. All symmetry and proportion crowned with chimney pots and with rows and rows of windows. Even on that grey day in February when the world seemed a bit bleak in a neutral, indifferent sort of way, The Workhouse had beauty. The red of the bricks and the buttercream of the Mansfield stone on the windows seemed to glow warm. The spooky thing is the House doesn't feel like just a building. It feels alive. I felt as if it spoke to me and there was a slight jolt, a spark of recognition. I felt the House was waiting for me. By the time I'd driven up the dangerously narrow lane and found my way into the staff car park at the back, I was feeling nervous and, unexpectedly, lost.

The Workhouse was empty that morning and I walked around with Sarah, the National Trust Learning Officer. I've almost forgotten how large and confusing the building is to newcomers. I'm so familiar with it now but back then

I felt bewildered and tiny, like a child. If Sarah had been called away, I think I would never have found my way out again. The House isn't really that big, but there are so many rooms, one leading into another, that all look the same; and steep narrow twisting staircases and long corridors. In those days it was empty. We have a lot more objects in the House now, but back then there was only the large table in the committee room, the range in the kitchen and the beds in the women's dormitory. Otherwise the House was one cavernous blank canvas. Being in the House when it's empty can feel like being in a dream sequence. That's how I felt on that first day, as though I was lost in other people's dreams. It wasn't scary as such, but unsettling.

I keep describing The Workhouse as empty when I first visited and it was in one sense. The lack of furniture, the bare walls painted cream and pale brown downstairs and the more institutional dark greens and browns upstairs, the endless windows and high ceilings gave a feeling of space and light. There was very little in the way of scent either. It wasn't musty or stale but there weren't any of the familiar smells of a lived-in place. The House seemed half asleep with its peeling walls and empty grates. Yet each room was sort of humming with the voices and stories of the people who'd lived and worked there. An odd kind of silent echoing that made the hairs on the back of my neck stand.

Over the years I've taken on many volunteer roles at The Workhouse. I've been a room guide and led tours of the House. Played the roles of Matron, teacher, and female pauper for school visits. (I even played a male pauper on one memorable occasion.) I do a lot of research on The Workhouse in the nineteenth century and I'm slowly coming to an understanding of what life would have been like for the pauper inmates.

I have always been fascinated by social history. Growing up, I loved to listen to Mum's stories and the best were about her childhood and family in Nottinghamshire. I think this lies at the heart of my passion for The Workhouse, the reason why I have been a volunteer here for so many years, and why I became one of the Workhouse Storytellers. I am drawn to the stories of the women and families who found shelter here, women who could have been my grandmother or my mother – women who could have been me.

In the nineteenth century the House operated like a terrace of tall, three storey separate dwellings with the Master's quarters in the centre. It wasn't a prison but it was run like one. The principle of segregation meant that men and women went in and out of their separate wards and yards and their allotted space would have felt quite small and confined. The doors, both outer and inner, were kept locked. They weren't free to be alone or to wander The Workhouse as we do today. The locked doors and high walls outside meant a young woman wouldn't have seen the men or the women on the old and infirm wards. Children were more visible. Younger ones would have been with their mothers and even those old enough to be living in the separate children's wards would have been seen through the schoolroom windows or working and playing in the afternoons.

But they would have heard the others, even if they couldn't see them. Sound carries and echoes, bouncing off the flag stone floors and whitewashed brick walls. I imagine a fairly constant din of footsteps and voices and the noise that went with the varied forms of manual labour that both men and women did all day; endless chores of stone breaking, scrubbing floors and washing clothes. Only the dreaded oakum picking was quiet and that too would be punctuated by coughing as the dust filled the pickers lungs. I imagine the House would have smelt of carbolic and cabbage.

Today, if I'm in The Workhouse on my own I can still feel very small, alone and hidden away; I think because my own life pales into insignificance beside the lives of the hundreds of paupers who lived here. But in the nineteenth century the paupers wouldn't have felt alone and they certainly wouldn't have felt invisible. The inner doors all had windows so they could be seen at any time if the Master or Matron chose to look in, windows that were often broken by the paupers according to the punishment record book. If they were working outside or enjoying a little bit of free time in the exercise yard they could still be seen from the outer windows.

Everything about life in The Workhouse was controlled. They followed a strict timetable of prayers, work, and sleep punctuated by meals. The Poor Law Board in London laid down their diet and although it was calculated to ensure they had sufficient calories it was monotonous and bland. It was only varied on special occasions such as Christmas or to celebrate Queen Victoria's Jubilee.

The daily regime must have been oppressive and dispiriting. Life was harder than we can imagine outside The Workhouse for those who were in extreme poverty. If you came into the House you were given warm clothes and shoes, fed three meals a day, with meat three times a week, you had a bed to sleep in, and a sound roof over your head. But you paid a heavy price. You lost your freedom and your sense of identity.

I always feel the House is unhappy. Not that it was an unhappy place to live in, but that the bricks and mortar, the fabric of the building itself, is sad. It doesn't seem to like what we've created for it, the role we've given it. As though it's always wanted to be a place of refuge and sanctuary and love in a more wholesome way. Of course, The Workhouse was, theoretically, intended as a refuge, but not in a caring way. Or rather, in a Victorian sense of caring, the "spare the rod and spoil the child" form of caring. The "you've made your bed and now you must lie in it" sort of caring. It was a punishment as well as a refuge. It really was a crime to be poor and even though the system recognised that there were blameless poor, children and the old and infirm, they were still tainted by poverty like an inherited disease. Their condition was something to be cured.

This taint, this unfair and cruel feeling of shame, is an integral, though fragmented, part of my own history, and perhaps why I feel such a connection with The Workhouse. In researching other people's histories, I've come to think quite a bit about my own, and how poverty and family dynamics are so much a part of who we are.

I never met my maternal grandparents, they both died before I was born. My grandmother died when my mother was young and when she spoke about this she made it sound as though she were only about twelve. In fact, she was nineteen when she lost her mother, still very young but not quite the child she suggested. My grandfather remarried three years later and my mother never forgave him.

But there was bad feeling between them before then. She described him as a cruel man and a bully. There was the unspoken implication that he was an abusive husband and a cold father. Mum was always self-conscious about her education, or lack of it. But she was bright, encouraged by her teacher to stay on and study to be a teacher herself. Instead, at my grandfather's insistence, she left school at fourteen to go to work. My mother would probably have denied being a "Daddy's girl," but I sometimes wonder if she was in fact just that when she was very young.

I was always envious of Mum's large family. Dad is an only child and I have only one, younger sister. I wanted a family like that of the March girls in Little Women and used to ask Mum to send me away to boarding school where I might find one. She tried to tell me that growing up in a large family, especially one steeped in poverty and hardship, wasn't necessarily the warm, loving environment I fondly imagined.

One of her older sisters, Annie, was like a second mother to Mum. But Annie was hard on my grandmother. Mum used to relate a story of how Annie came across my grandmother working when heavily pregnant with my Mum. She was scrubbing the front steps and finding it very difficult in her condition. Annie had not forgiven her mother for conceiving again and refused to help, saying my grandmother had made her bed and must lie in it, or words to that effect - a very nineteenth century attitude. My mother clearly felt that Annie was unfair, that she should have felt sympathy for my grandmother, who was clearly unable to stand up to her husband. But I think that my mother also believed in the principle of, "you've made your bed and now you must lie in it." And I think she applied it to herself as much as to anyone else.

Although Mum keenly felt the loss of her mother and spoke of her as though they were very close, I do wonder if that was really the case. I always sensed Mum felt guilty about her mother; feeling that for most of her childhood she'd not taken her mother's side against her father. She gave the impression that she wasn't proud of the person she'd been at home. One of the few stories she told of my grandfather was how, at Christmas, he would tie half walnut shells to their cat's paws and let off firecrackers to make it "dance." I have a memory of her telling me she found this funny at the time but as an adult she was ashamed of joining in the cruelty to the poor animal. But that might be a false memory that's become mixed up with Mum's story of her sister, who was a surviving twin and born deaf. Mum was definitely ashamed of the way she and her siblings had behaved badly to their sister, teasing and bullying her, and wouldn't talk about it very much.

My mother never shared my interest in old things and the old ways of life. I am always looking backwards, but Mum had decided to turn her back on her past, especially her childhood. If I romanticised about a kitchen range she'd just say she remembered the chore it was for her mother to have to black-lead the range at home every week. At one point in my life I bought an old-fashioned wrought iron bedstead, painted cream with brass rails and finials. This was the trend at the time, second hand chic. My mother hated it because it reminded her of the beds of her childhood. She used to tie a string around the finial on hers and pretend it was a telephone.

We've had beds in the old and infirm women's dormitory from the beginning; this was one of the few rooms the National Trust "furnished" when The Workhouse opened in 2002. They're actually hospital beds but the Trust felt they were close enough to the original artefacts and could be safely used to recreate the nineteenth century dormitory. They stand in rows along both walls, dark cast iron bed frames with straw filled mattresses and pillows encased in ticking. They are covered by a rough dark grey woollen blanket that is itchy to the touch, and a row of single hooks runs along the wall above them where the thick creamy calico nightshirts hang. The straw makes the beds rustle when you sit on them. They smell fusty and organic and they're surprisingly comfy. Try one if you visit The Workhouse.

It's easy to imagine life as a pauper inmate when you sit in this dormitory. There are no cupboards or wardrobes because they had nothing to put in them. If necessary they shared a bed, top and tailing with another pauper, although this was probably how they slept at home. Being one of nine, Mum always had to share her bed with a number of her sisters. Some of the beds would be prized because they were closest to the mean little fireplace. Not that they were guaranteed a fire. If the Matron thought it cold enough they might be permitted one, but only a single small bucket of coal and that would not have lasted long.

Other beds were despised because they stood beneath the windows. The Workhouse windows are unusual. There are many of them and they are large but divided into small panes. Only a small square of glass in the middle of the window can be opened. Turn the latch and it swings out and upwards. There is a metal pole attached to each one with a series of slots at the end that is fixed onto a hook at the bottom of the sill to hold the window open. The Matron decided whether they had the window open or shut and she locked it into position. Just as she locked them in the dormitory at night, having first made sure that any candles had been extinguished. If they needed the loo in the night, they used the bucket.

This was their bedroom but they had no say in when they went to bed, whether they had a fire or the window open, and they weren't allowed a light if they were scared in the dark. When I think how young some of the women were, eighteen or nineteen and often in the House with a new born baby, I feel certain they would have been frightened.

There was nothing of their own in this room. They wore a Workhouse nightshirt the same as all the others and they hung their Workhouse dress on the hook at night, along with all the other identical dresses. I often wonder what the women dreamed, if they weren't so tired that they just slept like a log until morning. In their dreams they were free. But how long would it take for them to begin to forget who they were? How often did they rue making the bed that brought them into the Workhouse?

For most of our lives my sister and I wondered why our parents married. They never seemed happy. Mum used to tell me stories about her boyfriends. She was very attractive, beautiful in a Hollywood glamorous way, while I was a plain child and thought I looked nothing like her. The account she gave me was that she met my dad when they were both on the rebound. Mum always said that she was attracted to Dad because he was a decent man, an honest man. And he'd always been a good provider. This never felt like a satisfactory reason. It's only now that I can begin to understand. The Workhouse has taught me about my mother as much as it has about the women who lived there in the nineteenth century.

When Mum died my sister and I came across all sorts of things from her past. There was one single photo of our grandfather with his dog at his feet; Mum said he always had a springer spaniel. And there was another one of a small woman we believe to be our grandmother, clearly walking beside somebody. We assume she was with Grandfather, but the photograph had been torn in half, and only the image of my grandmother remained.

One of the worst things my sister and I had to do was to sort through her clothes. In a shoebox on a shelf in her wardrobe I found a pair of old, black, patent dancing shoes.

The box had "dance shoes" written on it in black felt tip pen. They were wrapped in thin white tissue paper. They were for ballroom dancing and still had some sparkle on them. Mum loved dancing, the foxtrot was one of her favourites, and she used to go into Nottingham to the Palais de Danse on a regular basis.

She met my dad at a dance. I was touched that she'd kept the shoes for so long, especially as we were something of a nomadic family, moving house every two or three years and the temptation to clear out old things would have been a strong one. The sad thing is that I don't believe she kept the shoes as a romantic gesture, a reminder of meeting my father. I think she kept them as a fragile thread that led back to the woman she'd been in the past and the bed she left unmade. I believe Mum married my Dad to escape her life of poverty and to give her a fresh start and the chance to be a new, better person. I also think this backfired and suspect she always felt she'd made the wrong decision. But she'd made her bed...

It was a hard decision, but I gave the shoes away to the local charity shop in the end. I can't imagine anyone will buy them. Who would want a pair of second hand dancing shoes over fifty years old? Only a daft storyteller like myself, so I guess they've been recycled in a refuse centre somewhere. I did keep her ballroom dancing medals though. They are still in my parents' house, but my Dad doesn't know much about them. Clearly, she didn't win them with Dad as a partner.

The stigma of poverty, the feeling that if you were poor you were a lesser, worthless person, was very real to Mum. Perhaps she felt it all the more because it was only my grandfather who was the black sheep. The other members of the family did well for themselves. My great grandmother ran a successful grocery store and another branch of the family had a shoe shop. My mother was always bitter that grandmother was expected to buy shoes from them but was never given a discount. They had to pay like anyone else even though their financial circumstances were well known.

In spite of her best efforts, mum left me with a rather romantic, rose tinted picture of her childhood that The Workhouse has not shaken. I envied her so many siblings, so many stories, so much life. And that's the sense I have of the women who found refuge in The Workhouse as well. Incredibly they survived and many of the records show they found friendship in the House. It was an odd combination of family and institution.

But in the end, how can we really know what it was like to be a pauper inmate in The Workhouse? How can we be sure of anything in history? Even the most straightforward of facts can be interpreted in more than one way. Much in the way my mother's memories of her childhood sometimes jarred with other memories she'd mention or stories she'd tell. Where does the story end and truth begin?

Today I use those stories in my own writing even though I'm sure Mum wouldn't approve. How my grandmother made her own bread, and nettle beer, or how my mum got stuck in the outside toilet at the bottom of the garden. Or had a whipping from her mother when she was caught scaring the next-door neighbour out of her wits by rolling potatoes across their shared attic. A whipping that was unjust really, as it was Auntie Annie and her friend who used to play that particular game and Mum was the one that got caught on the only occasion they let her tag along.

I feel privileged to be able to spend time in The Workhouse, to bring the people who lived and loved there to life by telling their stories. Researching their histories is a curiously intimate task, rather like unmaking their beds, and I feel very close to the women of The Workhouse. This has also brought me closer to Mum and I wish she were still here so I could reassure her that I love her unconditionally and understand a little of how her early poverty scarred her.

So you see, The Workhouse has given me two gifts. As one of The Workhouse Storytellers I've found my voice as a writer, something I've always wanted to do but never been brave enough to try. And I've had a rare glimpse of my mother from the days before she married my father, the woman who danced and could never bring herself to throw out her dancing shoes.

© Katrina Burrup

Complicated Magic
by Katrina Burrup

I was six years old. A small girl with dark hair, big eyes and an accent nobody could understand. Moving house was scary, but leaving Orkney was scarier. It was a safe place where everyone knew everyone and you were expected to leave your doors unlocked in case someone called whilst you were out. There would often be a bucket of scallops or a note inside to say a friend had called by. I knew we were going on the ferry, with our car, to the mainland, then down to England! I stood on deck, smelled the salt air, and watched our island home disappear. The journey was long and seas are always fairly rough off the North Sea coast, so I felt pretty sick. Mum let me sleep with my head on her lap. I don't remember the drive down; I must have slept again. Sleep was, and still is, my default response to motion sickness.

Greet House was immense. I had never seen such a big house, and as I got out of the car and looked up, the house loomed over me. It seemed to stretch up to the sky! My fear was instantly replaced with excitement; this house was ours? MINE??!! Were we rich? We must be important!

I knew this was going to be an adventure. I thought this place must be filled with magic....and it was. The orchards with trees to climb and fruit to pinch. Vegetable gardens, greenhouses, the lushness of all the growing things, it was wonderful. Adventures were everywhere, and one of my best was the day I discovered the Medicine room and winding toilet.

Outside my bedroom was a door that connected with the unused part of the house. It was locked but the key was always on our side. I'd sneaked a peek through the door before but never gone more than a few steps... Today it was quiet and my parents were busy; perfect!!

The temperature changed as soon as I went through. The walls were so cold, and the whole feel of the building was different on the "other side". I hoped I would find Narnia or Oz, places I was reading all about at bedtime.

There was the stair-case that ran through all floors, but I didn't dare go up, and down just led to my dad's office. So it was on down the corridor, into the middle section of the building, where huge rooms were all empty and sad, with piles of office supplies and odds and sods of furniture. In one corner, behind the open door, was another door. There were so many doors I nearly missed it! What a thrill... My heart was beating like a hummingbird's, and I was trying to breathe and walk very quietly, just in case I was caught sneaking about. I had to see what was behind the door. Would it be a secret passage? Or a ghost? I was totally convinced that Greet House would give me definite proof one way or another of the existence of all things supernatural. After all, if this place wasn't the very best place for sad miserable spirits to hang on, then nowhere was!

There was neither a secret passage nor ghosts, but it was still amazing. It was a big walk in cupboard, lined with deep wooden shelves and filled with all manner of glass bottles.

Some were huge, like the ones my dad made wine in once, and some were tiny and dark. They were filled with liquids and powders in all kinds of colours. The bright red one was stunning, and was three quarters full of God knows what. All the bottles had brown, peeling labels, with faded script. It was such beautiful writing, just like the writing in the ledgers I'd seen down in the office. I touched the labels and imagined I could go back in time. At that moment, I felt so connected to the building. It was mine and I belonged there.

I knew these were medicines, but I pretended I had found a stash of magic potions! I never opened them, I knew they might not be safe and I would be in a whole heap of trouble if I broke them and made a mess, but I spent long hours staring at the jewel colours in the bottles and imagined all the magic I could do with these potions. It was a secret, my secret, and I loved sneaking through there.

I opened another door, just across from the amazing room with the jewelled bottles. It led to a very short, winding corridor (it seemed long when I was small and walking very slowly). When I saw what was there, I was so confused. All of a sudden, in this tiny little cubicle, there's a square box toilet. How random...no bathroom, just a loo? It wasn't like any I'd seen before; the seat was set into a big wooden box and the chain dangled ominously from a gap in another wooden box, this one up high. I knew that hole would be full of spiders. Yuk! Plus, there were tiny glass windows, about the size of bricks, in the ceiling above the toilet as well as in the tiny winding corridor leading to it. Who would put windows over a loo? This toilet absolutely fascinated me. I wanted to use it, but I thought something would get me if I did! Remembering that day makes me smile inside. That mix of fear and excitement encapsulates my childhood.

Then there were the days I had to sit in the office with

my dad whilst he worked. He was the boss, the Officer in Charge of the house, which was now a residential care home for the elderly. He always had a full jar of chewy buttermints so it wasn't too bad....and of course, the biggest perk, I was allowed to read the ledgers.

They seemed huge, those massive, worn tomes with hard leather backs, corded spines and thick creamy coloured paper that smelled old when I turned the pages. The ledgers were filled with names and dates, the records of people who had lived here when it was The Workhouse. They were all written in the same flowing script as the medicines upstairs. I was learning how to join my letters at school and I couldn't imagine how much practice it would take to make my writing look so beautiful.

I always looked for the children's names. I imagined them; I wondered about their faces and hair. At one point, I found names of babies that had died once and it made me feel sad.

Again, I felt a connection with the house, as though I, too, was part of its life.

I learned so much living there. I learned about history, and the way people lived. There were all sorts of old, everyday knick-knacks lying about, as well as some truly impressive antique furniture. The boardroom table was enormous; I'm sure it sat at least fifty people. It must've been a banqueting table once upon a time. There were stone hot water bottles that we used as doorstops long before shabby chic made them popular, and brass bed warmers, and open fires in almost all the rooms.

There were also antique phones still installed on the middle floor corridors. They were disconnected externally, but still wired up to each other. My dad used to prank me by winding the ringer from our quarters when he knew I was playing in the main part of the house. Once he let it ring and ring till I answered it, then shouted, "BOO!" I totally popped my pants!

The gardens and the kitchens were my play areas too, and as an only child I was often looking for someone to pester. I fondly remember nagging at the cooks for a treat. They made the most wonderful teatime sandwiches and cakes and their white uniforms always smelled of warm flour when I hugged them. I wanted to help my dad and the head gardener water the greenhouses, and I learned how to tell if the peas, tomatoes and sweetcorn were ripe. I helped harvest the produce, often popping raw peas into my mouth, fresh from the pods, as I went along. I picked pears, apples, and gooseberries, too. It all tasted incredible; fresh and soaked in sunshine and love. I had birthday parties in the garden, on long trestle tables set out under the Bramley apple trees, laden with every kind of treat you could imagine. My particular favourite was the pink and white coconut ice my mum made, piled up in chunks, just begging to be nibbled on.

The staff were all so kind to me, even though I must've been in the way. I developed a lifelong love for vegetable gardening and cooking from spending my days with them. I still get a rush of pleasure when I'm pulling back the silk from an ear of corn, or shelling peas. It's an instant hit of nostalgia and I hope that feeling lasts forever. Some of the staff kept in touch after Greet House closed, and we are still in contact now. Sadly, the head gardener passed away some years ago now. He was a very talented man with a warm smile and a big heart and I miss him still.

There were places I wasn't allowed to go. I was curious, but by then I knew there were limits to how much disobedience would be tolerated. The stable block was strictly off limits, and even with my curiosity at its peak I never went there alone. My mum took me in once after a long week of constant nagging, and it was nothing special at all, but I know now, this was used on occasions as a morgue for the residents that passed away. No wonder nobody wanted me wandering in there!

The villas Minster and Firbeck were where the residents lived, and those were also out of bounds, though I didn't mind one bit. The dementia patients scared the hell out of me. I had a run in once with a very poorly lady, who shouted at me and threatened me. She must have thought I was someone else, bless her.

I was allowed to come up with Dad when the Minster School came at Christmas, though. They gathered in the main room of Firbeck and sang carols for the old ladies, and that was lovely.

Christmas was the best at Greet House. The ceilings were so high; we had a thirteen foot, real tree every year and my dad had to stand on a step to lift me up to put the Angel on top.

I remember one year, walking into our dining room, and there was every single gift on my list, so many presents that Father Christmas didn't have time to wrap them. A typewriter, a box of lollipops, Barbie dolls, a Superman outfit. There were so many things...We had a very good life, plenty of money and food, and I had everything I ever wanted; pony riding, gymnastic lessons, a maid who cleaned up after me, I was so privileged.

The opposite end of the building was separate to us, and once I saw a child playing behind some bars in the garden. I was very put out! Who was this person and why were they here? Here where nobody was meant to be? This was glossed over by my parents. I was so protected by them,

I had no idea till later in life that there were occasionally families housed there whilst they waited to be given a permanent home. To me it was just my home and a place for the old ladies to live.

It makes me feel very uncomfortable, embarrassed, and a bit guilty to think that I was living such a naïve, well provided for life, when I know now that conditions in the far end of the building were cramped and horrid, with only a teeny fenced off yard, whilst I skipped about like a princess. That child I saw playing in the garden was living in desperate circumstances, while just beyond the fence, I was living in my own magical place. It seems to me that The Workhouse continued to divide us, just as it had in the olden days.
It's a hard truth for me to swallow that the history of the house was so complicated, right up to its closure. And not just the history of the house; these truths have impacted on my experience of my memories. The joy I remember I felt living there as a child is complicated by the knowledge I have now, of what the place was for so many others. I guess that must be the same for most people. Once you have adult knowledge, it's pretty impossible to put it aside. But today, when I'm there, I feel the beauty, the magic, and the innocence I had when I was a child, and I'm so incredibly grateful for the gift of that moment in time.

Leaving was awful. Greet House had been my special home for nearly four years. Not that our new house wasn't nice, it was, 3 bed detached in a quiet cul-de-sac with other children my age. It was all very "nice" but Greet House wasn't nice, it was exciting, adventurous, it had a grand status that made me feel special. I was scared to not be special...

I loved it and I still do, it's hard to explain the depth of my feelings towards my old home. I miss it, I'm incredibly grateful that it has been preserved, but also, I had latterly, a sense of loss, a feeling it was taken from me. Of course I know it was never really "mine" but I wished so hard it was. In moments of self-reflection I understand what I'm truly mourning is the loss of my childhood, my innocence and my fierce belief in magic. The childish conviction I had then, that good would always win, in the end. Leaving was the end of my fairy-tale and the beginning of a very real life, like waking from a perfect dream. In the years after Greet House closed and the building was empty, before the National Trust bought it, I used to wish that we could win the Pools and buy it. I dreamed of living there again. I think I believed I could recapture my childhood and have my happy ever after if I could just "go home"

I used to worry a property developer would buy it and tear it apart from the inside, killing its heart and soul. The restoration has allowed me to have that small piece of my childhood kept safe forever and I will be forever grateful for that.

HISTORY'S DRAMAS
BY KEV TROUGHTON

When you're a Drama teacher, you spend a lot of time looking for stories; great stories that could become the starting points for great pieces of Theatre. Audiences love a good story, of course, whether it's derived from fact or fiction. Often, though, stories that are based on real, historical events and people have a particular power to involve and affect an audience.

There's something very moving in knowing that the characters on stage actually lived, and that the events that are being acted out actually took place.

Imagine then, being able to perform those real-life stories in the place where they originally occurred. This was the opportunity that we had in Southwell, following the National Trust's opening of the renovated Victorian Workhouse.

I knew of The Workhouse, of course; I passed it every day on the way to and from work. But when I first came to teach in Southwell, it was just an empty shell, last used in the 1970s. So when the National Trust took over, and plans were announced to open it to the public, I was on the doorstep before the renovation work was even finished. There were two of us teaching Drama at the Minster School at that time, and Su and I were regular visitors, forging a link with the Education Team at The Workhouse and beginning work on a series of exciting Site Specific performances by A Level

Drama students.

The starting point was always the same; the students visited the building to soak in the atmosphere, and to explore the rooms, the cellars, the out-buildings and the courtyards. Then, lots of time spent on research. The implementation of the Poor Law in Victorian Britain was highly bureaucratic, and the original documents are all there to study. All the names and personal details of the inmates, all the minutes of the Board of Trustees' meetings, all the punishments that were inflicted on the paupers.

Always the research led to a focus; some particular story or fragment of a story. For one performance, it was an entry in the punishment book, detailing how an old woman was fitted with a wooden clog, after she had repeatedly escaped over the wall. For another, a reference to a pregnancy in the strictly gender-segregated building. The story could then be developed, the characters fleshed out, and decisions taken about which rooms and spaces in The Workhouse would be best for each section of the story to unfold.

Usually, the performances happened in more than one place, and the audience followed a carefully planned route around the building and the grounds. Sometimes, there were students acting as guides for the audience, sometimes the audience were treated as though they were inmates themselves, and were shouted at and hounded from place to place as they followed the performers. The student actors loved the opportunity to use the building; it has such atmosphere that it almost became another character in the drama. Fundamentally, it's the sadness of the place that overwhelms you, the hundreds of people who spent years of their lives locked into that forbidding place, because the prevailing view at the time was that their poverty was their own fault. Many times, we wanted to shout back through the years, to make those in charge understand, 'Don't you see that this woman is obviously mentally ill?', 'What's the point of treating a small child like that? What do you think you'll achieve?'

For me personally, the human stories always came alive in the re-telling, but never more so than when the Education Officer of the Workhouse approached us to provide actors for a video presentation, that was to be shown to visitors on arrival. A small child was needed, and my own daughter was chosen. Seeing her, mud-splattered and dishevelled, walking up the long driveway towards those high, grey walls, brought an even deeper personal resonance for me of injustices suffered and the importance of the constant fight for a more enlightened social policy.

As 2016 draws to a close, we are hearing many clamorous voices, trying to roll back the hard fought social advances of the last 100 years; endless talk of benefit scroungers, angry words and hard stares directed at those who are trying to escape from warfare and devastation, threats of walls and deportations. The lessons that can be learnt from places like The Workhouse are hugely valuable. If we don't learn from history, we are doomed to repeat it, and what better way to learn than to experience it in a personally affecting way as a performer or audience member.

Many former drama students keep in touch on social media, and their openness, acceptance and inclusivity are a joy to see. Maybe their experiences in Southwell help to mould those attitudes, at least a little.

Great stories, and many great acting performances too. But also, behind all that, the looming, atmospheric presence of The Workhouse itself, still speaking to us after nearly 200 years.

© Katherine Patuzzo

Cooking with Care
by Katherine Patuzzo

As long as I can remember I have loved cooking. My own mother was a very good cook and as a child I loved her Sunday roasts. She would start cooking very early in the morning to feed her family of eight. My parents were Italian and I loved to be in the kitchen with Mum and watch her as she made her own pasta, as it wasn't widely available in the 1950s. My Dad made her a rolling pin out of a spade handle. My sisters and I still laugh about it now! But this was typical; Dad made the most out of what we had during more austere times.

My mother cooked with love, which was passed down to her by her own mother. Eventually, I was able to use my own love of cooking in my job at Greet House.

By 1974, I'd been working in London as a nanny for eighteen months, and that was at an end. I'd worked for a family with three children, and looked after the baby, who was about nine months old. The other two children were school age. It was a mews house, so it had five stories. My bedroom was at the top of the house. I remember there were lots of stairs. It wasn't a happy time for me; I felt quite lonely, but fortunately one of my sisters lived in London so on my days off I would go and spend my time at her house.

One day, I saw an ad in the paper for work back in Nottinghamshire. When I applied for my new job in 1974 I thought, "Yes! This is for me!" My first role at Greet House was actually as a care assistant, as it was then a residential care home for elderly women. I jumped at the chance even though I had no experience of the elderly. I had never known my grandparents and I had never come across older people, so it was a bit daunting. Surprisingly, I had no idea of its history as a workhouse, even though I lived in a little village nearby called Hoveringham, went to school in Southwell and had been in the area for twenty-three years.

When I first started, my dad would bring me to work and pick me up at the end of my shift. I would work late evenings and early mornings. The first month I was there, sadly one of the ladies I helped look after passed away. I was very upset. One of the girls I was working with said I must go and see her in the mortuary. As a young woman, I had never seen anyone who had died and I was very apprehensive. I have to say though, it helped me come to terms with the reality I wouldn't see the lady again.

While I was caring for the elderly ladies, I saw another side of life; that we would all get old and some of us would need care at some points in our lives. As I was new to the job I learned from the older staff. My worst memory is of bath time, as the regimented regimes reminded me of a 'sheep dip'. This institutional pattern would not happen today and I am glad that times have moved on. However, I honestly believe that everyone at Greet House felt that they were doing the best for the ladies. My early experiences have taught me that older people are not valued in life. I wanted to care for them as I would like myself, and the people I love, to be looked after.

When the cook retired, I was asked if I would take a role in the kitchen. I loved the idea! I wanted to put my skills to use and cook for the ladies and I was determined to do the best I could for them. As one of the biggest care homes in Nottinghamshire, we worked really hard cooking for eighty people. We made all the meals from scratch and I had to order all the food and plan all the menus.

I am proud that the diet we provided was balanced, varied and healthy. The kitchen and store cupboards were located in the original Workhouse building and the meals we prepared were taken over to the ladies on hot trolleys by porters. I can still remember a typical day's menu: porridge and cereal with a hot breakfast (scrambled or poached egg, bacon and tomatoes); mid-morning milky coffee with biscuits; homemade pies (such as chicken or steak and kidney) and puddings with fish and chips on a Friday for lunch; mid-afternoon tea and biscuits or cake; sandwiches or beans on toast for tea with cake, jelly and ice-cream or blancmange for 'afters' and a hot-chocolate at 8.30pm before bed-time. I am pleased to say that most was eaten and not much was ever returned to the kitchen! I used to love baking cakes (I still do), and enjoyed making sponges for birthday teas. The only cakes I couldn't make were eclairs and that is something that has always stuck with me.

It wasn't all work and no play though. I loved working with Beryl and Sue and we had plenty of laughs, which will stay with me forever. We were a bit cheeky sometimes too! I remember sleeping off hangovers in the staff room and Beryl bringing me in some food to wake me up, or nipping out the back to have a crafty cigarette! Beryl would always arrive early at the weekends and would have breakfast ready for both the residents and ourselves. Sadly, Beryl has since passed away, but I know she would have loved to have told her stories of Greet House. She was a wonderful lady and such a character. When it was a hot summer day, you would find her sunbathing in the gardens in her swimming costume, which made me laugh. What happy memories! When it was quiet, Sue and I used to explore the main Workhouse building, daring each other to go down to the damp, horrible cellars. I remain close friends with Sue.

    I have the happiest memories of my years at Greet House. I left in 1981 to start my family (I have two girls) but continued to work with the elderly when I returned to work. When I visit The Workhouse if feels very familiar to me, like an old, fondly remembered home. Sometimes I would like to bring back those days, filled as they were with laughter and caring for others through food, just as I'd been raised to do. Today, most of my time is spent caring for my young grandchildren and I enjoy cooking for them. They love my pasta as much as I loved my mother's. And so the tradition continues...

© National Trust

Darkness, Darkness
by Dinah Wilcox

It was November when I opened the door marked "Private" that leads to the women's work yard. I know this place so well; I've been volunteering for nearly thirteen years. But I didn't recognise what I saw. It looked...dirty, unloved, frightening, alien. There were piles of what looked like dirt against the walls. Wooden barrels (what were they for?). A brazier. I think it's called "dressing the set" and I suppose I should have expected it, but it was still a shock.

Inside, everything was back to normal, at least in the volunteers' room. The coffee and biscuits were the same. The people were familiar, and there were other volunteers who, like me, had come to be extras. We exchanged the usual banter and jokes; but no-one really knew what to expect.

But then, unfamiliar people arrived; people with no knowledge of The Workhouse, people from the other film sites. I felt a bit annoyed, I suppose. This was MY Workhouse, or at least, ours. There were crew—hundreds of them, along with a huge cherry picker with a huge light on top. All very discombobulating. We couldn't wear our usual pauper dresses; apparently they dazzled the cameras. So we were put into a hotchpotch of costumes, none of which looked clean. But I was confident that the day would be exciting. There's been filming at The Workhouse before, and I've been involved in it. There's always a lot of sitting around waiting, but it's exhilarating, and I feel privileged to be part of it. We'd had a sort of trial run of this production and although we couldn't divulge details, it made for good dinner party conversation! I hardly spared a thought for Sarah, the pauper character I almost invariably take on when I'm re-enacting.

Sarah is, I suppose, my strongest connection to The Workhouse. As far as I know, no one in my family was born, or lived, in a workhouse. My grannie would say, "behave yourself or I'll send you to the workhouse," when I was being a bit naughty, but I had no idea what a workhouse was. I became a volunteer for the same reason as a lot of the others have, I suppose: retirement, more time, a wish to do something "useful", as well as because of a standing joke between me and my mother. Every time we visited a National Trust property she'd say to me, "Dinah, when you retire you'll have to buy a twinset and pearls and tell children not to play with the potpourri and sit on the chairs". What a notion we two had of National Trust room guides! She died before I came to The Workhouse; how thrilled she would have been to know that I'd had the chance to be a TV extra, and at a National Trust property at that!

At the end of day one, some of us were asked to "go to bed" in the women's dormitory. I was thrilled and excited to be even more deeply involved. We removed our dresses, and hung them up in the candlelight. Although the celebrities were talking, (and it was clear that they were deadly serious about what they were doing), the silence from us was palpable. By then a feeling of unreality was taking hold. I thought of Sarah. She came into The Workhouse as a teenager. How would she have felt, lying in the narrow bed, cold, the fire unlit and the window locked open? Even though we knew that the person playing Matron was another volunteer, still the swish of her skirts and the click of her heels increased our apprehension. We were finally allowed to leave just before midnight, the filming finished. None of us bothered to put our twenty-first century clothing on, we just drove home in our shifts, with a coat on top. I was so tired I hardly exchanged a word with my husband once I made it home. Like a pauper, I went to bed without a wash, still wearing my shift. As exhausted as I was, I hardly slept, knowing I needed to be up at five o'clock in order to "get up" with the celebrities the following morning.

It was pitch black; there are no lights on our street, a moneysaving measure. My journey back to The Workhouse took me close to the river. There was a thick mist, wet on my windscreen, the trees were dripping, and of course, there was no traffic. It's a very narrow lane to the building, and I crept down it. I was in my shift with a warm coat on top but I shivered constantly. When my mind wasn't occupied with the problem of keeping the car on the road, I thought of the day ahead. By the time I reached The Workhouse, perhaps I had a little sense of the dread that paupers must have experienced when they first saw the building.

In the car park, there was total silence except for the engine of the car belonging to the security men. I bade them good morning—no reply. I made my way to the door marked "Private" and clicked the latch. Inside, there was more darkness, utter stillness and total silence. The cherry picker light, which had shone like an oblong full moon the night before, was extinguished. I could just make out the shapes of The Workhouse walls, the pump, and the garden shed we'd had to use as the privy. (No using the toilets after filming starts, was the 21st century order.) It had been lit by a candle the previous day. Now it, too, was dark. I realised that I was desperate for a pee. But how was I to manage, dressed in a long shift, in total blackness? I was panicking.

As I stood dithering in front of the make-shift loos, there was a voice.

"Dinah, you can use the proper loos, they're open!" It was the House Manager, at an open window.

I couldn't see her, but I would have kissed her. I groped my way to the door of the Ladies and pulled it open. Two cheerful faces smiled at me, (how could they be so fresh-looking after a night in the House?), there was electric light, and a flushing loo! They seemed relatively unaffected by their night in the House, since all Health and Safety rules were adhered to, but then they were young, and they hadn't had that drive through the mist. We chatted about their overnight stay and everything felt good again...for the moment.

A little later, lying in that Workhouse bed again, waiting for the film crew to arrive and Matron to "get us up," I thought again of Sarah. She must have been a feisty girl; her name was listed five times in the Punishment Book for breaking the rules. She's a great character to play: lively, a bit cheeky, never crushed by the system. Actually, she must have been a bit of a pain—but when I'm in character, The Workhouse becomes a place of bothersome rules, and also of safety and shelter. It didn't seem like that in the moments I was waiting, though. Waiting for the swish of skirts to announce Matron's arrival. Trying to put on an unfamiliar costume in the half light. Helping, and being helped by, the pauper in the next bed. Let's hope that was authentic; they must have helped each other, surely?

Then came breakfast. It was filmed in the Committee Room with male and female extras and celebrities (six of them altogether), all filing up for their slop of gruel and hunk of bread. When we women approached the hatch we were told by Matron we were only to have a crust of bread because of telling an untruth. The atmosphere was oppressive; total silence save for Master and Matron shouting, and the celebrities conversing quietly with each other. They were miked up so their remarks were caught on film. Ours wouldn't have been, but still we remained silent. Maybe we were listening to what the celebrities were saying, talking about the nutritional qualities of gruel, their aches and pains, one remarking in amazement that he'd finished his entire bowl of gruel despite it being so disgusting! Although I knew it wasn't real, that I'd hopefully get something to eat later, it was the first time in those almost thirteen years that I had a real insight into what it felt like being a pauper. The hopelessness. The fear of going hungry. Only having cold water to drink. No wonder the pictures of paupers show them with bowed heads.

    I don't think it was just me who felt different. Often, when we're doing a re-enactment, you'll catch Master or Matron's eye and there'll be an almost indiscernible wink or twitch of the lip. Nothing like that today. Even when the cameras weren't rolling in our area, the stern personas remained. Not only did I feel antipathy towards the extra (not one of our volunteers), who continually kicked my carefully-gathered pile of leaves all over the yard, I also began to feel it towards Master and Matron. And I felt so sympathetic toward one of the women celebrities, who worked so hard. Perhaps I was beginning to turn into Sarah; I wanted to have a go at Matron for being so unfair to her!

    Well, I finished my part of the filming, handed in my costume without regret, put on my normal clothes and departed, back into normality. But I couldn't shake off the feeling. It took two days before I could sleep properly or join in a normal conversation. I loved it, but...

Postscript
By the time the series was shown it was May the following year. We were in France with my daughter and her partner; they had travelled from Australia. I hardly dared ask if I could watch the programme. It was agreed that we would all watch it, provided, said my daughter, "You don't say a word, Mum." Five minutes in, she leapt to her feet. "Mum, there's you!" She had keen eyesight; I was in the shadows. Each time she caught a glimpse, she uttered a sort of strangled yelp. After the programme, they had so many questions—about the filming, The Workhouse (her partner's Australian), my volunteer role... She seemed so proud of me. And we agreed that the television people had done a pretty good job.

Would I do it again? Too right I would!

SEEN BUT NOT HEARD
BY ROSE POWELL

I was adopted at birth by mum and dad. I discovered much later in life that my birth mother was only fourteen when she had me in 1941. I was born at the then City Hospital in Nottingham, which had only just been taken over by the local authority; it being seven years before the NHS came into being. The hospital had formerly been Bagthorpe Workhouse and Infirmary, and like the Southwell Workhouse it had a special wing for unmarried mothers. I'm sure my young mother would have given birth in that wing, and equally sure the purpose and stigma were still very much a part of the building. My private adoption was arranged by the fearsomely named Southwell Diocesan Board for Moral Welfare, which I now know to have been involved in most adoptions from Southwell Workhouse.

My personal story of the Southwell Workhouse starts with just a fragment of memory from sixty nine years ago. I was six years old when I saw my grandma taken to the Workhouse in 1947, but the trauma and bewilderment I felt that day lingers on down the years.

I have many memories of my lovely granddad; sitting on his knee by the fire while he read to me, him playing cards and dominoes with me. But the only memory of grandma that I have is of the day I saw her in a physical tussle with my dad, the kindest of men, as he was trying to calm her. She'd had a stroke I believe, and probably had dementia too.

My dad, who worked on the farm, mum and I, shared a tied house on Combs Farm, Farnsfield, with grandma and granddad, who was retired. Despite this I don't remember her at all, except for that one incident. I never saw her again or heard what became of her, although I now understand she died in early 1948. Little children in those days were 'seen but not heard.' I must have been playing in the garden when people came to collect her and she got upset. In the confusion everyone forgot I was there, or I'm sure I wouldn't have been allowed to witness it. I now know, from the records at The Workhouse, that it was the 5th December, but I don't remember it being almost winter. It's funny how one's most vivid childhood memories are usually of summer days.

How I wish that I'd been able to talk to dad about it! He was the strong, silent, man of the earth type who would sooner have died than discuss 'feelings.' If I had been able to talk to him it might have made things easier when it was my turn to take him to a care home, which nearly broke my heart. Sadly, or maybe not, his dementia was so bad by the time I eventually bit the bullet, that he scarcely realised. Thank goodness the scene when grandma was taken away wasn't repeated in my adulthood!

When I was adopted my mum and dad were thirty-six and forty-three years old, my mum being born in 1898 and dad born on Christmas Day 1904 in that same house. They had the Victorian working class horror of the Workhouse and the stigma of going there was palpable. Though Grandma would have gone to the hospital section of the Workhouse, the equivalent for the poor of a nursing home today. I don't remember anything specific they said, although I do remember that having to go to the Workhouse was spoken of with dread and I always felt it was something to be ashamed of.

I also remember passing The Workhouse as a young child on the bus from Farnsfield to Newark with mum, and her pointing it out as the place one should avoid at all costs. It seemed to me then such a horrible, grim looking, imposing building, standing gaunt on a slope. It made me shiver. I see it now as a beautiful Georgian building set in spacious grounds and green countryside. The disconnect between how you see things as a child and how you see them later is, I suppose, part of the journey to being a grown up adult.

Nearly thirty years passed before my next encounter with the Workhouse. By then I was a single mother with a school age son to provide for. I was lucky to have a good job as a civil servant, but it was full time, quite pressurised, stressful work. One day it sent me to Greet House, as it was called then, around 1976 or 77, to interview a family. There was a mum, dad and two children, I think, who had been placed there in accommodation for homeless people. I had never been inside the building before and had no idea it was used for that purpose. I hadn't thought about the place for years and, if anything, assumed it was closed down. At the time I remember being annoyed at having to go to such an out of the way place, as I knew it would take time to locate the people in charge, find the family, and take a claim for benefit that wouldn't be quick or straightforward. It was going to delay the rest of my visits that day and meant getting home to my son later than I always hoped for.

When I eventually arrived at The Workhouse, all my previous dread of the place as a child kicked in. I remember feeling oppressed and nervous as I climbed the bare stone steps. I can't remember anything about the circumstances that had led them there, but I remember feeling horrified by the large, cold room, with a few shabby facilities which seemed more out of the fifties than the late seventies. There were four hospital type beds made up with blankets and eiderdowns, an old-fashioned settee, an ancient cooker, a table and chairs, and very little else. I do know, though, that I would have been professional and done my best to help those poor people. I certainly wouldn't have let my horror at that stark room in such unsuitable surroundings show. I remember feeling guilty at being impatient for having to go there, and grateful that I had my own terraced house, decent food, and clothes for my little family. Any misstep and it could have been me! I cannot imagine how I would feel if I had to take my beautiful little boy there. I like to think that I'd cope – I always have – but would I?

If trepidation was my emotion as I drove in, it had been replaced by anger as I drove away. Anger that young children were put in such an awful place is all I can remember of that visit. I suppose that in this day and age they would be in some grotty bed and breakfast, in all fairness just as bad as Greet House in the 70s, or even worse, out on the street, sleeping in a car or the family broken up. At least that family were together, were safe, had fresh air around, and the kids had a play area.

Much later in my working life, in 1991 with my son grown up, I was working as assistant manager at a ninety-two bed, direct access hostel for homeless men with substance abuse and mental health problems in Sheffield. It was a Resettlement Unit, a 1960s building on the site of what had been a workhouse for vagrants known as a 'Spike.' These were used by men travelling around the country looking for work. They were given accommodation and food in return for labour in the workshops or gardens. In his book, 'Down and Out in Paris and London,' George Orwell wrote about his experiences of spikes in the 1930s. Even in the 1990s many of our older residents still referred to the place as 'Sheffield Spike' and called the men who ran it 'porters' just as they had been back in the day at Southwell Workhouse.

Another difficult and stressful job! I suppose I'm just a 'people person' and was never going to settle for a safe, boring job at a computer terminal. All the people who worked there were civil servants with no special training in dealing with such needy men. The shift workers who did the day to day running of the Unit were former steelworkers, miners, or servicemen who saw their primary role as keeping order and dealing with any trouble.

It was part of my job as management to try to instil more 'caring' attitudes, an unpopular idea with some of those staff, to say the least. All the training any of us had was a few days on various courses dealing with the nature of addiction, alcohol, drug abuse, mental ill health etc. I remember one called Difficult, Disturbing, and Dangerous Behaviour, when we learned that if someone kicked off it was better to keep an escape route open, or have access to the panic button!

We had many men who carried on the old traditions and travelled from one Unit to another, settled for a few days, weeks, or months, and then moved on. The problem for them was that we were a 'dry house,' (no alcohol allowed or you were kicked out, even on Christmas Day). Men who were in a bad way would be admitted, see a doctor, dry out, be fed three meals a day and recover, until they couldn't hack it any more, fell off the wagon, or just got itchy feet. It was my job to 'resettle' any men who showed an interest in it. Most of the old boys had reached the stage where they were beyond any hope of intervention in their chaotic lifestyle, but I had some limited success with a few of the younger ones, although the after support they had was non-existent, and it sometimes felt as though we were setting them up to fail again. I found this revolving door a source of deep frustration with the job.

In addition to 'resettlement,' it was also my job to arrange activities. I organised trips out to the seaside, or the countryside. I got free tickets to the World Snooker in Sheffield once, and we took a trip to the World Student Games, always with the reminder that if anyone got drunk they would be out on their ear later. If we had residents young and fit enough to get a football team together, I got them a game against the Probation Service users. It was good for the men to feel 'normal' for a change and part of society. It helped them to bond as a group and most importantly, it got them out of the Unit for a day having fun. And, truthfully, it also got me out for a day having fun!

One activity, which I didn't enjoy much, but the men loved, was bingo on a Friday afternoon. I learned not to buy any worthy prizes, like writing paper or deodorant; all they wanted were the giant bars of Cadbury's Dairy Milk you could buy then. Nothing with nuts, of course, due to the dodgy state of their teeth! Aftershave was out of the question, because its alcohol content meant it would have been drunk, and they couldn't have any sprays, which would have been sniffed. For the same reason we had to be careful with boot polish, and typists' correcting fluid could also be sniffed. It was the early nineties! No one is a 'sniffer' these days – they would be on legal highs like the synthetic cannabis, Spice. With our lack of real expertise, except for our wonderful doctor, we muddled along using a common sense approach, and there were a lot of days when I despaired. But, that said, there was never a dull day, and there was the occasional hopeful moment. I learned a lot in those years!

It was said in the homeless sector that after five years,

workers are 'burned out' and have to move on. Luckily for me, when I'd been there four plus years and was fifty-three years old, the government decided to leave the sector to the homeless charities and gave me the offer that couldn't be refused; 'here's your pension, shove off!'

Looking back, I can see that we ran rather an enlightened regime. There was nothing we could do about the dormitory accommodation, but we did our best to help and support our residents, or provide a few treats. That's obviously in direct contrast to the times of the Victorian Workhouse, when inmates were punished for being poor and the only activities they had was work and more work.

What I also learned was that our residents, so terribly damaged in many ways, could be lovely human beings; courageous, loyal and funny. We also had, obviously, some less than lovely human beings, as there are in every strata of society. Our residents also faced stigma, like the original inmates of the Workhouses. Some of them were just unlucky in life or unable to face reality without the help of alcohol or drugs, but all of them were just ordinary human beings with frailties, like any of us.

Places like our unit no longer exist and most homeless provision these days has to be through referral, which is one of the myriad reasons we see so many homeless sleeping out in towns and cities. Workhouses were indeed hard places, but the times were hard, and in a minimal way the basic needs of the poorest in society were met. The Victorians had a strong moral sense of duty to care for all society, not always kindly perhaps, but they did it.

It's amazing how many times in my life Workhouses or their successor institutions have played a role. I think that people should know as much about social history as about 1066 and all that. It's only by knowing what happened in the past that we can hope to avoid repeating the same mistakes.

How times have changed already from the early nineties of last century, let alone the century before! We are certainly more knowledgeable and think of ourselves as more enlightened, but are we really? It seems not. There is outrage because a handful of refugee children look older than people think they ought to. Attitudes to welfare have hardened recently, and too many seem more and more intolerant of the disabled or less fortunate. Anyone who has looked at some of the tabloid press or an internet comment stream lately will see how cruel people can be. In these days of food banks, cut backs, and austerity, I worry that the basic needs of the most deprived in society are not being met.

The voices of need through time may yet come back to haunt us.

With Special Thanks To:

The Southwell Workhouse

The Arts Council England

Museum Development East Midlands

National Trust

Move, Teach, Inspire

The National Trust is a conservation charity founded in 1895 by three people who saw the importance of our nation's heritage and open spaces and wanted to preserve them for everyone to enjoy. More than one hundred and twenty years later, these values are still at the heart of everything it does. The National Trust looks after historic houses, coastline, forests, woods, fens, beaches, farmland, moorland, islands, archaeological remains, nature reserves, villages, gardens, mills, and pubs; special places throughout England, Wales and Northern Ireland for ever, for everyone.

The National Trust relies on the support of its members, donors, and volunteers, as well as income from grant-making bodies and commercial activities such as retail and catering, to look after the places in its care. The donations generated by sales of this book will go towards helping preserve the nation's heritage and makes places like The Workhouse accessible for generations to come.

To find out more about the National Trust and the exciting plans for our 'Re-imagining The Workhouse' project please visit the website www.nationaltrust.org.uk

Many thanks for your support.

global words
What's Your Story?

Global Wordsmiths is a community interest company which provides an all-encompassing service for all writers, ranging from basic proofreading to development editing, typesetting, and ebook services. Our education and cultural programme offers a holistic range of services for all ages, including writing, photography, and art workshops designed to suit the current curriculum, as well as a full range of publishing services from concept and design through to publication. Our community focused work involves delivering writing projects to underserved and under-represented groups across Nottinghamshire, giving voice to the voiceless and visibility to the unseen.

To learn more about our work, visit:
www.globalwords.co.uk

Other books by Global Words Press:

Women's Stories, Women's Voices
The Victorian Vale by Farmilo Primary School
Times Past: Young at Heart
In Different Shoes: Stories of Trans Lives
Patriotic Voices: Stories of Service
From Surviving to Thriving: Reclaiming Our Voices
Fractured Voices: Breaking the Silence
Don't Look Back, You're Not Going That Way
Peace by Piece
Speaking OUT: LGBTQ Youth Memoirs
Late OutBursts: LGBTQ Memoirs